BEHOLD THE RAVES!

"Uncommonly fascinating . . . intricately involving. . . . Cuts through suspense novel clichés with solid characterizations and a witty touch of romance."

—*Publishers Weekly* (starred review)

"A slam-bang of a thriller . . . scratches the scabs of U.S. history, while focusing on the dark side of current politics and corporate business . . . Fast-moving plot lines . . . ample characters . . . explosive finale . . . will definitely leave readers wanting more."

—Copley News Service

"Roars like a white-hot blast. . . . The pace is warp speed and wonderfully relentless. The fascinating plot twists and turns and is all too real. . . . As a twenty-year NYPD veteran I was amazed at the reality of the crime scenes. It was as if I was back in NYC myself, working alongside Lieutenant Fink, a great cop. . . . A truly great read."

—Ed Dee, author of *Bronx Angel* and *Little Boy Blue*

more . . .

"Extremely exciting. . . . Steven D. Salinger demonstrates incredible degrees of talent with his debut novel. . . . Readers will be chanting 'encore!' from the new giant on the scene."

—***Midwest Book Review***

"Steven D. Salinger is the newest star on the thriller horizon."

—**Peter Maas, author of *Underboss* and *China White***

"A well-crafted thriller that will grip readers from start to finish. . . . A large cast of interesting characters are brought together by cleverly contrived circumstances for a fast-paced denouement. Along the way, numerous plot twists provide genuine suspense."

—***Library Journal***

"[A] lightning bolt of a tale. . . . Deftly combines police procedurals and international intrigue. . . . Salinger pulls the whole thing off with panache and attitude to spare."

—***Chicago Tribune***

"Intriguing . . . a real page-turner, filled with suspense and strong, memorable characters. I can't wait to see the movie."

—***Bookviews***

"Shockingly good. Succinct, hard driving, and relentless, with unfailing authenticity and always—to the very end—just one more surprise."

—Michael Weaver, author of *The Lie* and *Impulse*

"A gripping story of suspense built around a strong page-turning plot, memorable characters, and a situation that seems entirely plausible."

—Abilene Reporter-News

"A gripping tale from a major new storyteller . . . a first-rate thriller with a knockout setup that hooks you so deep you won't put it down."

—Michael Connelly, author of *Trunk Music* and *The Poet*

"A really good thriller that will grab you and keep you until the final page . . . satisfying . . . . Genuine suspense and a fast pace add to this well-written novel."

—*Sullivan County Democrat* (NY)

"A cold-eyed romp. . . . Too intelligent for Rambo and Chuck Norris, Salinger writes a refreshingly unhysterical story around the MIA question."

—Chuck Logan, author of *The Price of Blood* and *Hunter's Moon*

STEVEN D. SALINGER

Behold the Fire

WARNER BOOKS

A Time Warner Company

WARNER BOOKS EDITION

Cover design and illustration by Thomas Tafuri

Warner Books, Inc.
1271 Avenue of the Americas
New York, NY 10020

Visit our Web site at
http://warnerbooks.com

 A Time Warner Company

Printed in the United States of America

Originally published in hardcover by Warner Books .
First Paperback Printing: November, 1998

10 9 8 7 6 5 4 3 2 1

For my mother and in memory of my father

ACKNOWLEDGMENTS

The author wishes to express his gratitude to the following people who provided valuable insights and invaluable encouragement during the creation of this book.

Henry Dunow of Harold Ober Associates

Rob McMahon of Warner Books

Lynn Baier
Helene Hovanec
Estelle C. Ladrey
Alexander J. Londino
Bill Minkin
Paul Pines
Allyson, David and Gretel Salinger
Ana Carrasquillo Salinger
Antonio Salinger
Paul Stern
Bonnie Waitzkin
Fred Waitzkin

And Isaac spake unto Abraham his father, and said . . . Behold the fire and the wood: but where is the lamb . . . ?

Genesis 22:7

PART ONE

CHAPTER ONE

The elevator did a little jig and the doors slid back. Mel Fink stepped off and saw two kids in blues down the hall. He walked over, pulled back his coat and watched his gold shield stiffen their uniforms. It was funny how he still got a kick out of that. And this. The crime scene. Another murder. A new beginning.

There were three locks on the door and no signs of forced entry. Taking out his handkerchief, Fink followed his nose into the living room. He could hear Barton's voice.

The body was sprawled on the carpet. As advertised: white male, late forties, circa six foot, one ninety. Fink reached into his pocket and pulled out the latex gloves, a ritual he enjoyed about as much as putting on a condom.

Crouching down next to the body, he noted the hair weave, the quality suit, the gold Seiko. He poked some skin—eighteen hours, maybe less—and examined the nasty multiples on the neck. A wire job. Fink hadn't seen one of these in a while. *Muy español.*

Switching modes, he ran his eyes slowly over the body, letting the picture imprint. He looked around. No drag marks. No signs of a struggle. An open wallet with cash and credit cards meant *Sayonara* robbery. He thought of a T-shirt he'd seen the other day: Life's a Bitch/Then You Die.

Sensing Barton watching from across the room, Fink tried to make pushing up from his crouch look effortless. He nearly pulled it off.

"Okay," he said, snapping a glove, "fill me in."

"Franklin Grelling," Barton began, flipping open his pad. "Forty-eight. Lived here alone. Divorced. Vietnam vet. Doesn't show for important meeting at his office this morning, doesn't answer phone, doesn't respond to beeper. Very punctual guy. Secretary calls building management. Super comes up, catches a whiff and dials 911. Super's a Guatemalan. Swears he touched *nada.*"

"Yeah, sure. And?"

"Grelling worked for Parker Global, the big defense contractor. Parker does a lot of classified Pentagon shit, but they're insisting that Grelling was borscht, a traveling salesman with a fancy title. Lightweight rockets, small arms, Third World countries. Took down low six figures . . . just like you, Lieutenant."

Barton shifted his feet. "Doorman says quiet guy, away a lot, crisp fifty at Christmas, no girlfriends. Lab boys got some good prints, but I'll lay odds they're either Grelling or the super, or both. You want the bet, Lieutenant?"

Fink glanced down again, resisting the urge to massage his neck. Grelling's face was bloated, like a fish dragged up from the ocean floor. Barton was good. A little too black, maybe, but this was a new generation. Fink had a feeling he was going to like this case.

"Come on, Magic," he prodded, "show me something."

Barton shot him a look. "Our perp is a male," he said.

"Probably working solo. No forcible entry, so Grelling either let him in or Mr. P. had a key. We'll question the building staff when we get the TOD, but I wouldn't hold my breath."

"So?"

"No feds yet, so maybe Parker Global is being straight about his job. There's something, though. Wire is up close and personal. The apartment's clean, but I'm thinking coke. Because a) Grelling worked Central and South America, and b) there's something very Colombian about his neck. Also, there was talk. He knew something about something, or at least somebody thought he did. See the chairs?"

"Yeah. Or what?"

"Lovers' quarrel," Barton said, offering green tic tacs, taking some himself when Fink declined. "Remember that torture job out in the Hamptons? The art dealer's place? Egil Vesti, the kid's name was. Is that worth points?"

"Only if you come up with the art dealer."

Barton suppressed a smile. "Andrew Crispo."

"Swish," Fink conceded, holding up three fingers.

"They burned the kid's body," Barton continued, "but they strangled him first. Slow and vicious, just like this. The fuckers enjoyed it."

Fink heard something in the tone. "Meaning what?"

"Our perp's a white boy," Barton said, showing some tooth.

After everyone left, Fink peeled off the gloves and began wandering through the crime scene, the same procedure he'd been following for twenty-four years, ever since first joining the force. As always, he moved deliberately, running his hands over surfaces, feeling textures with his fingertips, lifting his chin and sniffing the air, casually scanning the walls, the floors, the ceilings: absorbing random details—

color schemes, photographs, leftovers in the fridge. Fink never knew what might send out a vibration, deliver an insight, give him a feel for the life that had ended here. This one had shared some uncomfortable features with his own. He found himself wondering if Grelling had any kids.

In truth, Fink wasn't sure if these solitary walks helped him solve cases or not, but he attached an almost mystical importance to them. Besides, he admitted to himself, reaching into a closet and absently fingering a green silk necktie, his shift was over and he had nothing much to go home to: dirty dishes, dirty laundry, bills he couldn't afford to pay and messages he wouldn't want to return.

He drifted over to the dining table and gently lifted each of the fruits in a cut glass bowl. The apples were wax. The pears and bananas were wood, a harder wood than the balsa of a kid's model airplane but almost as light. The last of the wax apples was a candle. For some reason, Fink was tempted to rub it, like a new baseball, or a magic lantern. Instead, he put it back and walked away.

The bedroom felt like a trail gone cold. A queen-sized bed with only one pillow, a framed Impressionist print—Manet or Monet, Fink always got them confused. No photos anywhere. Grelling must have been a lonely guy.

In the bathroom, Fink flipped on the light and caught sight of himself in the mirror. He leaned closer, studying his face. Where had these new lines at the corners of his eyes come from? Maybe it was the light. Maybe he was just tired. He looked down, checking the tile floor. He tapped his foot. It wasn't tile, it was linoleum.

Grelling had no girlfriends, the doorman had said, but Barton had suggested a lovers' quarrel. Fink looked in the mirror, checking to see how the flesh under his chin was holding up. It seemed okay: not great, but about the same. He needed a shave. It occurred to him that Grelling could have had a thing with another guy in the building, like some people used to say about Koch when he was mayor.

Fink found himself examining his eyes again. Crow's-feet they called them. He reached up and touched some. Clint Eastwood had them. So did Robert Redford. Paul Newman had bad ones. Christ, he smiled, he was starting to sound like Joan Rivers. Smiling only made them worse.

He took out his pad and wrote "Maid." From the look of things, the apartment had been done in the last day or so. Fink wondered what maids got for working in a place like this. Probably just like wise-ass Barton said: low six figures. Everybody in the goddamn city made that these days—everybody but cops. Cops like Mel Fink, anyway. He couldn't even work up the energy to be bitter.

Something about the maid was tickling him. Three locks and no forced entry. Keys? Was that it? Could she have lent her keys to someone, or had copies made, or said something to a boyfriend? Sure, but where was the robbery?

There was blue gel oozing from a white toothpaste dispenser standing on the sink. Mentadent. Peroxide and baking soda, the latest thing. Fink still used Stripe. Not that he liked it; it was just another old habit. Stripe had been his son's favorite.

He reached out, grasped the ungainly plastic dispenser and flipped it in the air, remembering the first time he'd brought Stripe home, and the look on the kid's face when he squeezed the tube and saw the different colors coming out.

Fink pulled the mirror and scanned the contents of the cabinet. He shook his head and chuckled, remembering how he'd told the kid—who was what at the time? Five? Six?—that Stripe was a new invention the Japanese had come up with, and how they could do the same thing with paint. In another year, Fink had told him, Americans would be buying cans of striped paint, all different colors, any combination they wanted. The kid had believed him.

Fink switched off the light and closed the mirror, expecting to hear a click but feeling instead the silent pull of a magnet.

Though there was still a bad odor, the air in the living room had settled down. The stain on the carpet was turning black, starting to look more like India ink than blood. As Fink turned slowly in place his eyes were drawn to a dim corner he hadn't noticed before. There was something on the wall: a picture, or maybe a map. Even in the dark the shape was vaguely familiar. When he got close enough to see, he recognized the deformed, grunge-covered fish hook that was Vietnam.

It was a full-color relief map, framed in lacquered bamboo. As Fink approached it he felt something like a soundless tone seeping into him. Acting on their own, his fingers began moving over the glass while his mind began spitting out bits of memory, like static. Before the channel had a chance to clear he pulled his hand back and turned away.

Taking one last look around, Fink discovered that he was feeling good again. Barton was dead wrong about this one. Grelling's murder hadn't been about drugs, and it hadn't been some lovers' quarrel. Fink would have Barton check out the maid, but that would be a dead end too. No, Barton was too young to understand, but somehow or other this case was about that map on the wall.

CHAPTER TWO

They came and banged on the bamboo bars. Johnson hadn't been sleeping, just floating. When his eyes focused, the old man was yelling at him and shaking the medic bag. Two of the others were aiming Kalashnikovs. He nodded and duck-walked out of his cage, staying very low, keeping his kidneys angled away from the rifle butts. He didn't want to start pissing blood again.

They straightened him up and hustled him over to the clearing. The mud was cool and squishy between his toes. There was a chill in the air tonight. He pulled his ragged shirt closed. Near the fire three VC in clean fatigues were standing by a beat-up jeep. The one offering cigarettes to the villagers saw Johnson, walked over and held the pack out to him. It had a wide V across the front. Johnson slid one out, bowed gratefully, felt saliva begin to flow.

The VC struck a match and cupped it. Johnson held the cigarette tightly and bent to the flame, sucking quickly to get it lit before his hand shook. He saw the red and white of the pack. Marlboro? He nodded a few times, stepped back, inhaled. The smoke scratched his throat deliciously and made him instantly dizzy. The VC turned away and began speaking to someone.

Johnson hugged himself and held each puff in as long as possible, letting the smoke from home rub against his insides like a warm cat. He ran a hand through his matted hair. An American cigarette. He tried to think how long it had been, but couldn't come up with a number.

The VC were talking excitedly with some of the village elders. It looked like a negotiation. Johnson assumed someone was hurt and these VC needed him to patch the guy up. It had happened often enough before. That was the main reason he was still alive. That and the fact that he'd been around so long he'd become like a village pet. The younger children even tossed him scraps. When no one was around, Mee Yang sometimes sneaked over and brought him milk or bread or snips of chicken.

The strangers seemed anxious to get going. Johnson supposed he'd be riding with them in the jeep, though he hadn't even known they were near a road. The only thing he knew for sure was that he hadn't heard any fighting in a long time so they had to be far from any fire zone. He figured he was still in Cambodia, but that was only a guess. He'd been captured near the border, but they'd moved him so often it wouldn't have surprised him to learn he was in Laos or even the North. He didn't much care; wherever he was he was still alive, with a Marlboro in his hand. He sucked in another puff. It tasted like the chrome on a Cadillac.

The jeep bounced along a dirt trail. There was blackness and trees and mud. No one talked. Johnson had his medical kit wedged between his feet. He used one hand to keep the wet leaves off his face and the other to sit on. The hard metal seat reminded him of how the kids in high school used to make fun of his big ass. They wouldn't recognize him now, that was for sure. They wouldn't be kids anymore, either. Some of them probably had their own kids by now. He wondered if he'd ever have an ass again. The jeep hit a rut and he pushed off and caught himself before his butt smacked against the seat. Fucking war, he told himself. Goddamn fucking war.

The road got smoother. Johnson glanced over at the driver, trying to think of some way to wangle himself another Marlboro. Without looking, the driver passed the one he'd just lit over to Johnson. Two Marlboros. Whoever was hurt had to be damned important. Johnson looked up. Between the leaves high fast clouds were smudging a full moon.

CHAPTER THREE

Barton was sitting at his desk making a quarter roll over his knuckles.

"Used to be silver," Fink said, taking a seat.

"What's that?"

"Quarters. Dimes too. Up until '64 they used real silver."

"How about nickels?" Barton asked, putting the coin away.

"Nickels were always nickel," Fink told him.

"Sixty-four, wasn't that the year you were in Nam?" Barton asked.

Fink looked at him for a moment. "What have you got for me on Grelling?"

"Zilch. No one in the building saw anything. You should have taken my bet on the prints, though."

"Why's that?"

"You would have lost. *Nada.* Grelling and the Guatemalan super."

"Any luck tracking down the maid?"

"I'm working on it," Barton assured him.

"You talk with his secretary, the one who called the building?"

"Secretary? Bite your tongue, Lieutenant. She's an executive assistant, and I thought I'd leave her for you."

Fink looked at him.

"Rhonda Cohen," Barton explained with a sly smile. "Fink? Cohen? A dollar and a dream. Hey, you never know."

"Get me a rundown on Grelling's service record," Fink said, pushing to his feet. "And where he worked before Parker Global. When do we hear from the coroner?"

"I'll check. Why?"

"Because, Detective Barton, we're trying to solve a murder. Turns out Grelling carried over two million in life insurance."

Fink's phone rang. He grabbed it, said hello.

"This is Captain Reynolds," a gruff voice declared. "I want to see you, Lieutenant. In my office. Now."

"I was just on my way out to an interview, sir."

"The Grelling case?"

"Yes, sir."

"That's what I want to see you about."

"Yes, sir, but I'm afraid I'm already late." He glanced over at Barton, who was pretending not to listen.

"All right," Reynolds said, "we'll do it over the phone. Who's the interview?"

"Grelling's executive assistant, over at Parker Global headquarters."

"What's his name?"

"Rhonda Cohen."

"Oh, I see," Reynolds snickered. "Well, we wouldn't want to keep a princess waiting."

Fink breathed in through his nose, but didn't respond.

"Where are we on Grelling?" Reynolds asked. "Bring me up to speed."

"Well, Captain, I'm working this with Detective Barton, and he—"

"Motive," Reynolds demanded.

"It's early, sir, but Detective Barton suspects narcotics or a lovers' quarrel."

"What do you suspect, Lieutenant?"

"I suspect I'm going to miss my appointment, sir."

"Just one more thing, Fink," Reynolds said, uttering the name with the same snide, mocking tone that had provoked Fink into dozens of schoolyard fights.

Fink bristled. "Sir?"

"Parker Global Corporation is a major player in this city," Reynolds declared. "That's major with a capital M. Their toes are not to be stepped on. Do we understand each other on this, Lieutenant Fink?"

"We do indeed, Captain."

"Ms. Cohen?" Fink asked, showing his gold shield.

"Go ahead," she said, looking up from her desk, "make a remark."

"About what?"

"I'm black," she said.

"Excuse me, Ms. Cohen, I hadn't noticed."

"That's a new one. Sit down, officer . . ."

"Fink. Lieutenant. I'm white."

"I know," she said sourly. "I was married to one."

The offices of Parker Global were a disorienting combination of earth-tone marble, bright plastic and indirect lighting. The decor complemented Rhonda Cohen's long, beautifully boned Somali face: dark skin, almond eyes, aquiline nose, high cheekbones. A band of red African cloth held up her straightened hair like a bundle of black wheat.

"We could talk in the lounge," she suggested. "The coffee and donuts are free."

Fink nodded and stepped back. When she stood he saw that her body was too short for her head. Also, she was narrow above the waist and thick below. Full of surprises, Fink thought.

The donuts were good. Fink finished a cinnamon and then, with Ms. Cohen's encouragement, took a chocolate-glazed. She skipped the donuts and sipped a tea to which she'd added two spoons of Cremora. It looked like milk of magnesia.

Rhonda Cohen, née Buttman, had worked for Frank Grelling ever since he'd become Assistant VP/Regional Small Arms/Central and South America a little more than two years ago. She'd been with Parker Global for six years. She liked it: good pay, good benefits, no hassles, three weeks vacation plus sick leave and personal leave, both of which could accrue. Mr. Grelling was fluent in Spanish, which was a real plus. He didn't spend much time in the office and Rhonda "never ever" saw him outside of it. Fink wondered if that was because he'd never asked, but let it slide. As his executive assistant, she set up Grelling's trips, handled his correspondence, processed the orders and followed through to delivery. Personally? He seemed like a lonely guy. Had an ex somewhere in Florida, a couple of grown kids. No close friends that she knew of in the company. Didn't smoke. Drank, but never came back from lunch drunk. No vices that she was aware of. It wasn't all his hair. Sometimes he had dandruff.

"Doesn't sound like the kind of thing anybody'd want to kill him for," Fink remarked, licking a fingertip.

Rhonda agreed, though she'd always sensed there was something mysterious about him.

"Mysterious how?"

"Like he was haunted by something. He'd been in the war."

"He ever talk about it?"

No he didn't, but sometimes he'd be talking to her and then suddenly fade out and stare off into space for a few seconds, like he was far, far away. Rhonda had spent two years married to a cokehead, she recognized pain when she saw it. She had no kids, thank God. She wondered if Fink worked with any eligible, straight black men.

"Detective Barton," Fink told her, brushing sugar from his hands. "I'll send him around."

"Really? Is he nice?"

Fink shrugged. "Not to me."

CHAPTER FOUR

Johnson had patched up a few tiger wounds before, though usually all a striper left was pieces. Pieces of kids, mostly. But this guy on the cot was no kid, and he was seriously messed up. There was blood everywhere. Johnson did a quick inventory of the wounds. Incredibly, the claws hadn't hit anything vital. He pulled over the lantern and went through the pack on the floor. His own kit had almost nothing, but these guys had plenty. Good stuff too: most of it American. He pulled out some bandages and antiseptic and went to work.

The real shock came when he began cleaning the caked blood from the man's face. His hand froze. It had never even occurred to him that the guy might be an American. He forced himself to get right back to work. Maybe the VC didn't know. The guy looked to be about forty, was probably an officer. Poor bastard wasn't even in uniform. They could shoot him as a spy. Then again, it wouldn't matter what the guy was if he was dead.

Johnson got the bleeding under control. It wasn't hard; most of it had stopped by itself and the rest was down to just oozing. He cleaned and sutured the wounds, taking well over a hundred stitches, the majority on the face and arms. Johnson had always been good with a needle and the more he worked the steadier his hand became. The stitches were textbook. But the guy's pulse was very weak. He'd lost too much blood. How he got here, what his unit was, why he wasn't in uniform, why these VC were so concerned about him—none of that mattered. The only thing that mattered was that he'd soon be dead.

Johnson had seen plenty of people die, a few during his time with the platoon, and a lot more since. Seeing Death didn't frighten him anymore. He and the old bastard had a nodding acquaintance. He thought about that now as he sensed something hovering in the darkness on the far side of the hut. Johnson lifted his patient's wrist and checked the pulse, leaned closer and listened to the shallow, raspy breathing. He looked across the hut and nodded. The old bastard wouldn't have long to wait.

Johnson had always done his best to save people, even enemy people. He'd been trained as a medic, and what medics were supposed to do was keep people alive. No matter how much pain he'd seen, life had always seemed worth fighting for. Maybe that was why he was still alive. As his Mama used to say, What else we gonna do? For all he knew, she was still saying it. For a moment he almost heard her voice.

He looked down. There was a soreness around his eyes. The lantern was casting irregular light on the dying man's face, making his skin glisten. The poor guy was drenched with sweat, his body fighting with everything it had. He couldn't have been a prisoner very long because except for his wounds he was in primo shape. Probably on some top secret mission, the kind of thing that could make the difference, turn the war around. End it, even. Johnson ached to talk to the guy, and ached even more knowing he never would.

After all Johnson's time in captivity he'd gotten used to living like an animal, but he'd never gotten used to watching people die—especially children or healthy specimens like this one—people whose lives could have been saved by something he didn't have: some antibiotic or, like now, some more blood. And this one was an American officer: a captain or a major, or maybe a colonel.

Hoping to get his patient to drink a little water, Johnson leaned closer and gently raised the man's head and shoulders. But he was hard to lift and one of the VC came over and helped prop him up, holding him almost like he knew him. Johnson poured a few drops from a canteen. The guy coughed out most of it, but swallowed some by reflex. His whole body was hot.

Trying to lift him had made Johnson acutely aware of his own frailty. When captured he had weighed one seventy-five. Now he was maybe one twenty: little more than skin, bones, scabs and nappy hair. A scarecrow like him—he should have been the one dying, not a healthy sucker like this, an officer on a secret mission. He glanced across the hut and sent the lurking presence a thought: Fuck you, Mr. D.

Johnson laid his patient back down and patted the man's face with a sponge. Maybe the water had helped; his breathing seemed a little better. Maybe— Who was he kidding?

Suddenly Johnson was overwhelmed by a sense of terrible loss. He knew it was crazy, feeling like this for a guy he'd never even met. But it was such a waste, such a stupid goddamn waste. He began to rock back and forth, his eyes burning. He struggled desperately to get hold of himself. In all this time he had never cried. Not once. But it had been so long since he'd seen another American, and so much longer since he'd actually touched one. It had been so damned long since he'd had a real conversation or heard any news from home. And he was just so goddamn tired.

His body was wracked by a series of involuntary sobs which he tried to mask as coughs. One of the VC held out a cup and he took it, nodded thanks, sipped. The warm liquid tasted like sparks. It was some kind of liquor. He felt it slide all the way down to his stomach, like hot oil. The VC encouraged him to drink more, but he couldn't. He handed the cup back.

Embarrassed by his show of weakness, Johnson busied himself with his patient. He discovered a dog tag hanging from a thick gold ankle chain. The guy's name was Ransom, Everett G., and he'd been born in 1948, the same year as Johnson. But what was even spookier was that they had the same blood type.

Ransom had gorgeous veins, officer's veins. Johnson had no trouble inserting the needle into Ransom's arm, but he had a hell of a time with his own, jabbing himself repeatedly until he got it right. The first moment his blood began flowing into his patient Johnson felt a kind of satisfaction he'd never known. If he could actually save this guy's life—well, he wouldn't even dare allow himself to think that far ahead. All he could think about now was keeping the flow going. Ransom had a watch, a big gold Rolex, but Johnson's body would let him know when it was time to stop. Though momentarily strengthened by excitement, he knew that Colonel Ransom needed more blood than Johnson's scrawny body could provide. But he also knew that every precious drop that flowed through the plastic tubing was increasing the colonel's slim chance of survival. Best of all, Johnson could feel the old bastard in the corner shifting irritably on his haunches.

It had been ages since Johnson had been able to do something for one of his own. It felt so absolutely right. He knelt there slowly opening and closing his fist, encouraging the blood to keep pumping from his skinny arm, feeling himself becoming enveloped by a soft cloak of well-being, sensing in place of his lost blood a new, expansive peace coursing through his veins. He felt like Sidney Poitier reaching out from the moving train to save Tony Curtis in that movie, what was the name again? They were both prisoners. Down south somewhere. He used to know the name . . .

He knelt there staring down at his fellow American, their arms close together, until Ransom's face began to blur. Waiting until the last possible moment, he took the alcohol-dipped cotton ball he had prepared, reached over and retracted the needles, felt a tiny burn and slid down and curled up on the floor. He felt lighter than a feather. He saw the shy, sweet smile of Mee Yang. She was tiptoeing over to bring him some milk. Her smile shimmered like a soap bubble as his mind filled with a soft golden light.

CHAPTER FIVE

"This must be a very difficult time, Mrs. Grelling," Fink said, rising too quickly from behind his desk and banging his knee.

She brushed off his office chair, checked her hand, sat down and crossed her legs. "Frank and I were divorced a long time ago."

She had to be at least forty, but Fink would have guessed thirty-five. She bore an uncanny resemblance to a Puerto Rican girl he'd had a desperate crush on in high school: same fiery eyes, same dark wavy hair, same olive skin, same proud bearing.

"Your accent," Fink said, rubbing his knee, "I'm trying to place it."

"And?" she asked, her lips parting in anticipation.

Fink watched the tip of her tongue slowly exploring the perfectly beveled edge of a bright front tooth.

"And?" she asked again.

He snapped out of it. "Bogotá?"

She smiled. "Bad guess. Santurce. It's a suburb of San Juan. I haven't lived there in— They told me Frank was murdered. Your name is Mel, right?"

"Yes, Mrs. Grelling. This is just routine," he assured her, pulling out a form. "I'll try not to keep you long."

"Frank had a lot of insurance. I'll be in the city a while. Ask your questions."

Marissa Montero and Lieutenant Franklin Grelling met in 1963 while he was stationed in Puerto Rico. They were married two months later. She was seventeen, he was twenty-four. Frank had gone through the University of Arkansas on an ROTC scholarship and owed the army three more years. Eleven months after they were married he got shipped to Vietnam, leaving her with one baby and a second on the way.

"You were there too," she said to Fink.

He looked at her.

"Vietnam, it does something to the eyes," she explained, offering an open tube of Mentos. He took one.

After Grelling shipped out she moved back in with her folks, to save money and for the company. When he was rotated home Frank seemed subdued but okay. Her folks had a small place. The babies cried a lot. Both girls. A month later Frank volunteered for a second tour in Vietnam. This time when he came back he was a different person. Restless. Bitter. She never understood what had happened to him over there and he never talked about it, except in his sleep when he mumbled on and on in some language she couldn't understand. Frank was great with languages, but he'd forgotten how to laugh. A year later they were divorced. It was friendly. He always sent her enough money, more than enough. The kids got postcards from all over the world, saw him once or twice a year. In her opinion he never recovered from the war. She had no idea who might want to kill him or why. No, as far as she knew, he never used drugs. He used to drink rum and Coke. She didn't think he had girlfriends, but maybe he did. She hoped so, for his sake. He sold firearms but the police must already know that.

"We do," Fink confirmed. "Why did he carry so much insurance?"

She sighed. "Some women get flowers or cookbooks, I got insurance. I guess Frank wanted to be sure his kids would be taken care of. Me too, maybe. That first year we had? It was good." She paused. "Did he die fast?"

Fink snapped his fingers. She blinked. She had great eyes.

"You said Frank was fluent in Vietnamese," he said.

"I said he was fluent in something. I wouldn't know Vietnamese from chow mein."

"I don't have any more questions," Fink said.

"I have a few," she said.

He looked at her. She looked back.

"I remind you of someone," she said. "Who?"

He angled his chair. "A girl I went to high school with."

"Pretty?"

"Gorgeous. Her name was Felicita."

"Was it serious?"

"I'm afraid not." He smiled at a fleeting memory. "What kind of man was your ex-husband, Mrs. Grelling?"

"Frank was a decent guy," she said. "My name is Marissa, by the way. Are you taping this conversation?"

"No."

"Good." Her voice softened. "Now that you know all about me," she said, "what's your story?"

He sat up straight. "Mel Fink. Forty-eight. Divorced ten years. My daughter's in college, my son died. I like being a cop."

"Died of what?"

"Leukemia. Thirteen years ago. He was eight."

"Sorry."

"Everybody's got sorry," Fink said.

"True," she said, "but we shouldn't brood."

"Was I brooding?"

"No, but it's something you have to guard against."

"And how do I do that?"

She locked on to his eyes. "You could take me to dinner tonight."

"It would be my pleasure," he responded reflexively, surprising himself.

"Eight o'clock," Marissa Montero Grelling said, standing and smoothing her skirt. "Better write the address."

An hour later Fink was still at his desk, tracing the scars on its aging surface with a pencil and remembering Felicita Encarnación bouncing along chilly sidelines in a bulky sweater and crisply pleated skirt, performing exuberant leaps and tantalizing cartwheels, thrilling his teenage heart with glimpses of bare midriff and flashes of satin panties.

Felicita Encarnación . . .

Using an eraser, Fink drew a small lopsided heart on the desktop. He stared at it for a moment before wiping it away and brushing the rubber flakes from his hand. Felicita had been thirty years ago, more than thirty. He had been so crazy about her he had never even asked her out.

He dropped the pencil to the desk and caught it on the first hop. Marissa Grelling, he reminded himself, was not the cheerleader type. Marissa Grelling was a murder suspect with a seven-figure motive.

And Mel Fink was a cop.

He checked the time. It was still early enough to call and cancel the dinner. That would be the smart thing to do. He had almost decided to do it when it occurred to him that he had never worn that designer tie his daughter, Eileen, had sent him last year.

He looked across his desk and conjured up Marissa Grelling's sultry image. She claimed to have seen Vietnam in his eyes, which he knew was a crock. But he had sure as hell seen something in hers. What he couldn't decide was whether it was teenage sparkle or the hissing of a lit fuse.

Either way, it was about time he wore that tie.

CHAPTER SIX

Johnson awoke to a warm breeze, white walls and the smell of flowers. He assumed he was dead. It was a wonderful, peaceful feeling, exactly as he'd imagined it. He was lying on his back between clean white sheets. An overhead fan turned lazily, making the same tiny squeak with each revolution. He watched it awhile, enjoying its unhurried pace, its steadiness, its absolute predictability. This death business was okay.

What he hadn't expected was such a strong physical sense. Different parts of his body were slowly making themselves known to him. His tongue felt heavy, his lips were dry and his eyes were sticky. He felt crusty, as if his skin was thin and brittle. He lay there staring at the fan and wondering if he should try to move, finally deciding there couldn't be any harm.

So he tried to sit up. It didn't work, and as he fell back down a girl started to scream. Her voice was so loud that he thought it was coming from inside the room. He rolled his head toward the sound and saw a young girl who looked almost exactly like Mee Yang, which convinced him he was dreaming. He wondered why she was screaming. He heard loud footsteps. Instinctively he pulled his body into a ball and covered his face with his arms.

He felt the presence of a heavy shadow.

"Hey, Doc," a voice called from above, "rise and shine."

The voice was so loud, so full of energy. It was a voice he had never heard before. But he was happy they spoke English here. Slowly he began to uncoil, feeling the rapid patter of his heartbeat as if it were the only thing in his chest. When he opened his eyes he saw a huge white face with many fresh scars. Good stitching, he thought, then came fully awake.

"Colonel Ransom?" he croaked, struggling to sit up.

The face broke into a wide smile and remained stationary, while hands gripped Johnson from both sides, pulled him gently and then propped him up against pillows. His body felt clean but frail. He wasn't dead.

"You are one scrawny bird," Ransom laughed, tilting the bed as he sat by Johnson's legs. He was wearing a white shirt and blue jeans. "There's some soup on the way," he said, "but how's about some water first?"

Johnson nodded. His throat was dry. He glanced around the room. Mee Yang was gone, if indeed she had ever been there. Ransom's accent was vaguely familiar. After a moment Johnson came up with it: Mama's cousin Rentin. That was his name: Rentin. Big guy with reddish hair. Drove an old green Buick all the way up from North Carolina once with the muffler attached with a wire hanger. Rentin. Mama's cousin.

Ransom held out a teacup which Johnson took with both hands. The water was lukewarm and felt almost solid going down. It tasted like life itself. Johnson sipped very slowly.

He wet his tongue and ran it around the inside of his mouth and over his lips. Wet had never felt so good.

Ransom was watching him with the happy fascination of a kid studying his first goldfish. "You been asleep a long time," he said. "I'll bet you're hungry."

"Where am I?" Johnson asked.

"You're with me," Ransom declared. Scars all over his face were curling into miniature smiles.

"How long did you think it was?" Ransom asked him.

"I don't know," Johnson replied. "I guess I just stopped thinking about it."

He was sitting up in the clean bed, his body washed and powdered and altogether strange to him. Everything itched, as if his skin was burlap. He and Ransom had been talking for a long time. His stomach felt as heavy and solid as an iron kettle. Mee Yang had brought soup and bread and coffee and two cookies; these last he'd insisted on eating by himself. After carefully separating them, he'd joined the two halves with the filling into one bigger cookie which he'd proceeded to nibble one tiny luxurious bite at a time. It had made him feel like a kid again.

Ransom had laughed. "That's one thing you're going to like for sure," he'd said.

"What's that?"

"They make DoubleStuf now."

"Who does?"

"The Oreo folks. They still make the regular ones, but they also make them with double the filling, like what you were doing. DoubleStuf. I'll get some for you."

"Double stuff," Johnson said again now, shaking his head and feeling his face stretch into a wide, uncontrollable grin. He tried to imagine what the package looked like: clear plastic with long stacks of black cookies, cookie after cookie stuffed to overflowing with sweet white filling. For some reason the idea made him deliriously happy. He began laughing and crying at the same time. How could it have been twenty-four years?

CHAPTER SEVEN

Snosset pressed print and heard the reassuring beeps and whirrs and tiny hiccups of modern technology applying itself to the task at hand. He listened to the regular thwipping of the greenish perforated paper moving with jerky precision, a kind of New Age electronic music, page after page unfolding and refolding, arranging itself into a neat continuous stack to be picked up or Fed-Exed or interofficed somewhere to cover another politician's corrupt ass. High-tech toilet paper, Snosset thought, that's all I do. That's all I am.

Leaving the uncomplaining machine to its work, Snosset closed his eyes, leaned back and stretched the muscles in his neck, wondering how the hell he ever got to be fifty years old.

For two decades now Snosset had been inputting and compiling, cross-checking and analyzing, measuring his life in useless printouts for snot-nosed kids with hard bodies and intact dreams. The phone calls and memos had already started for this new Senate committee, all these ambitious little aides thinking up clever new ways to reorder the data and score some brownie points with the senators. Well, they could design runs till kingdom come, they could merge-purge till the cows came home, but for Snosset the blunt, undigestible truth was that twenty years after the war ended there were still dozens of American men unaccounted for and fewer people each year who gave a damn. And that was only half of it.

The other half, the bigger half, was Calvin Snosset, unnamed co-conspirator, living with the fact that if it hadn't been for him one of those poor bastards might never have been captured. If not for Snosset, the guy would probably still be alive today, with a wife and kids and who knew what else. A life. If Snosset hadn't freaked. If, if, if.

But maybe, just maybe, Snosset thought, this new Senate committee would be different. Despite himself, Snosset was determined to give it one last try, to go all-out, not because he had any faith in politicians, but because the one man he respected in Washington was the committee chairman: Senator Antel Grantham of Alaska, the Sisyphus of the Senate, who'd been rolling boulders up Capitol Hill for more than twenty years. Since the early seventies, the craggy Alaskan had been a lonely voice pushing for national health care, a balanced budget, decriminalization of drugs and a universal higher education loan program. Back home they loved his unyielding crustiness, but here in Washington he was a pariah, even within his own party. Though he habitually lost, over the years Grantham had taken on the pharmaceutical industry, the oil industry, the auto industry. He had even done battle with Snosset's own federal employees over their exemption from Social Security. He'd lost that one too. But most important, as far as Snosset was concerned, was that for twenty years Senator Antel Grantham had kept the fire burning for the

POW/MIAs, doggedly fanning the shrinking embers, refusing to let the issue die. As Grantham had challenged last Sunday morning on *Meet the Press*: "Too painful? What in heaven's name are you talking about? Childbirth is too painful; does that mean the human race should not reproduce? I swear I do not understand what is wrong with some of our people. We left thousands of our children over there in Southeast Asia and we are obligated to them, to their families, to our nation and to our conscience which is the voice of God to account for them."

When he'd heard that, Snosset had leaped up from his chair applauding, tears streaming down his cheeks. The rest of the committee could go get stuffed, but any request from Senator Grantham would be handled instantly. Instantly. There would be no such thing as a break or lunch or quitting time as long as data for Senator Grantham was running. And when the run was complete, Snosset would close up his office and deliver it personally. The media could call the senator "Old Granny" all they wanted—Snosset's grandmother had been the finest creature God had put on the earth since His own son. Snosset didn't have a son, or a daughter either. He'd had a wife, but Vietnam had taken care of that.

The machine stopped. The official master list of POW/MIAs arranged by state and subdivided by congressional district was complete. After twenty years, Snosset knew every name on the list by heart. He could recite them in alphabetical order—last name, first name, middle initial. All of them save one. There was one name he couldn't bear to say out loud, the one that was etched in his conscience.

Officially, the total of missing servicemen on the MIA list remained at more than two thousand, but the official number was a fiction, characterized by Senator Grantham as "a cruel hoax." In the years since the war countless reports had been investigated, crash sites had been visited, evidence had been sifted, remains had been painstakingly identified. One by one, names had fallen from the list like dry leaves from a tree. The public didn't know it, but the tree was almost bare; less than a hundred aging leaves remained clinging to its branches. And Snosset's man was among them, his name cleaving to the tree as if nailed there.

Snosset decided to break for lunch. Before leaving, he clipped his beeper to his belt. The call from Senator Grantham would be coming any time now, and when it did Snosset wanted to be ready.

CHAPTER EIGHT

The conference table was littered with Styrofoam cups, plastic stirrers and crumpled napkins. The reporters were filing out the door.

"Shane," the editor called plaintively. "Come back, Shane."

It was a very tired joke, but Shane Reilly forced a smile and maneuvered her way back into the room.

Her editor, Mike Mitchelson, stood at the head of the table. "Shane, tell me the truth. You've heard that line before, right?"

"Yes, actually, I have," she smiled. She liked being alone with him. It made him nervous.

"Sit down," he said. "How tall are you, anyhow?"

She pulled a chair up to the table. "Five eleven."

He hitched up his pants self-consciously.

"You have an assignment for me?" she asked hopefully, nibbling her ballpoint.

"The Grantham Committee," he told her. "I'm putting you on it full-time."

She took her pen and punched a hole in a Styrofoam cup. "Lucky me."

"You'd prefer the flower show?"

"No, but I would prefer a breaking story."

"Something will break on this one. I've got a feeling."

"Really? Then maybe you should give it to Fleischer. He did the UFO thing last month. MIAs, UFOs, they're pretty much the same thing: random sightings, doctored photographs . . ."

"You ever meet Senator Grantham?"

"No."

"He's a good man."

"What?" she exclaimed. "Am I hearing right? Did Mike Mitchelson actually call a politician 'a good man'?"

"Look, Reilly," he said, sitting down, "stow the cynicism. If you don't want the assignment I'll give it to someone else."

"Sorry, boss."

"You're too young to remember Vietnam," Mitchelson said. "I understand that. But fifty-eight thousand American boys came home from that swamp in body bags, and the Pentagon still lists more than two thousand unaccounted for. It's a goddamn disgrace. Grantham is the only one trying to do something about it."

"Is that my angle?" she asked, making notes.

"No, that's too partisan. But you might try approaching it like unfinished business, a Saddam Hussein kind of thing."

She cocked her head, not connecting.

"The MIAs as a symptom," he explained. "Look, Reilly, I don't believe any of our boys are still prisoners over there. The poor bastards are all dead. They live on only as a cottage industry for crackpots. Unfortunately, your UFO analogy wasn't far off. But we abandoned these guys. The years right after the war, when some of them probably were alive, we turned our backs on them."

"The MIAs as a symptom of what?" she asked, writing fast.

"Maybe I'm getting too old," Mitchelson said, passing a hand through his thinning hair. "A symptom of national impotence? I don't know. We can't save these kids anymore, but at least we can give them an honest burial, tell them and their families that we're sorry. I think Grantham means to do that. It's a good thing."

"What about Saddam Hussein?" she asked.

"Oh, that was free association: a deep river of bullshit running straight from the Tonkin Gulf Resolution to the Elite Republican Guard." He picked up the remains of a donut, examined it, made a face and dropped it on the table. "I was just thinking about how Bush told the country that we had no argument with the Iraqi people, but that their leader, Saddam Hussein, was a new Hitler. So then he sends Stormin' Norman over there and kills maybe a hundred fifty thousand of those people with whom we had no argument, but leaves the new Hitler in power. And back home we wave yellow ribbons, wrap ourselves in the flag, chug beer and have parades. I don't know, Reilly. Grantham's a good man. You're a smart kid. It should be a strong story."

"Were you in the war?" she asked.

"Me?" He picked up a napkin and buffed a small section of the Formica tabletop. "Hell, no. I hid out in grad school, the same as Clinton and Quayle and all of my friends. Maybe that's another reason I feel guilty about this MIA business: Most of my generation did a lot less than they could. These MIAs did as much as they could. We owe them. Did you know Grantham lost his only son in the war? Poor kid stepped on a mine near Pleiku."

"How come I'm getting the assignment?" Shane asked.

"Grantham's old, but he's not blind. Try to get in to see him today. He'll appreciate those slacks."

"I'm a good reporter," she said, her face reddening.

"Here's your chance to show me."

CHAPTER NINE

Rhonda lowered her chin and looked up, giving the hunk in the blue suit her most seductive angle.

"I hope you're Detective Barton," she said.

He fumbled for his shield. "Right," he said, flashing it. "Who are you?"

"Rhonda Cohen." She fluttered her lashes.

"Wow."

"That sure beats some Whoopi Goldberg joke." She stood and showed him the rest, offered her hand. "You really single?"

"Say what?"

His hand was huge. She held it that extra half second. She'd gone the limit. The next move had to be his.

"Can we talk here," he asked, "or is there some place more private?"

"We have a lounge," she said. "The chairs are comfortable. Could I interest you in a cup of coffee and a donut?"

"Lead the way."

Which was a shame, really. She'd been hoping to have him walk ahead. He seemed so pleased with the front view. She hoped he liked big hips.

She aimed him toward the best chair and asked how he took his coffee, then went to fetch it. All men enjoyed being served, and since she earned more than he did, there was no harm.

She sipped her Diet Coke, trying not to leave lipstick on the straw. "You have questions," she said.

He uncrossed his legs and leaned forward. "Ms. Cohen," he said, "I need to ask you some things about Mr. Grelling."

She hitched herself higher in her chair, put her drink down, arranged her hands so he could see she had no ring. She wanted to appear concerned, interested, anxious to cooperate. She encouraged her eyes to speak to him on their own. I'll answer your questions, they said to him, then you ask me out. Do it, said her steady gaze, you won't be sorry. Then her eyes said something so brazen she had to look away.

He had a lot of questions. She answered them all, trying to make it sound as if she'd liked Mr. Grelling more than she had. She was sorry he was dead, of course, and curious as to why, but the fact was he had always been a cold fish.

Barton wanted copies of all Mr. Grelling's invoices from the past year. She told him she would need clearance for that, but she had been authorized to give him a list of Mr. Grelling's clients and his sales volume by country, region or type of product. She could access any or all of that through her desktop computer. She tried reminding him telepathically about tonight.

"How about personnel files?" Barton asked.

"Those too," she assured him. She knew the code. She paused. Was he interested in something in particular?

"I was just wondering," he said, coming to the edge of his chair.

"Yes?" The sight of his long fingers dangling between his legs made her breath catch.

He hesitated, sat back. "How many employees does Parker Global have?"

She exhaled. "Worldwide, a little over seven thousand."

"Could your computer tell us how many of them have died, say in the past year?"

"I should think so," she replied. "Why?"

"And what they died from?"

"If it's recorded in their file, sure." She leaned forward, intrigued. "What exactly are you thinking?"

"I'm thinking . . ." He took a breath which lifted his wide shoulders. "Do you like muffins, Miss Cohen?"

"Muffins?"

"I know this little place in the West Village that makes homemade muffins."

"Muffins," she said, suddenly flustered. She began fiddling with a button on her blouse. "When exactly were you thinking of these muffins, Detective Barton?"

"Tonight, Miss Cohen. I was thinking of the muffins for tonight. If that's convenient."

In her confusion she recalled having plans for tonight, something to do with her hand, her mouth. "Well," she said, trying to sort it all out, "we could go back to my desk and check my calendar."

"Let's." He smiled. He had great teeth.

While she worked the computer he leaned over her shoulder. She hoped he was sniffing her Joy and not her Secret. Keeping her elbows in tight, she accessed Mr. Grelling's personnel file. Its last entry was "DXNC," which Molly in personnel had to translate for her as "Deceased Not Natural Causes."

Following Barton's suggestion, Rhonda went to the search mode, entered "DXNC," set the time parameter for the past year, and hit the enter key. The screen hiccupped and flashed up "unable." She tried it three more times with the same result.

Barton asked if Mr. Grelling spoke any languages other than English and Spanish. Rhonda was sure he did. She'd heard him on the telephone a few times jabbering away in something like Japanese, except that it wasn't Japanese. She assured Barton she could recognize Japanese. Well, it was easy enough to check. But when she tried to call up Mr. Grelling's personnel file again she couldn't do that either.

"That's funny," she said, feeling foolish, "I must be doing something wrong. We could go up to personnel, I'm sure Molly knows how to do it."

"I'll go myself," Barton told her. "You just point me in the right direction."

Rhonda didn't want him going up there by himself. "It's a little tricky to find," she said.

"I'm a detective," he reminded her.

Rhonda smiled, but she was furious with herself. Molly in personnel had recently separated from her husband. Rhonda had overheard the boys in the mail room saying that Molly had the best legs in the office.

"I don't even know your first name," Rhonda said, handing Barton an engraved business card on which she had written her home address and telephone.

"Don," he told her.

"As in Donald?"

He hesitated. "As in Donatello," he said. "I don't like to say it because people think I was named after a turtle. I'll see you at eight o'clock."

She sat there smiling until he stepped onto the elevator,

then grabbed the phone and punched in Molly's extension. If that bitch so much as stood up, Rhonda was going to tear her eyes out. And why the hell hadn't she been able to get that DXNC to work? What was it, a secret?

CHAPTER TEN

As Johnson's strength increased he began to explore his new surroundings. The compound consisted of six buildings surrounded by a high wooden fence. There were towers at each corner which were always manned by armed guards. It reminded Johnson of a small Old West fort, except that here the wood was bamboo and the fence was surrounded by Cambodian jungle. He counted about thirty soldiers, all of them Asian and all dressed in camouflage fatigues without any insignia. After the first few times Johnson ventured out, the soldiers took no notice of him, though their eyes continued to linger over Mee Yang, who stuck to Johnson like a shadow. She fussed over him constantly, never letting him out of her sight except when he closed the bathroom door. She even slept on a mat on the floor next to his bed. In their short time here she had learned more English than he had learned Khmer in all his years of captivity. It made him feel like a dope. He'd learned many individual words, but she was already getting the gist of his conversations with Ransom. She claimed to be nineteen, which he supposed was possible. He had delivered her and it didn't seem that long ago, but his sense of time had gone haywire. On those rare occasions when he'd allowed himself to think about it—curled up on the straw inside his cage unable to sleep, or during one of the many forced marches through the jungle—he'd never been able to come up with a number. Now he realized that he had existed in a place outside of time, using what little energy he'd had to survive from day to day. In that narrow world there had ceased to be a past or a future, only a localized clarity surrounded by blurs.

In fact, it was this whole idea of time that he was having the most trouble adjusting to. He wasn't used to thinking about it, wasn't comfortable with it. He got rattled at the thought of making decisions. He couldn't come to terms with the apparent fact that he was more than forty years old, especially since each day now, as a bit more of his strength returned, he felt himself getting younger. He still thought of himself as a nineteen-year-old who'd been lost for a while. When he tried to zero in on how long he'd been a prisoner his thoughts started shooting off in too many directions and he had to stop and steady himself. He was bursting with all kinds of questions, but he was too timid to ask them: of Mee Yang, or Ransom, or even himself.

He spent a lot of time in front of the TV. Among a host of amazing devices, Ransom had a TV which he claimed received signals bounced off a satellite in space and picked up by a black metal dish on the roof. It sounded like something out of *The Twilight Zone*, but it brought in stations from all over the world, including one from Atlanta called CNN: the Cable News Network. Johnson imagined thick metal cables snaking all over the world distributing news the way a hose carried water.

At first everything on the screen went by much too fast

for Johnson to follow—color and noise all splashing together in a rushing waterfall of sight and sound. He would sit in a large leather chair working a wonderful new toy Ransom called "the remote." Mee Yang would sit at his feet in blue jeans and a T-shirt, her knees drawn up to her chin, anxious to see everything, encouraging him to keep changing channels. "Less suff," she would say, mimicking Ransom's goofy phrase, "channel surfing." And once he started, she would tap his leg excitedly with her hand, urging him to go "Fassa, fassa!"

Johnson believed that it was her boundless, childish enthusiasm that was slowly but steadily restoring him to health. Thanks to her prodding, he was gaining weight. He loved to sit quietly and watch her brush her long hair. Her skin and her hair were like two different types of silk. When she shaved him with a straight razor he would lean back against her, close his eyes and try to distinguish the soft scents of her fresh young body from the sharp menthol of the shaving cream.

"You fucking her yet?" Ransom asked him over breakfast one morning.

"No," Johnson mumbled, embarrassed because she was sitting right next to him and because he'd been thinking about it so much lately that he'd had to start bathing himself.

"Your plumbing all right?" Ransom asked, reaching out his fork and spearing a sausage.

"Sure," Johnson replied. "Everything's, you know . . . fine."

Up in the corner a metal box with a fluorescent purple light was busy electrocuting insects, each random flash and angry buzz making Johnson wince. Ransom called it a "zapper."

"You don't want her, no problem," Ransom said, squeezing the muffins, trying to decide. "I'll send her back and get you another one."

Under the table a hand grasped Johnson's knee. He jumped.

"Mee Yang is fine," he said. "Really. Just fine."

The hand relaxed and slid to the inside of his thigh. His leg began to tremble.

Ransom cut a piece of sausage with his fork and dug it into his scrambled eggs. He glanced up at Mee Yang and spoke to her in harsh, rapid Khmer. She answered him timidly, her eyes downcast. He said something else, almost a bark. She stood, touched Johnson's shoulder, left the room.

"Now we can talk," Ransom said.

"What did you say to her?"

"I told her to take a bath and wait for you in bed."

"She's just a kid," Johnson said.

"Does she get your dick hard?"

"Yes."

"Then fuck her. That's what she wants, believe me."

"You think so?"

"I know so. I just asked her. She was afraid you didn't like her anymore. Seems you won't let her bathe you." He chuckled. "You should have seen the look in her eyes when I said I'd send her back."

Johnson shifted in his chair. "It's been a long time," he said.

"It's like swimming," Ransom said. "You don't forget. Remember, I was a prisoner too."

Ransom's scars were healing well, though at first glance the left side of his face looked as if someone had been playing tic-tac-toe on it. There was one scar on his forearm that was still a little raw, but that had been the deepest. Johnson noticed that his host was starting to favor his right side when talking to people.

A sudden zap, a small flash: one less insect.

"What do you really do?" Johnson asked him.

"I do what all businessmen do: I trade things. Take some more eggs."

"Thanks." He was trying not to think about Mee Yang. "The sausage is super," he said. "Where's it from?"

"Nebraska, I think. The jam is British. I like these tiny jars. You?"

"Great. I don't want you to take this the wrong way, Colonel," Johnson said carefully, "but there's still . . . I mean, some things . . ."

"What do you want to know, Doc?"

"Well, for one thing, if the war ended so long ago, how come you're still here?"

"I like it here. The weather's good for my sinuses. I run a successful business. I'm addicted to Asian pussy. Did you try the marmalade? It's got those little pieces of orange peel."

"Drugs?" Johnson asked.

"Sure. What do you need?"

"No. I mean, is that your business?"

"My business is trading," Ransom said, "just like I told you." He stood and topped up both their mugs with coffee.

"Have I ever traded drugs?" Ransom shrugged. "Sure. I trade drugs all the time. Last month I moved a trailer filled with Zantac, Imodium, Tolinase and Prozac. You want profit margin, Doc, work with the pharmaceuticals."

"How about opium?" Johnson asked.

"There's action in opium, but it's seasonal," Ransom replied matter-of-factly. "You know what's moving right now? Apple computers. Windows. Game Boys are still hot, especially Super Mario." He stirred his coffee. "Don't get me wrong; opium is good. But I prefer the perennials: Marlboro, American blue jeans, Revlon, munitions, VHS porno tapes with big-titted white girls. When you're a hundred percent we can talk about all this stuff." There was a small flash and a zap. He glanced up and jabbed his finger at the ceiling. "Right now, if you don't mind a little advice, you should drag your MIA ass upstairs and get yourself some of that."

"Can I ask one more question?"

"Shoot."

"When can I go home?"

Ransom gave him a funny look. "*Mi casa, su casa,*" he said, spreading his arms wide. "You are home."

"I mean the States," Johnson said. "My real home."

Ransom took a deep breath and released it slowly. "You can't," he said gently. "You poor fuck, you can't go home. Don't you understand? The war ended too long ago. Take my word for it, nobody back there wants you."

"My mother wants me," Johnson said. "I know she does."

"You're right," Ransom sighed. "I forgot you still had a mother. Mine . . ." He pulled out his pen. "Write down her name, her last known address, where she worked. I'll see if we can find her."

As Johnson struggled with the pen, Ransom muttered something about going home, then abruptly crossed the room and started rummaging through a desk. He returned with a few things and straddled Mee Yang's chair. Laying a newspaper flat on the table he took Johnson's hand and one by one pressed his fingers against an ink pad, then carefully imprinted them on a blank space near the top of the front page.

"What's this for?" Johnson asked.

"A little going home experiment," Ransom explained. He folded Johnson's note and put it in his shirt pocket, then began rolling up the newspaper.

"Look, I've got to go away for a while," he said. "I'll be

gone a week or so. Problem with a supplier. Fuck the little girl every way you can think of. When I get back we'll talk. You saved my life, remember?"

"You saved my life too," Johnson reminded him. "We're even."

Ransom stared at him for a moment, his eyes suddenly flat. "We'll never be even," he said. "Never."

"I want to go home," Johnson whispered.

"I know, kid," Ransom said softly, slipping the rolled newspaper into a plastic sleeve and tucking it under his arm. "We all want to go home. Now go get laid."

PART TWO

CHAPTER ELEVEN

Marissa had hoped the surroundings would calm him. It was so lovely here, the Gold Room at the Helmsley Palace: so opulent, so refined, so Old World. But it was all wasted on Herbert Trang, who hadn't even reacted when she'd pointed out the exquisite little balcony over the entrance. For musicians, she'd explained, recalling how Leona had shown it to her that first time. And now Leona was in prison somewhere in Connecticut for evading taxes and Marissa was here, sliding the silver-plated ring from a lime green linen napkin. Fate.

That's what she was trying to explain to Trang; that it was fate, that there was no need to keep his family in Texas, that he was reading too much into Frank's death, that being alone was only making things worse for him. Trang was a wreck. In the weeks since Frank's death he had convinced himself they were coming after him next.

"Why would they do that?" Marissa asked, her tone suggesting that his concern was childish.

She encouraged him to look around. The room, she told him, was a replica of the ballroom at Versailles. But he couldn't seem to focus on anything she was saying. He winced at the slightest sounds: the clinking of a dish, the snap of a newspaper, muffled laughter from a nearby table. She complimented him on his tie. He fingered it nervously, tried to smile. When she offered him the basket of miniature croissants he shook his head and hid his hands in his lap.

"I was the one who arranged the sales," Trang reminded her anxiously. "Frank only handled—"

"We really cannot discuss this," she said softly but firmly.

"But—"

She leaned in, smiling fiercely. "Let's get this straight, *compadre.* You did nothing wrong. Neither did I. We don't know who killed Frank and neither do the police. I think you should have some fruit." She signaled for the waiter.

"We should try to talk to them," Trang pleaded. "You could—"

"No, I could not," she hissed. "The last thing we want is to draw attention to ourselves." She reached into her purse. "Here, I've brought you more Valium. They'll calm you down and help you sleep."

As he slipped the bottle into his suit pocket the pills rattled against the plastic-like tiny castanets.

"What are you doing tonight?" she asked him.

"Nothing. I don't know. I'll probably order in, watch some TV, try to relax. Why?"

She took his hand, felt his fear. This was not good. Trang was coming apart. Surprising, really, for a person who had survived a war, albeit as a child. Clearly, she had misjudged him. She hated cowardice in a man. Hated it.

"Promise me," she said, "you will not discuss this with anyone." She squeezed, trying to transfuse some of her resolve into him. "Anyone."

"I won't," he assured her. "You know I won't."

"Good," she said, patting his hand. Rancid cooking oil, that's what he smelled like. It was wilting the flowers.

"Trust me," she urged him, staring directly into his frightened eyes. "I've seen this before. What you're feeling now is the worst of it. It's like a fever, running its course. One more day and you'll be fine. I'm sorry about the shipment too. These things happen. We'll make it up to them."

She sat back. "Here's the waiter. What you need is some fresh citrus. Don't say no; we can never get enough vitamin C."

She ordered a fruit cup for him. After the waiter left she carefully lowered a spoonful of honey into her tea. She held it there patiently, watching it dissolve, admiring the steadiness of her hand.

The buzzer affected Trang like an electric shock. He waited while the shiver worked its way through his body, then he turned down the TV, padded over and pressed the intercom. Even with the Valium his chest felt tight. He could hear his heart thumping.

He spoke into the little metal grate: "Yes?"

"De-liff'ry."

Trang recognized the doorman's accent. Miguel. Manuel. Something like that. Puerto Rican.

"What is it?" Trang asked cautiously.

"Shy-neese."

"Okay, send him up." He released the button, felt for his wallet, panicked momentarily when it wasn't there but then remembered that he'd left it inside on the dresser. Mother of God, he hadn't felt like this since he'd been a child and they'd come and dragged his uncle away screaming. He'd never seen the poor man again. He stopped, lifted a foot, adjusted the heel of his slipper.

The apartment felt hollow without Mary and the kids, but Trang was glad they were safe. Texas. What could be more American than Texas? He'd call her later and talk with the kids and they would be home in two more days and yes, he had booked the limousine for the airport. Marissa was probably right; he wasn't used to being alone, that was a big part of his problem. Paranoid fantasy, she called it. Still, every time he thought about Grelling he felt a constriction in his throat. Now why had he come into the bedroom?

To his relief, the wallet was on the dresser, exactly where he'd left it. Now why did he need it? Oh. He couldn't even remember what he'd ordered. Whatever it was, he hoped he'd insisted on no MSG. Not that they ever listened. His stomach had been funny lately and MSG always gave him the runs.

Trang was sick of Chinese food, but he'd tried eating out twice this week and he couldn't handle it. He'd felt too exposed sitting all by himself and he'd nearly gone crazy waiting for the food to arrive. He couldn't understand how some people could do it all the time, just sit there like that. Maybe you had to be a Buddhist. His uncle had been a Buddhist, for all the good it had done him.

Trang was glad he was at home. Everything was familiar, comfortable. He was lucky to have all this. The Valium was starting to kick in; he felt lighter. All this worrying was stupid, he knew that. There was no evidence that Grelling's death had anything—anything at all—to do with the company. Besides, if that shipment had been the problem, they would have come after Trang first. He had been the salesman, after all. Grelling's end had been boilerplate. And when somebody had a problem with an order . . . Well, okay, these people couldn't, but still, Trang reminded himself, there were—

He jumped at the sound of the doorbell. Damn, he was on

edge. Maybe he should go out to the massage parlor later. He could call and try to reserve that little Korean girl again, the one with the strong hands and the tickling tongue. Tina. What a good idea. Except that he'd have to stop at the ATM for cash: Otherwise it could appear on some monthly statement Mary might open. Careful, careful.

The doorbell rang again and he tucked in his shirt and hurried inside, working out the logistics. He could have the cab stop at the ATM and wait for him. Like a little doll, that girl. Tina. And so anxious to please. Maybe he'd surprise her this time, pull her into the tub. Why not? He worked hard, he deserved a little recreation.

He crossed the living room, feeling a new bounce in his step. No, Marissa was definitely right. It couldn't have been that shipment. Those people were realistic. They didn't want trouble. Especially not now, when they were pushing to normalize relations. And what could they have expected? Some of that stuff was more than twenty years old. Why else did they think the price was so good? No, Grelling must have been into something else on his own. Greed, Trang reflected; greed was a terrible thing.

He checked the chain, turned the locks, opened the door a crack and peeked out. A nondescript kid, seventeen, eighteen maybe, probably illegal, holding the standard brown paper bag with stapled menu. Sneakers, blue jeans, creased white busboy's jacket. The food smelled good. Chicken with black bean sauce, that's what it was. And ten-ingredient fried rice. Plus they always sent two fortune cookies. He could take one to Tina, devise some clever way to open it.

"How much?" he asked

"Fifteen seventy-eight," the boy said, staring down at the hall carpet.

The delivery boy's hair looked like someone had used a pot and shears. A country bumpkin. What the hell, Trang thought, make the kid's day: Give him a twenty and tell him to keep the change. He smiled. If Tina performed like last time he'd be giving her a lot more than that.

He slipped a twenty from his wallet and transferred it to his left hand. If Grelling had been this careful, Trang told himself, he'd probably still be alive. Proceeding methodically, he slid the wallet into his back pocket, planted his left heel firmly to prevent the door from opening too wide and grasped the edge of it with his left hand so he could slam it instantly. Then, with his right hand, he unlatched the chain and opened the door about a foot. It squeaked. The kid glanced up, looking nervous: probably anxious to get back downstairs before someone stole his bicycle. Actually, he looked more Vietnamese than Chinese. All poor people looked the same.

Trang plucked the twenty from his left hand and passed it out with his right. "Here," he said, "keep the change."

"Sank you, sank you, sank you," the kid gushed, excitedly stuffing the bill into his jacket pocket while holding out the brown bag.

But just as Trang was reaching for it, the bag slipped from the boy's grasp. Instinctively, Trang released his grip on the door and lunged for it. There was a frozen fraction of a second when Trang, helplessly off-balance, saw the fist flying toward his face. He felt an explosion and then there was nothing until he awoke with something stuffed in his mouth and his arms and legs tied to a chair. Struggling to suck in air through his nose, he looked around desperately. He was at home. The TV was on. His head ached, his wrists burned. It was hard to breathe. He sensed someone behind him. There was a quick blurry motion past his eyes and then he felt something thin and hard against his neck. When it began to tighten he couldn't even scream. He knew it wouldn't do any good to thrash about, but he couldn't help it.

Chapter Twelve

As he was unbuttoning his collar, he heard across the darkness what sounded like the chirp of a small bird. He froze, savoring the growing intensity in his body, now nearing seventy but still lean and hard and fully functional. When she peeped again, things in him jumped.

He removed his gold eagle cuff links, the ones given to him by LBJ, and slipped them into a jacket pocket. Then, folding up his sleeves, he walked over and nudged up the rheostat, bathing the room in a soft fuzzy light.

She was standing against the far wall. Her demure pose—head down, arms in back, one foot turned in ever so slightly—called attention to her Mandarin-collared red silk dress. There was a lovely sheen to her long black hair, gathered at the top so it would fall like dark rain when he pulled the satin bow. His eyes traced down the line of mother-of-pearl buttons, all the way down to the white lace socks and clean white sneakers.

He dropped to one knee, clapped softly and held out his

arms. She looked up, saw him motioning for her and walked toward him, stopping a few feet away. He waved her in closer and, after some encouragement, she reached out and placed her hands in his. He held them lightly, feeling their subtle vibrations reverberate through him like the tinkling of a harpsichord. He watched a wonderful pale vein throbbing along the side of her delicate neck.

He pulled gently at her fingers, drawing her closer, breathing in her subtle odors. He lifted and examined her hands, admired each finger, held his breath and listened to the air passing through her nose.

With infinite care he began unbuttoning her dress from the bottom up. The room's temperature seemed to rise along with his hands. After the fifth button, he paused and slipped a forefinger into the elastic waistband of her pink silk panties. He lowered the front an inch, two, three, until, reflexively, she drew back. He stared up at her, his hooked finger maintaining the pressure. Her eyes darted from his gaze like a pair of skittish tropical fish. But it had been enough. She inched forward and returned her belly to where it had been.

He was immensely pleased to see that she had been properly prepared, that she understood that she must do precisely what this nice, white-haired man wanted or she and her parents would be thrown back into the hold of a filthy ship, returned to a life of grinding poverty: that throughout her life she would have to bear the shame of having failed her family in its hour of need. A difficult concept to grasp, perhaps, for a child of—how old was this one?—eight, nine, ten at the most. Difficult, yes, but clearly—demonstrably—not impossible.

While pulling the panties back above the little igloo of her navel his fingertips brushed along her belly. He swallowed hard, raised his hands to her throat and undid the final buttons. The dress fell away, exposing the tiny, puckered nipples of her narrow chest. He peeled the fabric from her shoulders. Instinctively, her arms crossed.

With her dress gone, her breathing became irregular. She began to sniffle. The strain of pressing her thighs together was making the flesh vibrate. He slipped his hand sideways between her knees and twisted. After a short hesitation, she made an awkward movement and her thighs parted.

He gazed up into her sweet face. Tears were welling up in her eyes. Her throat was producing tiny, involuntary squeaks, each piercing him like a needle of pure joy.

He hooked his forefingers into the sides of her panties, leaned forward and brought his face alongside hers. Her odor was intoxicating.

"Jen," he whispered into the little seashell of her ear.

His voice startled her, shaking tears loose to form a single curved rivulet down one smooth cheek.

"Jen," he whispered patiently, again and again until she understood.

"Jen," she repeated in a thin, quavering voice.

He ran an index finger up the channel of her tears, brought the finger to his mouth and licked its salty, animal warmth.

She had no trouble with the next sound, or with putting the two syllables together.

"Jen-uh," she said, sniffing hard and venturing the flicker of a smile because she knew she had it right.

He was leisurely exploring the waistband of her panties when she mangled the last syllable.

"Jen-uh-RAL," he corrected her, pulling her panties up very high and holding them, revealing the outline of her vagina.

"Jen-uh-RUH," she responded, tears flowing freely now.

Smiling and nodding, he encouraged her to say it over and

over while he eased the panties down over her little buttocks and carefully freed them from between her thighs.

He had some trouble getting her to accept the panties into her mouth, but he was gentle and persistent. He took special care to tie the silk ribbon securely.

He was leading her by her doll-like hand to the bed when the harsh cry of the telephone startled them both.

It took him a few moments to free himself from the hot sticky mist and get to the phone.

"Yes?" he growled.

"Good afternoon, General." It was Harold Schaeffer, Parker Global's CEO. "I'm sorry to disturb your nap, but there's been another killing. I thought you should be informed."

"Who was it?" he asked impatiently.

"Herbert Trang."

"Damn," the old man muttered, dropping into an easy chair, grabbing a nearby riding crop and angrily slashing at his shoe. He looked over. She sat huddled at the edge of the bed, exactly where he had placed her. Her eyes, wide with fear, were riveted on the crop in his hand. He tossed it away and gave her a flutter-fingered little wave.

"—found him in his apartment," Schaeffer was explaining. "Apparently, he was a mess. They say—"

"Spare me the details." The general glanced about the room, searching in vain for something she might play with.

"Do you think it's connected to . . . that problem?" Schaeffer asked cautiously.

"Proceed on the assumption that it is," the general advised.

"I'm expecting the police to arrive any minute," Schaeffer said. "What do you suggest?"

"Trang's personnel file," the general said, his eyes fixed on her even as his mind was scanning for danger. "Excise all exotic languages, just as we did with Grelling. Then give the police anything they want."

"Consider it done," Schaeffer assured him.

"And Harold, I think you should call Marissa."

"Jesus, of course. Thank you for reminding me. Oh, one last thing, General," Schaeffer said. "When can we expect you back?"

The general checked his watch. "I'll see you in my office in exactly one—" His eyes returned to the bed. The poor thing was shivering. "—better make it two hours."

Chapter Thirteen

A willowy blonde swished by. Jared's hand went into his pants pocket and rubbed the raised lettering of his business card. After three weeks, he could read the top lines by feel: "Jared P. Hansen/Special Investigator."

In the fifteen minutes he'd been sitting at the bar nursing a Heineken, Jared had spotted two congressmen, one assistant attorney general, and two deputy undersecretaries. And those were just the ones he recognized.

He took another sip of the beer. The once-frosted mug was now merely wet. He wondered how Zeiss was getting here. If he had a car maybe Jared could catch a ride back to Capitol Hill, save himself the cab fare. He glanced at his watch. Five more minutes and he'd have to order another brew. Zeiss would cover the lunch, but Jared would almost certainly have to pick up his own bar tab. He wondered if he would have saved anything by ordering a Bud. Place like this, probably not. Over by the entrance, a young White House aide was attracting a lot of outstretched hands. It bothered Jared that he couldn't remember the guy's name; in this town you had to know the players. He picked some more cashews from the mixed nuts in the wooden bowl. Okay, maybe it wasn't the White House, but "Special Investigator, U.S. Senate Select Committee on POW/MIAs" would look pretty damn good on anybody's résumé. True, he was little more than a glorified gofer, but who had to know? Besides, the job had already produced some very tangible benefits: Jared had screwed more women in the past two weeks than in the previous two years.

The place was getting crowded and the bartender was giving him looks, so Jared broke down and signaled for another beer, foraging for more cashews the moment the bartender turned away. He figured eight bucks a beer, plus tax. For two beers, in this kind of place, he didn't see any way to avoid handing the bartender a twenty and just walking. Which would leave him with barely enough cash for the cab ride back. He decided to think about something else.

Special investigator for a Senate select committee: not bad for a twenty-three-year-old with a B.A. in government from Illinois-Urbana and a handful of graduate credits from Georgetown. With a father who owned a video rental store, a mother who wrote "Low Impact/High Fiber," an aerobics-nutrition column for the local Winnetka paper, a sister who—

Jared felt a rush as Zeiss ambled through the door. There was just something about the guy: a naturalness, a sense of power, the way he always looked exactly right, in sports clothes or workout clothes or today's three-piece suit. Most people gave off a sense of their ethnic background, but Zeiss simply looked American: the kind of sandy-haired kid Norman Rockwell would have painted eating a hot dog, with his baseball mitt next to him on the bench.

The bartender approached with a bottle and a fresh mug,

but Jared waved him off, stood up and dropped a ten on the bar.

"Sorry I'm late," Zeiss said as they were seated at a small but private table for two. "I got hung up in traffic. You okay?"

"Fine." He moved the little vase of fresh flowers. "This is a nice place."

"A little trendy for my tastes," Zeiss confided, casually unfurling his napkin and draping it across his thigh. He passed Jared a menu. "Don't look at the prices. My treat."

Jared studied Zeiss with the intensity of an acolyte, excited to be sharing the same air with him. It wasn't simply that Zeiss had recommended him for the Senate job a few days after their chance meeting at the health club. To Jared, who'd been here only six months, the nation's capital was like an intricate chess problem. Never having learned chess, he felt overwhelmed. But it was clear to him that Zeiss, who couldn't have been much more than thirty, was an expert. Jared was hoping to learn by osmosis.

They spent twenty minutes on small talk: the gym, the weather, the latest Sharon Stone movie, the mess in Russia. Their entrees arrived.

"So," Zeiss said, shifting his tone into serious, "how's the job going?"

"Fine. Listen, I can't thank you enough for—"

Zeiss shook his head. "I assume by now you've met the other staff, shaken hands with the senators, been assigned some space?"

"Yes."

"And discovered that you have almost nothing to do."

"Well, it's important work," Jared protested, fluffing himself up. "We're still in the preliminary stages, but—"

"Not with me," Zeiss said with sudden menace. "Save the

K-Y for Barbara and Marianne and Luisa. With me you talk straight and listen hard. Understood?"

"Sure. Absolutely." Jared grasped his knees to keep his hands from shaking. Barbara, Marianne and Luisa. Those were—Jesus, how the hell—?

Zeiss broke into a grin. "Don't look so worried. I needed a target for a kid I'm training. I didn't think you'd mind."

"Hey, that's okay," Jared assured him, relieved to hear he was simply an exercise. Still, it—

"Relax," Zeiss told him. "The assignment was over at six P.M. yesterday." He grinned. "I don't even know what you did last night."

"He followed me all day?" Jared asked, his memory flipping through faces like a Rolodex.

"Did I say 'he'?"

"No. I just assumed . . ."

Zeiss raised his napkin to cover his smile.

Jared decided it was time to shut up. He went to work on his veal chop.

"When I was a kid," Zeiss said, using a fingernail to fish a tiny piece of cork from his glass of *Macon Blanc*, "I used to watch little girls play double Dutch. You know what that is?"

"I think so," Jared answered cautiously. "Two jump ropes at once?"

"Two ropes going in opposite directions. Anyway, it looked so damned complicated. And yet here were these little black girls making it look easy. You know what I'm talking about?"

"You're not talking about jump ropes," Jared said.

"So I started watching these little girls," Zeiss continued, picking up his knife and fork, "and I noticed that they never jumped right in. They always stood outside the ropes—listening, watching, getting themselves into the rhythm of the game. That was the secret. They watched. They listened. Before they jumped in."

Jared wanted to say something, but Zeiss was carefully deboning his fish.

"Senator Grantham," Zeiss whispered, coaxing a piece of flesh from a long thin bone.

Jared leaned closer, holding his tie.

"Watch," Zeiss said, displaying the sliver of fish on his fork. "Listen."

CHAPTER FOURTEEN

"So you believe it's simply a coincidence," Fink said, feeling about three inches too low in the billowy white chair.

"Absolutely," Harold Schaeffer replied, sitting high, scrubbed and prosperous behind his enormous polished desk.

To Fink, the chubby Parker Global president looked as if he'd undergone a kind of a liposuction in reverse, and had himself injected with money.

"No connection, then, between the two murders?" Fink asked.

"Certain common elements, of course," Schaeffer granted, admiring the long gold pen resting in his pudgy, manicured hand.

Fink leaned forward, pulled his suit jacket free, sat back. The cushions closed in around him like a Venus flytrap. "Here's my problem, Mr. Schaeffer," he said. "We average six murders a day in this city, rain or shine, but we see very few strangulations by wire. Now we've got two of them a few weeks apart. And our victims weren't bored suburban teenagers looking to intensify their orgasms, Mr. Schaeffer, these were both Parker Global executives, both involved in the sale of weapons to Third World countries."

Schaeffer dismissed this with a casual flick of his pen. "Different parts of the world," he said, "different product categories." He looked at a watch thin as a communion wafer.

A secretary entered and handed Schaeffer a note. He glanced at it and fed it into a shredder.

"Can I offer you some refreshment, Lieutenant?" he asked, delaying her departure.

"A little cooperation would be refreshing."

She closed the door behind her.

"Now, now," Schaeffer tsked, "Parker Global is only too anxious to cooperate."

His grin reminded Fink of a Heidelberg sausage maker he'd once busted for slashing a hooker. Fink squirmed in the grasping chair, pissed at himself for deliberately wearing his best suit; compared to Schaeffer's it looked like something pulled from the "Help Yourself" carton at the Tabernacle Mission.

"Where's that computer run you promised us last week?" Fink asked, putting an edge on it.

"Ah," Schaeffer smiled, "I think you'll find this quite interesting, Lieutenant. We discovered that the 'Deceased Not Natural Causes' designation was instituted quite recently. Company-wide, there is only one such entry."

Fink held up two fingers and wiggled them.

"Of course," Schaeffer conceded with a bow of his gleaming bald head.

"Somebody tampered with both personnel files," Fink said, "Trang's and Grelling's."

Schaeffer's smile froze. "If true, Lieutenant, that would be shocking."

"I'll bet."

"What makes you think there's been tampering?"

"Languages," Fink told him. "Your file on Grelling lists only Spanish, Trang's only French."

"And?"

"And we know they were both fluent in others."

"Really? Which others?"

"Why don't you tell me?" Fink suggested. "Show me a little of that good old Parker Global cooperation. Or maybe I should speak with General Robbins."

The smile never wavered. "The general is a very busy man, Lieutenant." He picked up his angular, lightweight phone. "Let me see if I can't get our chief of security, Anthony Rotelli, to assist you."

Tony Rotelli was a big, burly, ex–Los Angeles detective with blue-green eyes, a cauliflower nose and whiskey splotches on his cheeks. He and Fink hit it off instantly.

"My instructions are to cooperate with you fully," Rotelli told him with a conspiratorial smirk as they slid into a corner booth at a nearby coffee shop.

"Meaning?"

"Give you lots of watermarked paper, blow smoke up your ass, even offer you a job."

"What kind of job?"

"That's up to me. What are you packing, by the way?"

"Thirty-eight Smith & Wesson Captain's Special."

"All my guys have Glocks," Rotelli told him. "State-of-the-art."

"They use them much?"

"Never. But it's a hell of a weapon. Makes them feel like they've got a second dick. I could get you one."

"I don't need two dicks." Fink pulled a few stained sugar packets from the metal holder and tossed them under the table. "Now what is it you're not supposed to tell me, Tony?"

"Jesus, Mel," Rotelli cried in mock anguish, "whatever happened to foreplay? Aren't we supposed to trade war stories, bitch about our ex-wives, shit like that? You married?"

"After," Fink told him.

"Okay, so Parker fucked with the personnel files." The security chief shrugged, loosening his tie and releasing the two buttons over his belly. Long black hairs poked through his undershirt like weeds. "You got your pencil? Here it is. Trang and Grelling both spoke French, Spanish and Cambodian. Trang, of course—gook that he was—also spoke Vietnamese. Grelling knew Vietnamese too, also German and Thai."

"They ever work together?" Fink asked.

"Nope."

"You sure?"

"Far as I can tell. They had to cross paths at least twice a year, though. Once at the annual sales meeting, once at the fair."

"Fair?"

"International arms fair."

"So they probably stayed at the same hotels."

"I'll check."

"Which of them did you know?"

"Grelling, but only by sight. You ever see his wife?"

"Yeah. You?"

"Couple a times."

"They were divorced," Fink said.

"I heard that. But she was around. Hard to miss her. Hot-blooded Latin type. Legs."

"I noticed."

"You question her?"

"Yeah."

"Why am I getting an itch?" Rotelli asked him, reaching vulgarly under the table. "You mother, you did more than question her."

"A little more," Fink smiled, looking down at his hands.

Rotelli chuckled. "You sure you don't want a Glock?"

"What's with the languages?" Fink asked him.

"Hey," Rotelli shrugged, "you're the detective."

The waitress delivered two coffees and gave Rotelli a chocolate cannoli on a wet plate. "We sold outa cheese," she said to Fink, "we got cherry or prune."

"Forget the Danish," Fink told her. "Plain pound cake, toasted."

He poured a few drops of milk from the tin into his coffee. When it didn't curdle he poured in more. The mug was chipped.

"I don't think it was Parker," Rotelli volunteered, returning to the murders. "Not that I give a shit."

"Who then?"

"*Quién sabe?* Maybe Trang and Grelling were running something together on the side. Me, I'm just grateful they weren't snuffed on premises. The London suits are serious about a job for you, by the way. They had me get your records from NYPD."

"That stuff's confidential. How'd you do it, just for curiosity's sake?"

"A phone call and a Benjie."

"You overpaid," Fink told him.

"Company policy," Rotelli smiled, eating. "We always overpay cops."

"How's the cannoli?"

A small piece remained. Rotelli pushed the plate away.

"Come to a Greek diner and order cannoli, serves me right. My wife watches me like a hawk. I got blood pressure."

"I'm divorced," Fink told him.

"My third trip down the aisle," Rotelli said, slapping his belly. He brought a fist to his mouth and burped. "You got kids?"

"One girl in college."

"Three boys. One cop, one fireman, one chiropractor."

"Who do you think is killing these guys?" Fink asked him.

"Look, my job is to show a lot of uniforms downstairs and keep an accurate record of visitors. My biggest problem is boredom. Believe me, anybody wants anything from PG, they don't break into headquarters."

"Meaning?"

"Nothing here. You want some PG product, go hijack a trailer, rob a warehouse, drive to Virginia and buy it over the counter. You want intelligence? All you need is a Touch-Tone phone and the right codes. That's not me, by the way. We got a separate division: Industrial Espionage. Bunch a nerds with thick glasses. They all eat yogurt with little pieces of fruit in it. Fuckin' world. I'm still hungry."

The waitress delivered the pound cake, badly singed around the edges and greasy everywhere else. It looked about as appetizing as a dead cat. Fink set it aside and glanced around. The Parthenon wallpaper was faded. The ceiling panels were stained. Schaeffer never ate in places like this.

"There's a Parker Global connection," Fink said, thinking out loud.

"Listen, Mel, if PG was behind it I'd smell something. The fact is, PG doesn't kill people; our clients kill people. Aren't you gonna eat that cake?"

"Be my guest."

Rotelli broke off a corner of the cake and tried it. "Dry," he declared. "Could use a little ice cream. Strawberry, maybe."

"Good idea." Fink raised his arm for the waitress. She forced a smile, stubbed out her cigarette, shuffled over. Her white ripple sole shoes were scuffed.

Rotelli ordered the ice cream.

The waitress peered down at Fink. "You guys are cops, am I right?"

Fink held up three fingers.

"Because," she confided, "I would like to lodge an official complaint."

Rotelli covered his mouth and coughed. Fink reached inside his jacket and pulled out his pen and pad. "Regarding?" he asked her, flipping to a new page.

She sidled closer, cocked a hip, whispered: "The Pink Panthers."

Fink squinted up at her. She might have been pretty once. "Who?" he asked.

"The Depends crowd," she told him, inching closer. "You know, the pink panthers."

"Gray panthers," Fink corrected.

"Whatever." She was chewing gum. "The point is, the old farts steal all the Sweet 'n Low. I know 'cause I handle resupply."

Fink narrowed his eyes, made a quick note.

"The women stuff 'em in their purses," she confided. "In their bras. I'm talkin' handfuls."

"And the men?" Fink asked her.

"Pockets, or down the front of their pants. I'm serious. It's disgustin'."

Fink motioned her closer. She smelled of Windex. "I want you to contact my boss on this," he told her, writing on a new page. "Maybe he can mount a sting operation. Here's his name and number. Promise me you'll call."

"Captain Reynolds," she read, then folded the paper carefully. "An' who should I say?"

"Detective Barton," Fink told her. "But you can call me Don."

After she left, Rotelli leaned across the table. "You're a real prick," he said with undisguised admiration.

Fink shrugged, mildly embarrassed.

"So," Rotelli asked, "which do we talk about first, the department, the wives or the war?"

"How about that job offer?" Fink suggested, putting away his pad. "My daughter's thinking about graduate school."

"Plus you're gonna have to spring for the wedding," Rotelli reminded him. "That's why I had sons."

CHAPTER FIFTEEN

Snosset hated it when secretaries put him on hold without telling him who he was holding for. He'd been eating corn chips when the phone rang and now he saw that his fingers were leaving greasy prints on the receiver. In the fluorescent light, the phone in his hand gleamed like a black bone.

"Mr. Calvin Snosset?"

"Speaking."

"My name is Bob Cardanzer. I work for Senator Antel Grantham of Alaska."

Snosset's heart hiccupped, but he held himself in check. "In what capacity?" he asked warily.

"Chief of staff."

"Yes, sir," he said, wiping his free hand on his slacks.

"Mr. Snosset," Cardanzer said, "I'm sure you are aware of the senator's activities on behalf of America's MIAs."

"Yes, sir."

"Well, the senator has received some evidence which—"

"This is an open line," Snosset warned him.

"Excuse me?"

"We have to be very security conscious here at the Pentagon," Snosset said for the benefit of all those listening in. A call from Capitol Hill figured to have taps at both ends.

"I see," Cardanzer replied.

"We should meet."

"Fine. Can you get away this morning?"

Snosset kept them circling in an area of the mall where a gurgling waterfall provided enough ambient noise to subvert any listening devices. A nearby Gap for Kids was running a sale. Women were swarming.

". . . keep this in the strictest confidence," Cardanzer said as they came back together after having split for a stroller.

"I never met you," Snosset assured him under his breath. "What do you have?"

"I can't discuss the evidence," Cardanzer said hurriedly.

Snosset became dubious. "We're not talking fuzzy photos again, are we? Or pencil sketches from Thai bar girls?"

"No, nothing like that. Please, Mr. Snosset, I don't want to play Twenty Questions. The senator needs to know if you can get us one man's file without alerting anyone in your section."

"Sure I can." He stopped before a music store, pretending to study the life-size cardboard Madonna in the window. "I'll deliver it to your office myself, this afternoon." He leaned closer. "What's the man's name?"

Cardanzer looked around furtively, took a deep breath and whispered: "Army Corporal Isaac Prometheus Johnson."

Snosset kept stabbing the key all over the steering column, but he couldn't locate the ignition. He'd had the car five years. Finally, he hugged himself, bent forward and laid his forehead against the cool hard plastic of the wheel. From somewhere deep inside himself he heard his mother's voice: "When God wants to punish us, Calvin, He grants our wishes."

Corporal Isaac Prometheus Johnson.

Zack Johnson.

Alive.

Snosset laced his fingers tightly and held on as another storm cloud of emotion burst over him and left him wet and trembling. He pressed his eyes closed. The jungle closed in around him like a fist.

I won't be long, Johnson promised, I just need to set the kid's leg. You stay out here and cover my ass, okay, Cal?

Sure. Okay. Fine, Snosset answered irritably.

The sun was blazing. Goddamn gook kid. Who cared about a goddamn gook kid? Only bleeding-heart Johnson. Snosset wanted to get the hell out of this vill and back to the platoon. He didn't trust any of these people. Any of them. This was supposed to be a straight-up recon patrol, not a goddamn mercy mission.

You okay? Johnson asked. You want to come inside with me? He was smiling. Johnson was always smiling. Snosset's stomach started to heat up.

Fine, dammit, I'm fine. Go ahead and do what you have to do and let's haul ass before the damn bugs eat me alive.

I'll be quick as I can, Johnson promised.

But he wasn't.

Snosset hated standing there in the scorching sun, feeling things staring at him from the trees. He was pouring sweat. His feet were itching like crazy. The mosquitoes were having a field day. There were sounds everywhere. Down in his stomach someone began blowing on a glowing ember. He shifted his feet. Come on, Johnson, he pleaded silently, let's haul ass. He started thinking about the birthday party they'd thrown for Erickson the week before. Somebody had copped some primo Thai sticks. Everybody'd gotten zonked. Erickson had passed out smiling, his head hanging off to one side. Smiling. He'd been nineteen. The next day, Snosset had been behind him on patrol when there was a roar, a whoosh, and Erickson's head went flying up in the air like a jack-in-the-box. The splatter didn't hit until a second later: water and blood and bits of—

Snosset froze. What was that? Footsteps? A VC patrol? Without warning, somebody started shooting a flamethrower inside his stomach: short, searing bursts. He bent over, steeling himself against them. Somewhere overhead a bird screeched. Maybe they'd seen him. He tried to listen, but the sound of his heartbeat was squeezing out everything. He was drowning in his own sweat. He turned in place, instinctively raising his barrel and fingering the trigger. He sensed dozens of the little slant fuckers slithering around out there like leeches. It was time to hump.

One wall of his stomach burst into flame. He gasped, held his breath. He opened his mouth to call Johnson, but caught himself. Was he nuts? Call out like that? He'd be dead before he even heard the zing of the bullet. Maybe he could ease himself over there and— No, he could sense Charlies all around him now, like ants. Johnson, goddammit, he screamed silently, get your black ass out here!

He could breathe, but he had to keep it shallow. One side of his stomach was crumbling, making his muscles twitch. He was desperate to warn Johnson, but he couldn't, not with all those rifle barrels nosing through the grass searching for him. Couldn't call out, couldn't chance crossing the open ground. Be a sitting duck. Target practice. Even if he made it to the hootch they'd lob in a grenade and turn everything inside to toast.

He kept scanning the brush for a rifle barrel, listening for a snapped twig. High above him a bird kept screeching. He looked up, but couldn't see a goddamn thing but glare. He was tight everywhere except his asshole, which had begun to pulse urgently. He was trying, but he couldn't control it. Christ, he was going to shit his pants. Eyes swiveling, he backed urgently into the brush. Holding the rifle with one hand, he hurriedly unbuckled his belt, wrenched down his pants, squatted just in time. Pressurized diarrhea, like a fire hose. Whole thing took maybe five seconds. Tore off some leaves, wiped himself, pulled up his pants, moved away a few steps—all the time listening, listening, rifle ready, shoot the fuckers. Sounds everywhere. Rustling leaves. Birds squawking. Monkeys screaming. Voices? Footsteps? Neon sign in his head flashing red alert. Sirens wailing. Trust your body. His body was in these bushes. These bushes were good. They were safe. As long as he didn't go back out there . . .

He twisted his torso. Flames were snapping at his insides like maddened dogs. He had to get out of here, back to the platoon, go get help, get help, get away, get safe. He started to inch backward, slowly at first, one careful step at a time. He hit a branch, nearly tripped, spun around and began running, faster and faster, slashing at the grasping leaves with his rifle—

Snosset raised his head, rubbed his eyes, looked around. He was safe. His stomach was heaving. He was sitting in a car. His car. In a parking lot. He took a series of deep breaths, stuffed two Tums into his mouth, and kept telling himself he was safe, he'd just been dreaming again. A few minutes and he'd be okay; his heart would slow down, he'd stop hyperventilating, he'd be right as rain. Right as rain. What had he been—?

Back to the office! He had to get back to the office! For Senator Grantham.

Snosset wedged his mind back on track. Zack Johnson

was alive! ". . . everything you have in your files on this man," Grantham's man had said. Okay, okay, okay. What was the best way to do it? What would arouse the least suspicion? Yes, he'd print out everything from 1968. Zack had been in June, which would stick him right in the middle of the run. Perfect! He rewarded himself with two more Tums.

He reached out, found the ignition, turned the key. The engine caught. Another memory opened and sent him into a free fall. He grasped the wheel with both hands. The report! That damned incident report. When they couldn't find Johnson he'd had to help the lieutenant write out an incident report. He'd said that Johnson—

He had to get rid of the incident report. Okay, okay, okay. He shifted into reverse and carefully backed out of the space. More accidents in parking lots than anyplace else. Accident report. He'd been a frightened kid then, but now, almost twenty-five years later, now he knew exactly how to do things. Exactly. He shifted into drive, pulled up to the stop sign and, his eyes clear with purpose, headed out onto the Beltway.

When Snosset entered his office he saw a strange woman sitting at his console. Instinctively he grabbed the phone, punched in the two-digit security code and ran to block the door.

"Please," the intruder cried, now standing with her arms out in front of her, "I—"

"Take one step," Snosset warned her, brandishing a three-hole punch, "and I'll . . ." His heart was racing. He couldn't catch his breath. She looked exactly like his ex-wife. "Bitch," he hissed at her. "Bitch."

The door burst open. Things rushed past: boots, uniforms, noise. Snosset found himself staring down the barrels of automatic weapons. He directed their attention to his ID badge.

"This is my office," he declared. "It's a secure area. I found this woman—" He jabbed at her— "accessing my files. Arrest her."

Some of the guns shifted. The woman's hands were up. She looked terrified. "Thorsen," she said, "Ingrid R. I was sent here by—"

"Lying bitch." Snosset turned to the young lieutenant. "She could be armed. You guys have Tasers?" He wanted her hurt.

"Everybody stay cool," the officer said, his gun drawn but pointed at the floor. "We'll get this sorted out."

"Colonel Bradley," the woman whimpered. "He let me in. He—"

The lieutenant picked up Snosset's phone. "What's his extension?"

She told him. He pressed the digits, spoke, listened, hung up. "The colonel's on his way," he announced. He sounded relieved. "In the meantime, miss, why don't you, you know, put your hands down?"

Snosset was nervously checking his computer. The bitch had been in his files.

"We may have nothing more than a misunderstanding here," the lieutenant confided to Snosset. "But this whole sector is classified; you were right to call it in. Do you know this Colonel Bradley?"

"I report to a Colonel Bradley," Snosset admitted. This lieutenant looked like a high school kid. The whole security detail looked like Mouseketeers.

Snosset ran a hand over his computer, trying to reassure both of them. Their files had been violated. His arm was shaking. He must have hit it. Why were all these people in his office? He wanted them out, needed them out. He had to find that incident report, erase it, print out 1968 for Senator Grantham.

Colonel Bradley swept in, his face flushed. He looked around, then murmured something to the lieutenant. Snosset felt the tension in the room dissipate. The security detail filed out. The colonel went over, whispered something to the woman and she left too.

"Snosset," the colonel asked, "you didn't touch her, did you?"

"No. What was she doing here?"

"We needed some information in a hurry," he said, adjusting his uniform.

"What sort of information?"

"Routine inquiry," Bradley said, absently squaring up some papers on Snosset's desk. "I called down, but you were out."

Snosset nodded, though he knew Bradley was lying. If anyone had called, his beeper would have gone off.

"You're absolutely sure no one touched her?" the colonel asked, his natural aggression returning. "No Tail Hook scandals for me, Snosset. I'm up for review next month."

"I came in, saw her at my console and initiated security procedures," Snosset explained, struggling to ignore the thumping at his temple. "No one touched her." Snosset hadn't touched a woman in twenty years.

He stuffed a hand into his pants pocket and grasped his Tums. He felt worn out. Maybe he had overreacted. "What information do you need, Colonel? I'll get it for you right now."

"No, no," Bradley said, waving him off, "don't worry yourself. Ms. Thorsen already faxed it upstairs." He forced a smile. "It was only one little file. From 1968. June."

CHAPTER SIXTEEN

The long black limousine was crouched by the curb like a huge cat, silently breathing white smoke into the chill night. A light rain had the sidewalk shining like glass. Trying to honor her late-night rule of never stopping in the street, Adelaide slowed her walk to a snail's pace and peered at the car's dark windows, hoping to catch a glimpse of whoever was inside. Celebrities sometimes liked to come back and visit their old neighborhoods. She'd seen Diana Ross once, passing by in a long white limousine, and Smokey Robinson, and Berry Gordy twice, in black ones like this. And she would never forget the afternoon she stood at the curb holding her little Isaac's hand as Muhammad Ali—sitting up proud and tall on the back seat of a big yellow convertible—passed not six feet from them. Next to her baby, that man was the most beautiful thing she had ever seen in her life, and when he had turned to her and waved she had burst into tears. Thirty years and she remembered it like it was yesterday, praise be Jesus.

She shook her head and inched along the immaculate limousine, resisting the temptation to reach out and touch it. Sixty-two years old and never set foot inside one of these things. Well, she thought playfully, maybe whoever's inside will roll down the window and offer a tired old woman a ride home. Wouldn't that be a pip? She smiled at her own foolishness. Sure be a good night for it, though, with her back troubling her again and her ankles swole up and the cold nipping at her face like the devil's own bats. Earlier tonight, after her cleaning job was finished, she'd been feeling so low she had actually thought about not coming by to tidy up the church and say her nightly say to the Lord. But of course she had, and of course she felt better for it.

A gust of wind snatched up a loose sheet of newspaper and sent it bouncing down the gutter like tumbleweed. Her teeth started to chatter. She hiked up her worn cloth collar and buttoned it. Come on now, she wordlessly urged the limousine as she came alongside the rear window, where's your manners?

An insect-like buzz gave her a start. The rear window slid down like a motorized blade. She stopped and stared. Inside was dark. Smoke drifted from the open window. She saw the glow from a cigarette.

"Good evening, ma'am."

A soft voice, sounded like a white man.

"Who is that?" she asked, for some reason looking anxiously about the deserted street. The streetlights were all fuzzy from the cold.

The rear door swung open. She jumped back, clutching her purse with both hands. She thought about making a dash for the church until she remembered that she'd locked the door.

"Please," the man said, "get in."

"Who is that?" she asked again, taking two small, backward steps. "What you want from me?"

She heard noise from down the street. A trio of boys came around the corner. Oh, my dear Jesus, she thought, sucking in her lips, trying to decide what to do. Her heart was fluttering like venetian blinds in a breeze.

"Please, Mrs. Johnson," the voice from the dark interior urged, "get in the car now."

I'm in your hands, Lord, she reminded Him as she bent down, stepped into the limousine and sat down. An arm reached past her and pulled the door closed. A solid metallic thwunk locked all the doors at once. The man next to her said something in Chinese and the car started to move. She slid back in the seat. It smelled so rich in here. She felt shabby and misplaced.

"I hope you don't mind if I smoke, Mrs. Johnson," the man said.

"How you come to know my name?" she demanded.

There was no reply.

She was trying to mask her rising fear with a bold tone. "You're not from around here," she declared.

"No, ma'am," he answered politely. "I'm not."

He pressed something and a wide dark window rose and shut out the driver. It was warm as toast in here, but her bones felt chilly. She leaned forward, worried that her damp coat would get this fine leather all wet. She couldn't see the man's face, but a glow from his cigarette revealed white skin, dark hair, hard eyes. The car moved smooth and steady as a train. She couldn't even hear the motor. Marshaling her courage, she asked him where he was taking her.

"It's a raw night, Mrs. Johnson. I'm taking you home. Please sit back," he said gently. "You'll be more comfortable."

She sat back carefully. It felt even better than those big

easy chairs Dr. Harris had in the waiting room where she went for her back.

"How you know me?" she asked. "And how you know where I live?"

"Let me get you something to drink," he suggested, reaching down and pulling open a small refrigerator. A light came on.

"I don't drink," she told him, startled by his face.

"Dr. Pepper," he said. "I know you like Dr. Pepper."

"How you know that?" His face looked like he'd been in a knife fight, a real bad one. He wasn't anybody's celebrity; with scars like that he was probably some Mafia.

He popped the can, poured some into a glass and handed it to her. She sniffed it and then took a sip. It was Dr. Pepper all right, but her stomach wasn't up to it. She thanked him, but gave it back. This whole thing was spooky. She didn't like spooky things.

"What you want with an old woman like me?" she asked him pointedly.

"This friend of mine," he told her, "he wanted me to make sure you were okay."

"Which friend is that?"

"Someone you knew a long time ago."

"What's his name?"

"He asked me not to say. It was a long, long time ago."

She didn't believe him. Some kind of mischief was going on here. A light began blinking outside her window. The car slowed, then turned. She didn't recognize anything.

"Tell me the truth," she said anxiously. "What you want from a poor old woman that never hurt nobody?"

"I'm here to grant you a wish," he said.

"What wish?" she scoffed, gathering her coat around her knees. "Wait a minute!" she declared, jabbing a finger in his direction. "You sound like that fellow used to be on the TV, that John Barefoot Tipton. Is that who you are? The Millionaire?"

"No, ma'am," he laughed.

The car stopped. She looked out her rain-streaked window and saw her building. It looked old and tired. Her apartment would be empty. He had been telling her the truth.

"Do I have to go now?" she asked.

"Not at all. Shall we ride around for a while? Would you like that?"

"I surely would," she said. "If it's not too much bother. I've never been in one of these fancy things."

He put down the big window and said something Chinese to the driver and they started off again. She watched the neighborhood sail peacefully past, the project buildings tall and silent, the all-night groceries lit up, the streetlights flickering like stars. It was funny how the car windows had been dark on the outside but from in here she could see through them just fine. When the car dipped into an underpass lined with orange lights she looked around the interior, trying to study everything so she could remember it later. While her companion sat back and lit another cigarette, she reached out and ran her hand lightly over the leather upholstery, the telephone and refrigerator, the little TV, the polished wood trim. His window opened a crack and sucked out the smoke and let in a tiny chill.

"I saw Diana Ross once," she told him. "In person."

"I'll bet that was exciting."

"Not like Muhammad Ali," she said. "That was the best. When we saw him he was the champ. It breaks my heart to see what's happened to him now."

"Life," the man said.

She knew what he meant. "The Lord works in mysterious ways," she told him.

"Yes, ma'am."

"His wonders to perform."

"Yes, ma'am."

"You seem like a good man," she observed.

"I'm not," he assured her.

He sounded like he meant it. "You planning to harm me?" she asked.

"No, ma'am. I told you, I'm planning to grant your wish."

"Don't talk foolishness. You don't know my wish."

"No, ma'am, but the friend who sent me thinks he does."

"Only the— Hold on a hot minute," she said, getting a wild idea. "Are you an angel?"

"No, ma'am," he laughed.

"You speak Chinese."

"Do angels speak Chinese?"

"I wouldn't know, but Americans surely don't. Hey, I know! Maybe you're like that Clarence in that Christmas movie, the one with Jimmy Stewart. Is that it? You have to do something good down here on earth before you can get your wings?"

"No wings for me," he told her.

"What's your name?" she asked, brushing a wisp of damp hair from her forehead.

He shifted in his seat. "Everett," he finally said, then added, very softly, "My mother called me Ev."

"Where is she?"

"Cancer," he said. "A long time ago. I wasn't there. I never knew my father."

"Oh my. I'm sorry. Lord Jesus, there's so much pain in this world. I lost my only child."

He was silent, but in the darkness she could see him nodding his head slowly, as if he was thinking hard about something. Her coat smelled musty.

When he spoke again his voice was little more than a whisper. "I'll have to be getting along, Mrs. Johnson," he said apologetically, leaning forward and tapping the glass partition. "I have to get back."

"What about my wish?" she asked.

"A week from tonight," he told her. "I'll call you around midnight. We'll talk about it. In the meantime," he said, holding a paper bag out to her.

"What's this now?"

"Hershey's Kisses."

"My favorite," she gushed, accepting the bag. "My oh my. Isn't this something?"

"There's some money in there too," he said. "To pay off the TV and the furniture, buy a few things."

"I can't take your money," she said, trying to give the bag back to him.

He grasped her outstretched hand with both of his. "Please," he said.

He wouldn't let go. How long had it been since a man held her hand? She'd forgotten how it could make her go all soft inside. And she with her skin all dry from the ammonia.

"All right," she said, feeling old and foolish, "I don't want your money, but all right."

Still he held on. His hands were warm and soft. She felt embarrassed that her hair was such a mess. When the car stopped he bent down and kissed her hand like she was some Princess Di.

"I don't understand any of this," she said, bewildered. "Jesus knows I truly don't." Her building was here again.

"A week from tonight," he reminded her. "We'll call you." His voice turned harsh. "And don't you go giving all that money to the church. Ten percent is okay, but the rest is for you. Promise me."

After she promised he reached over and opened the door. As she stepped out the cold made her a little dizzy. The ground seemed tilted.

She heard the car door close behind her and without thinking she rushed back and tapped on the darkened window. It slid down.

The words came pouring out of her. She couldn't help herself. "Just tell me one thing," she said, bending to the open window, "one thing and I'll leave you be. I don't care what you say you are or what you say you ain't, but have you seen my little boy? Is he all right up there? Will I be with him soon?"

There was no response.

"Answer me, Ev," she pleaded, gripping the edge of the glass. "Is my baby all right?"

"Yes, Mrs. Johnson," he said softly. "Zack is fine."

She stepped back, stunned. The window closed. The car moved slowly off, its tires crunching. Her eyes began to burn. She pressed her purse and the bag of Kisses to her chest and began walking mechanically toward her building, as if in a trance, telling herself that the Lord works in mysterious ways His wonders to perform.

The elevator smelled sour, but when she closed her eyes it became a golden chariot carrying her straight up to heaven and her little boy's side. Praise be Jesus. Praise be Jesus. Praise be Jesus.

CHAPTER SEVENTEEN

Stupid country!

Bo had pedaled past the building twice before realizing that this was it; the fools had painted a name on the awning—The Leonardo da Vinci—but no number. And naturally the bill from the restaurant had a number but no name.

He leaned the old bicycle against a lamppost reeking of urine—stupid, filthy country—and hurriedly snaked the chain through both tires and secured it with the combination lock. After checking that nothing was leaking, he lifted the still-warm bag from the wire basket and carried it into the lobby.

A black doorman raised a sleeve trimmed in tattered gold braid. Bo displayed the bag and told him the apartment number.

"Feeding time for the hippo," the doorman muttered.

"Not understand," Bo replied.

"Ain't nobody talkin' to you," the doorman snapped, turning his back. "Delivery," he announced into a speaker. "Chinese."

The speaker squawked in reply.

"Elevator's that way," he told Bo, indicating with his chin, then called after him: "And don't you be sneakin' aroun' slidin' your damn menus under no damn doors," and when Bo didn't respond, added, "You hear me, Chop Suey?"

Swine, Bo told himself, jabbing the up button with his thumb, imagining that it was the black man's windpipe. Americans were all arrogant swine. Bo's political instructor had been right: Capitalism was a disease, an addiction, a corruption of the spirit. Where was that stupid elevator?

When it finally arrived, Bo stomped in and hit the floor button with the side of his fist. Chop Suey, the insolent black fool had called him. Bo hated this stupid country, hated these stupid people, hated this stupid job. Chop Suey! He kicked the elevator wall hard enough to crack the wood paneling. That calmed him.

The elevator came to a stop. He located the apartment, smoothed his hair, rang the bell.

The door opened. Bo's jaw went slack.

She was gigantic, breathtaking, magnificent. Her enormous torso was sheathed in a wrap delicate as an Ao Dai, its dark fabric accentuating the smooth, rice-white skin of her shoulders.

As a youth, shunned by the other children and compelled to watch helplessly as his tubercular mother wasted away to a skeleton, Bo had invented a secret companion, a dream creature overflowing with health and flesh, in whose imagined arms he had found his greatest happiness.

And now here she was, the incarnation of his most secret fantasies.

"You look like you've seen a ghost," she told him. "Are you okay?"

He tried to answer, but the sight of her filling the doorway rendered him speechless.

"You need to sit down," she said, stepping back and holding open the door. "You better come in."

She was everything he had ever dared imagine, and more. Her curled yellow hair was like spun gold. Her eyes were the blue of the Tonkin Gulf. Clumps of soft flesh hung from her upper arms like succulent fruit. He held out the bag of food to her like an offering.

"I wasn't, like, expecting visitors," she said, taking the bag and putting it on a table. "The place is such a mess."

Bo's legs were moving, but they felt strange, distant, weak. As he came alongside her he entered a fragrant cloud of sandalwood and exotic spices. When she bent to clear a chair of magazines one of the straps slid from her shoulder, loosening her bodice and affording Bo a glimpse of riches so vast they forced a groan from his throat.

"Sit," she said, straightening up and self-consciously adjusting the strap. "I'll, you know, get my purse."

He obeyed mechanically, his eyes following the hypnotic swaying of her immense body. She had the same graceful silhouette as the huge bell in the Buddhist temple near his village. Bo had seen a trio of women about this size on a TV talk show. They had all been sensuous, but the stupid American audience had ridiculed them. Still, none had been as—

Her return snapped him from his reverie. He jumped to his feet. She turned her face away, apparently embarrassed by something. At first he did not understand. When he did, his hands ran to cover himself.

"What's your name?" she asked shyly, still not looking at him.

"Bo," he mumbled, struggling to flatten his stubborn erection against his thigh.

"Is that like bow tie?" she asked, allowing herself a peek.

He sat down and shook his head. "No tie," he croaked, staring down at his hands.

"Or is it like Beau Brummel?" she asked. "That's French."

"I know French," he assured her without looking up.

"*Je m'appelle Tiffany*," she volunteered shyly. "Did I say that okay?"

He looked up. Creamy white ankles rose from fluffy pink slippers. This was madness. He was on assignment.

"Miss, please to pay bill," he said, and forced himself to add, "I must go."

"Oh." She sounded disappointed. "How much is it?"

"Bill is—" he replied, looking around for it, but seeing her seated on the sofa made him lose the thought. There was so much of her. He felt puny and ridiculous.

She crossed a monumental leg. "How old are you, Bo?"

The back of her slipper swayed free, revealing an exquisitely curved heel. His breath caught. Her foot was so tiny!

"Bo twenty-four," he replied uncertainly. Her knee was a luxurious mound of white dough. He wanted desperately to reach out and knead it, to fall to his knees and rub his cheek against it, to—

"Tiffany twenty-nine," she said, tugging ineffectually at her hem. "You're so slim and trim," she told him. "You make me feel like a whale."

"Yes, like whale," Bo agreed solemnly. "Beluga whale. I saw in aquarium once. Boy and girl. Smooth white skin. Blue eyes. Most beautiful creatures in world."

Her cheeks reddened, her hips shifted. "I'll bet you work out all the time," she said.

"Work every day," he told her. "Deliveries."

She covered her bare knee with daintily folded hands. "Where are you from, Bo?"

"China," he lied.

Her voice dropped. "I guess all the girls tell you how incredibly cute you are," she said. Her voice shrunk to a whisper. "Nobody ever comes here. Would you look at me one more time?"

He did. She reached up and brushed back a stray golden hair. A giant breast rolled beneath the thin fabric like an ocean swell.

"People look at me all the time," she said, averting her eyes. "But not like that."

Bo was having trouble breathing. "You please to pay bill," he stammered, struggling awkwardly to his feet. "I am go."

She rose from her chair and carefully smoothed her dress. His eyes followed her hands ravenously. She was more desirable than any two women he had ever seen.

"Don't go," she murmured. "Please?"

He imagined himself sinking into her and never coming out. He took an unsteady step backward. "You pay bill now?" he asked weakly, searching for the door.

"Later," she whispered. "Look at me, Bo."

Then, staring directly into his troubled eyes, she hitched the straps from her shoulders, peeled down her top and reached out to him.

He flew to her.

Bo locked the front door and walked back through the restaurant.

"You are late," Old Han snapped without looking up from his stacks of cash and credit card slips.

"Bicycle," Bo replied, placing the money on the table. "Chain slip off and—"

"Sit!"

Bo sat. Thoughts of Tiffany poured in, filling him with little bubbles.

"Stop that grinning," the old man barked. "I have important news."

Bo tried to clear his mind. She wouldn't go.

"I have received a message," Old Han told him. "You are to begin a new job."

"When?" Bo cried.

"Tomorrow."

Bo's mind reeled. Tomorrow! But—

"—continue to sleep here in the basement," Old Han was saying. "You will now have to travel by subway. You must carry nothing which connects you to me. Nothing. Ever." He stared at Bo fiercely. "Do you understand?"

"Of course, Elder Han." Bo's heart leapt. He would be remaining in New York!

"Not a slip of paper, not a card, nothing. You understand me? If you are caught they must think you are simply another illegal alien."

"I understand, Elder Han." Did the old fool really think a trained agent required notes to remember names and numbers? Tiffany's address flashed through his mind. He tried to push it away, but it kept coming back.

"—an excellent hotel," the old man was saying. "One of the very best. You are a fortunate young man."

"Yes, Elder Han. Fortunate indeed."

The old man leaned closer, bringing the sour smell of boiled cabbage. "Oh," he said, "there is one more thing. Whatever you earn, you must give me half." He pointed a long fingernail, curved from a lifetime without labor. "Half of everything, do you understand? Not one penny less."

"Half," Bo repeated obediently.

"As if any amount could compensate me for the danger of having you here," the old man grumbled, carefully aligning his stack of dollar bills.

"My superiors will be informed of your generosity," Bo assured him, thinking of the smelly cot, the filthy washroom, the table scraps, the ill-fitting clothes . . . He heard the delicate tinkle of her laughter—

". . . your true purpose here," the old man was saying. "Nor," he quickly added, "do I wish to know. See that you do not dishonor me," he said sternly.

"Yes, Elder Han."

The old man kept talking. Bo floated back to Tiffany, wondering if it had all been a dream . . .

He had been too excited to satisfy her the first time, but she had not complained. Instead, she had placed his hands on one of her enormous breasts while she bent over and reawakened him with her mouth. Before she had progressed too far he had squirmed free, rolled her over and entered her again. It was glorious. She began moaning, then heaving, then kicking the air. Just when her thrashing became so frenzied that he feared being thrown, she grasped his buttocks, dug in her nails and began—

"Do you understand?" an angry voice demanded.

"What? Excuse me, Elder Han, I—"

"The subway tokens," the old man said irritably, "they must come out of your half."

"Yes," Bo replied. "Of course."

Subway tokens! It would be a happy day when he snapped this old fool's neck.

CHAPTER EIGHTEEN

It started to drizzle while they were walking to Zeiss' car. It was early afternoon, but the sky was already dark. Zeiss had won all three games of squash, playing with a ferocity which had only added to Jared's anxiety. The committee staff had received another stern warning from the chief counsel this morning: Keep your mouth shut or go to jail. Talking to Zeiss like this could mean years of stamping out license plates for ten cents an hour.

"The FBI is convinced it's a fake," Jared said, hoping to get it over with quickly.

Zeiss picked up the pace. "The FBI does what it's told. We're interested in what Grantham thinks."

Jared was nearly jogging to keep up. "My information is all second- and third-hand," he apologized. "Senator Grantham doesn't talk to anyone."

Zeiss stopped short. "You mean he doesn't talk to you." He paused, staring hard. A raindrop hit the side of his nose. "Right?"

"Right," Jared admitted. If this was such a good job, why was he feeling so scared?

There was a rumble of distant thunder. Zeiss glanced at the sky, adjusted the towel around his neck and started walking again. "Okay, you can't get to Grantham," he said, "but are you at least talking to his staff?"

"Yes," Jared assured him, making a skipping attempt to synchronize their steps. "Every day, whoever I can, just like you said." They turned a corner and it suddenly occurred to him that if Zeiss could have had him followed, why not the committee?

"Does Grantham think the prints are genuine," Zeiss reminded him, "that's today's question."

"I'm not sure," Jared replied, glancing back over his shoulder. Nothing. "The word is, he's got other people looking at them."

Zeiss stopped. "Which other people?"

"I don't know."

"Find out." He started walking again.

"I will," Jared promised. "I'm trying. I'll stay on it. The newspaper was sent from Zurich, by the way. Federal Express. A girl—"

"She's been vetted. It's a dead end. The bastard's smart."

"You think he's in Switzerland?" Jared asked.

"Who?"

"Johnson, the black medic."

"He's not the issue," Zeiss said. "Who's behind it? What are they really after? That's what we're working on. You're supposed to be helping us."

Jared was dying to ask who "us" was, but he didn't dare. "The newspaper was genuine," he offered instead. "That's been confirmed."

Zeiss made a short, angry gesture. "Get real, will you

please? Why bother to fake an *International Herald Tribune*?"

"But fingerprints," Jared said, darting around a garbage bin, "how can you fake fingerprints?"

"In more ways than you can imagine, Horatio. But who said the fingerprints were faked? Listen, my high school science lab had a rattlesnake that had been preserved in alcohol for forty years."

"You mean—?"

"Why not?"

"Jesus," Jared shuddered, envisioning a severed hand floating eerily in a sealed glass jar. "Why would anybody—?"

"You tell me," Zeiss suggested, stopping at the curb and indicating with his chin the garage across the street.

"Destabilization?" Jared ventured.

Zeiss began jogging in place, waiting for the light to change. "Explain," he said.

"To raise doubts? To undermine people's faith in the government? To make the nation relive the whole Vietnam thing all over again? A psychological form of terrorism?"

"You come up with all that yourself?" Zeiss asked, his tone more amused than condescending.

"Sure," Jared lied. He'd overheard two female aides speculating about it in the office.

A jagged streak of lightning appeared overhead, followed almost immediately by a deep rumble. The sky was a dense gun-metal gray. The nearby Washington monument looked ghostly, its ring of American flags hanging soggy and lifeless. Large, intermittent raindrops began to splatter in the street. The light changed. Zeiss patted him on the arm and began trotting, his sneakers slapping against the wet asphalt. Jared followed, unable to shake the image of a black hand bobbing in a jar like a hideously bloated spider.

CHAPTER NINETEEN

The rain had been lashing the compound for days, huge swaying sheets of it beating against the house, pummeling the leaves, splashing the saturated earth. The wailing of the wind was eerie and intense. The deep rumbles of thunder made everything tremble. Indoors and dry, Johnson was possessed by a childlike delight. He was crouched by a window, peering out through binoculars at a guard tower, watching the relentless water pouring off a sentry's poncho and remembering how, as if in another life, he had endured storms like this huddled in a corner of a wooden cage, shivering with chills, burrowing under the sodden, sweet-smelling straw, staring at big droplets falling rhythmically from bamboo bars.

Mee Yang came over and snuggled up next to him. He stroked her hair, closed his eyes and saw her rushing about barefoot with rainwater pouring off her wide straw hat, her wet blouse clinging to her spine as she bent and gathered up wide thick leaves to spread across the top of his cage.

He especially cherished the image of her with one arm raised to hold her hat in place as she flitted on tiptoes back to her hut. Who could measure how much it had meant to have someone care about him like that? With life and death so evenly balanced, those few ounces of leaves had tipped the scales.

Pulling him back to reality, she took his hands and rubbed them slowly and deliberately against her small breasts and belly while she mimicked the exaggerated pelvic motions she studied so intently on Ransom's pornographic videos. After a few minutes of this, she led him upstairs, shut the door, pushed him onto the bed, wriggled out of her clothes and, puffing out her narrow chest, demanded in newly mastered English: "How you wannit, big boy? Mouse? Beehine? Or sow-fees-aizin pussy?"

For Johnson, it was all like a dream. These days he often found himself drifting off without warning, his attention arrested by little things, ordinary things, that he had been away from too long. He was particularly fascinated by shapes and textures; at breakfast sometimes he would become lost in the embossed pattern on a paper napkin or the coarse surface of a cereal or the alternating patches of dark and light on a piece of toast. Everything seemed new and wondrous. During their walks outside the compound he would stop and stare at a bird or a lizard or a beetle, the movement of a single leaf in a gentle breeze, the passage of clouds overhead, the complex pattern of sunlight sifting through the jungle canopy. Every day was a miracle. His sense of freedom seemed to have given time a three-dimensionality, making it something he could hold in his hands and admire, something that was his.

If left to its own devices his mind was liable to wander off anywhere, but Mee Yang was his anchor. Whenever and wherever he wandered she was always there to bring him back. With Ransom away, her timidity had disappeared. In his absence she had appointed herself the grande dame. Lightly holding Johnson's arm, she marched about the compound with her chin unnaturally high, inspecting things, asking questions. He loved when she discovered some unfamiliar thing and found out what it was. Her eyes would go wide with delight and for a few moments she would become a child again. But it amazed him how quickly she adjusted to new things. While he was still marveling at everything, she now handled the TV and the household appliances like she'd had them all her life.

The only part of the house that was off-limits to them was Ransom's office. He'd locked it when he'd left, but even with him gone there seemed to be life in there. Above the constant hum of the room air conditioner, Johnson often heard the phone ringing, garbled voices leaving cryptic messages on the answering device, the efficient beeps and whirrs of mysterious machines. Mee Yang always gave the office a particularly wide berth, as if Ransom's spirit was lurking behind the door, ready to pounce. She avoided all Ransom's private space—his office, his bedroom, even his dining room chair—as if it was haunted.

Johnson was awakened by a commotion downstairs followed by heavy footsteps on the stairs. Gently removing Mee Yang's arm from his neck, he went to the door, wrapping himself in a towel on the way. A moment later Mee Yang—fully dressed somehow—slipped in front of him and stepped into the hall to confront an agitated guard who spoke to her rapidly but deferentially. After hearing him out she turned to Johnson.

"Wife having baby," she said. "Try all night, but baby not come. Man want Doc come get baby out."

Johnson sent Mee Yang for the medical kit, rinsed his face

and pulled on his clothes. Everything around him seemed to have come into sharp focus.

The guard drove the jeep, Johnson in front, Mee Yang in back. The air was warm and thick. Heavy rain clouds hung just above the treetops. The birds sounded nervous.

Two old women were tending to the prospective mother, but Mee Yang shooed them back. The woman was so exhausted she could barely move her eyes. Johnson felt her belly. The baby was turned the wrong way. Afraid to reach inside and try to turn it around, he had Mee Yang and the old women hold her down while he pulled on rubber gloves, said a little prayer and made the incision. The one previous time he'd performed a cesarean the baby had been dead, but this day he lifted out a healthy little girl, red and prune-skinned and, after one crisp slap, screaming. He passed it to the two old women with the placenta still attached, gave the mother a shot of morphine and bent confidently to his sewing. Before he'd taken three stitches he heard the mother snoring.

When he finished he noticed Mee Yang studying the baby with solemn interest, as if trying to divine its secrets. Johnson peeled off the gloves and washed up. He was tingling. It seemed appropriate that his first case since becoming a free man was to help bring a new life into the world. Maybe, he thought, when he got back to the States he could keep doing stuff like this, work in an ambulance or something. It was too bad nurses were all girls. He tried to recall exactly how many babies he'd delivered, but his memory wouldn't cooperate. He couldn't remember Mee Yang as a baby at all, only as a skinny little girl gathering green leaves, running lightly through the rain with one arm up holding on an oversized hat.

When they got back to the compound Ransom was yelling furiously at the head guard, but when he saw Johnson he waved and broke into a grin and jogged over. He was still wearing his suit and tasseled loafers.

"Welcome home, Colonel," Johnson cried, hopping from the jeep. The two men hugged and slapped backs.

"Come on," Ransom said, stepping back and squeezing Johnson's shoulder, "let's talk over lunch. I'm sick of airline food."

"How was the trip?" Johnson asked.

"Look at all this mud," Ransom said. "What happened? This place is like a swamp." He lifted his trouser legs and began prancing gingerly between puddles. "How was the trip? Except for New York it went fine."

"New York?" Johnson exclaimed. "You were in New York?"

"No, but there's some trouble there. I'm trying to stay the hell out of it."

"Serious trouble?"

"Serious enough to have gotten two guys killed already." He made a gesture of disgust, then brightened. "Wait till you see what I picked up for you in Zurich. Come on, princess," he urged Mee Yang, who was hanging back. "I even brought a present for you."

"Something nice?" Johnson asked hopefully.

"Baseball caps," Ransom said. "Can you believe that baseball caps are the latest craze? I picked up two: one from the California Angels when I changed planes at LAX and—" He was trying not to smile— "Hey, Doc, you ever hear of a team called the Tigers?"

"Detroit?" Johnson exclaimed. "You were in Detroit?"

Ransom hopped up to the porch. "Ba-by, ba-by, ba-by," he sang while performing a spirited but clumsy version of the twist, "where did our love go?"

Ransom was at the sink preparing a fresh fruit salad.

Johnson took a deep breath. "Listen," he said, "you smuggle stuff, right?"

Ransom stopped working. "Sure."

"All kinds of stuff."

"Pretty much."

"From all over the world."

Ransom's shoulders delivered a so-what shrug. He went back to squeezing papayas.

"How hard would it be," Johnson persisted, "for you to smuggle people? Two people, I mean. Into the U.S."

Ransom sniffed one of the colorful fruits. "Not hard."

"Could you get us papers?"

"Sure." He began expertly peeling the thick skin from one of the fleshy fruits. "But is that what you want, Doc? To sneak back home like a criminal?"

"Don't you sneak back home like a criminal?"

"Yeah, but I am a criminal," Ransom declared, his knife working a little faster. "You said so yourself. I smuggle things."

"I didn't mean to—"

"No offense taken," Ransom assured him, his knife paring steadily. "Let's give it a little while, okay, Doc? Another week or so. But like I told you, anything you want. You want to sneak back in, I'll take care of it. Little Miss Saigon too."

"Why do you call her that?"

Ransom put down the knife and turned to face Johnson. He had a funny smile. "Maybe I'm jealous."

"Of Mee Yang?"

"No, not her. She's a nice kid, but come on, Doc . . ."

"What then?"

"Get out of here," Ransom said, turning away and grasping another fruit. "I've got work to do."

Chapter Twenty

Fink burst awake gasping for air, the crackly smell of burning thatch clogging his nostrils, the pressure in his head like a wall of noise. He forced his eyes open and felt the madness slow, loosen, pass. He began to see things. Marissa was curled up beside him, fast asleep and hugging a pillow. They were in her suite at the Helmsley Palace. It was still dark outside. He picked up his watch. There was a canyon of time before he had to meet Barton. He sat on the edge of the bed and waited for everything to come floating back into place. His mouth had the coppery taste of fear.

In his sleep she had been running toward him again, the fear-crazed little girl with the outstretched arms. Tonight she had been wearing his daughter's face, from that time when she'd run to him wide-eyed, naked and shrieking, a terrified nine-year-old whose bedtime shower had suddenly turned scalding. In that fractured moment before his senses had clicked and his arms had opened for his own flesh and blood, he had seen running toward him the little

Vietnamese girl in the heartbreaking newspaper photo, her child's skin burned by napalm, her child's eyes wild with terror.

In Fink's mind, the two children had fused together to symbolize all the horror in his world. In his dreams a naked little girl with arms outstretched was always running toward him, sometimes wearing his daughter's face, sometimes the other's, sometimes both. This recurring image replaced all those from the war and from the city's irredeemably mean streets: all the dead and mutilated bodies, all the burning, all the cruel, senseless sufferings of old and young—all of it reduced to a single terrified little girl always running running running toward him through his dreams. He hadn't seen her in a long time, but here she was, back again. Maybe it was all this MIA talk coming from the Senate. Maybe it was something else.

"You okay, *hombre*?" Marissa asked, patting his shoulder.

"Yeah. I couldn't sleep."

She propped herself up on one elbow, reached for the phone and pressed a digit. "Room service? Send up a bottle of *Veuve Clicquot*, a pot of regular coffee, a bowl of fruit—whole fruit, not fruit salad—and some Oreo cookies . . . What do you mean? . . . No, I don't want petit fours, I want Oreos . . . Well, then get them!"

She replaced the receiver with a smack. "Believe it or not," she groused, "when Leona was here this was a luxury hotel."

"How did you afford it?" Fink asked, rubbing the back of his head.

"I did some work for Frank's company. I told you. With their corporate rate, this costs about the same as the Y."

"Who's paying for it this time?" he asked.

"Why, you offering?"

He laughed. With what his daughter's college was costing, a room at the Y would be a stretch.

She fumbled around the night table and lit a Virginia Slims. Fink breathed in deeply. A former smoker, he liked the smell of tobacco on her breath, the taste of it in her mouth. Passive smoke was better than none.

She turned on a light, stood and stretched. Though naked, she looked nothing like the prepubescent in Fink's dreams. Marissa's body was full but solid, with no sharp edges. Most of the women's bodies he saw were wrecked: ugly tracks on the arms and legs, scabs, bruises, gashes, gunshot wounds, waxy skin, glazed dead eyes. Marissa's was a delight.

The smoke floating in the air was making him hungry. He reached to the night table, unfoiled the chocolate mint they'd left on his pillow and began sucking it. He looked around and scratched his naked belly. Under different circumstances he might have felt genuinely happy.

The toilet flushed. Water started running in the sink. No, the nickel had dropped when Rotelli mentioned seeing Marissa around Parker Global headquarters. Clunk: end of fairy tale. The truth was, he'd been suspicious from that first day in his office, when she'd come on to him like a cheerleader. It was almost comforting to find out she was on Parker Global's payroll; it explained so many things. She hadn't flinched when he'd asked her what she did for them. Years ago, she'd explained, a business favor she'd done for Frank had evolved into assignments with Spanish-speaking clients: serving as a translator, tying up loose ends, writing background reports on middle-level government officials. Her assignments took her to Central America, mostly, South America, sometimes: Panama, Nicaragua, Paraguay, El Salvador, Belize, Peru, Argentina, Uruguay. She had no complaints; she enjoyed traveling and PG always paid her well. PG paid everyone well.

Licking the last of the chocolate from his teeth, he walked to the window and gazed down at the spires of St. Patrick's Cathedral. The best thing about religion was the buildings.

Park Avenue was nearly deserted. The only traffic was scavenging yellow cabs whose headlights successively illuminated the lone pedestrian, a tiny, dim figure rummaging through a garbage bin.

Sure, Fink thought, he'd be back pounding a beat if it turned out Marissa had anything to do with Grelling's murder. But he trusted his instincts: also his common sense. Besides, she'd been in Florida when Grelling caught it. Outfits like Parker Global didn't go around killing off their own salesmen; it wasn't cost-effective. If Trang and Grelling had been involved in something extracurricular—which was how Fink was leaning—there were better ways for PG to handle it than having them strangled. Besides, if PG was into that kind of stuff Tony Rotelli would have smelled it. Rotelli was a pisser. Fink reminded himself that he was going to pick up some pastries from Ferrara's before they met next time.

Flashing lights caught his eye. Down on Park a blue-and-white had stopped by the garbage bin to shoo the vagrant on. Fink felt for the guy.

As for Marissa, *quién sabe*? A reasonable explanation was that she was enjoying herself with him and keeping her ears open for PG at the same time. At her suggestion, they were together every night now. Whether PG was paying her for it was immaterial, since thanks to Grelling she was now a millionaire. Millionairess, he corrected himself. And he'd never had an affair with a real one before. So why, he asked himself sincerely, didn't he just stop worrying and enjoy it while it lasted? Because, he answered, everything was a little too neat; it all made a little too much sense. His damned instincts again. Still, it always paid to be careful. He was glad he'd asked that guy at Immigration to check Marissa's passport file for him, not that he'd expected it to turn up anything unusual. Lots of trips to Central and South America, as advertised, especially Peru and Paraguay. Funny, he'd always associated Paraguay with German, not Spanish: ex-Nazis, stuff like that. Wasn't Mengele supposed to have gone to Paraguay? Or was it Argentina? Or was that Eichmann?

The knock at the door caught him by surprise. He was reaching for his gun when he remembered room service. Still naked, he went inside, ran a hand through his hair and opened the door a crack. A starched Asian kid was out there behind a fancy cart. Fink told him to wait, closed the door and went for Marissa.

"Sign for it, *caro*," she called from the shower.

Out in the hall, Bo gripped the handles of the food cart and asked the hovering spirits of his maternal ancestors for their blessing. The child of a dutiful country girl sold into prostitution during the war, neither she nor Bo knew the identity of the man who had sired him. While slowly tightening the wire, Bo had fantasized that first Grelling, then Trang, was his father.

But he did not like the idea of killing a woman, even an American one. His mother had suffered enough for all women. Fortunately, the nightly presence of this policeman had restored his enthusiasm for the task. Bo thanked his maternal ancestors for providing another American male old enough to have been a soldier in Vietnam. He would disable the policeman first, then return to him after disposing of the woman. He wanted to kill him very slowly. He had told Tiffany that he might be working late tonight.

Bo dropped his hands below the level of the cart and grasped the metal bracelet on his left wrist, slipping his index finger through the plastic ring and testing the retractable wire. He would explain to his superiors that he had not known that the man was in the suite. As long as Bo killed them both and got away cleanly there would be nothing more than some grumbling. He reminded himself that the man would be carrying a gun, most probably in a shoulder holster. Perhaps, Bo thought, he would keep the gun as a souvenir, the way American GIs used to keep his countrymen's ears.

He heard a sound from the other side of the door and concentrated on preparing himself. In another moment he would be inside with them, setting out the food and watching for the man to turn his back. Two seconds was all Bo would need. Less. He smoothed his white jacket, squared his shoulders and waited for the door to open.

Fink stepped into his slacks, taking extra care with the zipper. After making sure his ankle holster was out of sight, he opened the door all the way. The waiter wheeled in the cart and set it up by the table in the living room, next to the sofa. The way the kid's eyes were darting around the room, Fink figured he was new here: mixed, from the look of him, what they called an Amerasian; maybe even one of those Vietnamese boat people. Fink smiled at the kid. He always liked seeing people getting a new start in America: a Statue of Liberty kind of thing.

After securing the cart, the kid lifted a silver cover and showed Fink a dark circle of Oreos. There was a large basket of fruit and an ornate coffee service which included a vaguely patriotic arrangement of Sweet 'n Low, white sugar packets and Equal. Despite the waiter's repeated urging, Fink had no interest in inspecting any of it. The champagne's gold head poked rakishly from a silver pail, its neck draped with a white cloth. Fink told the waiter they would open it themselves. The kid nodded, but he looked disappointed when Fink declined to come over and inspect the label.

It seemed to Fink the kid was taking a lot longer than necessary to get the job done, almost as if he was stalling. Hearing the bathroom door open, Fink told him to hurry up.

The kid handed Fink a pen and the check, then suddenly reached under the cart. Reflexively Fink stepped back and tensed. The kid pulled out a copy of tomorrow's *Times*. Fink walked over, told the kid to turn around, and used his back to write on. The total was a little over two hundred dollars, more than half of it for the wine. The Oreos were twelve. Fink decided that a twenty dollar tip, though outrageous, was probably appropriate, so he wrote it in and totaled it up. He signed "M. Grelling" and handed it back. The kid was good; he didn't even glance at it as he left.

The shower stopped. Fink latched the door, slipped off his pants and removed the Velcro holster, then strolled to the center of the living room and stood there naked, his arms outstretched, thinking that, all things considered, this was not a bad way to live.

CHAPTER TWENTY-ONE

The lights were flickering insistently, but the people crowding the lobby of the Kennedy Center were reluctant to return to their seats. For most of them, the networking during intermission was the most important part of the concert.

Standing off by himself, Antel Grantham, the senior senator from Alaska, was admiring a young woman's bare and beautifully reticulated back when a familiar pattern of military ribbons slid over and blocked his view.

"I was wondering when you'd appear," the senator remarked.

"We've got a problem," General Olden said.

Olden was attached to the Pentagon. He and the senator went back more than twenty years. Olden had served with Grantham's son in Vietnam.

"Kennedy would have hated this place," the senator sighed, staring down the long row of massive chandeliers. "No grace, no delicacy, no style. His father would have liked it. I didn't know you enjoyed Mozart, Buzz."

"Screw Mozart," the general grumbled. "Come on, Antel, I've got a car outside."

"What about my driver?"

"I sent him home."

"You have anything to drink?"

"Wild Turkey for you, Chivas for me."

"I'll get my coat."

General Olden poured two fingers of bourbon and an equal amount of scotch. Both men were tall. They sat facing each other diagonally in the limousine. The general, the heavier of the two, had unbuttoned the blue jacket of his air force uniform.

"We headed somewhere in particular?" Senator Grantham asked.

"I just told the boy to drive us around for a while. And don't you go looking at me like that, ant hill. He's white. Shit, for all I know he's gay. Happy now?"

"You must be pissed off," Grantham observed, gently shaking his glass. "You normally don't start calling me 'ant hill' until your third drink."

"To your very good health, Senator," Olden said, raising his glass.

"And yours, General." He took a sip. "Tell me, Buzzard, how many stars does it take to requisition a vehicle with leather seats? I hate this velour crap."

"Can we get started?" Olden asked.

"Do your worst."

"Isaac Prometheus Johnson," the general said.

"Am I supposed to feign shock?" Grantham asked. "The FBI is a sieve. Did they send you to tell me the prints are a forgery?"

"Did who send me?"

"The boys with more stars."

"The boys with more stars—your construction, not mine—sent me to convince you to keep Corporal Johnson's name out of your hearings."

"Spare me, Buzzard, please."

"That's what I'm here for, Antel, to spare you."

"From what? Embarrassing the mighty heroes of Desert Storm? The conquerors of the Elite Republican Guard? Where's their sense of shame? My God, Buzz, this man has been a prisoner for twenty-four years."

"I don't think so, Antel," Olden said. "That's what I've come to tell you. Our people don't think he's been a prisoner for twenty-four minutes."

"The hell you say!"

"You ready for another drink?"

Grantham covered his tumbler with his hand. Time to listen, ant hill, he counseled himself. Olden's appearance to plead the Pentagon's case was no surprise, but Grantham didn't like the way this was starting. The story was supposed to go like this: The Pentagon has been spending a hundred million taxpayer dollars a year to ensure that not one American boy had been left behind in Southeast Asia, and now we discover that despite the other side's repeated denials, this brave American soldier has been held captive . . . It was such a four-corner solution that there had to be a damn good reason why the Pentagon was rejecting it in favor of what sounded disturbingly like character assassination. Grantham hoped to hell he was wrong. He'd read the file: Corporal Isaac P. Johnson wasn't some white-collar whistle-blower running to the media with tales of ten-thousand-dollar toilets; he was a poor black kid from Detroit who'd gotten sucked into a lousy war and gone out and done his duty. An army medic, for chrissakes. Where were the Pentagon's brains? Had they forgotten the story of David and Goliath? If mishandled, this could turn out to be a public relations nightmare . . . Unless there was some essential thing he didn't know. He'd better find out now, before CNN broke the story and left him no room to maneuver. The last thing Grantham wanted was for his hearings to be turned into a media circus. Live TV coverage was wonderful, but only if all the surprises were known in advance. Biden was probably still having nightmares over Clarence Thomas and Anita Hill.

"Let's start with Nixon," Buzz suggested.

"Good," Grantham agreed, "then we'll have nowhere to go but up."

Olden refused to rise to the bait. Instead, he conceded that all the government numbers on Vietnam—Nixon's as well as Johnson's—had been massaged. "When the war ended," he said, "we were officially carrying twenty-four hundred men as missing, but of course half those guys were KIA/BNR."

"I know," Grantham said ruefully. His son, Samuel, had been on the KIA/BNR list: Killed in Action/Body Not Recovered. Lieutenant Sam Grantham's platoon had been crossing a rice paddy after a firefight. The mine he'd stepped on hadn't left enough of him to bring back. There was no ambiguity; seven of his men had seen him die. Grantham raised his drink only to discover he was no longer holding a glass.

"Don't start brooding on me, Antel," the general warned, "we've got a lot of ground to cover."

The senator cleared his throat. "Where's that coffee?"

"The boy is getting it now. Didn't you notice that we'd stopped?"

"Get on with it," Grantham said irritably.

"Okay. Cut to Paris, January 1973. As part of the Paris Accords, Kissinger signs a secret codicil which promises North Vietnam four point seven five billion in U.S. aid. The war ends. Five hundred ninety-one U.S. prisoners are released. Bands play, flags wave, tears flow. Everything seems fine. But a few months later Watergate explodes, Nixon resigns and our government reneges on the aid. We won't even discuss it with the North Vietnamese. The only thing we'll discuss are the mostly mythical twenty-four hundred missing men. Uncle Ho's people become recalcitrant. We want information about our MIAs and they want their fucking four point seven five billion. We stonewall each other for years, though every once in a while, just to keep the dialogue going, they produce some wreckage from a downed jet or throw us a few American bones. Rumors persist of POWs being held in secret jungle prison camps. For some reason, the American public wants to believe that we left American boys over there."

He stopped to take a drink. "You with me so far, Antel?"

"By the way, Buzz, what's the latest total of men still unaccounted for?"

"Off the record?"

"Yes."

"Less than forty."

There was a knock on the window. Olden opened it and the driver handed in a bag. A minute later the car was moving again. Grantham broke off the little plastic tab and slurped. It was getting late, the caffeine would be good for him.

"Year after year," Olden continued, "we've investigated every report, no matter how far-fetched. Rumors, sightings, blurry Polaroids, anomalies on computer-enhanced satellite photos—you name it. What else can we do? We have to follow up on everything. Meanwhile, Antel, in the twenty years since the war not one of these reports has turned out to be genuine. Twenty years, Antel, and not one POW, not one MIA."

"Until now," the senator submitted.

"Exactly." Olden paused to pour some scotch into his coffee.

The car was moving at an unhurried, almost stately pace. The boy was a good driver. Grantham wondered idly how old he was. No, Sam would have been older. Much older.

"I assume you've read the Snosset report," Olden said.

"Test me. Johnson and Snosset were on a two-man recon patrol. Corporal Johnson went into a hut to treat a wounded civilian: a little boy with a broken leg, if memory serves. PFC Snosset, standing guard outside, heard noises which he subsequently identified as an approaching enemy patrol. When informed of the danger, Johnson elected to remain with his patient but ordered Snosset to evacuate. When Johnson failed to return to camp and the search party came up empty, he was listed as MIA, possible POW. Did I leave anything out?"

"No, but you'll admit the report does raise some questions."

"Sure it does. It allows for the possibility that Johnson went over to the other side. But honestly, Buzz, is that your take on it?"

"No," Olden admitted. "My guess is that Snosset heard an enemy patrol and bailed out, abandoning his buddy Johnson. That might be why Snosset has worked for us all these years handling the POW/MIA files. It's a little too neat, I admit, but things sometimes happen that way."

"And so?" Grantham prompted.

Olden took a deep breath and sighed. "So Corporal Johnson was most likely captured by the enemy. I admit that. It's what happens after the capture that gets murky."

The car had stopped. The senator glanced out the window and was startled to see the deep gash in the ground that was the Vietnam Memorial. Grantham was outraged that Buzz would do this: A father's grief was not negotiable. He rapped his knuckle on the glass partition and said "Drive."

The car stayed put.

"Forgive me, Antel," Olden said gently. "I was ordered to take you here. I know we both want to honor these men, but if this man Johnson was a collaborator . . ."

A bitter sadness was seeping from the grave-like trench and filling the car. "Evidence," Grantham demanded. "I have the man's fingerprints. What have you got?"

"Twenty-four years," Olden responded. "Think about it, Antel. We debriefed every one of the five hundred ninety-one returning POWs. Not one of them mentioned Isaac Johnson or anyone fitting his description. Officially, we carried him as missing, but our assumption was that he was dead, probably killed back in '68 by that VC patrol. Antel, where in the hell has he been all these years?"

"I don't know, Buzz, but since when in this country does disappearance equal guilt?" Grantham was still smarting from their proximity to the Memorial.

"There's more," Olden offered. "We've had intermittent reports of an American medic working with—"

"Where?" Grantham demanded.

"Laos."

"No, where are these so-called reports?"

"In the files, Antel. We—"

"If they were worth a tinker's damn, you'd have them here."

"Fair enough," Olden conceded. "They're all low-confidence sightings. But now that—"

"Now that some real evidence has turned up," Grantham shot back, "the boys with more stars are scrambling to cover their collective khaki ass."

"Maybe," the general granted. "Maybe that's true, Antel. But maybe this Isaac Johnson never showed up in any POW camp because he spent the rest of the war patching up enemy soldiers and sending them back in to kill some of the boys whose names are carved on that granite wall out there."

"General," Grantham declared with barely controlled fury, "that is truly . . ." But he couldn't find an adequate word.

Olden slumped back against his seat. "Jesus, Antel," he groaned, "the war's been over twenty years and look at us."

"Look at yourself," Grantham suggested. "Cards on the table, Buzz. We both know what the Pentagon is afraid of. If Corporal Johnson has been alive all these years, the media will ask, how about all the others—the mythical two thousand? And you know what, Buzz? I know just who—"

"Let's walk for a while," Olden said, hurriedly drawing a forefinger across his throat. "I hate arguing in a cramped space."

"My legs could use with a stretch," Grantham agreed, reining in his anger.

Olden stepped out and headed off away from the Memorial. Grantham followed. The grass was damp and rubbery. The moonlit capital looked like a schoolroom diorama. A chill wind was sweeping by close to the ground. Grantham felt old and brittle. The loss of his wife four years ago had been a terrible blow, but the loss of their son twenty years earlier had been much worse, creating a permanent void inside both of them. The long black wall behind him was exerting the steady pull of a distant vortex.

Both men buttoned their coats. Neither spoke until they were far from the car.

"I don't know if it's bugged or not," Olden said, "but I didn't want you mentioning any names. If they are listening, that argument we had was good. Now when we go back and you've agreed to keep this Johnson thing quiet I'll look like a hero."

"You know I won't agree to that," Grantham told him.

"Yes you will, Antel. I wouldn't have signed on to be their errand boy unless I was sure."

"You must know something I don't."

"Damn right."

"Let's have it."

Olden remained silent for a few steps. "Antel," he began, "you have no idea what a can of worms this is. I don't know all of it, but what I know is bad enough."

"But do you believe that Isaac Johnson is alive?" Grantham asked impatiently.

"Yes."

"And the prints? Any question?"

"No question," Olden said, "the prints are genuine." He reached out and took the senator's arm. "Both sets."

Grantham stopped and turned to him.

"That's right," Olden said. "There was a second set of prints on that newspaper."

"Not another MIA," Grantham exclaimed.

"Yes, Antel, and we've got to make sure he stays that way. Johnson is a mystery to us, but we've been aware of the other one for years. Come on," he urged, "let's keep walking. I'll tell you what I know. Believe me, Antel, this other guy is poison."

Chapter Twenty-Two

"You sent for me, Captain?" Barton asked.

Captain Reynolds didn't look up from the document on his desk. "Take a seat."

Barton sat, but kept his jacket buttoned. Reynolds continued reading. The office was crowded with plaques and commendations, all of the bullshit variety. It was common knowledge that Reynolds had come up administratively and had served virtually no time in the field. Rumor had it his favorite assignment had been internal affairs. Another rumor was that when he'd been in Nam some of his own men had tried to frag him.

Reynolds pressed his intercom and asked his secretary to hold all calls. "We're not having this conversation," he began, signing something with a flourish and putting it aside. He looked up, measuring Barton with hooded eyes. "Is that understood?"

"Yes, sir."

Reynolds had a dark beefy face that suggested Africa far

more than the polyglot West Indies of Barton's people. The captain's hair was nappy and black, with an oily sheen that came from cheap pomade. It occurred to Barton that if his sister had ever brought a man like this home their mother would have chased him out with a broom.

"I know your record," Reynolds said. "You've been on the fast track since the academy." His voice was gravelly, but he wasn't a New York native. "You married?" he asked.

"No, sir."

"Seeing someone?"

"Uh, yes, sir, pretty much."

"She a sister?"

"Yes, sir."

"Good, I like that." The captain chuckled, wobbling his high-backed leather chair. "I keep an eye on certain brothers," he continued, swiveling within a narrow arc, "the ones who have what I call P.P." He paused. "Pro-mo-tion po-tential," he said. "You," he declared, sighting Barton's nose along a yellow pencil, "are on my list."

Barton nodded, trying to look flattered.

"I see they've got you working with Mel Fink," Reynolds remarked, leaning back.

"Yes, sir."

"Fink's a hard-ass. You agree with me?"

"I'm not sure what you mean, sir."

"Fink's not a team player. He's a synagogue of one, so to speak. You with me now?"

"Yes, sir." It didn't make sense to disagree with a captain, especially if you didn't know where he was headed.

"Don't get me wrong," Reynolds said, buffing his fingernails on his shirt, then inspecting them. "Fink knows his job." He sniffed hard twice, bending his nose up sharply each time.

Barton shifted in his chair.

The captain clasped his hands on the desk and carefully arranged the rest of himself behind them. "Here's where it's at, Barton," he said. "Fink should never have been assigned to the Grelling case. It's too sensitive. Fink lacks finesse. You following me, Barton?"

"Not exactly, sir. As far as I can see, Grelling was nobody."

"Neither was Trang. But in our business, Detective, two nobodies sometimes add up to a somebody."

"Parker Global," Barton offered.

Reynolds tapped index finger to temple. "See," he said, "you think. You have sense. That's what got you on my list."

Whatever this guy wants, Barton thought, I'm not going to like it.

"Let me lay it out for you," Reynolds said, returning to his formal pose. "Parker Global is considering moving their headquarters outside the city. That would be very bad news: hundreds of jobs, millions in tax revenues. Not to mention that another major corporate defection at this time would be seen as a slap in the face of the mayor. In a word, Barton, we want Parker Global to stay put."

"Yes, sir."

"But it seems that Fink is more interested in hassling their senior executives than in solving the unrelated murders of two of their employees."

Barton wondered if he'd heard right. "Sir?"

"Spit it out, Barton."

"The murders are clearly related, Captain."

"Listen to me, Barton. A man with P.P. learns to grasp certain things instinctively. Asserting this position is important to Parker Global and inconsequential to us. What we say to the press does not necessarily have a damn thing to do with the actual investigation, now does it, Barton?"

"Not really, sir, no."

"We can't pull Fink off the case, much as we'd like to. Just because he's made a few lucky busts over the years, some of his friends in the circumcised press see him as a Yiddish Kojak. So okay, he stays. But he has to be monitored. That's where you come in."

"Sir?"

Reynolds ignored the alarm in Barton's voice and held out a business card. "Here's my direct office line. On the back I've written my private number at home. When you've memorized the numbers, destroy the card."

Barton reached over and took the card. "Yes, sir, but—"

"It's imperative that I be kept current."

"But why not ask Fink, sir?"

The captain's eyes narrowed. "Because I'm asking you, Barton. There's plenty of room for a smart young brother to advance in this department, but I need to see if you're one of us. It always helps to have a rabbi, Barton. You ought to know that."

"Who else would know of our arrangement, sir?"

"No one, and it damn well better stay that way, unless you want to spend the next ten years in a toll booth— Don, isn't it?"

"Yes, sir."

"You'll keep me informed of all developments in the case, Don."

"Yes, sir."

"On a daily basis."

"Daily?" His voice was close to a wail.

Reynolds stood and extended his hand. "Oh, and Barton, stop giving out my name to waitresses."

"Sir?"

Rhonda hadn't stopped fussing since he arrived. She was making Barton nervous, the way she kept flitting into the living room to deliver yet another appetizer: nuts, raisins, cheese, crackers, salsa, guacamole, tortilla chips—arranging and rearranging things like twigs in a nest. She was wearing a low-cut black unitard beneath a loose-fitting multicolored silk thing open in front but very long in back, its many ends lifting and trailing through the air as she moved about. Her promised quiet little dinner for two was turning into a major production and Barton wasn't in the mood for it. As good as Rhonda looked, all he could think about was how that ugly bastard Reynolds was turning him out like a whore. Barton didn't owe Fink anything, but the idea of being Reynolds' snitch—anybody's snitch—filled him with disgust. He'd taken a long shower after he'd gotten home, but he felt like he needed another one.

Rhonda could see he wasn't relaxed. She redoubled her efforts, turning up the Lite FM and surrounding him with ever more appetizers: party mix, sesame sticks, yogurt-covered raisins, glazed apricots. Nothing was working; if she pulled her top down any lower she'd fall out of it. She'd wanted everything to be perfect tonight. This was their third date and she'd managed during the first two to keep both feet on the floor: not that she'd wanted to, but she had been determined not to be too easy. Rhonda knew herself; Don was gorgeous; once she let herself go she'd be totally out of control.

Which was what she intended tonight. She'd tweezed her eyebrows, shaved her legs, sprayed and perfumed everywhere. She felt like a tigress. She'd scrubbed the apartment and bought fresh flowers and packed away all the stuffed animals and broken out the new Ralph Lauren sheets. She even left that new frilly thing from Victoria's Secret hanging in the bathroom.

But his head was someplace else: either back at the office or—God, don't You dare!—thinking about another woman.

Rhonda was desperate not to mess this up. There had to be something he liked. There was a pack of those frozen pigs in a blanket she could heat up in the microwave. It was worth a try. She glanced down; the coarse fabric of the unitard was keeping her nipples hard as bottle caps, but he wasn't even looking. Pigs in a blanket, she reminded herself.

Barton picked up a yogurt-covered raisin, examined it, put it back. Sure he'd been warned about Reynolds, but what was he supposed to do? The son of a bitch was a captain. Barton thought about his own career: maybe he should have stayed in the air force, signed on for the extra years, tried to become a pilot. Who knew? By now he might have been flying the friendly skies and taking down a hundred large.

He adjusted his jacket. The little card in his wallet felt like a ball and chain. Memorize and destroy—what did Reynolds think this was, Mission Impossible? Goddamn affirmative action, Barton thought bitterly, that's where bastards like Reynolds came from. It was too bad those guys in Nam missed with that grenade. Daily reports! Barton couldn't believe he was going to have to call that slimeball every day. Like he was on fucking work release.

"Pigs in a blanket," Rhonda proclaimed, materializing before him with yet another plate.

"No, thanks," he muttered, barely glancing at it.

"They should be crisper," she lamented. "That's the thing with a microwave. I could still put them in the toaster oven."

He shook his head, staring down at the floor. Rhonda moved a few things and put the plate on the coffee table. Then she knelt down in front of him and put her hands on his knees, arranging herself so that he could see straight down to her belly button.

"Hey," she said, squeezing his knees.

He looked up and seemed surprised to find her there. His eyes passed and then returned to her breasts.

At last.

"So?" she said, using her palms to trace slow circles on his knees.

"What?" he asked. "I'm sorry, Rhonda. I'm kind of out of it tonight."

"Is there anything I can do?"

He looked into her eyes. "That could be a dangerous question," he said, finally showing signs of life.

She looked up into his eyes. "Is there anything I can do?" she asked, going for it.

He reached out and gently brushed her cheek. She inched closer, her belly tingling, her fingers climbing his thighs like determined spiders. He kissed her and she heard herself emit a little squeal. A moment later she felt herself grasped under the arms and lifted off the floor and there she was, out of control.

The bed was a mess. Rhonda was wet everywhere. Her thighs were sore in the loveliest way imaginable. She looked over at him lying there with his hands behind his neck and ran her eyes greedily down his body.

"Okay," she said, "now tell me what happened today."

"You don't want to hear it," he assured her, staring at the ceiling. He'd been enjoying the silence.

"Listen to me, Donatello," she said, poking a rib, "here's the deal. When you get tired of me, you walk. I won't come running after you. I promise. Fair enough?"

"More than fair."

"Now tell me what happened today."

"I got a call from a Captain Reynolds," he began.

Rhonda listened carefully. As she understood it, Don's dilemma was not whether to make the daily calls to Captain

Reynolds—he had no choice—but whether to reveal the arrangement to Lieutenant Fink. The problem wasn't really that Fink was white, though of course that was part of it. The truth was, Barton admitted, he'd never allowed himself to trust anyone. That approach had worked pretty well for him, but now . . . well, what did Rhonda think?

She thought two things. First, she had a soft spot for Fink because he'd brought them together. Second, the quicker he and Fink solved the case the sooner Don could stop making daily calls to Captain Reynolds. As long as he was asking her advice, she thought he should tell Fink.

"Weren't you supposed to feed me?" he asked.

She rolled off the bed, stood, shook out her hair and pretended to yawn, carefully holding in her belly while giving him her best profile.

"I get the bathroom first," she said, "then I'll make dinner."

She was tearing lettuce in the kitchen, her whole body pumped with endorphins and humming with well-being, when she remembered something that she'd wanted to tell him. She called to him through the serving window.

"Excuse me?" He was sitting in an easy chair wearing only his slacks, looking good enough to chew.

"Paraguay and Peru," she called, "those were the two missing countries."

"Would you back that up for me, please?"

"Remember that list I gave you last week? Mr. Grelling's clients?"

"Sure."

"Well, after Mr. Trang died I got a call asking if I'd given it out to anyone—the list, I mean, and—I don't know why—something told me to say no."

"Who was the call from?"

"Mr. Schaeffer's secretary."

"And he is . . . ?"

"The capo."

"But I thought General Robbins—"

"No, no, no. The general gets top billing, but Schaeffer runs the show."

"So you said no, about the list."

"Right. And Mr. Schaeffer's secretary said, 'Good, we've prepared an updated one.' Then she came down—personally, mind you—took my old list and gave me the new one."

"What's the difference?"

"Paraguay and Peru are no longer on the list. I checked the computer. They'd been deleted from there too. That took some doing."

He walked over to the serving window. "What does that mean?"

She turned to face him. She could feel her shorts riding up in back. "I don't know," she told him, "but I can probably figure it out. You know, if you want . . ."

He had entered the kitchen. "I want," he said.

She tugged hard on her T-shirt. It wouldn't stay down. He had a funny look in his eyes. "Oh," she remembered, backing against the wall, "I have to tell you about Subic Bay."

"About what?" he asked, coming closer.

"Subic Bay. It's in the Philippines."

"Can it wait?"

"Yes. Sure. Absolutely."

CHAPTER TWENTY-THREE

"Looks like you were right," Shane Reilly said to her editor, her long fingers nervously rotating her drink.

Mike Mitchelson stirred his Jack Daniel's with his pinkie, sending the high-octane smell itching up into his nostrils. "What was I right about this time?"

She leaned across the booth. "Grantham," she whispered, "he's on to something."

"Okay, tell me."

"I go over to his office this afternoon," she said, "just to snoop around, and there's all this activity. Everybody has these forced smiles. Nobody has time to talk to me."

"Okay. So?"

"Grantham's door is wide open but he's not there, so when Bobby Cardanzer comes into reception, I say, 'Hi, Bobby, where is he?' And he gives a little hitch, stops cold and says, 'Where is who?' When I say 'The senator,' he seems relieved."

"And from this you deduce . . . ?"

"There's another 'he,' " she said urgently, "one I'm not supposed to know anything about."

Mitchelson took a sip of his bourbon. His gum still burned where he'd jabbed it with his toothbrush. "You're making a hell of an existential leap here," he cautioned her.

"Here's something else," she offered. "After Cardanzer left, I sidled over to Grantham's secretary and asked her, very *entre nous,* when they first found out about this guy. Now you tell me, boss, how would you expect her to respond to that?"

" 'What guy?' "

"But she didn't. She shooed me away, told me she didn't have time to talk."

"Interesting, but still awfully thin," Mitchelson responded.

"I know it's awfully thin. That's why I wanted to keep it out of the newsroom." She clasped her hands and hunched her shoulders. "I got to thinking: The boss knows how it's done. He was here with Woodward and Bernstein, back in the old days."

Mitchelson felt a tremor; when had Watergate become 'the old days'? " 'I shall wear the bottoms of my trousers rolled,' " he recited wistfully.

"Who is T. S. Eliot?" Reilly shot back. "Poets for four hundred."

Mitchelson looked across the table. Her eyes were sparkling. No one had the right to be so young, so pretty. What the hell.

"Okay, Reilly," he sighed, "I'll give you my best contact at the FBI. He owes me. If there's anything going on, he'll know about it."

A man picked up on the first ring. "Yes?"

"Agent Fredericks?" Reilly asked, trying to suppress her excitement. "My name is—"

"Listen," he interrupted, "I have to go out now. You want to meet me, that's fine. If not, that's even better." He gave her the address of an Arlington IHOP, described his tie and said he'd be there in thirty minutes.

He was.

At first glance, Agent Fredericks looked like he should be retrieving shopping carts in a Safeway parking lot: tall and thin, but with a double chin and thick, distorting glasses.

"How's your boss?" he asked after ordering prune juice and dry whole wheat toast. He sounded as if he'd once had an accent.

Shane ordered decaf and cheesecake. When the waitress left, she said, "Mike says to tell you 'Regards from Atlanta.' "

"No kidding? He must like you. You're what, five eleven?"

"Exactly. You've got a good eye. Mike also said that you're the best man in the Bureau."

"At what?"

"He didn't say."

"You watch much TV, what's-your-name?"

"Reilly. Shane. No, not much. You?"

"I finally got cable, last month," he said. "I've been watching the Weather Channel a lot. I don't know why."

"I won't use your name," she promised him.

His flicker of a smile made her realize that she didn't know his name. "Fredericks" was probably a code to tell him the source of the call. She wondered how many names he had.

He selected one of the plastic dispensers from the little rack on the ledge and carefully poured a moat of pancake syrup around his whole wheat toast.

"Can we talk while we eat?" she asked.

"Be my guest."

She took a breath, held it, took the shot. "We know about him," she said.

"Who's that?" he asked, casually extracting his utensils from their paper napkin cocoon.

"I have a high-level source inside the committee," she confided.

With surprising delicacy, he cut off a Chiclet-sized square of toast and carefully saturated both sides with syrup. He had long bony fingers. Then, timing the drips perfectly, he delivered it neatly into his mouth. He chewed thoughtfully.

"Mike said you'd help me out," she told him.

With a disquieting smile, he submerged another little toast square in the syrup.

"I'm talking about Senator Grantham's committee," she told him, feeling completely out of synch.

"Which one is that, ma'am?"

"POW/MIAs."

He nodded, releasing the pressure on his fork. "And that's the committee where you have this source?"

"Exactly."

"And what did this source tell you, exactly?"

Her fingernail began scraping graham cracker crust from her cheesecake. "They've found one," she whispered.

He started carving again. "One what?"

"An MIA," she whispered, and when that got no reaction, quickly added, "or a POW."

He shook his head as if embarrassed for her.

"I need a second source," she told him, feeling like a moron but determined to see it through. "You know, to confirm." Why was she so bad at this? She began to disfigure her cheesecake with her fork. "Mike said—"

"Mike said check it out with Fredericks," he said harshly. "But there's nothing to check out, Stretch. Why aren't you eating?"

She glanced down. Her ravaged cheesecake looked like tapioca pudding.

"What did Mike tell you about Atlanta?" he demanded.

"Nothing," she admitted sheepishly.

"That's what I figured." He came down a notch. "What he knew wouldn't matter now, but it mattered back then."

"Gay" flashed through her mind, surprising her. She stared down and poked her index finger through the filmy surface of her coffee. It was cold.

He wiped his hands on his napkin and pointed to the gold medallion on her neck chain. "That's nice," he said. "You mind?"

She leaned forward. He reached out and examined both sides of the little coin.

"St. Christopher?" he asked, releasing it and sitting back.

"St. Patrick. My great-grandmother brought it over from Ireland."

"Swell," he said indifferently, then got up, brushed his hands together, pointed to the check and left.

"I don't know why he was so nasty," she said to Mitchelson. She was all folded up and grumpy in his corner chair.

"Maybe he was under surveillance," her editor suggested.

"I doubt it."

"Why?"

"For a second there, I thought he was going to put his hand down my blouse."

"Fredericks? Not likely. Besides, I thought you said he never touched you."

"He wouldn't even shake my hand."

"So?"

"My medal," she said. "I had to lean forward so he could look at both sides."

"Show me," Mitchelson said.

"Oh, Jesus," Shane said irritably, untangling her legs, leaning forward and grasping the little gold medallion. "Oh, Jesus," she exclaimed as her finger felt a tiny piece of tape.

She reached back and hurriedly undid the chain. Weird little currents were shooting through her body. Something was written on the tape.

"Don't touch it," Mitchelson warned. "Lay the whole thing down here on the desk." He began pulling open drawers. "I've got a magnifying glass here somewhere."

CHAPTER TWENTY-FOUR

Reverend Ainsworth had a thousand things to do, but he stood up, forced a smile and invited Adelaide Johnson to have a seat. He knew why she was here, of course. He'd been expecting this meeting for a long time. It was only fair that the woman be paid something for cleaning up every night. He realized that, he accepted that. But it wasn't in the budget. Collections were down, down, down and the cost of everything was up, up, up. Still, Reverend Ainsworth understood how things were with Sister Johnson. She was getting on in years, she wasn't going to be able to keep her regular job much longer, and the Social Security wasn't going to be enough. While they exchanged pleasantries the whole sad meeting played itself out in his mind like a scene in a bad TV movie. He'd hear her out and then offer her as much as the church could afford, which would be far less than she was hoping for and considerably less than she needed, and then he would have to explain and explain and watch her smile give way to disappointment or, worse still, bitterness or, worst of all, tears. It was a shame, really: The sister did have such a nice smile today, almost a glow. But what could he do? Times were hard, that was the thing. He talked to his flock about heaven, but like everyone else he had to contend with things down here on earth first. Sister Johnson would simply have to understand. If he did it right, maybe he could keep her from crying. He always felt so helpless when the old ones started to cry. It suddenly occurred to him that now, with Brother Thompson gone, they were short two baritones in the choir. If it wasn't one thing, it was another.

He centered his leather-bound, gilt-edged Bible on his desk, rubbed one of its many silk ribbons for luck, and asked her how he could be of service.

As her story unfolded he thought it must be Alzheimer's. She was a little young for it, but he'd seen it often enough with shut-ins and people who lived by themselves. The tricks the mind plays, he marveled, smiling and nodding as she spun out a ridiculous but harmless tale about some white man taking her for a ride in a limousine, though he had to admit that a scarred angel made for an interesting image. Maybe she wasn't going to ask for money after all. Not this time, anyway. All this limousine talk reminded him he had to get his car in for that oil change.

Reverend Ainsworth pursed his lips and did that thing with his eyes that made his brow furrow. He knew where the story was going, of course. All Sister Johnson's stories revolved around her little Isaac, like that one about the day they met Muhammad Ali. At least this one was new. He'd been through enough of these to know not to interrupt, though when she said the angel promised to telephone he was tempted to ask her to get the area code. But of course he would never do that; those kinds of thoughts were simply his way of keeping himself focused; blasphemy required intent. Several times during her presentation he had offered a sympathetic shake of his head or a soft and carefully modulated "Mmmmm-mmmmm," like it was a ham she had cooked up instead of a fairy tale. He was about to give her a "Do tell" when she got to the Hershey's Kisses.

"I wanted you to have some for yourself, Reverend," she said. "These here are Kisses from heaven," and she reached into her purse and took out a plastic sandwich bag—one of those with the green stripe to show it's really closed—and laid it on his desk like it contained diamonds.

"That's very kind of you, Sister Johnson," he said, making like he was admiring them. "Six," he said. "My, my. Thank you very much indeed." He'd allow himself one, maybe two. The doctor said to avoid sweets, but how often did he get Kisses from heaven?

"—same as the money," she was saying.

"What was that, Sister?"

"If it was up to me, Reverend, I'd give more, you know I would. But that angel made me promise."

"Well, we can't go around breaking promises to angels," he agreed, allowing himself a paternal smile, even though she had a good dozen years on him.

"Ten percent," she said, struggling to her feet and handing him an envelope.

It was sealed, but it had some weight to it. He laid the envelope down on his desk, feeling guilty for not having realized how far this fantasy of Sister Johnson's had gone. Poor woman had probably emptied her bank account, might not even realize she'd done it. This Alzheimer's was a nasty business, a nasty, cruel business.

"Sister Adelaide," he said gently, patting the envelope and enjoying the bittersweet feeling that came from resisting temptation, "how much money is in here?"

"Twenty-five hundred dollars, Reverend."

"My, my, my," he said, shaking his head. "It must have taken you years to save up that much."

"Never have saved that much," she told him. "Most I ever had saved was, let me see—" She moved some fingers—"fourteen hundred and sixty-three dollars and some cents. 'Cept for that time the government sent me that check for my little Isaac. You remember that, Reverend. I wanted to send it back but you had me to keep it and buy that memorial plaque with my boy's name on top and all the empty spaces for the church, the one's still right out front in the entryway."

"Yes," he said. He did remember that now, though he wasn't proud of it. That was years and years ago, right after he'd arrived here. Poor woman couldn't believe her son was dead. Wouldn't believe it. Far as he knew, they never did find the body. Terrible thing, war. Terrible. Her hat seemed a bit crooked.

"Now Sister Adelaide," he said, hefting the envelope, "I appreciate this gesture, but I can't have you going into your savings—"

"That's not my money," she insisted. "That's what I'm telling you, Reverend. Ain't you been listening to me?"

"Of course I have, Sister Adelaide. Every word."

"That there in the envelope is the ten percent the angel told me to give you. That's holy money. You know me, Reverend. I don't play no numbers. I don't have that kind of money."

"Ten percent? Are you saying . . . ?" He slit open the envelope and experienced the momentary light-headedness that always accompanied the sight of large amounts of cash.

"Twenty-five thousand dollars," she told him, "that's what the angel give me in that Kisses bag. I counted it five times, but it always came out the same."

Recovering his equilibrium, the Reverend determined to

bring this sad charade to an end. He asked her what she'd done with the balance of the money.

"In the savings," she told him. "I was so nervous I called me a car service to carry me there this morning. They made me to fill out a special form 'cause there was too much."

"Too much?"

"Seems like there's a limit on how much you can put in. I never knew that. Ten thousand dollars, the man said. But no way I was taking the rest of that money back out with me, so I filled out his form."

"In that case, you must have your bankbook," he said, seeing an easy way to straighten this out. "May I see it?"

"You can come see it anytime you want, Reverend." Her voice dropped to a whisper. "I put it back in the 'partment in the hiding place, along with one of the bills. I had to keep one of them, don't you think?"

"Oh, certainly." He admired the way she had her story down pat, but he had things to do. "Which bank was it, Sister Adelaide?"

He called them. It took a while, but once he'd established who he was the assistant manager confirmed that Adelaide Johnson had this morning made a cash deposit of twenty-two thousand four hundred dollars.

But there was one strange thing, the banker confided to the stunned Reverend Ainsworth. He hadn't noticed until after she'd left the bank, and he was sure to catch some flak for it, but on the form, where it asked for the source of the funds, the lady had written "Jesus."

Chapter Twenty-Five

Rotelli, waiting at the bar, saw the box and smiled. "Bribe?" he asked hopefully.

"Cannoli," Fink told him. "From Ferrara's. I was down that way."

"How many?"

"Six. Two for me, four for you."

"You saying I'm fat?"

"Respect," Fink assured him.

"Order a drink," Rotelli said. "Lunch is on me."

They carried their glasses to the table. Rotelli's son—the middle one, the fireman—was in the hospital in Modesto. It wasn't serious, something with his knee, but his department had scheduled a hearing to determine if the injury was job-related. He'd been playing basketball in his backyard.

"Ten years ago no one would have said boo," Rotelli grumbled. "Today," he said, dismissing the present with a disgusted shake of his head. "Okay, Mel," he said, snapping out of it, "what have you got?"

"Not much more than an itch," Fink admitted. "But here's what I'm thinking. Who can get into almost any building in New York, no questions asked?"

"Just about anybody," Rotelli replied. "I'll bet a buncha fuckin' Arabs could drive a tanker of jet fuel into the U.N. garage."

"Probably," Fink granted, "but I'm talking residential buildings. Who has easy access?"

"Repairmen," Rotelli offered.

"Not really. They have to show work orders, permits—all kinds of crap."

"Messengers," Rotelli said. "Fed Ex, UPS, the crazies on bikes."

"Yeah, but most of the time they leave the stuff at the desk, let the doorman sign for it."

"True," Rotelli conceded. "How about pizza?"

"Bingo. Food deliveries. That's what I'm thinking, Tony. What a great cover. Who ever notices those guys? On any one night, a building like Grelling's or Trang's must get, what, forty or fifty deliveries, right?"

Rotelli pulled a tiny device from his pocket, pressed a button, spoke into it: "Memo to Danbury. Food deliveries."

"Your guys must be working overtime," Fink remarked as Rotelli slid it back into his pocket.

"Not mine, paesan," Rotelli chuckled. "Yours. We hire off-duty cops." He selected a breadstick. "General Robbins and your friend Schaeffer are getting double coverage. Eight others are getting round-the-clock."

"You think they know what this is about?"

"That's the strange part," Rotelli said, hunkering down and dropping his voice. "A few of the lesser all-stars talked to me. They're scared shitless."

"What do they know?"

"They know it's related to the company, but nobody can

figure out how. Grelling and Trang were nickel-dimers. You in a pasta mood? Try the angel-hair. Otherwise the veal. You don't want wine, right?"

"Right."

"Good," Rotelli said, "I can't bring myself to pay thirty bucks for a four dollar bottle of Chianti, even when I'm not paying."

"You're from the old school, Tony. The kids today—"

"Fuck MTV," Rotelli said. "They give you, what, half a second to look at a broad. *American Bandstand,* that was a classy show. The camera used to pan around until it found a good ass, a nice pair a tits, and then just follow it around the dance floor."

Fink laughed, shook his head, made a "give me" motion with his hand.

"All right," Rotelli said, "what do I hear. Hey, everybody cuts corners these days, am I right? Downscaling," he said disgustedly. "Anyway, most of our assembly work was moved to Mexico a few years back, so naturally a lot of the shit we deliver nowadays is defective. Okay, so customers send it back, get replacements, take credits. That happens all the time. Who would be pissed enough to kill salesmen? Nobody can figure it out. I had the yogurt fruits punch their keys to see if any of Grelling's or Trang's clients had major problems recently. They came up empty."

"How about Paraguay?"

"Paraguay wasn't Grelling."

"I know, but there's a drug thing one of my guys is working on. I'm curious how big a customer they are."

"Humongous."

"Seriously?"

"Too big, maybe," Rotelli said as the waiter appeared.

Fink held the thought. "Too big how?" he asked after they'd ordered.

"At first I thought they must have been getting ready for a war," Rotelli said, "but I checked back and they've been buying like that for years. Them and Peru."

"Them is Paraguay?"

"Right. So?"

"So nothing. How bad is your son's knee? We talking ligaments or what?"

When the waiter brought the appetizers, Rotelli burned his fingers on a zucchini stick. He plunged the hand into his water glass.

"Can you find out exactly what they're buying?" Fink asked, reaching over and sopping up some of the overflow with his napkin. "Paraguay, I mean."

"I don't know. Goddamn oil. Watch the mushrooms too. All I saw was that they had yukes up the gazonga."

"Yukes? Watch your tie."

Rotelli opened a button on his shirt and stuffed in the tie. "Yukes. EUCs. End-user certificates."

Fink didn't understand.

Rotelli pulled his hand from the water and stared at his dripping fingers as if they had let him down. "Any time we ship to a foreign country," he explained, "we have to file a yuke with the feds, listing who will be using the shipment: the end user."

"So the guy taking delivery can't go out and sell it to someone else," Fink offered.

"Right. Otherwise Jordan, say, could buy shit from us and sell it to Arafat."

"Don't they?"

"None a my business," Rotelli shrugged. Then, "Probably." He dried his finger on his slacks. "Listen, Mel," he said, "you gotta see the big picture. Some of the shit we produce they can't get from anyone else. Plus, they need our foreign aid. See, they buy our stuff with our money. So, at least from what I hear, there's not as much fucking around as you might think. But it's like everybody's Sicilian; nobody talks. Omerta. How's the daughter? Where is she, anyway?"

"Michigan."

"U or State?"

"U."

"Smart cookie, huh? How you gonna handle her graduate school?"

"I don't know."

"Money," Rotelli said, shaking his head. "Fuckin' world."

Part three

Chapter Twenty-Six

General Robbins sat behind his cherrywood George Washington desk and listened stoically as Schaeffer explained that Fink was getting warm. Last week the pushy detective had started asking about end-user certificates. Now he was demanding to see them, specifically the ones from Paraguay and Peru. Schaeffer was stonewalling, but Fink was dogged; it was only a matter of time. By themselves, of course, the certificates wouldn't tell him much, but he was getting too close for comfort.

Yes, Fink was still seeing Marissa, but he was either too smart or, more likely, too cautious to tell her much of anything—assuming that she was telling them everything he was telling her. Schaeffer was personally reviewing the videotapes, but so far they contained nothing useful. Captain Reynolds was continuing to resist the most logical solution, claiming that removing Fink from the case could precipitate a departmental scandal. Rotelli was dangling the job offer and Fink was nibbling, but he hadn't bitten yet. If he did, that would simplify their problems considerably, at least on this end.

Grelling's former assistant, Rhonda Cohen—the most likely source of the leaks—had been transferred to a position which precluded access to sensitive data. Unless the general felt differently, Schaeffer saw nothing to be gained by dealing with her now. She was black and a discrimination suit at this time could—

Robbins flicked his hand impatiently. Schaeffer skipped ahead. The good news was that there had been no further violence, though all stepped-up security measures were being maintained. Schaeffer reiterated his belief that no one at Parker was responsible for the unfortunate incident that had apparently triggered the attacks. And, he hastened to add, despite the current political discomfort, the company was enjoying its best quarter ever. He wondered if the general had been following the progress of the stock.

"Anything else?" Robbins asked, looking at his watch. It was nearly time for his nap.

Schaeffer paused, cleared his throat. The real danger was the unpredictability of this Corporal Johnson situation. Senator Grantham had agreed to keep the fingerprints under wraps, but his cooperation was conditional; he'd made it clear that if the press got wind of either Johnson or, worse still, Ransom, all bets were off. The others on the committee would toe the line, but Grantham was a wild card.

Schaeffer paused, searching the general's face for worry, concern, misgivings of any sort. None were there. The general was calmly making a note on a pad.

Schaeffer continued in a hushed voice. If Johnson somehow showed up at the hearings and started talking about Ransom's activities . . . Or even worse, if Ransom himself surfaced . . . If that happened, not only the Subic Bay operation, but the entire network—

"I'm aware of the situation," the general assured him. "Preparations are under way to resolve it. Naturally, given the logistics, they require a little time. Now sit down, Harold, and stop wringing your hands."

Schaeffer felt twenty pounds lighter.

"And Harold," Robbins said, "don't worry so much about Lieutenant Fink. We should continue trying to recruit him, of course, but if it becomes necessary, we can go far higher than your recalcitrant Captain Reynolds."

He reached over and twisted a cigarette into his ivory holder, an affectation he'd borrowed from FDR: "The last President," Robbins liked to say, "who wasn't afraid to win a war."

Schaeffer sat back and crossed a leg, recognizing Robbins' wish to smoke and reflect in silence. The general was one of the few men who could make a pin-striped suit look like a military uniform. Everything about the man suggested discipline, iron resolve: certain victory. It was an article of Schaeffer's faith that if Robbins had been given the command rather than Westmoreland the Vietnam War would have been won.

"What would they have us do," the general suddenly asked, walking to the window and gazing down at the world, "cede the future to the Japanese and the Germans? To the Mongol hordes? Is that what they really want, Harold?"

"They don't know what they really want, General." Schaeffer expected another attack against "that pussy-whipped draft-dodger in the White House," but Robbins surprised him.

"Balance of trade," he continued, "that's what it's all about, isn't it, Harold?"

"Yes, General."

"And what do they expect us to sell to the rest of the world, Harold? What do we produce in this country these days, besides cigarettes and vulgar entertainment? This company and the few others like it are essential to our nation's continued leadership. Essential." He turned to Schaeffer. "Worldwide, Harold, how large was our industry last year?"

"Six hundred billion dollars, General."

The number seemed to have a calming effect on Robbins. He returned to his desk, slid his reading glasses into place and broke the red seal on a manila folder.

When Schaeffer left, the general pressed the intercom and asked his secretary to get Marissa Grelling on the phone.

"What a pleasant surprise," Marissa said.

"Our Asian friend," Robbins asked, "is he at home these days?"

"I'll check."

"Thank you. Oh, and if you do make contact, don't mention this inquiry."

"All right. Is there a problem?"

"No, no, not at all. An administrative detail. How quickly can you get an answer for me?"

She glanced at her watch and calculated the time difference. "With luck, later this afternoon."

"Fine. If I'm out, please leave a message on my voice mail."

"You're sure nothing is wrong?"

"Absolutely sure. Are you still working on that other matter for me?"

"Of course, but those things cannot be rushed."

"I quite understand."

Marissa replaced the pay phone, reset her beeper and returned to the table. Her skin was tingling. The old bastard was up to something. The question was, what?

"Problem?" Fink asked, holding her chair.

"I'm not sure."

Her espresso was cold. When she asked the waiter for a fresh pot, Fink caught his eye and signaled for the check. He had to be downtown for a court appearance. This fancy lunch had been Marissa's idea.

"You're upset about something," he observed.

"Business," she assured him, staring at the remains of her lime sorbet, now reduced to a sad little green ball submerged in its own melt. During Frank's second tour in Vietnam—the year his eyes went hollow—General Robbins had been his commander. Marissa never blamed Frank for what happened; she couldn't. What had come back from that second tour was a husk. For years she had no one to blame for the end of her marriage, the breakup of her little family. Then, thanks to Frank, she met General Robbins. It had taken her years to gain the old man's confidence, but now, it seemed, all that distasteful service might be starting to pay dividends. She would have to be very careful . . .

"Want to talk about it?" Fink offered. Ten more minutes and he had to be out of here.

Marissa didn't seem to hear him.

Jewelry tinkled as a quartet of old women at the next table argued over who should pay the check. A busboy slipped among them scraping crumbs from their tablecloth with a special silver tool. Places like this made Fink uncomfortable.

There was a collective murmur of delight as the room suddenly flooded with sunshine. Fink glanced up. The greenhouse roof was sparkling and the restaurant now seemed more like some country glade than a town house in midtown Manhattan.

Marissa didn't notice as the waiter poured her espresso and slid a gold-tooled leather folder near Fink's elbow. Fink motioned for him to wait, dropped his MasterCard into the folder and handed it back. It was about time he paid for a meal. They hadn't ordered wine, so how bad could it be? He glanced at his watch. The subway station was four blocks away. He still had to review the file.

"An associate who is rigidly set in his ways," Marissa mused, fingering her pearls, "suddenly breaks his pattern. Would you regard that as significant, Lieutenant?"

"Probably," Fink replied. "When one of our people—a snitch, say—does something out of character, we always pay attention."

"*Bueno*," Marissa declared, apparently coming to a decision. She looked down, saw the espresso, pushed it away. "We'd better get the check."

"I took care of it," Fink told her, feeling more satisfaction than the gesture warranted.

The waiter returned. "Excuse," he whispered to Fink, "would Monsieur please provide us with another card?"

"What?" Fink asked, confused. He thought everybody took MasterCard.

"A small problem with the authorization," the waiter confided. "I am sorry for the inconvenience. Any other card will do."

But Fink's only other card was Visa, and he'd long ago exceeded his limit on that one. He opened the folder, retrieved his MasterCard and looked at the check. He didn't have enough cash. He sensed other patrons beginning to stare.

"*Mira*," Marissa called to the waiter, holding out her gold American Express. "I told you this gentleman was my guest."

"Yes, Madame," the waiter murmured, taking her card with a bow. "My apologies, Monsieur," he said to Fink, backing away.

"Goddamn it," Fink muttered, stuffing the useless plastic back in his wallet.

Marissa laid her hand over his. "I asked you, remember?"

Her touch made him shrink. A spurt of rage tried to cover his humiliation but failed. He pulled his hand away, crumpled his napkin, stood. "I've got to go," he announced. "I'm due in court."

"I'm taking a cab," she said. "Let me give you a lift."

He slid his chair back into place. "I'll see you tonight," he told her. Then, forcing a smile, he added, "Thanks for lunch."

CHAPTER TWENTY-SEVEN

Jared beeped Zeiss from a pay phone on Connecticut Avenue, then stood there depressing the mechanism with his thumb, pretending to carry on a conversation while he waited for the return call. It didn't take long.

"Yeah," Zeiss said, "what's up, *amigo*?"

"They're sending me to Detroit," Jared said. "Today."

"I'm listening."

"My assignment is to collect Corporal Johnson's mother and fly her back here."

"All by yourself?"

"Far as I know."

"Who set it up?"

"Bobby Cardanzer from Senator Grantham's office. That's why I thought I'd better call."

"You did right. What else?"

"Well, the word I get is that Johnson's mother called the senator and told him her son is coming to the hearings."

"Jesus Christ. Any idea when?"

"Next Thursday."

"That's nine days from now. What's the rush to get her?"

"I don't know, but I hear Grantham has been talking with reporters. The buzz is that the Johnson story is about to break."

"How are you getting to Detroit?"

"They've got me on an army plane out of Andrews in a few hours."

"Real VIP treatment."

"Yeah, I guess." Jared was pleased that a military flight impressed Zeiss, but he was still disappointed over missing out on all those frequent flyer miles.

"What happens when you land?" Zeiss asked.

"A car and driver. We get the lady and her luggage, hightail it back to the airport and fly right back here."

"Which airport?"

"How many does Detroit have?"

"What kind of plane?"

"They didn't say."

"And what happens when you get back here?"

"Other people take over. I'm only like a courier."

"What time do you leave Andrews?"

"The army guy said sixteen hundred hours. Made it sound like a secret mission. What do you think it's all about?"

"I don't know, *amigo*, but it looks like you're moving up in the world. Listen, if that's it, I've got to run. I'm off on a trip myself."

"No kidding? Where?"

"A few time zones further than Detroit. I'll be gone four or five days."

"What if something comes up?"

"If it's today, you'll probably get me. After that, you'll have to talk to whoever calls back. Don't ask any questions, just pass along whatever you've got."

"Okay," Jared grumbled. "But seriously, you think this is a good thing for me, this assignment?"

"I think it's dynamite," Zeiss told him. "*Bon voyage, amigo*. Don't forget to fasten your seat belt."

"This better be important," General Robbins fumed, watching the girl slip off the bed and scurry into a shadowy corner.

"They're sending my kid to Detroit to bring Johnson's mother back to D.C."

"When?"

She squatted down and began pulling at the gag.

"Sixteen hundred today. From Andrews."

"Hang on a minute." The general put the phone down, strode over and pulled her roughly to her feet. Disdainful of her blubbering, he dragged her over and threw her face down on the bed, wrenched her arms behind her and tied her wrists together. Then, for good measure, he hauled off and gave her bare bottom a fierce slap. She gave a muffled shriek and twisted away from him.

"Proceed," he said into the phone, shaking the sting from his hand.

Zeiss repeated the operative portions of his phone call with Hansen. Robbins listened carefully, making notes. When he was sure he had it all, he thanked Zeiss for the call and wished him good hunting.

The general stood there fitting this troubling new development into information he'd already received from other sources. He didn't like the way it added up. A connection between Johnson's mother and Ransom was virtually certain, but its nature was unclear. Zeiss had asked the key question: Why the hurry to get her to Washington? There had to be more to that than senatorial courtesy.

He looked across the room. The little vixen had rolled over on her side and pulled her knees up to her chest, but she wasn't trying to go anywhere, only ease the pain. She was crying. He was sorry he'd slapped her so hard, but he'd been angered by that mole on her back. Imperfection always infuriated him. At least she was quiet. What he had to do now was going to take some time. She would simply have to wait. Maybe she'd cry herself to sleep. With Zeiss and his team shipping out tonight he would have to find someone else to handle it. When it rains, it pours. Who used to say that? Creighton Abrams. Hell of a soldier, old Cray. Best tank man since Patton. Except that even Cray, when it had come right down to it, had turned out to be a little soft in the center. Better than that poster-boy Westmoreland, but still too soft. Even after twenty years, Robbins bristled at the thought of America having quit a war.

He gathered up his reading glasses, his pen, a notepad. It was still exciting as hell, this planning of missions. He had to admit there was a nice symmetry about these, almost like the Mormons pulling two teeth at once. He glanced over. She looked sweet curled up like that, her back fluttering with each breath.

He walked over and sat on the edge of the bed. She turned her head and looked up at him. The pink ribbon holding her gag was wet and had lost its silken beauty. When he reached out and began stroking her hair, she surprised him by wriggling closer. Any port in a storm, he thought, enjoying the sound of her soft, puppy-like whimpering. He raised his hand and let her hair sift through his fingers.

He became aroused, but in an unfamiliar, meditative way. Indulging an unexpected impulse, he rolled her onto her belly and, studiously avoiding the unsightly mole, untied her wrists and then, when she remained calm, undid the ribbon holding the gag. He removed the panties from her mouth and set them like a damp chrysanthemum on the night table. She gazed up at him with undiluted gratitude, then tucked her arms and legs into the fetal position and nestled closer.

"Do you speak English?" he asked, smiling down at her.

She stared back quizzically, uncomprehending.

"Do you understand what I am saying?" he asked her, enunciating clearly.

"Sank you," she offered, pressing her palms together and nodding vigorously. "Sank you."

"What else can you say?"

"Sank you," she repeated hopefully. "Sank you."

He rolled her onto her back, gently pried her hands apart and placed them at her sides, leaned over and straightened her legs.

"Here's my problem," he said with a sigh, gazing off into space.

While his hand roamed lightly over her skin he laid out the facts of the situation, explaining his interpretation, weighing the alternatives, considering the personnel available, and finally, once he'd settled on a course of action, assessing the possible consequences. Through it all, she remained wonderfully still, not squirming even as his fingers absently caressed the flesh along the insides of her thighs. She was not the prettiest little girl, though she had a somber, round-faced beauty to her, but it had been a long time since one had given him this much pleasure. Perhaps he had slapped her a bit too hard. If she behaved from here on out he'd find some way to make it up to her. He used to have a box of candy around here somewhere.

He lifted his index finger to his lips. "Shhhh," he whispered, rising from the bed, pausing a moment to make sure she stayed still.

She lay there on her back with her arms at her sides, her legs spread slightly, her belly rising and falling, her eyes calmly following him as he went to the phone.

"I'll be back to you in a minute," he promised her in the same soothing tone.

CHAPTER TWENTY-EIGHT

A full moon hung above the dining room skylight. The overhead fan was stirring the thick air like soup. Mee Yang was inside watching TV. They'd had duck for dinner, with a fruit sauce. Ransom was smoking a cigar.

"You want some more brandy?"

"Sure." Johnson held out his glass. He was sleepy, but Ransom was still talking.

"The Swiss, by the way, Doc, maintain one of the finest armies in the world. Did you know that?"

"I didn't know any of that stuff," Johnson said, feeling ignorant again. "I'm not even sure where Switzerland is."

"Easiest place in the world to find," Ransom smiled, slurring his words a bit. "Just follow the money."

"What money?"

"Any money, long as it's large denominations. Sooner or later it all ends up in Switzerland." He nudged the ash from his cigar. "That's not really true, Doc, but it's a reasonable approximation. Remember you asked me about drugs once?

Where do you think the biggest drug companies are headquartered? One guess now, Doc."

"Switzerland?"

"Bingo. Ciba-Geigy, Sandoz, Pfizer, Hoffmann-La Roche. The list goes on and on. The Swiss are amazing. It ain't just cuckoo clocks, Doc. People talk about the Jews, but the Swiss—"

A loud whoop from inside startled them both. When Johnson arrived, Mee Yang was pointing frantically at the screen.

"Dachshund on TV," she cried.

Johnson looked, expecting to see a long dog, but saw only a woman news announcer. He was befuddled.

"Dach-shund," Mee Yang insisted.

Ransom came in and she blurted something to him in Khmer. He tensed.

"What is it?" Johnson asked.

"She says she saw your son on TV."

"That's nuts." He went over and put a hand on her shoulder. She squirmed away and hid her face. He looked at the screen. A man was standing before a national weather map. There was a large splotch of green crawling over most of America's midsection.

"I don't have a son," Johnson said to her. He tried it in Khmer. She wouldn't look at him. "Colonel?" he asked.

"She didn't see your son," Ransom explained, "she saw you. They must have showed an old photo of you on TV."

"Me? On TV? Why?"

"Somebody must have identified your prints."

"I don't understand."

Ransom explained that he'd Fed-Exed the newspaper with Johnson's prints to Senator Grantham in Washington.

"You're the one who wanted to go home," Ransom reminded him.

"What do we do now?" Johnson asked.

There were two loud beeps from the office. Something was coming in. Ransom trotted inside. Johnson went over and knelt down beside Mee Yang.

She looked at him through red eyes. "You have wife in States," she accused him.

"No," he insisted.

"Damn yes. I see Doc son on TV."

"No. That was me."

"You bullshit. Boy young like me."

Johnson heard his name and turned. The screen was filled with an old black and white photo of him. He remembered the day that picture was taken, the same day he got his corporal's stripes. Which explained the funny look on his face: not a grin exactly, more like a kid trying to look like a man. He stared into the eyes on the screen and felt himself floating backward in time, reliving the excitement of the promotion, the congratulations of the guys, the weight of the extra stripe on his sleeve, the prospect of more pay.

"That you?" Mee Yang said, tugging at him. "You?"

He nodded, though in truth it didn't seem possible. The kid in the photo was so incredibly young. This picture, he realized, was coming from halfway around the world and half a lifetime away. Johnson tried to snap himself out of the past and concentrate on what the announcer was saying. But the photo suddenly vanished, startling him, and they switched to a live shot of two men standing outside a big, government-looking building. They looked cold.

"Off," Ransom barked at Mee Yang.

The TV picture swirled down into a tiny white dot. There was a burst of sparks from the zapper. Ransom seemed agitated.

"I should have asked you this before," he said to Johnson, "but now it's important. I know you're a medic, but are you a CO?"

"You mean a conscientious objector?"

"Yeah."

"No, I don't—"

"So you'd have no problem using a weapon?"

"No," Johnson assured him, "but—"

"Good," Ransom said, nodding his head and rubbing his hands together. "That's good, Doc. Real good."

"What's up?" Johnson asked.

"It looks like I screwed up," Ransom said. "Big-time."

"Can we fix it?"

"Yeah," Ransom said with an unfamiliar smile. "Sure we can fix it."

He walked over and crouched next to Mee Yang. As usual, they talked too fast for Johnson to understand. They seemed to be arguing.

When Ransom straightened up he turned to Johnson. "I told her it's up to you," he said.

"What is?"

"I stay," she declared, coming over and hooking Johnson's arm possessively.

Ransom ignored her. "That telex I just got," he said. "We're going to be having visitors."

"When?"

"My guess, a few days. You and I have to talk, Doc." He motioned for Mee Yang to go upstairs.

She stamped her foot defiantly, clutching Johnson's arm like a spoiled child. Johnson kissed her forehead. She smelled like wet flowers. "Go ahead," he said gently. "Please."

She stared at him searchingly for a moment, then released his arm and reluctantly climbed the stairs.

Ransom was at the desk in his office, pulling out papers, spreading charts, making notes—moving like a dynamo.

"They must have found my prints too," he said, as if that explained everything.

"But they didn't mention you, Colonel. I—"

"We'll have plenty of time to talk once the defenses are set," Ransom told him. "Go upstairs and decide what you want to do with Miss Saigon, then come on down and give me a hand."

"Doing what?" He had never been in here before. It felt strange.

Ransom was rifling through a drawer. "We've got to cover everything: the roofs, the fences, the towers, all the open areas. They could do a high altitude flyby anytime."

"Who?"

Ransom appeared to be talking to himself. "The key's going to be the perimeter." He glanced up. "Come on, Doc, get it in gear."

"What should I do?" Johnson asked, confused by the pace of events, the vision of his former self still glowing somewhere in his head.

"Talk to her. Let her stay or tell her to go," Ransom said, savagely pulling open another drawer and finally locating what he was looking for: a set of diagrams. "Oh, Doc," he said, placing both hands on the desk and leaning on them, putting his body on hold, "one more thing." He stared at the ceiling. "She says she's pregnant."

The jungle was alive with sound and motion, the night air frantic with stinging insects and sharp, overlapping smells—fresh-cut vegetation, gasoline, paint, metal, old plastic. Johnson and Mee Yang worked with a team of ten men inside the compound while Ransom had everyone else outside. The object of the exercise, as Ransom explained it, was to make the compound invisible from the air and impregnable from the ground. At this stage, speed was more important than precision. Working in near darkness, green paint was slopped over the roofs, camouflage tarps were hung between buildings and spread out along the tops of the fences, branches and leaves were strewn everywhere.

Johnson was enjoying the strenuous work. It had been so long since he'd sensed his body as a smoothly functioning machine. He liked the feel of sweat soaking the band of his Tigers cap and dripping down his sides. He was proud to be able to wield a machete and unravel a tarp and splatter paint as well as the soldiers and, though he slapped furiously at them, he was pleased that the insects found him so desirable. At one point, wrestling with an unwieldy tarp, his eyes stinging with sweat and dust, he glanced up and saw Mee Yang darting across a roof, moving like some graceful, sure-footed jungle cat. The idea of her soft belly carrying the first stirrings of his child filled him with awe. Everything was good and real and important again. He worked along with the steady rhythm of his blood, every few minutes smiling involuntarily as he recalled the look on her face when he told her yes, he would take her to the States with him; the colonel had promised. "In States we have babies," she had said triumphantly, "we have air-condition house, we have TV with remote, we have fuck, fuck, fuck."

Johnson swung his machete with gusto. Everywhere around him there was noise and purposeful activity. Mee Yang was somewhere on the roof, in her jeans and T-shirt and Angels cap, spreading branches and leaves. Ransom was out preparing the perimeter. Johnson knew they were in danger, but he had never been happier in his life. He looked up at the clustered stars and thought, irrationally, Let the bastards come.

CHAPTER TWENTY-NINE

They were the first ones on board. Jared had been amazed to learn that Mrs. Johnson had never been on an airplane before. Sensing her anxiety, he helped her off with her coat, chose a window seat for her, helped her fasten her seat belt, answered her questions. There was a cold draft coming from outside. Thinking she might like something warm around her shoulders, he pulled a blanket from an overhead compartment and arranged it for her.

The plane was a converted 707, with seats up front for eight passengers and everything from the wings back cordoned off with canvas webbing and rigged for cargo.

The crew appeared, their hat brims beaded with rain. After introducing himself, the pilot said their flight time to Andrews would be about two hours. Some last-minute cargo was coming on board, but he didn't expect that to delay them unduly. If all went well, they should be airborne in about twenty minutes. Due to a scheduling snafu, it now appeared they might be the only passengers.

The co-pilot showed Jared the small galley, pointing out the ice, soft drinks and various snack foods. He reminded Jared that there were no cabin attendants. Playing the good host, Jared went back and asked Mrs. Johnson if she'd like something to eat.

"I'd take a Dr. Pepper," she said, her eyes bright as a schoolgirl's, "if it's not too much bother."

"Would a Coke be okay?" he asked her, suspecting a very limited selection.

"Sure thing."

Pleased to have the run of the plane, Jared went forward imagining that this was his private jet. A man with his own jet didn't have to worry about frequent flyer miles. There was no Dr. Pepper but, enjoying the cozy claustrophobia, he prepared a tray with plastic glasses, napkins, assorted snack packets and two cans of Coke. While returning to his seat, he noticed a lone workman kneeling in the shadows of the tail section. The man seemed to be securing a small crate which, judging by the care he was taking, contained something valuable. It pleased Jared to think of himself accompanying top secret military equipment. It helped compensate for the disappointment of a bare-bones flight.

They sat and snacked. Mrs. Johnson began to talk about her son. Isaac had been a good-natured little boy who loved goldfish and stray animals, who nearly cut off his index finger with a can opener when he was nine, who laid out the hymnals every Sunday in church, whose favorite TV show was *Bonanza,* who had done well enough in school to go to college. She never did understand why he decided to join the army right out of high school. He'd been so young. She suspected he liked the idea of wearing that snazzy uniform for the girls. Getting away from Detroit probably had something to do with it too. They had never had the chance to travel and well, boys like to roam around some, she knew that.

And Isaac said the government would give him money for college when he got out. She hoped they kept their word. They were calling so many of the young boys in those days, she recalled. Every time you turned around the war seemed to be getting bigger and bigger, more boys dying.

She had worried, of course; all mothers do. But she had prayed for Isaac every single night since his birth, so God knew her boy well, and she had been sure He would watch over him. That was why, even when they came around and told her Isaac was missing over there, she knew he was all right. All these years she knew it. Felt it in her heart, her bones. And that was why, that night when Ev showed up and told her that Isaac was fine—

"Ev?" Jared asked.

"That fellow he's over there with," she explained, then caught herself. "Oh my, they told me not to talk. But you're the government, right? I can talk to you."

"Of course," he assured her, trying to hide his excitement. "I'm a special investigator. You can tell me anything."

"I wonder if he'll even recognize his old mother after so many years," she fretted.

"Of course he will," Jared assured her. "You were telling me about Ev."

"Oh yes. Well," she said, the bounce back in her voice, "you talk about the hand of God, look how He brought these two boys together to help each other. And one colored and one white, and both been prisoners too. It truly is a miracle, praise be Jesus."

Both been prisoners? "This Ev," Jared asked, trying to sound casual, "is he American?"

"Yes. Didn't I say that?"

Jared couldn't believe what he was hearing. Two POWs! Zeiss would go ballistic when he heard this. If only Jared could catch him before he left on his trip.

"Would you like another Coke?" he asked her.

"No, thank you, young man. And I shouldn't be eating all these nuts and raisin things."

He excused himself, hurried forward, stuck his head into the cockpit and asked if he had time to go make a quick phone call.

"How about the lady?" he was asked.

"She can wait here. I won't be long."

"We can't be responsible for her," the pilot objected.

"I'll be gone maybe five minutes," Jared pleaded.

The pilot glanced over to his counterpart, who shrugged.

"Great," Jared said. "Thanks."

When she saw him putting on his coat she became alarmed. "You're leaving me here all by myself?"

"I'll only be a few minutes."

Her eyes darted nervously about the empty cabin. He reminded himself that he was her escort.

"Let's go together," he suggested. "It's not far."

She liked that idea. He helped her up. It took a minute to get her coat on. Then, despite his assurances, she refused to leave her suitcase; it contained some of Isaac's favorite things. He carried it for her. They had to hurry.

"This Ev fellow," he asked as he led her down the metal stairs, "does he have a last name?"

She spoke above the wind. All she knew was Everett. His mother had called him Ev. She'd died of cancer. He spoke Chinese.

A sudden gust brought stinging rain. "Watch your hat," he cautioned her, anxious to get them inside.

He sat her on the far side of the waiting room and trotted over and made the call to Zeiss' beeper. While he was waiting for the call back, a large family led by an army officer came in shaking water from their coats. The bulky officer, who looked like he'd played tackle for West Point, marched straight over to Jared. There was gold braid on his cap.

"You in charge here?" he demanded.

"No, sir."

"Well, who is?"

"There's an office right outside. That's where we—"

"You on the flight to Andrews?"

"Yes, sir."

"How many in your party?"

"Just the lady over there and myself. Two of us."

The officer checked out Mrs. Johnson.

"You with the military?" he asked Jared suspiciously.

"No, sir."

"Who is? Her son?"

"Yes."

He dropped his voice. "What's his rank?"

"Corporal," Jared whispered back.

The officer spun about, told his wife to wait right there and then, to Hansen's relief, stormed out. Zeiss would be calling back any second. Mrs. Johnson was busy with the children.

Five minutes went by. Jared was becoming rattled. The six kids, all small and all active, were making a lot of noise. Where was Zeiss? The room was stuffy. The windows were fogged. A little boy was climbing on Mrs. Johnson's suitcase. She seemed delighted. The mother looked harried. A little girl's nose was running.

The officer returned, approached Jared, removed his cap. "Son," he said softly, "can I speak with you for a moment?"

"Yes, sir."

"I'm Colonel Burke. That there is my wife, Norma, and those are our kids. We were all confirmed for this here flight, but now they're saying they're two seats short."

"I'm sorry," Jared said, glancing toward the phone. Zeiss should have called back by now.

"See, the thing is," the colonel said, "Dwight, our oldest, is only ten. I can't be sending two of them off by themselves. You see my problem?"

"Yes, sir, but—"

"Good. I appreciate that, Mr. . . ."

"Hansen. Jared Hansen."

"Jared, there are two first-class seats available on an American flight into National leaving in forty minutes."

"American?" Jared had a frequent flyer account with American. He caught himself. "Seriously, Colonel, I'd really like to help, but I don't have the authority—"

"Look, son, I'm due at the Pentagon at oh six hundred tomorrow. The fellow inside tells me you're with the Congress. Here's my card. If you can't get reimbursed from those boys on the Hill I'll get the army to cover it, for you and the lady. You have my word."

"I really don't think—"

The phone rang.

"That's for me," Jared said, turning away.

The colonel caught his arm. "I'll go confirm that flight for you," he said as the phone rang again.

"Honestly, I'd really like to—"

The colonel had a powerful grip. The phone rang a third time.

"Here's my card," the colonel said, and slipped a card and a fifty dollar bill into Hansen's shirt pocket.

Another ring. Jared said okay, pulled free, dashed over and grabbed the receiver. Dial tone. He clicked it a few times. Nothing. He whirled around, but the colonel was already gone. He fumbled for his Sprint card and punched in the numbers again. In his haste, it took him four tries to get all the digits right.

Minutes passed. The phone wouldn't ring.

The colonel returned and started herding his family toward the exit. "I've arranged a ride for you folks over to American," he called to Jared.

Jared supposed it would be okay. The colonel had bullied him, but "military emergency" sounded good, and there were benefits; they would be flying first class, he'd get the miles, he had an extra fifty in his pocket. Still, something was nagging at him. She had her suitcase . . .

"Oh, Colonel," he remembered, running over. "There'll be a car waiting for me at Andrews, right at the gate. Would you please send it to meet the American flight at National?"

"Sure thing. And listen, I owe you one." He pumped Jared's hand and turned to his family. "Come on, people, we've got a plane to catch."

Jared paced. Mrs. Johnson hummed. The phone was silent. More minutes passed. A lieutenant came in and announced that their car had arrived.

"It'll have to wait," Jared told him. "I'm expecting a call."

"I'm sorry, but if you want to catch that American flight you'll have to go now. When the call comes in, I'll tell them you had to leave."

Jared was drowsy when they landed at National: too much food and five glasses of champagne. The free drinks had helped him float through Mrs. Johnson's stories. Nice as she was, he was looking forward to passing her along and letting someone else hear about Muhammad Ali's limousine and Reverend Ainsworth's sermons and little Isaac's goldfish experiments.

But, as Jared had feared, there was no one there to meet them at the gate. They went to the baggage claim, but none of the hand-held cardboard signs there had his name either. He collected her suitcase from the carousel, found a comfortable place for her to sit, and went to find a pay phone. It was only eleven o'clock, but it felt much later. He shouldn't have had that last glass of champagne. The question was, who should he call? He didn't want to try calling Zeiss from a crowded airline terminal. He could call Andrews, but who would he ask for? No, he decided, his best bet was Senator Grantham's office. No one figured to be there, but maybe the answering machine would have an emergency number. At least they would see that he'd checked in. He could go on record about the military emergency.

When someone answered on the first ring he was momentarily tongue-tied.

"Speak up," the woman said, surprisingly brusque.

"Mr. Cardanzer, please."

"Hold."

He peered through the swirling cross-currents of people, located Mrs. Johnson and tried to give her the thumbs-up sign, but she was looking at everything but him. His head ached.

A new woman came on the phone. Mr. Cardanzer was in conference and could not be disturbed. If she could have his name and number . . .

"The thing is," he explained, cupping a hand to his ear, "I'm at a pay phone and—"

"Look, I don't mean to be rude, but we're trying to deal with a situation here. Now if you will—"

"I'm a special investigator," he declared, afraid she was about to cut him off. "For the Grantham Committee."

"If you're on staff, you had better get your ass over here," she said, and hung up.

They had some difficulty getting into the building, especially with the unwieldy suitcase. The security guard summoned his supervisor, who studied Hansen's ID and then made him fill out a special form for Mrs. Johnson. The champagne had done bad things to his head.

Their footsteps echoed through the long empty corridors. When Mrs. Johnson stopped to chat with a cleaning woman, Jared put down the suitcase and wiped his brow with a handkerchief. His arm was sore. His ears were ringing. The old lady was fresh as a daisy, but he felt dusty and rumpled. This was no way to show up at a senator's office. He reminded himself that he had to fill out reimbursement forms for the plane tickets and— Oh, Jesus, he'd forgotten to get a receipt from the taxi! His head was throbbing. What the hell could she be talking to a cleaning woman about?

Senator Grantham's office was crowded and noisy. No one even glanced up when he and Mrs. Johnson squeezed in. Jared found a chair for her against a wall, put the suitcase on the floor next to her, and dragged himself over to the reception desk.

"Is Mr. Cardanzer out of his conference yet?" he asked.

The woman held up a hand to silence him. She pressed buttons on her blinking switchboard, looked up, said "What?"

"Mr. Cardanzer—"

"Meeting," she said. "You'll have to wait. Harry!" she cried, and passed a slip of paper to a reaching hand. She saw that Jared was still there. "What?"

"Reimbursement form."

"Now?" she asked, incredulous.

"I just got in," he explained. He dropped his voice and leaned closer. "What's going on?"

The woman held up an index finger while she fielded another call. People were hurrying in and out of doors on either side. Everyone looked grim.

"There's been a terrible accident," the receptionist said. "We've lost one of our committee staff."

"Who was it?" Jared asked, reflexively crossing himself.

"Hansen," the woman said. "First name Jared. He was—"

"That's me," he declared.

"What's you?" the receptionist asked.

"I'm Hansen."

Several people near him stopped short. The room got quiet.

"Weren't you on a plane?" the receptionist asked, squinting at him.

"Yes."

"From Detroit?"

People were staring at him as if he were a Martian.

"Yes, but—"

"That plane crashed," a man said. "We heard there were no survivors."

"Not my plane," Jared assured him, thinking they were all crazy.

Then it hit him. Oh, Jesus. All those kids. A numbness spread through him. He leaned against the console. Thoughts were crashing inside his head like surf. How could—

Bobby Cardanzer burst from the senator's office, looked around wildly, rushed over and grasped Jared's arm.

"Johnson's mother," he said urgently.

Jared turned and pointed. She was sitting right where he'd left her: her face down, her lips moving, reading her Bible.

CHAPTER THIRTY

Shane sat in front of her TV working the remote with one hand and holding her third glass of Chardonnay in the other. She was alone. Her parents were a continent away in San Mateo. The paper should be hitting the newsstands right about now. As she continued switching channels, a sense of elation rippled through her: She was going to beat TV to the story; there was a God.

CBS was the first network to break it, but instead of a tight-lipped bulletin from Dan Rather, as Shane had hoped, they settled for a repeating crawl across the bottom of the screen: "GI MISSING SINCE 1968 REPORTED ALIVE. DETAILS AT 11." As she flipped around, NBC, ABC and Fox all flashed similar messages. She tingled with excitement as she sensed her story—*her* story—buzzing through the air, rushing through wires, bouncing off satellites, reaching into millions of homes across America. Millions. She wondered what time it was in England.

CNN switched live to their chief Washington correspondent. Using the White House as a backdrop and braving a drizzle, he smoothly summarized her front-page story in tomorrow's *Washington Post,* crediting the paper but not the reporter: not *her*.

"Shane Reilly," she said to the screen, hoping to prompt him. She felt like jumping in her car, driving over to the White House and kicking him in the ass. She swigged some more wine instead.

He finally did mention her name, but only because he was stalling until the research people in Atlanta could scare up some video from the files. They ended up going with the blurry army photo which accompanied her page-one story and some file tape from the 1968 Tet Offensive which, though not related to Corporal Johnson's disappearance, at least had occurred the same year. To Shane, the green-tinted night shots with streams of tracer bullets arcing through searchlight beams were eerily reminiscent of CNN's exclusive feed from Baghdad on the first night of the Gulf War. She took it as a good omen; Peter Arnett had won all sorts of awards for that.

On the story's third go-round CNN added file tape of returning POWs, the shots Shane's editor Mike Mitchelson had predicted, the ones he referred to as "KHCs," for Kiss, Hug and Cry.

Shane kept switching channels, grinning as her story popped up as the lead on every eleven o'clock news show, the same fuzzy black and white photo of Isaac Johnson flashing on channel after channel like a stuck frame on an old eight-millimeter home movie. But after seeing it a few times she suffered an awful epiphany; this thing on the news wasn't a story, it was only a headline. And they didn't give Pulitzers for headlines.

So while her answering machine was busy recording congratulatory messages, she booted up her laptop and made a list of the ideas streaming into her head. She saved them under the file name "Pulitzer," drank off one more glass of wine, went inside, took two Nembutal, set the alarm for six, slipped into her nightie and turned on the small TV. Koppel began his show with the announcement of Johnson's "astounding reappearance," and held out the carrot that ABC would have "late-breaking details" on the morning news. Shane was disappointed to learn that tonight's show would be about flooding in the Midwest: rowboats in streets, cats in trees, mud: bore-ing.

She changed channels, not wanting the day to end, and spent a frustrating few minutes alternating between Leno and Letterman before it dawned on her that their shows had been taped hours before her story broke. She switched off the set.

While brushing her teeth it occurred to her that she should have asked Grantham something else, something more. She rinsed her mouth and spat. But what? She realized that the sly old goat had charmed her with his smile. Why did she keep making the same damn mistake? Nearly thirty years old and still stuck on surfaces. The same way she had lost her virginity to that airhead model with the Grecian features and the blow-dried hair. Lost it? Hell, she'd nearly raped the poor guy. Very pretty and very bi and it had served her right when he'd left the next day with his photographer-cum-boyfriend for a shoot in Acapulco without so much as a phone call. Though the bastard might have found the time to call once since then. Maybe he would now, now that she was Brenda Starr. Assuming he was still alive. One of these days she'd get up the nerve to go get tested for HIV instead of simply scanning the daily obits for his name. Not tomorrow, though. She had much too much to do tomorrow.

Substance, that's what was missing from her work and from her life. She stared at herself in the mirror and had the almost mystical feeling that if she could get some substance into one it would seep into the other.

She flipped off the lights and got into bed. Replaying the interview in her mind, it now seemed that Senator Grantham had been pleased to discover that she knew as little as she did. Maybe that's why he'd been so quick to confirm it, to go on and on about the fingerprints. Dumb, dumb, dumb. She'd discovered an iceberg, all right, but all she'd seen so far was the tip. She rearranged her pillow, the pills kicked in, she made some burbling sounds and slid beneath the surface. Her last thought was a pleasant one: Millions of Americans were taking her story to bed with them.

Her story.

Hers.

CHAPTER THIRTY-ONE

Fink located a working pay phone on Forty-second and Sixth and put in a call to Marcia, his squad clerk at the precinct. He pressed a palm to his ear to block out the street noise.

"How we doing on Subic Bay?" he asked her.

"I'm fine, thank you, Lieutenant. And how are you?"

"Just give it to me," he told her.

"Not much to give. You were right about one thing, though. What was your quaint expression? 'Shitload'? Well, it sure was. More than a hundred tons."

"A hundred tons of what?"

"Materi-El, Lieutenant. The actual breakdown is classified. All I could get is that Parker Global contracted to remove the entire contents of several storage depots at Subic Bay."

"What about the contract?" Fink asked.

"Competitive bid. Parker didn't come in the lowest, but the Colonel Pisarcik I spoke with said that PG was chosen because of their 'extensive experience transporting hazardous cargo,' was how he phrased it. He sounds like an overripe banana."

"And?"

"He's requesting clearance to fax us the contract."

"Any details on how the stuff was shipped?"

"According to Pisarcik, that would have to come from Parker Global. All he knows is, the job was done and PG was paid."

"You did good, Marcia," Fink told her.

"Thanks, Mel."

Fink waited for a bus to pass, then asked the obligatory question: "How's Vinnie doing?"

"Same old same old," she said, the perkiness forced.

Marcia's husband, Vinnie, was an ex-partner of Fink's who became an alcoholic in his thirties, crashed a squad car and was cashiered out with a partial disability. Between the months-long bouts of drinking he attended AA meetings. Marcia was Fink's age, but looked ten years older.

"So what do you think," Fink teased, trying an old routine, "should we go to Vegas this weekend? Spend a few days in a heart-shaped tub?"

"I'll take a rain check," she told him. "What's next with Subic?"

"Call Schaeffer's office. Sound very official. Tell them homicide wants copies of everything relating to the disposition of the Subic Bay—what did you call it?"

"Materi-El. The Poconos have those too, you know."

"Which?"

"Heart-shaped tubs. Vinnie and I went there once, right after he got back from Vietnam. Jesus, Mel, you know how long ago that was?"

"Mel!"

A cab lurched to a stop, blocking traffic. Rotelli got out

and slammed the door. A van driver gave him the finger. Cars honked. It was midday in midtown, tempers were short.

"Hey hey hey," Rotelli said, hopping onto the curb and hoisting his pants back above his belly, "*Come va*?"

"*Va bene*," Fink replied. "*Qué pasa*?"

"Come on, take a walk." He indicated the park across the street.

The sky was dirty. There was a nasty chill in the air. Fink didn't believe in chance meetings.

As they entered the park a scruffy-looking black teen with Reeboks and dreadlocks fell in beside Fink whispering "Sense, sense, sense."

Fink kept walking, but the kid stayed with him, repeating his code word like a mantra.

"I think you're trying to sell me oregano," Fink told him.

"No, mon," the kid insisted, offended at having his integrity questioned. "Dis some righteous smoke. Good housekeepin' seal, mon."

Fink reached into his pocket. "How do you know I'm not a cop?"

"You aine no cop," the kid assured him, sniffing the air. "I an I can smell a cop."

"You must have a cold," Fink told him, showing the gold shield.

The kid wheeled and took off, his long hair swirling in his backwash.

"I worked narcotics two years," Rotelli said, pointing to a vacant bench.

"Like it?" Fink asked.

"What's to like?" Rotelli replied, easing himself down and unbuttoning the vest of his suit. He sat back and sighed. "Can you believe this MIA thing?" he asked.

Fink shook his head.

"Twenty-four goddamn years," Rotelli said, speaking for

both of them. "The poor guy must be a vegetable. Our fucking government."

"Yeah."

"And our fucking us," Rotelli murmured.

Fink looked at him.

"Nothing," Rotelli shrugged. "Not a fucking thing."

An elderly couple shuffled by, fragile as dried leaves. Their clothes were too big. Fink and Rotelli paused to watch them pass.

Rotelli sat up straighter, changed his tone. "I been thinking about your situation," he said, flicking something from his pants. "I don't know how the hell you do it, Mel. There's no money in homicide, for chrissakes."

"Yeah," Fink said, pressing his palms against the wooden bench seat and elevating himself for perhaps three seconds before one arm started to shake. In the army he'd been able to hold it for a minute, with his legs out straight.

"Middle age sucks," Rotelli said.

"That's what you wanted to see me about?"

"Fifty-nine fucking years old," Rotelli sighed. "Can you tell me how that happened, Mel? My kids are older than I used to be."

A squirrel dashed to the base of a nearby tree and halted, its body tense, its bushy tail twitching. Fink wondered how long squirrels lived.

"A grandfather," Rotelli said disgustedly. "More gifts."

"Let's talk about Subic Bay," Fink suggested.

"Nah, I'd rather talk about who's going to replace me in a couple of years."

"Before we turned the base over to the Philippines," Fink said, "Parker Global got a contract to dispose of all the old munitions. Couple of warehousefuls. Must have been tons and tons of that shit, am I right?"

"Three years," Rotelli said. "At sixty-two I get my full bennies. Three years, Mel."

"Now what was PG supposed to do with all that stuff? Was that spelled out in the contract?"

"How the hell would I know?" Rotelli grumbled. "Three years is not a long time, Mel."

"I bet they had stuff there left over from the big deuce," Fink said. "Forty-, fifty-year-old powder and shells and—"

"I don't get you," Rotelli told him. "I'm talking your future and you're talking old shells." He noticed a vendor's cart nearby. "You want a pretzel? A hot dog? I'm buying."

"Pretzel, if they're warm."

"Stay and watch my stuff," Rotelli said, pointing to a plastic shopping bag.

Across the cement path, a pack of growly dogs was frolicking behind a flimsy slat fence, bounding and sniffing and play-fighting on the sparse grass. Fink turned and watched Rotelli talking to the vendor. Rotelli didn't know anything about the Subic Bay deal, and didn't care. In three years he would start collecting two pensions plus Social Security. And do what, Fink wondered, filling his lungs with chill, doggy air: Take a bus once a week to Atlantic City to play the slots? Sign up at Arthur Murray? Sit home and watch *Jackpot Bowling*? The golden years.

Fink squinted up at the sky. It was a dirty gray, the color of squirrels.

Rotelli returned, his hands full. Fink moved the plastic bag and helped him set everything down between them on the bench.

The security chief used an index finger to even out the relish on his hot dog. Fink's pretzel was warm but stale. He broke off a small piece and tossed it to a pigeon waddling nearby. A moment later there were ten pigeons.

Rotelli licked his fingers, then wiped his hands with a

napkin. "Here, I brought you something," he said, pulling a hardcover book from his plastic bag and passing it over.

"*Principles of Modern Corporate Security,*" Fink read, hefting the volume in his hand. "Thanks."

He started to open it.

"Careful," Rotelli cautioned.

Fink opened the book slowly, saw the hollow filled with cash, closed it. "How much?" he asked.

Rotelli slurped Yoo-Hoo through his straw, staring off at the barren trees. "Ten grand."

Fink laid the book on the bench. The pigeons inched closer, bobbing and cooing. Their purple-gray feathers had an oil-like sheen. One of them was missing two toes.

"My boss wants you on board," Rotelli explained. "This is like a pre-signing bonus. No strings."

"That right?"

"Look, these people are damn good to me, Mel. They'll be good to you too."

"Where'd you get the money?" Fink asked, tossing more pretzel crumbs.

"Requisitioned it from petty cash. Why?"

"I'm not saying you," Fink explained, choosing his words with care. "This was that cue ball Schaeffer's idea, right?"

"Right. So?"

"You're good people, Tony. You've been straight with me from day one."

Rotelli shifted on the bench. "Right. So?"

"I don't want the book," Fink told him. "And be careful what you say, I think we're on *America's Home Videos.*"

"Bullshit," Rotelli fumed, spinning to face him. "You saying I would—"

"No," Fink assured him, "I know you wouldn't." He stood and brushed pretzel salt from his jacket.

Rotelli's face was turned away. He was breathing heavily.

"Ten years ago," Fink said, "you would have been on to a cocksucker like Schaeffer in a second and a half."

That hadn't come out right. An awkward moment later, Fink was relieved when Rotelli's beeper went off and he had to go.

Danbury, Rotelli's second in command, was waiting for him by the big marble console in the lobby. There were three uniforms behind the counter monitoring the lunchtime traffic.

"What's up?" Rotelli asked Danbury.

"Maybe nothing. But remember that memo you sent last week, the one about deliveries?"

"Right. So?"

"Well, since then I've been having the guys log them in and out."

"Right. So?"

"So here," Danbury said, pulling over a logbook and pointing.

Rotelli tilted his glasses. "This the one?" he asked. "Chinese, twelve-fourteen?"

"That's the one."

Rotelli glanced at his watch. Much too long. "And we're sure he didn't come out?"

"Jeffries here called me," Danbury said. "I called you."

"Jeffries," Rotelli barked, and a stocky young black man with an eye patch responded: "Sir."

"C'mere. You logged in this Chinese thing?"

"Yes, sir."

"And you been here ever since?"

"Yes, sir."

"No breaks at all? Think. Phone call? John? Smoke?"

"I been here the whole time," Jeffries assured him.

"You remember what this guy looked like?" Rotelli asked.

"Wiry little mother," Jeffries said. "For sure Asian, but not exactly Chinese. Carrying one of them brown shopping bags. The guy looked kosher to me."

"How old?"

"Twenty?" Jeffries guessed.

"What else?"

"Funny hair," Jeffries recalled. "Regular Chinese hair, but cut funny, like somebody'd stuck a pot on his head and . . ." He made a scissors motion with two fingers.

Could be a wig, Rotelli thought. Shit. He asked what the kid was wearing.

"Nothin' special," Jeffries replied, fidgeting.

Rotelli looked at him.

"Otherwise I woulda noticed," Jeffries explained.

"Says here he was delivering to forty-six," Rotelli read from the log. "Did you ask for a name?"

"Name?"

"Who the delivery was for."

"No, sir. With food it's just the floor. I got that, see? Forty-six."

"Okay," Rotelli told him, "you did good. It's probably nothing. My guess, the kid sneaked into a bathroom to take a dump. Anyway, Jeffries, you stay right here. The second that kid shows, you beep Danbury."

Rotelli led Danbury away from the counter and asked: "Did you alert the security desk on fifty-one?"

"I did that before I beeped you," Danbury assured him. "The kid never showed on forty-six, by the way; I checked with the receptionist. Oh, and here's your walkie-talkie."

"Okay, so fifty-one is covered," Rotelli thought out loud, hooking the bulky device to his belt. "That leaves four other executive floors." He patted his Glock. "I'll take fifty. You take forty-nine. Get a man up to forty-eight and another one to forty-seven. Make sure they're good men."

"Right." Danbury shuffled his feet. "Listen, boss, are you sure you wouldn't rather stay down here and coordinate—"

"Let's be thorough," Rotelli said, pressing for an elevator. "Make sure our guys have passkeys. Every office, bathroom, linen closet, supply room—the whole nine yards." He thought about calling Fink, then caught himself. Calling Fink for what? Who needed Fink and his—

An elevator pinged. Rotelli ambled over. A woman with a maroon briefcase came up and stood alongside him.

"Take the next one," he told her. "This one's got a problem."

"What sort of problem?" she wanted to know.

"Just do it," he growled.

She glared at him, held it for a moment and then walked to the next elevator.

Rotelli covered his mouth and burped hot dog gas. "Look," he said to Danbury, "tell the boys if they see anything, stay there and call it in. That goes for you too." He glanced over and raised his voice. "I don't want some bitch shot in the ass."

He inserted his override key so the elevator would take him straight up to fifty. Halfway there, he realized he was still holding the plastic bag with Fink's book. He thought about dropping it off somewhere but decided against it. He wasn't that goddamn old yet; one hand was still enough for some gook delivery boy.

The floor numbers flashed by overhead, climbing rapidly through the thirties and forties. Rotelli burped again. He used his free hand to hitch up his pants. Goddamn kid was probably running up and down corridors handing out menus. Then again, if he never showed on forty-six, and was maybe wearing a wig . . .

The elevator slowed. Rotelli glanced up. Fifty. He rubbed his nose and stepped off, ignoring the burning in his gut. The reception kiosk was empty; fine time for the broad to take a whiz, Rotelli thought, heading off down the corridor. The wife was always warning him about hot dogs. One of these days he'd listen.

"Routine check," he announced as he poked his head into a succession of elegant offices. The offices were not much larger than his, but Rotelli's had no view and no fancy modern art, unless you counted that page from *Playboy* taped inside his desk drawer, the one with the bare-titted New York cop fondling her nightstick: Carol something.

Rotelli froze. He'd heard something when he'd turned the knob—something subtle, fleeting, like the fluttering of a moth, the rustling of a paper, the scraping of a shoe. With a push, the door of the conference room swung open. Rotelli peered into the cool darkness. The sound, whatever it had been, did not return.

He reached in and pushed a bank of switches. Indirect fluorescents blinked on all around him. The room appeared empty.

Inside now, Glock in hand, door closed securely behind him, he circled the conference room, repeatedly bending to check beneath the polished racetrack table and its many matching leather chairs. His stomach was tightening up. It hurt to bend. He was too old for this shit.

He leaned against the wall and waited for the pain to pass. His face was wet and the cool air hitting it was making him shiver. He reminded himself that he still had to check the closets and the projection booth, told himself that if he had half a fucking brain he'd call Danbury, let somebody else do it. Yeah. Right. Because he was so old. Son of a bitch.

Straightening up slowly, he did something with his throat that made him burp again, a good one that eased the pressure inside his stomach. He raised the arm with the plastic bag and wiped his forehead. Christ, Rotelli, he thought, staring at the dark stain on his sleeve. Extricating his hand from the twisted plastic, he laid the bag on the gleaming table, warning himself not to forget it.

There were four closets. Moving stealthily, he approached the first of them. By the book, he reminded himself, figuring angles.

"Hello. You have reached the offices of Parker Global Corporation," a peppy male voice declared.

"Shit," Fink said.

"Your call is important to us," the voice continued. "If you are calling from a Touch-Tone phone and know the extension you wish to reach, please enter it now. If you are calling from a rotary phone—"

Fink rummaged through the cards on his desk until he located Rotelli's, then punched in the extension.

"Hello," a female voice said, "you have reached the office of the Director of Corporate Security. Your call is important to us. No one is free to speak with you at this time, but if you would care to—"

Fink hung up. He didn't want to leave any damn message. The old fart was probably standing in the lobby peeking up miniskirts. Or telling Schaeffer what he could do with his ten grand. Fink noted the time. He'd try again in a little while. Barton's hunch about Chinese food could wait.

The closets were all clean. Rotelli felt better. One of the other men had checked in following his floor sweep. Nothing. Danbury and the other guy would be done with theirs soon. So will you, Rotelli told himself. His pulse was banging away inside his temple, but he told himself it was good to get the heart rate up once in a while: kept you young.

He glanced around. The only thing left was that little projection booth. Ninety-nine percent it was clean. Rotelli hadn't heard another sound since he'd entered the room; he was beginning to wonder if he'd actually heard the first one. The gook kid had probably walked back out right past Jeffries' patched eye. Go hire the fucking handicapped.

The door on the projection booth opened easily, but it was dark inside and Rotelli didn't have a flashlight. He felt around for a light switch. Nothing. There had to be a pull cord somewhere inside. He didn't like the idea of ducking down and—

Something slammed him in the chest, throwing him backward, making him gasp, sending him crashing into a chair and then the floor. Through blurred vision, he saw a fast-moving shape and tried to bring up the gun, but something smashed into his kidney with an exploding jet of pain. He rolled away from it—he would kill the little fucker!—when suddenly his head was yanked back and he got his hand up but something cold went around his neck and—goddammit!—his face smacked the carpet—something cutting into his neck, his wrist—dammit—pressing the gun barrel against his cheek—couldn't pull it free—shit—couldn't—maybe . . .

He twisted his trunk hard, swung back an elbow and caught something solid with it, heard a grunt. The pressure on his neck loosened and he sucked in air as he lurched away and pulled the gun free. But he couldn't get the bastard off his back, couldn't get the gun turned— Something had his wrist! He flung himself into the air and tried to land on it, but the pressure on his neck returned worse than before and this time all his elbow caught was air, air, air.

Christ—couldn't breathe—strong little—couldn't— Oh shit . . .

CHAPTER THIRTY-TWO

"I didn't think it was that cold out," the doorman remarked, noting the ski mask.

"Tiff'ny is in, please?"

"Oh, it's you. Hang on a second." He buzzed, waited. "Mr. Lee," he announced, and nodded for Bo to go on up.

She was standing by the open door in her pink robe. He rushed past her into the bathroom where, after hurriedly locking the door and stowing the plastic bag in the laundry hamper, he began anxiously peeling the ski mask from his overheated head, slowing only at the area around the eye where the dried blood had glued the wool to his skin. Feeling as if he had been freed from a suffocating cell, Bo gratefully sucked in deep unencumbered breaths, then sprinkled his face with deliciously cool water.

He examined himself in the mirror, testing the puffy, angry discoloration with his fingertips. It was ugly, but as he had suspected, nothing was broken. Closing his eyes, he sent a silent prayer to his maternal ancestors for the succession of miracles they had provided to save him today: the empty freight elevator, the deserted basement, the delivery bay door left ajar. He continued giving thanks until interrupted by a persistent knocking on the door and Tiffany asking if he was all right.

When he came out she gasped and covered her mouth, then rushed over and hugged him. Exhausted from hours spent huddled against the cold clammy wall of a subway tunnel, he abandoned himself to the luxurious warmth of her body.

"My poor baby," she crooned, gently stroking the back of his head and rocking him. "My poor, poor baby. Tell Mommy what happened."

His hands went beneath her robe and roamed her naked flanks. He became aroused.

"What happened to my baby?" she asked again, but with diminished urgency.

On the subway, he told her, he had been set upon by bandits, a gang of dark youths who had attempted to rob him. He had managed to escape, but not without injury.

"They picked on my Bo because he's small," she murmured, kissing his damp forehead. "Poor baby has a fever," she said, leaning back and taking his chin in her hand. "Now let Mommy look— Bo, that eye looks serious. We'd better get you to the emergency room."

"No," he said, burrowing against her. "No hospital. No doctor."

"I'll go with you, silly," she chided, patting his behind. She took his hand. "Come on, you can watch me dress."

He pulled free. "You not understand, Tiff'ny," he said. "Please to listen. We must fix here. No can go out."

She grasped his wrist, pulled him into the bedroom, sat him on the bed, marched to the dresser and unsashed her robe.

"I'm giving the orders now," she declared, selecting pink

panties. "That eye needs to be looked at. And we are going to report those muggers to the police."

"Eye not broken," he insisted. "Nothing broken. Must listen, Tiff'ny. Please. No doctors, no police."

She stopped wriggling. The frilly pink silk was only halfway up her thighs. "I've been really stupid," she declared, pushing the panties back down, stepping out of them and coming toward him, her robe open and flapping.

The sight of her made him moan. He reached out with both hands and captured a breast, raised it to his lips and began to suckle.

"My Bo has a secret," she whispered, resting her belly against him and stroking his hair. "And now Mommy knows his secret," she teased.

He stopped what he was doing. She licked inside his ear, making him shiver.

"My Bo has no papers," she whispered. "My Bo is an illegal alien. Isn't that right, baby?"

He resumed his sucking, nodding yes.

She began slowly gyrating her torso. "So if we went to a hospital—oooh, that feels so nice—my sweet Bo could be taken away from Mommy and sent all the way back to China."

His head moved up and down. He made a guttural sound.

She began rubbing herself against him more insistently. "Does that taste good, baby? I'm so glad. It's all for you, baby. Move your knee a little. That's it. Now suck a little harder. A little harder. Perfect. Mommy will care for baby's boo-boo all by herself. Right here. Is that what you want, baby? Okay, sweet thing. Oh! Here, try the other one. That's my baby. Don't be shy, baby, you know Mommy would do anything for you. You do know that, don't you? Oooh, yes. Does my baby want Mommy to get some warm water and peroxide and wash his boo-boo now? Are you sure, baby? Oh, I love it when you put your hand there. Will

Bo stay here and let Mommy take care of him? Promise? Oh, good, good, good. You feel how wet Mommy is for you? Don't stop. Are you sure baby feels strong enough for this?"

CHAPTER THIRTY-THREE

Shane was limousined to ABC's Washington studios to appear live on *Nightline* with Ted Koppel. Ted asked her a single puffball question before taking a commercial break. Then, for the rest of the show, she sat watching the monitor as Henry Kissinger in New York delivered a labyrinthine analysis crediting Corporal Johnson's "miraggulous" survival to "de piss prozess ve initiated so lonk ago."

By that first night the Isaac Johnson story had displaced everything. Everything. Tell us about him, the public demanded—NOW!—and the press fanned out with a vengeance.

Isaac Johnson's army record turned out to be not much different than those of a million other young men: a succession of dates and postings, routine medical records, a childish signature on a mimeographed form naming his mother as his beneficiary. The composite that emerged—from official sources, classmates, teachers, neighbors and army buddies—amounted to little more than a blur. More and more, it seemed that Isaac P. Johnson was someone no one had really known: a fuzzy picture in an old school yearbook, one of those other kids in the class, someone who had once lived down the block, a name engraved on a large brass plaque in a neighborhood Baptist church, above the legend "Gone But Not Forgotten."

Making matters worse, Johnson's mother was proving as elusive as the now-celebrated MIA himself. Though the press established that she had been working in Detroit as recently as a week ago, her current whereabouts remained a mystery to her co-workers, her minister and her neighbors in the housing project. To the frustration of a news-hungry nation, Adelaide Johnson had disappeared.

While a telegenic Pentagon press officer was treating each new Johnson tidbit as if it were a sacred relic, Shane Reilly was logging the air miles. Maintaining a tenuous lead on her scrambling competition, she managed to track down two far-flung members of Johnson's army platoon, one working as a rigger for Exxon on Alaska's North Slope, the other as a deputy sheriff in a small Oregon town. But despite their exclusivity, the resulting interviews turned out disappointing. Both men remembered Zack Johnson as "a decent guy who did his job"—hardly the kind of material to make the Pulitzer committee sit up and take notice.

"Who should I be talking to?" she had asked each of them, and each had mentioned the same name.

He was tucked away in a back booth trying to lose himself in the Life section of *USA Today* when a very tall, very glamorous young woman asked if she could join him.

"Sure," he said, stunned.

"Shane Reilly," she said, offering her hand across the wood-grain Formica.

"Calvin Snosset." He glanced around nervously. This was too good to be true. The only women who ever talked to him outside of work were waitresses, sales clerks and cashiers. She looked vaguely familiar, like a magazine cover or—

"Hey," he asked, "haven't I seen you on TV?"

"Well, let's see," she said, trying to sound casual, "I was on a news show last week with Henry Kissinger."

"Sure," he said. "Ted Koppel."

"You're amazing," she told him, delighted. "I was only on for a few seconds."

"He's short, isn't he?"

"Who? Koppel?"

"Kissinger."

"I don't know. He was in New York, I was here in Washington. With Ted," she added.

"Oh."

"But they say he's short," she agreed. "Kissinger, I mean. Really short."

Snosset looked around, wishing someone he knew could see them together, snap a picture. But the restaurant was nearly empty.

"You mind?" she asked, showing him a small tape recorder.

"What? No. Sure. I mean, yes, that's okay. You're a reporter, right?"

"*Washington Post.*"

"You have a card or something?" he asked. "Just so, you know . . ."

She rummaged through her bag, came up with an old plastic press pass with her name and paper typed on it. "How's this?"

"Fine," he said, taking it. "Thanks."

He surprised her by slipping it into his jacket pocket.

The waitress came over. When Shane asked if the grapefruit juice was fresh-squeezed, the waitress cackled.

"Orange, then," Shane said. "Cal," she asked, studying the menu, "would you like to share a carafe?"

He clutched his knees. "Sure. Anything you say." Sharing a carafe seemed so intimate.

She ordered egg beaters, dry rye toast, decaf.

He asked for the same. She'd actually called him Cal. Cal, like they were friends. He hadn't been this alone with a woman since his wife left him.

"Will you watch my stuff?" she asked, standing.

"Sure—" He tried to add "Shane," but couldn't.

The carafe was waiting when she returned. He filled their glasses, giving her more.

"What should we drink to?" she asked, raising her glass.

"You decide."

"How about the safe return of Corporal Isaac Johnson?"

"Sure."

She reached out and clinked. They drank. A few drops dribbled down his chin. He grabbed his napkin and the silverware spilled out. She laughed, but not in a mocking way. He shifted in his seat and felt her press pass against his thigh. He kept trying not to stare at her, but he couldn't help it.

"Isn't it exciting?" she said.

"Yes," he agreed. "What?"

She started the tape recorder. "Mr. Snosset, you were the last person to see Corporal Johnson before his capture."

"Oh," he said, "that."

"Weren't you?"

"I guess." She had him feeling inside out. "The last American, anyway. That's what you meant, right?"

"Tell me about him," she said.

"About Zack?"

She nodded encouragement.

"Zack was nice," Snosset said. It sounded lame. "He did his job. He was a decent guy." Lamer.

"Come on, Cal," she prodded. "That's what everybody says. But you knew him better. You went out on patrol with him."

"Just that once," Snosset said, anxious to be honest. "I didn't, you know . . ."

"Has he called you?" she asked hopefully, edging the tape recorder closer.

"No. I wish he would. But, I mean, I don't blame him. We weren't really what you'd call friends."

"Why not?"

"Oh, I don't know," Snosset replied, aligning his silverware. "We were different kinds of people. Maybe because he was a medic. That might have been it. He never should have been sent out on that patrol."

"Why was he?"

"I don't know. It was his turn maybe. It wasn't much of a job: checking the perimeter, seeing what was around. I guess it was okay to send him. The lieutenant, you know . . ."

"But you said he shouldn't have been sent. Why did you say that?"

He heard the words, but she was dissolving. He was seeing the jungle, the vill, Zack walking ahead through the tall grass with that funny lumbering walk he had, signaling for him to wait, going into the hootch . . .

"Cal?"

She reappeared, right in front of him. Startled, he looked down at the table.

"What happened?" she asked.

"When?"

"June, 1968."

"Zack got captured."

"Did you see it?"

"No. I . . . uh . . . I was gone."

"Why were you gone, Cal?"

"Because they were coming. The enemy." Snosset glanced up at her face. Her eyes were focused completely on him. What could he say to her? They were sharing a carafe.

"Did you see the enemy?" she asked him.

He sipped some juice. His hand shook. "See them, no. I heard them, though. They were close. But Zack was inside there. He didn't know. I was . . . I was . . ."

"You warned him."

Snosset grasped at her words. "I did," he confirmed, nodding energetically. "I did! I ran over to the hootch and called to him, told him we had to go." He saw himself in his uniform, with his rifle, young and brave and decisive.

"What was going on inside the hootch?"

"I don't know. He must have been fixing the kid's leg. 'Zack,' I called. 'We gotta go, man. Toot sweet. Charlie's coming.' " Snosset felt the itch of dry thatch against his back, the sticky heat, actually heard himself saying it. "But he said he was working on this kid, you know, this Asian child, and he wouldn't leave. Wouldn't leave. 'Go,' he said. 'Cal, you go ahead. I'll be along in a minute.' " Just like he'd told the lieutenant, just like it said in the incident report. The same lie. It wouldn't go away. No matter how hard he tried, it wouldn't go away.

"How close was the enemy at this point?" she asked.

"Yards. I mean, it was an any second kind of thing. They were all around me, everywhere."

"And then?" She nudged the tape recorder closer, nodding for him to continue. Her lips parted. There was a tiny piece of orange rind on one of her front teeth.

"He ordered me to go," Snosset said. "He outranked me," he explained. "I was only a PFC."

"And then?"

"I went for help, back to the platoon. It wasn't very far, a couple of clicks. Get the guys, get some firepower, and come back for Zack, that was the idea."

"But when you returned with the guys . . ." she prodded.

"He was gone. The kid with the leg was gone. The old woman, everybody. Gone. Even the goat. Did I tell you about the one-horned goat?"

"How long was it?"

"What?"

"Before you got back."

"Oh, Jeez, I don't know. Not long. Time, you know, in a situation like that, time gets . . . You'd have to ask someone else." He looked down and saw that their breakfasts had arrived. He tried the eggs.

"Are yours cold too?" he asked.

He called the waitress. "These eggs are cold," he told her. "Please heat them up."

She made a face but took his plate.

"Shane's too," he said.

Shane's too! He'd actually said it.

Fifteen minutes later Snosset poured Shane the last of the juice from the carafe. They'd been talking up a storm. She was so young, so alive. That was it: so alive.

"We should be going," she said, picking up the check.

"Let me take care of that," he told her, reaching.

She pulled it back. "My treat," she insisted. "Expense account. Oh gosh," she said, glancing at her watch. "You must be late."

"What happens now?" he asked.

She seemed surprised. "Regarding what?"

"Me," he said.

"I don't know what you mean, Cal."

"I mean, when your story comes out, will I be—will there be questions—I mean, a lot of reporters and—"

"Oh," she laughed, "don't worry about it, Cal. You will be a media star. I guarantee it." She took out a compact and checked her face. "I'm serious, Cal," she assured him. "People will stop you in the street. You are going to be swamped with offers. Oprah, Koppel, Geraldo, Sally Jessy, Montel, Ricki Lake—everyone is going to be after Calvin Snosset. You ought to consider getting yourself an agent." She was making funny expressions in the mirror. "For the book deals," she explained. "Stuff like that. Everybody writes books these days."

"Books," he said uncertainly. "Not me. I mean, I don't—"

"You don't have to," she assured him, snapping the compact shut. "Every publisher has a stable of writers. You think Amy Fisher can write? She never finished high school. 'You shot Joey's wife in the head,' they told her. 'We'll do the rest. Just sign here.' Believe me, Cal, that's all there is to it. You are going to be a celebrity."

"That's really great," he said, not wanting to dampen her enthusiasm. He slid from the booth. "I'll walk you to your car," he offered.

"No, you go ahead. I want to stay and make some notes." She extended an elegant hand. "It's been a pleasure. Really. Thanks. Oh, and Cal, is there a number where I can reach you? I know a good agent. Maybe I'll have him call you."

He gave her his home phone. "Thanks," he said, backing away reluctantly. "Thanks for everything. Bye, Shane."

Her smile was dazzling. She gave him a little wave.

The car started on the second try. Once past Arlington, the traffic thinned. Everyone was heading the other way. He found the exit he was looking for, eased the Dodge up to sixty, opened all the windows and let in the fresh chill air. He reached down and rubbed Shane's press pass against his leg. A wonderful calm settled over him. He had the road practically to himself. There were so many trees. It was a pretty time of year, fall. Maple syrup. Pumpkins. Reds and browns, yellows and oranges. The car was running fine this morning. Even that ping was gone. He felt a rush of affection for the old car. He smiled when the fuel light came on. It was nice of God to have sent her—Shane—to let them share a carafe, to let her call him Cal. He remembered the bit of orange on her tooth, the way her eyes glittered when she laughed, the way she looked right at him as if he were somebody nice.

He rounded a bend and there it was, way up ahead, the high bridge that spanned the water like a big steel rainbow. Even at this distance he could see it still had only the one metal railing. They'd been talking about strengthening it for years, but they never got around to it. They would now. See, he told himself, wiping one palm at a time on his pants and then gripping the wheel hard, you're performing a public service. But the terrible pressure in his head prevented him from laughing. The bridge was approaching very fast.

Sorry, he said one last time, and stepped down hard on the gas.

CHAPTER THIRTY-FOUR

Schaeffer indicated two overstuffed white chairs, but Fink pulled over a pair with tubular steel frames and black leather straps. Barton waited until his boss sat down. Fink had warned him not to say a word.

"We're all terribly upset," Schaeffer began.

"Fuck you," Fink told him.

"Now listen here, Lieutenant—"

"No, you listen. Tony Rotelli is dead because you bastards weren't straight with us."

"That's simply not true. Mr. Rotelli's death—"

"No more bullshit," Fink told him, the rage distorting his voice. "Now either you tell me right fucking now what's going on or Detective Barton here will be on his way to the DA's office. For starters, we've got obstruction of justice and—" Fink almost said "attempted bribery," but he didn't want to mention it in front of Barton. "—and if you piss me off any more, I'll press for negligent homicide."

Schaeffer shook his head in disappointment. "Lieutenant," he sighed, "we have cooperated fully. I assure you—"

"Go," Fink ordered Barton, jabbing a finger toward the door. "Right now. Tell the DA I'll be down to sign the complaint."

Schaeffer remained unruffled. "Please sit down," he said to Barton, then turned to Fink. "If the lieutenant will stop making empty threats, we can discuss this matter like reasonable men."

Fink crossed his arms, trying to rein in his anger. Schaeffer was right, it was an empty threat; no DA would present that charge to a grand jury. The strongest case against Schaeffer would have been the bribery, but Fink's star witness was laid out on a slab in the morgue.

Barton returned to his seat and made a show of flipping open his pad.

"Where would you like to begin?" Schaeffer asked.

"The Chinese delivery boy," Fink said. "Forensics has tied him to all three murders."

When Barton had first suggested a Chinese delivery boy, Fink had ignored him. Schaeffer wasn't the only one Fink was angry with.

"I wonder," Schaeffer remarked, "if perhaps Detective Barton's time wouldn't be better spent with our Mr. Danbury."

"I'm fine here," Barton assured him.

Fink shot Barton a look; the mouth again. "Why Danbury?" he asked Schaeffer.

"Mr. Danbury has replaced Mr. Rotelli as our chief of security," Schaeffer explained, "at least temporarily. I thought he and Detective Barton might coordinate efforts."

"That's not a bad idea," Fink mused, feeling ornery. Then, ignoring the resentment flaring in Barton's eyes—or perhaps because of it—he dispatched him to Danbury's office.

Schaeffer seemed to relax the moment Barton left. He ordered coffee for two, came out from behind his desk and settled into a swivel chair by the coffee table. He invited Fink to join him.

Fink went over, sat, glanced out the giant window. The sky all over the city was going dark, like some troubled kid's fingerpainting.

"Officially, lieutenant," Schaeffer said conversationally, "we know nothing about the killer. However, if I may speculate off the record . . ."

"Off the record," Fink agreed.

"We strongly suspect that the man you are looking for is not Chinese, but Vietnamese."

Fink raised an eyebrow.

"Almost certainly in this country illegally," Schaeffer continued, "almost certainly a trained agent, almost certainly sent here to . . . eliminate specific executives of this company."

"Tony Rotelli?"

"No. We agree with your hypothesis that the killer was here for someone else when Mr. Rotelli discovered him."

"Who do you think his target was?"

"We don't know, but we assume it was someone above Mr. Grelling and Mr. Trang in the corporation."

"You? General Robbins?"

"Very possibly."

Schaeffer didn't seem unduly concerned, but then again, there were two armed off-duty cops sitting out in his reception room.

"Why didn't you tell us this before?" Fink asked.

Schaeffer swiveled, pursed his lips, stared out the window. "We were in denial, I suppose. Initially, Grelling's death appeared nothing more than another senseless slaying in a city inured to them."

"Yeah, but then Trang was killed," Fink prompted.

"Yes, and immediately we began to search for a connection."

"And you found it."

"Perhaps. At this juncture all we have is a theory, Lieutenant. We have no hard evidence."

Fink waited, then asked sarcastically: "Are you planning to share this theory with me?"

"Certainly," Schaeffer assured him, nodding toward the door.

A moment later there was a knock, and a black woman in food-service whites rolled in a cart. Schaeffer stood, politely dismissed her and poured the coffee himself. The china cup and saucer he handed Fink had little pink flowers painted on it.

"Let's begin with a bit of history," Schaeffer suggested, making himself comfortable.

"I didn't come here for a civics lesson," Fink told him.

"Your man Barton is gone," Schaeffer said mildly, then surprised Fink by asking: "May I call you Mel?"

"Sure. What should I call you?"

"Hal."

It sounded strange, until Fink remembered that Hal was the name of the evil computer in the movie *2001*. He smiled.

"So, Mel," Schaeffer said, then paused to lift his cup, take a dainty sip, set it down, "I take it we have an understanding."

"What understanding is that, Hal?"

Schaeffer had the expression of a guy talking to a woman he used to fuck.

"I reviewed the videotape of your meeting with Mr. Rotelli in the park," he said, leaning to inspect the plate of petit fours. "I must compliment you, Mel. That was quite a performance. Such conviction! Such self-righteousness!

And most remarkable of all was the way you managed to keep your hands out of sight. If you don't mind telling me, how did you know the location of the camera?"

"I don't know what you're talking about," Fink told him evenly.

"Of course not," Schaeffer agreed. "After all, I could be taping right now. I'm not, but I admire your caution. We recovered the book, by the way. Mr. Rotelli had hidden it in one of the conference room closets. When it was brought to me it was still wrapped in the plastic bag . . . but empty . . . of course." He paused and glanced at Fink. "Not to worry; I had it incinerated before your people arrived. I saw no point in their discovering a book like that, with your prints all over it."

Fink kept his expression neutral as the pieces clicked into place; Schaeffer had noted the missing ten grand and concluded that Rotelli wouldn't have taken it, the killer couldn't have taken it, so Fink must have taken it. That explained the shit-eating grin.

"We never compromise our friends," Schaeffer explained. "Especially not now, with Mr. Rotelli's position vacant."

He rose and strolled to the window. "Mel," he said, staring out at the smudged sky, "General Robbins and I would prefer that you remain where you are until this case is resolved." He turned, adjusting a French cuff. "Is that acceptable?"

"Sure," Fink answered, thinking about Rotelli: fifty-nine fucking years old and going around like some eighteen-year-old grunt on recon patrol. Why the hell would he have done that? And why was Fink letting Schaeffer think he had bought him for ten grand? Why the hell not? He wondered what they were paying Captain Reynolds.

"Rotelli's gun was taken," Schaeffer said. "I'm told it was a Glock."

"Yeah," Fink answered, thinking of Rotelli laid out in a refrigerator with a tag on his toe.

"Right now, if you will excuse me," Schaeffer said, "I have to go brief the general. Next time you come by I'll make sure you meet him. It's not often one gets to rub elbows with a genuine American hero."

"Oh," Fink remembered, "you never told me: How do you know our man is Vietnamese?"

"Ask Marissa," Schaeffer suggested pleasantly, picking up a folder from his desk. "She's much closer to it than I am. Come on," he offered, "I'll walk you to the elevator."

Chapter Thirty-Five

Before the flare completed its sputtering descent through the night sky the forty people inside the compound had gathered up their gear and were moving to their assigned positions. They moved swiftly, efficiently, nearly silently. The loudest sounds were the scraping of boots and the thumping of heavy metal against wood as weapons and ammo were delivered and set in place. There was tension and urgency, but no sense of panic.

Ransom, his camouflage fatigues tucked smartly into his boots, his vest bulging, his face and upper arms smeared with dark grease, stood in the doorway conferring quietly with his four commanders. He sent each off with a solid handshake, a confident smile, a ritual squeeze of the shoulder.

Johnson fastened Mee Yang's flak jacket and adjusted her helmet, made sure she had extra magazines for her Uzi. She stared up at him, her eyes clear and bright.

"No worry by me," she told him, trying to sound tough. "Better worry by you."

Ransom checked his massive Desert Eagle Fifty, strapped it on, picked up his AK-47. Things in his vest jangled like spurs. The grease on his face looked like war paint. "Come on, kids," he called, leading them outside.

Mee Yang held her Uzi with both hands, Johnson cradled an AK-47 with one and grasped his medical bag with the other. The ground felt fragile, unfamiliar.

Ransom deposited them in a steel-lined foxhole, told them to stay put, and ran back toward the house.

When the last of the lights went out, the darkness brought a hollowness to Johnson's belly and a chill to his legs. He became acutely aware of the absence of human sound. Jungle noises were coming at him from everywhere, all mixing together, some rhythmic, some random: wind and rustling leaves and animal movement and insects. He thought he heard an ominous, distant creaking, like thick ropes straining, and he wondered if he was listening to his own nerves. He thought he recognized the sound of Mee Yang's breathing, smelled the sweetness of her breath. He inched closer and confirmed it, felt desire for her welling up inside him and stepped away. The darkness was so thick it seemed to have wrapped everything in sheets of black fabric. He felt around the foxhole with his free hand, getting the sense of it, relearning its dimensions. They had been down here for drills, but now that their lives depended on it he felt the need to know it more intimately, to touch it, to run his hand along its edges—in a weird sort of way, to make friends with it. A mosquito circling his ear reminded him that he'd packed a tube of repellent in his pocket. He made a soft buzzing sound, felt around and placed the tube in Mee Yang's hand. After she finished he rubbed some on his face, neck and arms, inordinately pleased with his foresight, hoping it was an omen. It occurred to him that he didn't have a photo of Mee Yang.

Everyone had been working sixteen-hour days. Ransom believed that the compound's defenses would be sufficient to repulse a determined attack, but just in case, he and small groups of his men had been spending several hours each day practicing hand-to-hand combat. Ransom had been coming in for meals with his skin glistening, his knuckles bloody and his eyes scary, reminding Johnson of those old guys who would come down to the schoolyard and challenge the neighborhood kids in basketball, then try to make up for their lost speed by playing dirty.

Ransom had assigned one of his best men to familiarize Johnson and Mee Yang with the compound's arsenal. Mee Yang had found the rifles cumbersome, but after three days Johnson had learned to assemble an AK-47 in total darkness: load and fire, switch from semi to full auto and lay down a good tight burst without the muzzle pulling up on him. Mee Yang had kept practicing with the Uzi. It was light and she seemed to enjoy saying its name.

Johnson had worried about aircraft. The compound was vulnerable from the air, Ransom conceded, but he had chosen its location carefully; it was outside the operating range of carrier-based copters and he considered it highly unlikely that anyone would send jet fighters this deep into Cambodian territory.

"Too many people would have to sign off on something like that," he had explained. "No, it'll be commandos. They'll be dropped in somewhere nearby and have to hump it through the jungle, which will limit their firepower. With any luck, one of our villagers will spot them and we'll have plenty of warning." It now appeared he'd been right about that too.

Rapid footsteps approached, their sound exaggerated by

the proximity of the ground. They stopped. Ransom asked them to make room and slid in, not bothering to feel around for the ladder.

"Okay," he whispered, their heads coming close together, their breath commingling. "We're set. All our people are hidden, so once it starts, if you see something move, kill it. I don't think there'll be more than eight of them, maybe only six. Chances are it'll be all over before any of them get close. Let's just stay alert. They saw the flare too. They can't get near this place without setting off something. I've rigged the house. If they get inside, I'll blow it."

"Where are the girls?" Johnson asked, suddenly remembering the two young whores Ransom had imported for himself that evening.

"Long gone," Ransom assured him. "It's four in the morning, Doc. What time did you guys go to bed?"

"A little after eleven."

"I'm glad somebody got some sleep. Listen," Ransom said, pushing up alongside, grasping Johnson's arm, keeping his voice low, "if something happens, there's an envelope for you inside my left boot."

"Nothing's going to happen," Johnson said.

"That's right, Doc. Not to us, anyhow." He squeezed Johnson's shoulder. "Like the song says, 'Only the good die young.' "

He took a step back. "Hey, Ling Ling," he called, the cockiness back in his voice.

"Whassup?" Mee Yang responded.

"You take care of Doc, okay?"

"Damn right," she said.

Ransom's voice dropped. "You're a pretty good woman," he said.

Johnson heard her boots scrape. "You pretty good cook."

The walkie-talkie squawked. Ransom's voice returned to normal.

"Everything's set," he said after clicking off. "Now all we do is wait. Anybody want a granola bar?"

Something squished under Zeiss' boot: a rotting fruit, some monkey shit, maybe a small lizard. He regained his balance and moved on, staying low, his rifle snug under one arm, his free hand keeping the leaves from his eyes. It was very dark. The ground was soft and damp. The loudest sounds were the swiping of leaves and the cracking of twigs.

Zeiss enjoyed moving through an alien landscape weighted down with the gear of death. He breathed in the rich jungle smells and understood that the way he felt now—his pores open, his senses sharp, his blood pumping—was what life was all about. He smiled, trying to imagine the look on Jared's face when he heard the explosion, turned around and saw that the back of the plane had disappeared.

Taking the point for the small column, Zeiss reached up and tugged at the straps of his backpack, working the weight higher. His shoulders were raw, which was fine; the pain was keeping him focused. He hadn't killed anyone since El Salvador: too long.

Zeiss reacted to the first whoosh of the flare's ascent by dropping down to one knee and freezing. Remaining motionless, he used the sudden illumination to study the target. They were still at least a quarter mile away. He was grateful for the flare; now he knew what they were up against. He had anticipated a defensive configuration, but he hadn't expected a jungle fortress.

As the light flickered down, details were absorbed, a revised plan of attack formulated. He signaled his men to gather round.

"Big fences are good," he assured the tight huddle. "They make the people inside feel safe. Ten minutes from now they'll have convinced themselves the flare was a false alarm." That brought chuckles.

The eight men pooled information. Each added useful insights. Finally it was time for orders. Zeiss spoke. The flare had come from the east, behind them. Consequently, he had decided on a wide circling maneuver which would allow them to approach the compound from the west. Once they got close enough, they would space themselves and wait for the first rocket. He designated two teams of three, the first to turn right when it got inside, the second left.

"I don't want to have to chase anybody through the bush," he told his best shooter, assigned to remain outside, "so after you drop them, put in an extra round just to be sure, in the head. Questions." He glanced around. There were none.

"Gentlemen, our orders specify an immaculate operation," he reminded them. "If it's inside that fence and breathing, we kill it. No exceptions. Now check your gear one last time. We move out in two minutes."

He took his second in command off to one side and asked for his assessment.

"The fence is high, but it's bamboo," the man said. "It'll go up like kindling. But we're going to have to move damn fast once we're inside. They figure to be dug in. We're going to take casualties."

"What's your estimate of force size?" Zeiss asked him.

"There were two in the northeast tower. Four towers, that's eight right there. All together, I figure fifteen, maybe eighteen."

"Four buildings inside, all wood. We carrying enough rockets?" Zeiss asked.

"Two launchers with six each."

"That should do it. You think they've rigged anything outside the fence? Booby traps? Trip wires? Mines?"

"Probably not. It's a pussy fence. Best be careful, though. You see how they camouflaged the whole place?"

"That's why we couldn't get resolution in the photos. This guy is no amateur."

"Neither are we, bro."

Zeiss grasped his shoulder. "Once it starts, you hang back with me. We'll go in last." He hitched up his pants, straightened the sheath on his thigh, checked the knife.

Something was keeping the other man from moving. Zeiss wondered what he'd left out.

"This guy supposed to be rich?" the man asked.

"We'll search the place before we torch it," Zeiss promised. "Anything we find gets split even."

"That suits me. What about wounded?"

"We'll deal with it," Zeiss said noncommittally. "You wearing your vest?"

"Yeah."

"Come on, then. We've got less than two hours before sunrise. Let's get it done."

The time was dragging. Johnson stared out into the night, slowly sweeping the darkness, trying to gauge distances by sound, checking and rechecking his weapon, making minute adjustments to his stance, his clothing. Ransom climbed out and padded off to check on something. Johnson removed his helmet and laid it on the foxhole's lip. His head was sweaty and the air cooled it. His ears felt like radar dishes. He kept hearing sharp things which turned out to be nothing. Mee Yang was silent as a cat. Ransom slipped back in.

A few minutes later there was a short flash outside the fence, followed almost immediately by a ka-BOOM, the noise shattering the night and sending ripples through the air. All around him Johnson heard the cricket-like chorus of weapons being readied to fire. He felt around anxiously for his helmet and discovered it already on his head. Ransom began whispering urgently into his walkie-talkie. Johnson reached out, found Mee Yang's arm.

"Worry by you," she said, pushing him away.

A second explosion, far from the first. Johnson winced again, shocked anew by the force of the sound. Floodlights came on outside the compound fence. Gunfire erupted from the towers. The area outside was aglow. Irregular shafts of light pierced the bamboo fence and striped the ground. Angry noise assailed Johnson from all directions. He hunkered down, pressing his shoulder against the wall and trying to make sense of the sound. Most of the firing was coming from machine guns in two of the towers. As he raised himself and peeked out, one of the towers exploded with a blinding flash that left bright spots dancing before his eyes, followed almost instantly by a brutal, cracking noise that sent a horribly sharp pain shooting through his eardrums. More explosions went off. While rubbing his eyes furiously, Johnson heard Ransom bark "Incoming! Incoming!" Johnson ducked and heard the whoosh of a rocket. His eyes became functional just in time to see a second tower burst apart: a multistage explosion that sounded like fireworks and sent debris whizzing into the air. He ducked as shards of metal came crashing down and lay hissing on the ground nearby. He thought he heard running. There was gunfire, but he couldn't see anyone. There were fires. He smelled burning. He grasped his rifle, desperate for something to shoot at, but everything seemed to be happening outside the fence.

The night began to reclaim the compound; in rapid succession, the outside searchlights were knocked out, each dying with a loud pop. Gunfire became sporadic. Burning fires and glowing metal fragments provided some illumination, but the change was so sudden that for many seconds Johnson was unable to identify anything. Then he picked out the top of the fence, and after that a few other details appeared. He rubbed one palm then the other hard against his pants, finding momentary reassurance in his own touch. Though he had been through this before, he had somehow forgotten what combat was like: the way shreds of thought flew through your mind, and how scary it was to sense death's wildly careening presence.

Ransom was talking nonstop, and though Johnson understood few of the words, he sensed an edgy satisfaction. Flares appeared above the smoldering corners where the destroyed towers had stood. Johnson glimpsed what he thought was a muzzle flash and then heard the shot and a cry from a tower. When it flashed again, he squeezed off a round to get the range and then switched to full auto and sent a burst exactly where he wanted it. Whether or not anything had been moving there before, nothing was now. Uncertain of how many bullets he'd used, he ejected the clip, inserted a fresh one, slammed it home.

Ransom barked into his walkie-talkie. The firing stopped. It was replaced by an eerie silence punctuated by fire sounds: hissing, crackling, patches of flame being shoved by gusts of wind. From beyond the fence to the east, a red the color of an angry bruise began to seep up into the sky. Amid the drifting smoke Johnson sensed a kind of breathlessness, as if the air was being crisscrossed with the energy of strained listening. He became aware of a vibration in the leg pressed against Mee Yang's, but couldn't determine its source. He asked her what Ransom was saying into the walkie-talkie.

"No one move," she whispered. "Wait for light. Maybe

not over. He ask how many us dead, how many them." Her tone changed. "What wrong your leg?"

Johnson squatted and located his medical bag. He didn't think any of the men in the two towers could have survived, but there might be some wounded somewhere. When Ransom fell silent, Johnson asked him.

"We have four dead," Ransom reported, "all from the towers. As soon as the light comes up I'll send men out to check, but right now they count five enemy bodies."

"You sound disappointed," Johnson observed.

"I am. You hungry?"

"Yeah."

"How about you?" Ransom asked Mee Yang, who was bent over.

"You cook good, maybe I eat," she replied, straightening up slowly.

"You okay?" Johnson asked her.

"Baby no like guns," she said.

"Stomach pains?" he asked.

"Worry better by you."

They climbed out into a fresh, sweet-tasting dawn, alive with the first peeks of sunlight and the reckless cries of birds. Random air currents carried the sharp smells of expended gunpowder.

Mee Yang went on ahead into the house. She seemed out of sorts, but Johnson assumed it was morning sickness compounded by the night's tension. He had experienced combat before, but this had been Mee Yang's first time; she probably wasn't used to tasting her own fear. He wanted to go with her, but she seemed to want solitude, and he was unnerved by all the feelings pulling at him simultaneously. He wasn't used to feeling so much, so strongly, so many things at once. Could this morning, for instance, really be so much more beautiful than other mornings? Could the air really taste that much better?

He followed along as Ransom toured the compound. Men were recovering bodies, clearing debris. A sense of relief was everywhere; they had been tested and they had prevailed. It didn't seem to have fully registered on them that some of their friends were dead. Johnson knew the realization would sneak up on them and hit them from behind.

Holding his rifle loosely, he followed Ransom toward the house, smiling as he thought first of Mee Yang carrying his baby, then of a big breakfast and a long peaceful sleep. His mind kept replaying the exhilaration of emptying his clip at that spot in the jungle.

Johnson trailed Ransom up the steps and across the porch, enjoying every creak and tremble of the familiar wood. It felt great to get inside, but as Ransom passed from the living room into the dining room a figure sprung at him from the shadows. Instinctively, Johnson moved to help, but Mee Yang's shriek spun him around just in time to deflect an arm with a knife as a big man, lurching forward with Mee Yang on his back, crashed into him and carried him thudding to the floor.

Down on his side, his teeth clenched against the rain of wicked blows to his ribs and kidneys, Johnson concentrated every ounce of his being on that driving wrist, grasping it with both hands as if it were a throat, his legs bicycling and kicking out wildly, trying to gain a purchase, trying to use his weight to force the knife to the floor, twist it loose, keep its death away from them. It was like fighting a thick monstrous snake. Pain was bursting over him from everywhere, but he knew if he broke his concentration—shots!—the knife would—

The arm gave and hit the floor and the knife came loose. In a single desperate motion, Johnson sprung at it, grabbed it and plunged it deep into the man's gut, then wrenched upward with all his might. When he looked up the man had no face. Mee Yang was standing over him with her rifle. She appeared to be in shock. He called her name.

"Worry by you," she said weakly.

Men were clambering through the door. Johnson momentarily panicked, but they were Ransom's men. He relaxed and discovered that the wetness he felt on himself was blood. The shots he'd heard must have been Mee Yang putting her Uzi to the guy's face and pulling the trigger. Jesus, where was—

"Colonel," he cried, struggling to his feet.

Ransom, standing on the other side of the room, was directing men to search the house. They rushed off. He limped over, cradling a badly bleeding forearm. "Medic," he called sarcastically, coughing and laughing at the same time. There was a crumpled body on the floor behind him.

Johnson pointed to the forearm. "That looks—"

"Ladies first," Ransom said, gesturing sharply with his chin.

Mee Yang was swooning. Her eyes rolled up and the weapon slipped from her hands. Johnson caught her as she fell, cleared some space with his foot and lowered her to the floor. She was ashen. Her pants were soaked with blood.

Johnson came down the steps slowly, his limbs heavy.

"How is she?" Ransom asked.

"She's asleep. Let's see to that arm."

They sat at the dining table. Johnson opened his bag.

"She lose the baby?" Ransom asked.

"Yeah." He carefully peeled away the bloody shirt Ransom had wrapped around the forearm. "Nice clean slice," he remarked when the wound was exposed. "You're pretty lucky."

"Damned lucky. If I don't get the arm up he cuts my throat. Nothing else, right? Just the baby?"

"Just the baby." Johnson spread a cloth and started cleaning the wound with peroxide. There was a lot of fizz.

"Who were they?" he asked, dabbing again and watching new bubbles form.

"Americans," Ransom replied, glancing over at the one on the floor, "but private. Sent by an outfit called Parker Global."

"These the ones you've been expecting?"

"Pretty much."

The wound was clean, ready to be stitched. "This is gonna hurt some," Johnson warned.

"Good, I deserve it. I should have figured they might have gotten inside the house."

"Why didn't they just shoot us?" Johnson asked, rummaging through his bag.

"They shoot us, how do they get away? These guys weren't kamikazes. The plan was to kill us quietly, create a diversion and sneak back into the jungle."

"How do you know?" He pulled on a pair of rubber gloves, tore open a glassine envelope and removed a long hooked needle, already threaded.

"Guy over there told me," Ransom explained.

Johnson looked at the body across the room. It had moved.

"He's alive?"

"Used to be," Ransom said. "His name was Zeiss."

"I didn't hear any shots," Johnson said, preparing to insert the needle.

"Didn't want to disturb you. He answered a few questions before I broke his neck. Jeez, that burns."

"Don't move. Yeah, it's coated with alcohol. So they're all dead?"

Ransom chuckled. "That one whose face you shot off isn't going anywhere."

"Mee Yang shot him."

"No shit? Good for her. Can't you go a little faster with that needle?"

"Yeah, but I won't. Now hold still and let me do it right. Why does that company want to kill us?"

"Not us, me. I do work for them. Setting up arms deals. Been doing it for years."

Johnson pulled the thread through, made it snug, took another stitch. "So?"

"I guess they decided I know too much. You want a drink?"

"Not right now. You go ahead." Johnson still did not understand. "Does this have anything to do with that trouble in New York?" he asked.

One of Ransom's men came over and reported. Ransom sent the man to get him a Snapple. "House is clean," he told Johnson. "Mee Yang is talking in her sleep."

Johnson smiled. "She does that."

Ransom shook the bottle and handed it back for the man to open. Two men were dragging Zeiss' body out.

"Look at this floor," Ransom lamented.

Johnson sat back and wiped his face with his sleeve. The sun was up. He was worn out. It didn't feel like morning, but it didn't feel like anything else either. He thought of Mee Yang sleeping upstairs, then resumed his stitching.

"This company you do work for," he said, trying to pick up the thread of the conversation, "you think they'll send more guys?"

"Won't matter," Ransom said, smacking his lips. "How soon will the princess be ready to travel?"

"I'd like her to rest for a few days, but if you're in a hurry . . ."

"A few days is okay. The hearings aren't for a week." He reached out with his good hand and mussed Johnson's hair.

Johnson pulled away. "You need a shave, Colonel. I've been meaning to tell you that."

"This is my new rugged look. Goes with the gun, don't you think?" He removed his huge automatic from its holster and laid it on the table. "Goddamn Israelis," he said admiringly. "Those people make some weapons."

"You work for them too?" Johnson asked.

"I wish," Ransom said. "See, Doc, the good thing here is that all these guys are dead, but their boss back home doesn't know it. By the time he finds out, we'll be having dinner with your mother."

CHAPTER THIRTY-SIX

Fink floated with the rhythms of the car, dimly aware that Barton had looped around the foot of Manhattan and was now heading north on the FDR Drive. Barton was edgy, but he was always like that after calling Captain Reynolds. Fink wasn't exactly on top of the world either. He'd received a letter from his mother. Writing on that same cheap nursing home stationery, she'd told him she was still playing the Florida lotto in hopes of attending Eileen's graduation, adding: "Who knows how much longer I'll be able to travel?"

Fink leaned back and closed his eyes. There was a draft through his closed window. He could smell the water. Thoughts sloshed about his head. Rotelli. Marissa. Schaeffer. Trang. Eileen's tuition bills. End-user certificates. His Visa limit. And through them all, the MIA story buzzed like a persistent mosquito. Fink couldn't get over it: twenty-four years . . .

Sure, Marissa had said, she could explain why Schaeffer

believed the killer was Vietnamese. Since Rotelli, she had come to the same conclusion. She had been about to mention it, but Fink beat her to it. Her ex-husband, Frank, had been involved with Herb Trang in a munitions deal: Vietnam, Subic Bay surplus, bargain basement prices. Trang got the order, Frank booked it and got the end-user certificates, Marissa flew down and squared it with the government honchos in Paraguay and Peru. It wasn't a big deal, not by Parker Global standards, but something had gone wrong and somebody in Vietnam must have gone ballistic. She didn't know the particulars, but there had been an accident. Yes, she supposed she could be a target and yes, she was in the building the day Rotelli got killed and yes, on the fiftieth floor. But hey, so were dozens of other people.

It was nice, driving without having to stop for lights. Soothing. Maybe, Fink thought, he should have been a state trooper: spend all day tooling along the Thruway, wearing a funny hat. Sunglasses. Boots.

"What are you smiling about?" Barton asked, coming out of his funk.

Fink breathed in salt air. "Rhonda Cohen," he replied, stretching himself carefully and opening one eye.

"I should be the one smiling," Barton told him.

"Yeah, but you're not." Fink reached into his jacket for the pack of sugarless gum. His mouth tasted musty. He offered one to Barton, who shook his head. Off to the right rose the masts of several giant sailing ships.

"You been to the Seaport lately?" he asked Barton.

"I took Rhonda last week. Mistake. Strictly for tourists."

Dwarfed by glassy skyscrapers, the restored Seaport complex was all lit up and crowded with people. "They don't pay us enough," Fink observed, chewing thoughtfully.

He'd been happier asleep. Marissa, Rotelli, Schaeffer, Eileen, his mother. Too damned much. Plus, this mysterious

MIA kept popping into his thoughts, delivering an uncomfortable—and inexplicable—sense of guilt. And now here it was again: here and gone. Not a clear image as much as a passing smear: a thin, haggard, hollow-eyed GI stumbling out of the jungle onto a highway, the sense of a truck bearing down. Fink suspected the image was from a movie. Isaac P. Johnson: The media was going nuts over him. You couldn't turn on the TV anymore. It was the only story. Like the rest of the world had stopped. Like Rotelli was still alive. Twenty-four fucking years . . .

The radio squawked.

"Ten eighty-five," Barton announced, stomping down on the gas, flicking on the siren, starting to weave. A red glow, like a dragon's breath, began pulsing from the front of the hood.

"Shit," Fink growled, reaching down and pulling the thirty-eight from his ankle. Ten eighty-five was the code for "Officer in need of assistance." "Where?" he asked, spinning the cylinder. Nice and smooth, seemed okay.

"Projects," Barton replied, driving with heavy-footed aggression, "right up here on Houston. Give us a chance to practice our Spanish: S.O.C.K.S."

He crossed into the exit lane and bounced up the ramp, swung hard left, slowed for the stop sign and then gunned it.

"Don't get crazy on me," Fink warned him, feeling prickly. Every cop in the area would respond; Fink had no desire to be first.

Barton made a sharp U-turn, squealed in by a hydrant and was out the door. Fink scrambled after him, getting into the building barely in time to see Barton go charging up a stairway.

Fink's legs were responding, but reluctantly. He entered the stairwell, heard Barton's footsteps clanging above him. Fucking gazelle. As Fink grabbed the banister he heard the door slam on the second-floor landing. He paused to pull out his gun and click off the safety, heard himself huffing and tried to pretend it was excitement. Goddamn building felt like a jungle: same wet heat, smell of rot, rustling sounds . . .

Fast and careful through the door, instinct kicking in. Lone working bulb gave the long empty hallway a dull brown glow. Allowed himself one deep breath and took off, hugging the wall. Suspicious eyes peering from doorways, roaches scurrying for cover. Heavy, overlapping smells: stale piss, greasy chicken, garbage, hot sauce. Where the hell were the sirens? Backup should have been here. Barton, that goddamn cowboy—

There! Last apartment. Shit. The cop was down, not moving, legs sticking out at a funny angle. Fink approached cautiously, realized he'd forgotten to hang out his badge. Fuck it. Noises from the apartment. Barton must have charged straight in, like it was a fucking game. No lights in there either. Squatted by the fallen cop, heard him moaning, patted his shoulder. Fabric wet and sticky. Too dark to really see, but it looked like—yeah, gashes on arms, legs—machete. Bleeding didn't seem too bad. No arterial spurts. Probably be okay. Fink caught an eye staring from behind a nearby door, glimpsed a dress. "*Por favor, señorita, nueve uno uno. Ambulancia. Emergencia policía.*"

The door closed, a lock turned. Maybe she'd call. It was worth the shot. Fink wiped his hands on the cop's shirt, then loosened the guy's gun belt, gave his shoulder a squeeze. Black kid, twenty-five, maybe less: a baby. Fink was forty-eight, and feeling it.

An unexpected wave of rage washed over him, leaving him alert but calm. Game time, he told himself. Keeping low, he entered the apartment gun first, eyes straining, ears itching. Narrow hallway smelled of tension, fear, used diapers. Baby crying somewhere in back, far away. Chair scraping on linoleum.

"Barton," he called, announcing his presence, maybe providing a diversion. His voice sounded so close it shocked him.

No answer. Nothing except the baby's wailing and Fink's own voice, both echoing.

Moving fast, staying low, he banged into some kind of cupboard. Dishes rattled. He froze, held his breath, wiped his palm against his pants. Heartbeat pushing against his eardrums and eyeballs. Twenty-four goddamn years. Squatted and reached out. Floor filthy. Baby crying so hard it couldn't catch its breath. Woman pleading in Spanish, trying to calm it. A toilet flushed in the apartment directly above.

Fink counted to three, darted around the cupboard and pressed back against the wall. An intermittent red glow from outside—ambulance?—was providing some light: not enough to see, just enough to tantalize. Where in hell was the backup?

"Police," Fink yelled again and heard feet shuffle somewhere in front of him, but not close. He scrunched down as low as he could, his knees beginning to rebel. Forty-eight fucking years old and crawling around in roach shit. Barton was—

What was that? Too many sounds. Too many sounds. Goddamn baby wouldn't shut up. Be just his luck to shoot it.

He inched forward, his left side scraping the wall, his gun hand free. Thighs sore from squatting, muscle in left one twitching. Breathing too hard, sweating everywhere. Damn shoes rasping like sandpaper. Hot. Sweat pouring, tickling nose, wiped it with sleeve. Feeling his way along wall, progress slow but steady. Pulsing red glow. Framed Jesus on opposite wall, arms outstretched. Hallway not more than three feet wide. Where the hell was the backup? Where the hell was Barton? Didn't like this at all.

Sirens outside. Two. Three. Finally. He kept moving. Maybe now the fuck will give himself up. Yeah, sure.

His fingers stopped, clutching molding. A doorway. An inch further, a door. It swung, squeaked. Woman inside began to shriek, hurt his ears. Everything at once. Sounds of scuffling down the hall. A yell. Someone hurt. Heavy footsteps approaching. Someone running. Whole apartment shaking. Woman screaming. Baby. Too heavy for Barton. Sounded like Refrigerator Perry. Fink ducked into doorway, rested cool gun metal against cheek. Ignoring the screams behind him, he dropped to one knee, braced himself with his free hand, and stuck out his other leg to block the hallway.

Something hit his ankle hard. Surprised grunt, loud crash, clang of metal. Fink launched himself at the sound, landing atop a man's wet back, but sliding off and carrying hard into the wall. Wielding his gun like a stone, he turned and swung at where the head should have been, but caught only bare wet shoulder. The body rose up roaring from the darkness like a Brahma bull. Amidst the chaos and noise, Fink grasped hair slimy as chicken fat, held on and swung again, this time feeling his gunned hand glancing off skull. As he raised the arm again, he heard metallic sounds; bucking ferociously now, the huge bastard was slapping about for his machete. Fink swung desperately, caught all head, sent it bouncing heavily against floorboard, heard machete fall, couldn't see shit.

A moment of absolute stillness, then woman sobbing. Baby wailing. Reality coming back one ugly layer at a time. Fink, gasping, shaking, hit him again just to be sure.

Straddling the wet hog-flesh, needing desperately to wipe the slime from his hands, Fink was struggling to catch his breath when he heard rapid footsteps behind him, twisted around and was run smack into hard, knocked against wall, stepped on, kneed, fallen on top of. Seeing stars, he held on to his gun and tried to grasp this new assailant. Body solid, cologne familiar.

"Barton?"

"Lieutenant?"

They struggled to untangle.

"Shit."

"You okay?"

Loud, animal moan from nearby.

"Cuff this son of a bitch, will you please?" Fink said, crawling free, jamming his gun back into its holster and then sitting with his shaking hands held out in front of him as if they were used flypaper.

He heard Barton shifting the perp's limbs, then the reassuring crunch of cuffs. Fink felt woozy, but he was still in one piece. Adrenaline aftertaste was making him nauseous. The baby's crying was giving him a throbbing headache. He should have shot the kid. Still could. He patted his holster with his wrist. Gun was okay. His shoulder was twitching.

"You all right, Wyatt?" he asked Barton.

"My arm." He sounded tired.

Fink looked over. The pulsing red neon made Barton's wet face shine like plastic. "Your arm what?"

"Back there, Pedro here grazed me with the blade. I better go check the guy in the hall, right?"

"Yeah yeah. Careful with the arm."

Fink shifted, trying to make room.

"Watch the floor," Barton advised. "Crack vials all over the goddamn place. It's like walking on M&Ms."

He moved off. Fink looked over at their prisoner, a huge, shadowy mound with the shape and stink of a beached walrus. This is what we risk our lives for, he thought, desperate for something to wipe the goo off his hands. He felt old and worn. Time to retire, he told himself. Let Barton and his pals have it all.

Fink sighed involuntarily, overwhelmed. So much crap. The suit would need dry cleaning. There'd be a shitload of paperwork. He'd have to call Marissa and explain, then go back to his place and shower, change, grab a cab and why couldn't that baby shut the hell up?

He leaned back and rested his throbbing head against the wall. Ten eighty-five, he called out silently, officer in need of assistance. He was sitting there reciting his badge number when flashlight beams began crisscrossing the hall like tracer bullets. About fucking time. He sat up. His hands were still shaking. Maybe someone could find him a goddamn paper towel.

A minute later two kids in blue did even better; they found the bathroom light switch. Fink squinted. The female cop shooed a woman out and motioned Fink to go ahead. He glanced up and saw, captured in an oblique rectangle of light, a smiling Jesus holding up two fingers like some bearded Cub Scout. Without using his hands, Fink clambered to his feet, went inside and shut the door with his foot.

It was as if someone had packed in the air with a trowel. The heavy, sick-sweet smell of used diapers was close to unbearable. A far corner was littered with the filthy things, the whole area crawling with roaches. Fink swallowed a hiccup of bile as he moved to the rust-stained sink and, using the heel of his hand, turned on the faucet. It spit a few seconds, then began to flow. He rinsed his hands, trying not to breathe through his nose. The water felt oily. Naturally there was no soap. Random spasms of pain afflicted different parts of his body. He wanted to pee, but some bastard had piled filthy diapers on the closed toilet, a huge brownish mound of them covering the water tank. Roaches were everywhere. Everywhere.

Without warning, his mind clicked into a strange, new, terribly calm zone, as if someone had moved the dial and switched his life to a new frequency. Methodically now, he turned and scanned the narrow room. No shower, no tub, the one small window covered over with cardboard. Leaving the tap running and shaking the water from his hands, he went over and locked the door, went to the toilet tank and, using both hands, cautiously raised the porcelain top and, gritting his teeth against the tickle of roaches, lowered it and its filthy cargo gently onto the closed seat cover.

He leaned forward and peered down into the murky water, couldn't see a thing. But when he pushed the rusty handle and flushed, the receding water revealed a package. Wrapped in black plastic, it clung near the bottom of the inside wall like a giant leech.

Before the spurting water could cover it again, Fink reached in, pried it loose and pulled it out. By the feel of it, a stack of bills, about two inches thick. Holding it delicately, as if it carried disease, he took it to the sink and laid it under the stream of water, then returned to the toilet, lifted the tank cover and carefully lowered it back into place.

He became aware of a lot of activity out in the hall. Moving quickly now, he went over and finished rinsing off the plastic package, using his fingers to scrub the gook off it. Finally, when he'd done as much as he could, he folded over the loose tape, dried the package against his pants leg and, his mind weirdly numb—he could no longer smell anything—jammed it into his left inside jacket pocket. Avoiding his reflection in the mirror, he bent over and splashed his face with cold water, trying to ignore the new pain throbbing in his lower back.

"You drop your shield?" one of the uniforms asked when he stepped into the hall.

"What?" Fink patted himself down, found the worn

leather case, slid it into the outside jacket pocket. He thanked the kid and began working his way down the now-crowded hall, nodding blankly in response to greetings, his insides tight, his limbs jittery, feeling strangely distanced from everything around him, like he was coming out of a jungle. The moving flashlight beams were affecting his balance. The package in his pocket seemed to be warm and breathing, like a small animal.

He forced himself to keep moving, zombie-like, through the hall, out the doorway, down the stairs. He pushed heavily with his shoulder, the safety door gave and he felt the ruffle of night air, the reassurance of hard gritty pavement beneath his feet.

The street was busy: lights flashing red and blue, white and yellow. Noise. It was hot and cold at the same time. There was no breeze. His knees felt soft. During the short trip from the apartment his package seemed to have tripled in size.

He was passing through the crowd when somebody he recognized came jogging over. O'Brien, one of his detectives. "Hey, Lieutenant, there you are." He put out his hand.

Fink shook it, heard himself ask: "Where's Barton?"

"Flesh wound. They're patching him up. Hey, you know who you collared?"

"Jabba the Hutt?"

"Almost. El Gordo, Lieutenant. Warrants going back two years. Word is, he supplies crack to the whole project. Looks like another citation."

"How's the cop, the one he cut up?" Fink asked. But he was running on fumes. None of this seemed real. Another citation. The lights kept flashing. His jacket felt dangerously lopsided. There was noise everywhere. He felt like he was going to puke. "I need to find Barton," he said.

"Over here," O'Brien said, leading the way. "They took

the uniform to the hospital. Word is, the commissioner's on his way there now. The mayor too. Election year. I hear he was cut up pretty bad."

"Bad enough," Fink said, catching sight of Barton sitting in the back of an open ambulance, bathed in bright white light, surrounded by shiny chrome and reporters and cameras. No shirt. Big bandage on his upper arm. Looking like a hero.

Fink remembered the smack against his ankle, then sliding off the guy's back, the slimy feel of— A wave of nausea swept over him. He stopped and grasped O'Brien's arm. "Listen," he said, "I can't deal with the press right now. El Gordo is Barton's collar. I just backed him up. Make sure he gets to the hospital to kiss the commissioner. I've got to go home."

"You okay, Lieutenant? I could go with you."

"I look that bad?"

"No, no," O'Brien said, "I just thought—"

"Just find a blue-and-white to drive me. You stay here. Tell Barton what I said."

Fink sat alone in the back. Car bouncing like crazy, needed new shocks. Hadn't been in one of these in . . . whew, a long time. Long time. Long. Time. Like being in a cage. Get home and close the door. Be okay then. Envelope rubbing against his heart. Damn city streets. Twenty-four fucking years. He could still turn it in. Could still—

"Step on it," he said, as much to himself as the driver. "I've got a date."

CHAPTER THIRTY-SEVEN

Bo was floating in a warm liquid world, his body drifting in graceful, effortless swirls. He stretched his arms up toward the surface and felt something moving down below his waist. As he came awake his erection grew to its full length inside Tiffany's gently moving mouth. She adjusted herself to accommodate it, shifting her body and emitting deep, satisfied, feline growls. He raised himself to watch her rhythmically bobbing blonde head, retaining the image as he fell back and sighed, giving his body over to her completely.

Moments later she positioned herself for a final assault: rising up on her knees, aggressively sliding the inside edge of one hand up between his buttocks, grasping his testicles with the other, lengthening her determined strokes.

He felt his orgasm slowly gathering itself, drawing strength from all parts of his body and concentrating in his groin. The bed was rocking with the same irresistible tidal rhythm as her hands and head and mouth. He reached down and urgently grasped her breasts as his pelvis began to shake and he heard himself whimper and then moan and then gasp and then cry out as the spasms began.

When his body finally went slack she released him and rested her soft warm cheek against his thigh.

"Good morning, baby," she said.

He stroked her golden hair. "Good morning, Tiff'ny."

She rolled over onto an elbow. "How do you feel?"

"Better," he said, sitting up and scratching his head, still a bit dazed.

"I woke you because I have to go to work," she told him. "But you'll stay in again and rest, okay?"

"No, Tiff'ny. Today I must go out. Do errand."

"But you called the hotel, baby. They know you're sick."

"Must do something else," he told her.

"Is it a secret?"

"Secret," he said. "Yes."

"Another girl?"

"No other girl. My swear."

"Well, your eye is almost all healed, but you better bundle up. Wear one of my sweaters."

"Okay. I do that. You wake me up big surprise today."

"Good surprise?"

"What you think, crazy woman?"

She sat up and mussed his hair. "Don't forget to take the key."

Bo found an isolated pay phone a few blocks away. After five days indoors, all the street noise was disconcerting. When the number answered he cupped his hand over the phone and identified himself in Vietnamese. The voice at the other end, initially relieved, quickly became angry: Where had he been?

"I was wounded," Bo explained. "I went to ground."

"Why did you not call?"

"No public telephone was available. You know my instructions."

"The police have been raiding Chinese restaurants all over New York. Your former employer is terrified. He is convinced the American authorities have him under surveillance."

"He is an old fool," Bo declared. "I cannot go back there."

"I understand, but where will you stay? Where have you been all this time?"

"I am in a safe place."

"All right, but you must report in every day at one of the appointed times."

"I will."

"It is very dangerous for you now. They are searching everywhere. Large rewards are offered for information. The man was a retired police officer. We assume you had no choice."

"No choice," Bo confirmed, sensing someone approaching from behind and spinning around with his fist cocked.

A middle-aged man jumped backward and interposed his attaché case. "You gonna be long?" he asked nervously.

"Yes," Bo told him, dropping his arm and bowing. "Much long. Sorry."

The man turned and walked off.

Bo waited until he was out of earshot. "Safe to talk," he said into the phone.

"It is good you are finally concerned about safety," he was told. "Reckless actions threaten to compromise all of us."

"Nothing has been compromised," Bo protested. "Perhaps it was unwise to send me to a place with such heavy security."

"It was you who told us she was never alone in her hotel."

"Yes, I know, but—"

"Let us not argue. Are you fully recovered?"

"My strength has returned, but it will be two or three more days before all traces of the injury are gone."

"Are you prepared to continue your mission?"

"Of course!"

"Do you require funds?"

"No." He glanced around, dropped his voice. "The retired policeman was quite generous."

"We heard nothing of that." The voice suddenly became alarmed: "You must not use credit cards!"

"I am not a fool," Bo huffed. "I use cash only."

"You must understand how anxious we have been. How many dollars do you have?"

"More than three hundred," Bo answered, choosing a number large enough to prevent a visit to Old Han, but not large enough to provoke jealousy.

"All right. Now listen carefully. Take no further action at this time. We expect to have a new assignment for you."

"Where will this assignment be?" Bo asked impulsively.

"We may know more when you call tomorrow," the voice replied, ignoring Bo's transgression. "But for now, I repeat, you are to take no further action."

"No action. Understood."

"You will contact us tomorrow without fail."

"Without fail," Bo assured him.

He replaced the receiver, zipped up his collar, dug his hands into his jacket pockets and, choosing a new route, headed back toward Tiffany's building. The call had gone well. He had expected far harsher criticism for his long silence. There had been anxiety in his controller's voice.

His hand felt around inside the pocket until it grasped the hundred dollar bill he had removed from the laundry hamper. He looked up and down the street for a store where he could exchange it for smaller bills. So many stores, so much obscene wealth, such a stupid evil country. Except for Tiffany.

He passed a large food market with a yellow window sign announcing a sale on Russian caviar. Next to it was a sign welcoming "Food Stamps," whatever they were. He noted the store's location but, feeling bitter toward anything Russian, decided to walk on.

On the next block he saw another possible store. Before he realized it, a strange idea had seized him and propelled him through the door.

The aroma inside was overpowering. A middle-aged Caucasian woman behind the counter asked if she could be of service.

"Yes, please," Bo said nervously. "I am wishing gift."

The woman smiled indulgently. "Is the gift for a man or a woman?"

"A woman, please."

"Friend or loved one?"

"Excuse?"

"Is this woman a friend or is she a loved one? Someone you love," she explained.

Bo lowered his eyes and crumpled the bill in his pocket.

"How about a nice heart?" the woman suggested.

He forced himself to look up. "Nice heart?"

"A heart-shaped box. Very popular with the ladies. This one, for instance. It comes in red or pink, with a matching satin bow. Does your lady friend prefer dark or sweet?"

"Excuse?"

"Dark chocolate or sweet chocolate?"

"I wish all chocolate," Bo told her.

"A mixed assortment, then. Fine. An excellent choice. Do you like this size, the one-pound? It's fourteen ninety-five, plus tax."

"No," Bo told her.

"Perhaps you would prefer something smaller," she said, moving to another section. "We have this lovely half-pound assortment for nine ninety-five or, for even less—"

"Not smaller," he said.

"Sir?"

"Loved one," he explained, spreading his arms. "Big."

"Oh," she said. "I see. Well, the largest heart we have is over here. Satin box and bow, lace trim, five pounds of assorted chocolates, nut clusters and fancy chews."

"How much price?" Bo asked, staring at the vaguely familiar pink shape.

"Forty-seven ninety-five," she said, "plus tax. It comes to a little over fifty-three dollars."

"You make me change?" Bo asked, pushing the crumpled bill across the counter.

She took the bill and went to the register. Bo stood there admiring the huge inverted heart, thinking of Tiffany's rear and wondering if he was losing his mind. As he breathed in the thick, heady chocolate air he imagined himself straddling her in bed, one hand reaching back and massaging the moist bird's nest between her thighs while the other was gently delivering one chocolate after another into her open waiting mouth.

PART FOUR

CHAPTER THIRTY-EIGHT

With Mee Yang clinging to his arm, Johnson followed Ransom through a wobbly metal tube connecting the 747 to the terminal, then followed him down a long blank corridor into a vast fluorescent room filled with people clustered around what looked like a fleet of miniature flying saucers, but were, he soon realized, some sort of luggage dispensers.

Johnson didn't feel right. The suit was pinching him everywhere. The hard shoes were making him unsteady on his feet. Mee Yang was gripping his arm like a kitten afraid of falling. Shrunken inside the oversized leather jacket Ransom had bought for her in Bangkok, she winced each time an announcement blared from the loudspeakers. Johnson was afraid that if anyone asked her a question she would collapse. Since leaving Cambodia, her English had gone to pot. On the long flight over the Pacific she had kept asking what would happen if they became separated: where could she go, what if her papers didn't work, would the American Khmer

Rouge beat her, rape her, shoot her? Nervous himself, Johnson had not been able to calm her.

Only Ransom seemed at ease in this alien place. His eyes were different here, more alert. Their piercing blue was more prominent now because of the full beard. He stood with his hands in his pockets, casually rocking back and forth on his heels. With a forged passport in his pocket and thirty fresh stitches in his arm, Ransom was amusing himself by openly staring at every attractive woman in his vicinity.

Mee Yang's suitcase appeared. Johnson reached for it, only to have her push him away and struggle with it herself.

"Kids," a short bald man next to Johnson commiserated.

Johnson smiled nervously and looked away, patting his pocket for the passports. He glanced around. All these people seemed so sure of themselves. He felt hopelessly out of synch, as if he was attempting to join a mysterious new dance that everyone else had already mastered. Everything itched, even his skin. It had been a long time since he'd been so aware of being colored.

He was having trouble holding on to his new sense of time. Just when he thought he was getting the hang of it, it would slip away from him. Past incidents kept intruding, making him lose track of where he was. He glanced over at Mee Yang. At their final dinner at the compound, Ransom had made them stand and hold hands while he—acting, he said, in the capacity of ship's captain—solemnly pronounced them man and wife. He'd then presented them with matching gold rings and U.S. passports in the names of Zachary P. and Mee Yang Johnson. When, at Ransom's urging, Johnson had kissed her, she had surprised them both by starting to cry. How long ago had that been? A week? Last year? He couldn't tell. Slow down, he told himself. Concentrate. Try. He struggled with it and decided that his marriage had been two days ago and half a world away. He allowed himself a deep breath.

They fell in behind Ransom on one of the inspection lines. Mee Yang's bag had built-in casters, so she was able to pull it along with one arm while holding on to Johnson with the other. After reminding her not to speak no matter what, Johnson silently quizzed himself on the particulars on their passports.

The line moved disconcertingly fast. Suddenly it was Ransom's turn. The customs inspector, a black man about Johnson's age, with a blue shirt, gold badge and colorful insignia, glanced at Ransom's papers, stifled a yawn and waved him through. Johnson stepped up, held his breath and handed over the white declaration forms and green passports, then leaned over and centered their luggage on the conveyor. He stared straight ahead, trying to ignore Mee Yang's nails digging into his arm. He felt all his muscles seizing up. The inspector flipped each passport open with one hand while picking at a tooth with the other. Suddenly he twisted his head away, handed the passports back and waved them through, turning his full attention to the finger in his mouth, which had apparently located something.

Ransom led the way outside and had them wait by the curb while he went for a car. It was nighttime. The air was heavy and warm. Johnson, bewildered by all the noise, the dense traffic, the bright lights, was finding it impossible to believe that it had been that easy, that he was home, that Mee Yang was really here with him. His eyes burning, he breathed in the strange-smelling air and squeezed Mee Yang's hand. All these people, all these lights, all this activity. The sidewalk seemed to sparkle. The terminal behind them had the futuristic curves of a spaceship, which added to his sense that they had passed through to another dimension. Everything inside him was fluttering. He discovered himself bouncing up and down on his toes, unable to contain his excitement. He kept telling himself that he was home. Home! He wished he had a handful of quarters so he could run to a phone and call his mother, tell her he was here, tell her about Mee Yang and—

"Get in," Ransom said, giving him a friendly push toward an open limousine door.

The car was huge. Johnson looked around anxiously before realizing that Mee Yang was already inside. He got in, slid over and, noting the dark window separating them from the driver, wrapped his arms around her. She nestled against him and he inhaled the reassuring perfume of her hair. Ransom climbed in. The door closed. As the car pulled out into traffic Ransom turned to Johnson and extended his hand.

"Welcome home, Doc," he said softly.

"We are really Merica?" Mee Yang asked timidly.

"Yes," Ransom smiled. "We are Los Angeles," he teased. "We are Hollywood. Mee Yang now American girl."

She asked Ransom something in muffled Khmer and he laughed. Johnson heard his name.

"She wants to know if she's still Mrs. Johnson," Ransom explained.

"Oh, wow. Tell her—"

"No, no," Ransom said, "you tell her." He leaned back, folded his arms and closed his eyes.

Everett G. Ransom had other things on his mind. He was feeling very strange. Unwelcome twenty-year-old memories were rushing in, tumbling into one another: the smells of chicken feathers and rancid cooking oil, the buzz of giant stinging flies, the iridescence of dried fish scales on his arms, the dead pasty look of fingers wrinkled from dishwater, the slack sunburned skin of his buddies as they stumbled in from the fields, the ugly green and red of Cambodian uniforms, cheap boots, dull suspicious eyes, sweat-stained rifle stocks . . . His arms being wrenched back, the crack of wood against bone, the taste of blood in his mouth. The dizziness. The fear. The constant, sickening fear . . .

The camp was run by Major Cao, a small, acne-scarred sadist who liked to rest his hand on the American forty-five he carried in a holster on his belt. Whenever any of the prisoners did something wrong, Cao lined them up and punished them all. He had a particular fondness for bamboo canes. All prisoners had to learn to count in Khmer so they could call out the strokes while they watched each other being beaten.

Ransom was the youngest prisoner. Cao put him to work in the kitchen. Day after day, while the other Americans tilled the fields, Ransom swept floors, washed pots, cleaned fish, plucked chickens, cadged food and stayed strong. His health became a source of communal pride, something the other prisoners drew upon to keep themselves going. Months passed, then a year. Slowly and unobtrusively, Ransom learned his captors' language and how to prepare their favorite foods. They began to take less notice of him. Most nights, despite the required body search, he managed to return to barracks with food hidden in his mouth. Crouched in the darkness, surrounded by outstretched hands, he would pull morsels from his cheeks and dole them out like a mother bird to her famished chicks.

He served the Cambodians and listened to their talk, never showing that he understood. Time passed. Months. A year. More months. No new prisoners arrived. The number of Americans dwindled from eleven to ten, then eight, then six. All the others had been pilots, officers. Ransom had been a supply sergeant. He bided his time, passing up numerous opportunities for escape because of what his disappearance would cost those he left behind. On the day he overheard that the war had ended he secretly approached Lieutenant Dai and asked when the prisoners would be going home. Dai said nothing, but the way he averted his eyes suggested the unimaginable: that they might never be going home.

When Ransom shared this with the other Americans that night they refused to believe him. He looked around, saw how fragile they all were and, after listening to their arguments, agreed that he must have misunderstood. They all laughed and forgave him.

But the next morning, when the commanding officer began bemoaning the camp's lack of ammunition, Ransom stepped up and bet his life.

"What does the honorable major require?" he asked in clear Khmer. "Perhaps I can be of service."

The startled officer studied Ransom through narrowed eyes, then listed his needs and asked sarcastically how much of it Ransom could provide.

"All of it," Ransom said with a deep bow.

The officer rose so quickly he toppled his chair. All conversation stopped. Ransom froze, his eyes fixed on the slatted wooden floor. He held his breath, listening for the opening of a snap, the rasp of steel against leather. He realized that he was no longer afraid to die.

They gave him a clean shirt and a pair of old shoes. The major promised increased prisoner rations if he succeeded, and severe punishment if he failed. Lieutenant Dai was given the jeep, issued a sidearm and ordered to take Ransom to retrieve the supplies. Based on Ransom's map coordinates, they were given two days for the mission. After that, the major warned, he would begin executing one prisoner per day.

The roads were terrible and the rain unrelenting. Ransom drove carefully. It took six hours to reach the spot. Once there, he sighted along the appropriate trees and unearthed the supplies exactly where he had helped bury them nearly two years before. Five separate caches had been buried in the area, but Ransom revealed only the smallest. He had no doubt the others were still there; everyone else on the detail had died in the helicopter crash.

The rain and mud made the task of excavating the plastic-wrapped crates exhausting. Ransom had forgotten how heavy ammunition was. The only good thing about the rain was that it kept the mosquitoes away.

The sun was a sinking red disk by the time they finished. His back and shoulders aching, Ransom dropped wearily to the ground. Dai reached over and offered a brown Chinese cigarette. It sputtered in the rain and tasted like sewage, but Ransom inhaled deeply. He was tired. The cool mud felt good. He fell asleep.

Awakened by something slithering across his face, Ransom clambered to his feet, brushing madly at himself. The sun was shooting harsh needles of light through the foliage. The rain had stopped. His skin was alive with insect bites. His hair was caked with mud. He turned and saw Dai sprawled across the jeep's front seat, sound asleep. His rifle was lying across some boxes in the back.

Ransom tiptoed over, picked up the weapon and backed across the clearing. He dropped to one knee and took careful aim at one of the Cambodian's fluttering eyes. As his index finger tickled the trigger he felt himself fill with a bristly satisfaction. He visualized the bullet bursting eye tissue soft as egg white, tearing through pink gelid brain and crashing through the back of the skull.

The temptation to squeeze the trigger was exquisite, but Ransom reminded himself that it would mean the death of all his friends. He held his aim a moment longer, then released his breath and lowered the weapon. After replacing it in the jeep, he was overcome by hunger. He went out searching for food.

The jungle was green and fresh and wet, thick with sweet smells. There were sounds of life everywhere. Ransom felt reborn. He picked mangoes.

"Sit," the officer told him when he returned, "I have something to tell you."

Ransom arranged the fruit on a leaf platter on the ground between them and sat on the exposed root of a nearby tree. The hole they'd dug looked like the crater from a mortar round. The bottom had filled with water and a huge, black, pincer-headed beetle was swimming awkwardly in it, struggling halfheartedly to get out.

"You could have killed me," Dai observed, nodding toward the rifle.

"The war is over," Ransom said. "You are not my enemy." He smiled. "Besides, if we do not return, Major Cao will kill my friends."

The officer leaned forward, selected a mango, took out his knife and began turning the fruit, deciding where to make the first incision. Without looking up, he said: "Your friends are already dead."

Time skipped a beat. Ransom felt amputated. Numb. Why was Dai saying this?

With practiced motions, Dai began peeling the fruit's thick skin. "The major planned to kill them when they returned from the fields yesterday," he explained.

"But why?" Ransom asked.

Dai shrugged.

Ransom asked how they were killed.

Dai raised a hand and made a crude swinging motion. "Ammunition is precious," he explained.

"But the war is over," Ransom cried. "Why kill them now, when the war is over?"

"I do not know," Dai replied, using his thumb to slide a thick slice of fruit from the knife to his mouth.

Life seeped back into Ransom's limbs. He glanced at the rifle and gauged his odds of getting to it as slim to none. Then he remembered the sidearm.

"You are not eating," Dai observed.

Ransom glanced down at the mangoes. Bile was churning in his empty stomach. He felt nauseous.

"My orders," Dai said, "are to collect the American supplies, if they exist, and then to shoot you. Here," he said, tapping the back of his head.

Ransom felt the hairs on his neck stand up. The shafts of sunlight now seemed barbed and cruel. Ten minutes ago he'd had the rifle in his hands. What a stupid bastard he was; he'd even dug up the ammunition for them. All the others dead. Only a fool would have believed anything that frog-faced son of a bitching major said: increased rations . . .

He looked over at Dai. The only thing to do was to make a run at him, wrestle him for the rifle. Shoot him, take the jeep and head for the border. Ransom slid his feet along the ground. He could reach Dai in two steps. If he didn't make it he would be dead, which would be okay too . . .

Dai was watching him. "I will not kill you," he said.

Ransom looked at him.

"I will take the supplies back to camp," Dai said. "Major Cao will be very happy."

"And me?" Ransom asked.

"I shot you," Dai said, making a child's motion with his hand. "Boosh, boosh. You are dead." He smiled, showing the wide gap between his front teeth.

"Colonel," Johnson said, shaking him gently, "I think we're here. Is this the hotel?"

The moment the bellboy left, Mee Yang grabbed the remote and flipped around until she found MTV. Instantly connecting to the hyperkinetic video, she began twirling around like a little girl. After a few spins she grabbed Johnson about the waist and toppled him over onto the bed. He fell back laughing at her exuberance, but before he could hug her she had popped up and started untying his shoes.

"What are you doing?" he asked, lifting his head.

"Sometime you big-time stupid," she replied, tossing the second shoe and grabbing his belt.

"Wait a minute," he objected, grasping her wrist and using it to pull himself into a sitting position.

"Wassamatta?" she asked. "You fraida girls?"

"You're still weak," he told her.

"Better worry by you," she responded, thumping his chest and sending him back down on his back.

She was at his belt again. "I need a shower," he insisted.

"Take too long."

"We can shower together."

She stopped and peered at him. "Merican girls do that?"

"Of course. Yes."

"Then we make baby?"

"Sure."

"Okay then," patting his stomach. "Good video," she said, directing his attention to the screen.

He looked at it, but it was going too fast for him. It made him feel old. "You happy?" he asked her.

"Shoe. Mee Yang real Merican girl. Happy like hell."

CHAPTER THIRTY-NINE

The speed limit dropped from fifty-five to forty. Fink tapped the brake to release the cruise control. His leg felt strange without the holster and his upper lip itched from the false mustache. He looked around. Standing out starkly against the night sky, the outlines of Atlantic City's hotel-casinos loomed up before him like giant gravestones in some space-age cemetery.

The Taj Mahal garage was jammed and he had to guide the rental car up six twisty, claustrophobic levels before finding an empty space. Overcoming his misgivings, he put on the clear glasses, checked himself in the mirror, hooked the beeper to his belt, patted his wallet, got out, locked the car, patted his wallet again and walked to the elevator.

He stepped out into a long wide carpeted corridor that had the look and feel of an airport terminal. A few hundred yards along, it opened into a high, mirror-lined rotunda dominated by an arrangement of colossal chandeliers. Fink was reminded of Pirra Mids, a watermelon-breasted topless dancer he'd had a thing with, who always ended her act by making her tassels rotate in opposite directions.

Hunching his shoulders, Fink stepped onto the down escalator. Pirra was good people. When she'd died freebasing tainted coke a few years back they'd called Fink in to ID the body. He watched the chandeliers recede. A lot of people he liked were dead.

The escalator deposited him on the casino level. The unique sound of massed slot machines came at him like a complex, metallic wind.

The woman in the poker kiosk asked him what stakes he wanted.

"Fifteen-thirty stud," he said, looking past her and down into the vast sunken room, table after oval table crowded with players, everywhere the clinking of chips.

"Name?" the woman asked, surprising Fink.

"Barton," he replied, shifting his weight.

"Initial?"

"D."

She entered it on a list. "Okay, Mr. Barton, I'm sure we'll have a chair opening up in just a few minutes. Feel free to stroll. We'll page you."

He thanked her and, anxious to get started, turned and went over to a nearby blackjack table whose unobtrusive chrome plaque indicated a hundred-dollar-minimum bet. When he climbed onto one of the middle stools none of the other players even glanced up from their cards. Joining them made Fink feel slightly soiled, like stepping into a dirty tub. His mustache itched.

The dealer turned up a hole card which gave her fifteen, dealt herself a picture, grasped a tall stack of chips and proceeded with a single smooth arc of her arm to pay everyone at the table but Fink. A rumpled-looking old man in the first seat yawned as he pulled in his winnings and added them to his pile of black and white hundred dollar chips.

Fink reached into his pocket, eased two bills from his wallet and laid them on the table. The dealer glanced over, reached across and took the bills with one hand while smoothly doling out four stacks of five chips each with the other.

"Two thousand," she said mechanically, before sliding the bills over a slot in the table and tamping them down with the plastic tool. "Bets," she said, tapping her fingers on the green baize.

Fink put out one chip. The dealer slid cards from the long plastic shoe, dealing Fink first a jack and then a ten. She dealt herself an eight. Beginner's luck, he told himself. When the dealer reached him, Fink moved his hand laterally over his cards. Her eyes shifted to the next hand.

The dealer turned up an eighteen. Fink's twenty earned him a chip. He pulled it back and kept his bet at one.

He was four hundred dollars ahead when he heard the page for "Mr. D. Barton, fifteen-thirty stud."

After playing out the hand, which he won, Fink slid from the stool. He wanted to tip the dealer, but all he had was hundred dollar chips, and he feared a tip that large might be remembered. So he said a quick "Thanks" and took off.

"I need to cash some chips first," he told the poker woman.

"You can use them here," she assured him.

"Superstitious," he explained.

She smiled knowingly and promised to hold his seat.

The cashier took the chips Fink pushed beneath the steel bars, stacked them on the marble counter, announced the total, and smoothly counted out twenty-five hundred dollar bills. Fink folded the bills, stuffed them into an inside jacket pocket and walked off feeling a little giddy. In the men's room, he locked a stall door and set his beeper to go off in twenty minutes. Heading back to the poker room he reminded himself that this was only the first trip, that he'd now passed two of El Gordo's stash of thousand dollar bills, but there were still three more in his wallet and one hundred forty-five more at home. Still, the wad of hundreds in his pocket felt like success.

A man wearing a leather-trimmed blue suit and carrying a walkie-talkie escorted Fink to his seat at the poker table. There were seven other players, plus the dealer. As Fink sat he casually placed three of El Gordo's bills on the table. With practiced motions, the dealer swept them up, spread them out, announced the total, pushed over the chips, stuffed the bills into the slot and began shuffling the deck.

For the first time since he'd arrived, Fink allowed himself a good look around. He'd read about "supermarket gambling," but he'd never understood the term until now. It was true; the staff here looked as bland as Grand Union workers. Even the cocktail waitresses, despite their abbreviated outfits, looked like middle-aged checkout clerks. Still, he reminded himself, he wasn't here to have fun. Officially, he wasn't here at all.

When he'd opened the slimy package he'd discovered one hundred fifty used thousand dollar bills. Once he'd convinced himself they were genuine, he'd had to figure out how best to convert them into normal denominations. He couldn't very well use them to pay for his groceries, and even in a bank, bills featuring President Cleveland were likely to raise eyebrows. Fink knew people who laundered cash, but involving others was the kiss of death. Most arrests—his and everyone else's—came from tips. If no one knew, no one could tell.

Atlantic City presented the perfect solution. Most guys on the force gambled, here in AC and elsewhere: sports pools, OTB, numbers, Lotto. And even if someone recognized him here, mustache and all, he could claim he was on the job.

The dealer tapped the table and everyone threw in a dollar ante. Fink's fellow players were five men and two overweight, overjewelried, over-made-up middle-aged women. Four of the men were Fink's age or older. The fifth was a kid in his twenties with curly red hair, freckles and a plaid bow tie who reminded Fink of Howdy Doody, a TV puppet he'd hated. Freckles kept playing with the huge, castle-like arrangement of chips in front of him.

The game was seven-card stud. Everyone was dealt two cards down and then one card up. Fink got a deuce up, which made him smile. His plan was to drop out of every hand as quickly as possible. A deuce was the lousiest card in the deck.

"Deuce bets," the dealer announced.

"What?" Fink asked.

"First round, low hand bets," the dealer explained.

Fink tossed in ten dollars, the minimum bet. Responding in order, three people called the bet, two folded. When it was the kid's turn he raised fifteen. He was showing an ace. The woman between the kid and Fink called the twenty-five-dollar bet. She was showing a queen. Fink, trying to make his departure look considered, covered his hole cards with one hand, bent up an edge with the other and peeked. Two more deuces. Three cards, three deuces. Fink called. The kid even grinned like Howdy Doody.

There were five players left in the hand, four more cards to go, and more than a hundred dollars already in the pot. The dealer burned the top card and dealt out a round of up cards, flipping the kid another ace, the woman a pair of queens, and Fink another deuce. Fink interpreted his four deuces as a sign that God approved of what he was doing.

"Aces bet," the dealer announced.

The kid bet thirty. The queens folded. Fink made like he was wavering, shook his head a few times, then called. The kid regarded Fink's pair of deuces with amused disdain.

While Fink rubbed his ankles together, two other players called, one showing two medium hearts, the other two high clubs. Fink figured they each had four to a flush.

On the next card one of the men hit a third heart and raised the kid's thirty to sixty. The kid, now showing aces and a ten, fingered his bow tie, looked down his nose at the three hearts and made it ninety. Fink, showing two deuces and a ten, made a show of hesitating, deliberating, agonizing, before calling. The kid winked at him. It was obvious that he considered Fink an absolute schmuck. The man with the clubs folded.

Three players: the flush, Howdy Doody and Fink. On the next card, the flush was dealt the ace of spades. Fink looked down to hide his excitement; now the most Howdy could have was a full house. Fink was going to beat the little bastard.

The cards, Fink warned himself, concentrate on the cards. All right. There was one more card to go. It was theoretically possible that the other guy could get four of a kind, but it seemed clear to Fink that he'd been betting the hearts. More important, without a pair showing he couldn't possibly have four of a kind yet, no matter what he had in the hole. So when the kid bet thirty Fink stepped up and made it sixty. The man with the hearts gave a look of despair; his flush wasn't going to be good enough. He examined his cards one last time and then threw them in. The kid looked lovingly at his aces and tens, grinned at Fink and raised to ninety. Fink brought his hand to his mouth to hide his smirk, felt the mustache and frightened himself. He tried to turn it into a throat-clearing and raised to one twenty. The kid called, studying Fink's up cards: a pair of twos, a ten and a five.

The dealer gave each of them a final down card. Fink left his conspicuously untouched. The kid picked up his three hole cards, squared them up and then slowly squeezed them apart. He grinned and bet thirty. Fink made it sixty, the kid ninety, Fink one twenty.

"Call," the kid said, casually tossing in chips. "Let's see you beat aces full."

"Two little pair," Fink told him, turning up his hole cards. "Both twos."

The dealer pushed the wonderfully ungainly mound of chips toward Fink. He'd won well over five hundred dollars on the hand. He tossed the dealer a red five dollar chip.

On each of the next three hands Fink folded on the first bet. When his beeper went off, he picked up his chips and carried them to the cashier's window. He got back to his car with six thousand two hundred dollars, all in hundreds. He cashed one of them to pay his two dollar state parking fee. It was hard to contain his euphoria: All together, he had laundered five thousand, won twelve hundred and been in the hotel less than an hour.

During the long drive back to the city Fink kept the cruise control at sixty-four and the radio tuned to an oldies station, at one point breaking into song to accompany Diana Ross and the Supremes' thumping sixties hit "Baby Love."

He was halfway through the Holland Tunnel when a familiar glare in his rearview mirror alerted him to the dark Chevrolet three cars back. One of its headlights must have been slightly out of whack. The realization that he'd seen that same glare a few times on the Jersey Turnpike registered as a deep rippling chill.

Fink clicked off the radio. Instinctively he reached down and felt for his gun. But it was back in his apartment, in the top dresser drawer, under the socks.

The grimy yellow tile on the tunnel walls slid by like the scales of a huge snake. Fink stole frequent glances in the mirror, trying to get a good look at his tail. No use. Cars.

Shadows. Glare. All he could tell for sure was that it was one man, small.

Fink exited the tunnel, eased over into an uptown lane and stopped at the red light. It was much darker out here. He lost sight of the Chevy, but sensed it lurking somewhere behind him. The light changed and he veered left and headed for the West Side Highway. Watching the rearview mirror, he spotted the Chevy a cautious half block back, far enough to allow Fink to make a sharp right into the local lane of the highway, pull over to the curb, kill his lights, and wait for the son of a bitch to come by.

It didn't take long. The Chevy slowed for only a moment as it came abreast, then accelerated past him. Fink pulled out and gunned it. He traveled a wild half block before realizing that his lights weren't on. By the time he located the proper knob, the Chevy had disappeared.

Fink squealed into the first side street, saw nothing, pulled over and slammed his fist against the wheel. All he'd seen was a New York plate with a Z, which identified it as a rental. The guy had looked Asian, but that might have been the light.

As Fink sat there, paranoia began entwining him like lengths of gauze. His first thought was internal affairs, Captain Reynolds' old stomping ground. The guy tailing him was a pro, but what had he seen? Had he followed Fink into the Taj Mahal garage and seen his disguise? Had he trailed him into the casino and seen him passing El Gordo's bills? For a moment Fink was consumed by the wildly irrational idea that it was the kid with the aces, and he saw the smirking puppet face and felt a surge of pure animal hatred. The fury-induced shaking subsided. He rolled down the window, peeled off the mustache and breathed in chunks of thick, fume-laden New York air. He envisioned himself turning in his gun and shield, getting the notice of suspension, sitting through the departmental hearing, watching twenty-four years fly out the fucking window. Son of a bitch.

Barton had been there with El Gordo. Could Barton have suspected something when Fink bugged out early? Said something to Reynolds? Fink didn't want to believe it was Barton. You don't do something like that to a fellow cop. Also, Barton had been straight with him about Reynolds from day one. And he'd given Barton the El Gordo bust, written him up for a commendation. Besides, what would be in it for Barton? No, it wasn't Barton, couldn't be Barton. Fink felt ashamed for even suspecting Barton.

El Gordo, that mountain of slime. Could El Gordo have tried to make a deal with the DA, offered to deliver a dirty cop in exchange for a plea? A detective lieutenant was a pretty good-sized fish. Fink reached into his pocket and squeezed the thick wad of hundreds. No, he didn't think it was El Gordo either. He'd been out cold the whole time Fink had been in the bathroom. Unless one of the women told him, the one with the screaming baby. Not likely.

No, the one he couldn't get past was Reynolds. All those years with internal affairs. And the bastard was taking green from Parker Global, Fink was sure of it.

Which raised another possibility: Parker Global and that shiny-headed bastard Schaeffer. They were smart enough and rich enough not to trust anyone. In which case, it suddenly occurred to Fink, they should be following Barton too. Barton was sharp, he was young, his reflexes were better; he'd probably pick up a tail faster than Fink had.

He had to talk to Barton. Tonight, this morning, whatever it was. The digital on the dash said four-ten. Jesus, he had a lot to do: return this goddamn car and call Marissa and talk to Barton and stow this cash. He'd better get home and see if anyone had tossed the place. He rubbed his jacket. The clump of hundreds felt like a tumor. The four deuces couldn't help him now.

Five hours: It had taken him five hours to pick up a tail. He was getting old. And sloppy. Goddamn it. He hit the gas.

Everything in the apartment was exactly where he'd left it. He retrieved his gun and hid the money. The answering machine was pulsing silent red accusations. He pressed the button: Marissa, Barton, his daughter, Marissa.

He called Marissa. She sounded worried. He checked in with the precinct and called Barton, then went inside and rinsed his face. His neck felt like thick dry rope.

"Where the hell have you been?" Marissa demanded the moment she pulled open the door.

Fink wasn't too tired to recognize fear masquerading as anger. Everybody was wired these days. "I'm sorry," he said. "Can I come in?"

She stepped back from the doorway. "I was worried about you," she said.

"Things are happening," he explained. "I've asked Barton to come over. We all need to talk."

Marissa walked over and turned off the big lamp. The city outside became a dense constellation of flickering stars. She looked both weary and sexy. As he started toward her, the phone rang. She answered, listened, covered the receiver.

"Are we expecting a Sergeant Palermo?"

Fink nodded.

"Please send him up," she said.

The sergeant arrived with a small aluminum suitcase, set up his gear and combed the suite, rhythmically waving what looked like a Geiger counter. After twenty minutes he'd removed six tiny microphones and two video cameras, one of which had been in the bedroom.

"State-of-the-art," he told Fink, displaying the microphones in his palm like a set of fancy buttons. "The cameras are sound-activated. I wish we could afford this kind of stuff."

"You got everything?" Fink asked, secretly relieved it was Parker Global and not IAU.

"Oh yeah," Palermo assured him, packing up.

Fink noticed that Palermo's bald spot was gone and wondered if the weird smell was that spray hair they hawked on late-night TV at fifty bucks a can.

"Log it all in," Fink told him. "Sorry to get you out at this hour."

"Overtime," Palermo smiled, handing Fink a form and standing there tenderly patting the back of his head while Fink signed.

"I didn't know," Marissa said after Palermo left, lighting one cigarette from another. Her hand shook. She was wearing silk pajama pants, a pink silk blouse and floppy red slippers. She was pale, drained.

"My mistake," Fink told her, dropping into a chair. His eyes felt heavy. "I'm getting careless."

"How could you have known?"

"Because I knew you were reporting to them," he told her, rubbing his eyes. "And I should have figured. I'm a cop."

She perched on a nearby chair, stared out the window. "Listen to me, Mel. I want—"

"It's okay," he assured her.

"Can I come sit on your lap?"

"Sure," he said, surprised. Maybe she had been more concerned about his disappearance than he'd realized.

She put her arms around him and nuzzled his neck. "You need a shave."

She smelled heavy, like perfume over perfume. He kissed her ear. Nobody was perfect.

The phone rang. She extricated herself, a little too quickly, Fink thought.

"Detective Barton and a lady," she said. "Should I order refreshments?"

"Sure. I'm going inside to brush my teeth."

"Who's the lady?"

"Rhonda Cohen. You probably know her. She was Frank's assistant."

At this hour, Barton's energy was disconcerting. Fink made the introductions and got him to sit down.

"You were Frank's assistant," Marissa said to Rhonda, shaking her hand warmly. "I hope you drink coffee."

"Tea."

Marissa went to the phone, Rhonda to the sofa.

"I had Palermo over here a little while ago," Fink told Barton. "He found video cameras and mikes. We'll send him over to sweep Ms. Cohen's place in the morning."

"Rhonda," she said. "Wait a minute. Are you telling me . . . ?"

"Nice people you work for," Barton said to her. "You say video?" he asked Fink, the idea sinking in.

"Somebody was tailing me tonight," Fink said.

"Who?" Barton asked.

"One guy, dark Chevy."

Barton looked at him.

"I rented a car," Fink explained. "Drove down to Atlantic City."

"Where?" Marissa exclaimed.

"Atlantic City. I had some business."

"I would have gone with you," Marissa said petulantly. "Did you gamble?"

"Yeah, I played a little poker."

"Well," she asked, "did you win?"

"Nobody wins," Fink replied.

CHAPTER FORTY

Johnson awoke with his knees drawn up, his shoulders hunched and his arms covering his face. Cautiously, he peeked out. Where was Mee Yang? He saw light under a closed door, heard sounds. She was in the bathroom. See? he told himself, and tried to laugh. Then he realized where he was, grabbed the phone, followed the instructions on the plastic card and dialed his mom's number in Detroit. Despite his urgings, there was no answer.

Unable to relax, he went inside, found the remote, turned on the TV and kept switching channels until he found CNN. A girl at a desk was talking about him again. Johnson watched open-mouthed as a photo of him nineteen and grinning in his army uniform was gradually transformed into a picture of a frowning middle-aged man in a business suit. It was magic, all right, but a strange kind of magic: The finished picture looked almost nothing like he did now. According to the girl on TV, this "computer-enhanced" photo was being distributed everywhere. Which, Johnson realized, reduced the chances of anybody recognizing him pretty much to zero.

"Colonel," he said the moment Ransom arrived, "I can't get my mom on the phone."

"Let me try," Ransom offered, but he had no better luck. It was three hours later in Detroit, he explained; she was probably already up and out. "Remember, Doc, she didn't know when you were coming."

Johnson nodded. The colonel was right; he had forgotten about that time business again. Still . . .

There was a knock at the door. Breakfast. The smell of morning food transported Johnson back in time to a sun-filled kitchen and a big glass of warm chocolate milk. Mama was standing by the sink making his lunch, her strong hands moving fast and graceful and in time with the song she was singing to herself. She had on that red and yellow apron with the—

"Listen to me," Ransom said, shaking Johnson's knee.

"What? Oh, hi, Colonel."

"You're not listening, Doc."

Johnson's eyes focused. "Sorry," he said, admonishing himself to listen to the colonel.

Mee Yang came out of the bedroom brushing her hair. She looked scrubbed and fresh. Seeing her made Johnson feel warm inside.

Bouncing over to the cart, she snatched a croissant and took a bite. "Colonel cook better," she announced, casually discarding it.

"You like waking up in America," Ransom observed.

"Merica fine. Doc snore." She rubbed Johnson's hair roughly. He looked up at her gratefully. "Eat firse," she said.

"Doc," Ransom said, "here's an envelope with your plane tickets and some cash. I've arranged for a car to the airport."

"Where are we going?" Johnson asked.

"I'm sending you and the princess to a friend of mine."

"Sending us? You mean you're not coming?"

"Not right now. I've got a few things to do first, business things."

"But we could help you."

"Not unless you speak Russian."

"But—"

"Look, Doc, those guys who attacked the compound were after *me*. We took care of them, but the people who sent them are still after me. I stay alive by keeping a step ahead of everybody." He squeezed Johnson's shoulder. "Give me a little space, Doc," he said gently. "I'm looking out for all of us."

For one awful moment Johnson's mind slipped and he was bound with rough ropes, lying helplessly on his side, staring out through bars. He shook free of it, but the prospect of being separated from the colonel frightened him. He did not understand why he had to keep flying, why he had to go to hearings, appear in front of all those people, talk into a microphone. He had nothing to say. He was bad with words. He just wanted to see Mama.

"I want you to meet my mom," he said to Ransom, trying to construct an argument against being separated.

"I already met your mom, remember?"

"Oh," Johnson replied, feeling foolish. "I forget things. I don't know why."

"Your flight is a little after ten," Ransom said. "You'll have to leave here about nine. They'll call you from downstairs when the car arrives. Everything is paid for. Put that money in a safe place, Doc. If you need more my friend will give it to you. Here's some for you, princess."

"Tonks," she said, reaching for the envelope.

Ransom held it an extra moment. "Mee Yang," he told her, "I'm counting on you to take care of this guy."

"Worry better by you," she said, tucking the envelope into a front pocket of her jeans.

Johnson reached up and began stroking her hair, studying individual silken strands, fascinated at how lovely each one was, how he could make hair slide over his finger, weightless and silent and dark as a moonless night.

"Mee Yang?" Ransom said.

"I take good care," she assured him. "Worry by you."

CHAPTER FORTY-ONE

Bo plunged his hands into his jacket pockets, hunched his shoulders and hurried westward, threading his way through the endless stream of people. The streets were dirty. The sky was overcast. The cold air smelled of exhaust fumes and bad food.

Once inside the bus terminal, he took the escalator up to the second floor, hurried to the designated corner and waited among a group busily making furtive pencil marks on printed red forms. The sign above the nearby booth said "Lottery." A few feet away a black derelict lay asleep on the floor, covered by torn pieces of cardboard that read "Sony."

Bo was considering buying a container of coffee to warm himself when his contact appeared.

"Walk with me," the man murmured in Vietnamese and led Bo into a crowded take-out restaurant on the lower level. Bo kept glancing back to make sure no one was following them.

"Have some soup," the man suggested, getting on a line.

"I recommend the tomato rice. Avoid the chicken: The noodles are soggy and tasteless."

"Thank you," Bo replied, studying the blackboard behind the counter, "but I think I will have the garden vegetable and a croissant."

"Take a scone," the man advised. "The croissants are an abomination."

They carried their trays around a crowded enclosure until they secured a vacant table and two molded plastic chairs. Bo's scone was thick and chewy. His soup was good but should have been hotter.

"You look well," the man said. "The injury was to your eye?"

"Yes. But as you see, it is nearly healed. My vision is unimpaired."

"Good." He drew in his chair to allow a large black woman to squeeze past. "I do not have much time," he said, "so please listen carefully." He dropped his voice. "As you know, things at home are bad. No one can help us. The Russians are bankrupt. East Germany has ceased to exist. Cuba is struggling to survive. The Chinese offer us aid, but to accept it would be to swallow poison. Rapprochement with the Americans has become imperative. Do you understand?"

"Yes, but—"

"Listen, please. For years now, our government has been secretly working to establish diplomatic and commercial ties with the United States. An agreement is quite near. When implemented, this arrangement will provide much for our people: more food, more medicine, better schools, better housing. We wish you to understand this."

"Why?"

The man glanced around cautiously. All the nearby tables were occupied. There were roaming beggars. It was noisy.

He leaned closer. "Do you follow the news?"

"At night I watch television," Bo told him.

"Have you heard about this American Corporal Johnson?"

"Yes." Who had not seen the ridiculous yellow ribbons? Seen the outrageous newspaper headlines and stupid magazine covers? Heard the idiotic theories?

"Then you should understand this," the controller said. "A normalization of relations between our two nations is possible because the Americans have chosen to forget their dishonorable war of aggression against our people. But now, with these crucial negotiations nearly concluded, the appearance of this missing soldier threatens to upset everything. If nothing is done, the American people will again be turned against us, the negotiations will fail and our people's suffering will continue."

"What has this to do with me?" Bo asked.

The man looked at him. His lips tightened.

"Oh," Bo said. "I see."

"We will provide you with his location."

"All right, but arranging this will take time."

"There is no time," the man said, stirring rice grains about his bowl.

"He will be heavily guarded," Bo pointed out.

The man stared down into the dregs of his soup. "Four days from today congressional hearings are scheduled to begin on national television. Corporal Johnson must not testify."

Bo brushed away the crumbs of his scone. He explained that four days would not give him enough time to plan a proper escape.

"Your last escape was miraculous," the man reminded him. "Your ancestors protect you well."

"I pray my good fortune will continue," Bo agreed. "But—"

The man looked up. Their eyes met. Bo's stomach went hollow. He thought of Tiffany.

"Everything will be done to insure the success of your mission," the man said, "but your orders have not changed; you cannot allow yourself to be captured. You will be provided with improved capsules. If necessary, you merely bite down hard and—"

"I have received instructions," Bo assured him.

"Here is a key to a locker upstairs. Do not approach it until instructed to do so. From now on you must call in every eight hours, without fail."

"All right."

"Do you require any money?"

"No."

"Time is critical. Should we need to contact you, we must know where—"

"Hey there, brothers!" A grizzled vagrant in worn jeans and a tattered military shirt stumbled over to their table. He reeked of urine and cheap wine.

"Please leave us," Bo's controller asked him politely.

"C'mon, li'l buddy," the drunk said to Bo, thrusting out a hand covered with a stained fingerless glove, "how 'bout helpin' out a Vietnam vet?"

Calmly but firmly, Bo advised him to go away.

The man turned belligerent, pulling back his hand and drawing himself up: "Says who, gook?"

"Go away now," Bo told him evenly.

"Who the fuck you think you are?" the drunk demanded, raising his voice and fixing Bo with watery, red-rimmed eyes. "Little pissant slant," he cried, taking an awkward swipe at the air above Bo's head. "I used to fuck your sister in the ass."

Bo avoided making eye contact. He had no sister. This

stupid American was not worth killing. Bo could sense people turning to stare at them.

"Here, my friend," Bo's controller called, waving a dollar bill at the man. "Now please leave us."

The derelict slapped the bill to the floor, nearly losing his balance. "Fuckin' slopes," he bellowed. His head swung back to Bo. "Look a'chew," he challenged, staggering closer and wiping spittle from his mouth with the back of a crusty glove. "I just might be your father!"

Bo stared up calmly into the burning, hate-filled eyes and kicked the man's ankle very hard. The man howled and fell, toppling a table and pulling an elderly woman down with him. She became hysterical. All around them people jumped noisily to their feet.

The vagrant rolled over and lunged, but Bo darted out of reach. The old woman scrambled free and people came and helped her up. Bo's controller was signaling urgently that they should go when two uniformed policemen appeared. One grasped the drunk's shirt, restraining him, while the other confronted Bo and his companion.

"What happened here?" the policeman asked Bo.

"This man demanded money," the controller said, pointing to the drunk, "and then tried to attack us."

"Fuckin' gooks," the drunk roared, struggling against the other policeman's grasp. "Broke my goddamn leg."

"Did you hit him?" the first cop asked Bo.

"Man crazy," Bo replied. "Fall down his own self."

The drunk was sitting on the floor hugging his knee, rocking back and forth, moaning.

"You have some ID?" the policeman asked Bo.

"Please, officer," the controller said, "we do nothing wrong. We are having quiet meal and—"

"Let's see some ID," the policeman said to Bo, holding out his hand. The crowd inched closer.

Bo reached into his pocket, uncertain what to do. He had no documents with him. He looked to his controller, who communicated nothing but fear. Still fumbling, Bo glanced around and selected an escape route. The policemen would not fire their weapons in such a crowded place. Bo would get away unharmed. Still, all these people had seen him. What if—

"Officer."

The policeman turned to a well-dressed man in his sixties and demanded, "What's your story?"

"These two gentlemen were having lunch," the man replied. "This creature on the floor was going from table to table, panhandling, cursing, threatening people. He fell down as a result of his inebriation. No one struck him."

"That right?" the cop asked, looking around for confirmation.

Several people nodded. A few mumbled in agreement.

"Okay," the cop said. "I guess we can skip the report." He turned to the crowd and raised his voice. "Sorry for the disturbance, folks. Go on back to what you were doing." He nodded to his partner, and together they got the drunk up and dragged him away. The controller snatched up his dollar bill and hurried off.

Bo was righting the plastic chairs when the businessman walked up to him and squeezed his arm.

"Next time," the man whispered, "kick him in the balls."

CHAPTER FORTY-TWO

Marissa's beeper went off while she was shopping at Bendel's. She found a pay phone, dropped in a quarter, took a deep breath and dialed General Robbins' number.

"Any luck with our Asian friend?" Robbins asked her.

"Nothing. My faxes are getting through, but nothing comes back. Do I keep trying?"

"Yes, please."

"Frankly, I'm mystified. He's never been this hard to contact. If I do get a reply, is there any message?"

"No message. We simply want to know where he is. I'm sure you can appreciate our concern."

"Of course. I'll keep trying."

"Thank you. Now tell me, how are you doing?"

"To be perfectly honest, I'm a nervous wreck."

"Once again, I urge you to consider full-time security. It's a sensible precaution. Several of us have it. We sleep better. I would be happy to arrange it for you."

"No, thank you. I'm being very careful. I just want to see

this over with. Have you managed to make contact with them?"

"Yes, and I have received certain assurances. But the truth is, I cannot bring myself to trust those people."

"Who can?"

"Exactly."

There was an awkward pause. Marissa held her breath, crossed her fingers. She understood that he had to bring it up. It seemed that she had been waiting forever for this moment.

"Did you have something else for me?" he finally asked.

She exhaled. "Yes," she replied casually. "It's an immigration matter: a small one. Do you still maintain an interest in such things?"

"Occasionally. Does this concern someone you have met with personally?"

"I wouldn't mention it otherwise. In my opinion, it's a most unusual case. But if you are too busy . . ."

"No, no. I can always find time for a friend of yours. What is the party's name?"

"Vinh." Marissa spelled it for him.

"And how shall we proceed?" he asked.

"Same as always. I will call your secretary and set up an appointment. It should be in the next few days, if that's convenient."

"Fine."

"Oh, one last thing, as long as we're doing favors. About those surveillance tapes . . ."

"Destroyed," the general declared. "Every one of them. By my own hand. That was shameful. I hope you don't think that I—"

"Of course not."

"Good. Well, I must go."

"Goodbye."

Marissa hung up the phone and stood there trembling, her hand gripping the receiver like a dagger.

CHAPTER FORTY-THREE

The tiny room smelled like old cabbage. Barton showed his gold shield.

"No want trouble," the old man behind the desk told him, waving a withered hand. "Many years here. Run honest business. Clean business."

"I'm sure you do," Barton said, trying to breathe through his mouth.

"Health inspector here last week. Permit in mail."

"No, that's—"

"Liquor license renew next month. Can pay now. No want trouble."

Barton was trying not to disturb any of the dusty, paper-stuffed shoe boxes crowding all the shelves around him. The place was a firetrap. "I'm with homicide," he said.

"What is homicide?" the old man asked.

"Murder. Dead people."

"Someone dead?" the old man exclaimed, recoiling in horror. "Here? My res'rant?"

"No, no, no," Barton assured him. The old man had the ugliest fingernails Barton had ever seen. "All I want is to ask you a few simple questions."

"Sure. Questions. No trouble."

"Do you keep a record of every delivery you make?" Barton asked.

"I have all records. All. Someone have delivery problem from this res'rant?"

Barton asked to see the slips from the days Grelling and Trang were murdered. The old man leafed through a shoebox and handed Barton two bunches of receipts, each secured with a rubber band. There weren't too many. The old man sat behind the desk and pretended not to stare. The older they were the more frightened they were, Barton reflected.

A few of the addresses were close, but no cigar. "This is all of them?" Barton asked.

"All," the old man assured him. "You want see register tape?"

Barton handed back the receipts. "No, thank you. You have been very cooperative." He turned to go and then, à la Columbo, turned back: "Oh, Mr. Han, one last thing. Do you have anyone from Vietnam working here?"

"This Chinese res'rant," the old man declared.

"I know, but I thought maybe you had someone from Vietnam. A young man. I'm not from Immigration, Mr. Han. This is a police matter."

"This Chinese res'rant. All worker Chinese. Officer hungry? Want something take-out?"

"No, thank you. Do you know any Chinese restaurant that has a young man from Vietnam working, doing deliveries maybe? There could be a cash reward."

"Reward? How much reward?"

"That depends. If it turns out to be the man we're looking

for, it could be ten thousand dollars, maybe more." The old man was just pulling his chain.

"Vietnam bad country," Mr. Han declared. "Officer have wife, girlfriend? I get menu. How reward paid, cash or check?"

"Cash." Barton handed him a card. "If you hear anything," he explained, backing out.

"Bring lady in," the old man encouraged. "I make special Chinese love drink. No charge."

CHAPTER FORTY-FOUR

When Bo got back to the apartment after work he found Tiffany sitting on the sofa with the pile of hundred dollar bills in her lap and the Glock in her hand. She was still dressed for the office. She had been crying.

"What is this?" she wailed, waving the gun.

"Nine millimeter semiautomatic," Bo told her, approaching cautiously, making soothing gestures. "Please, Tiff'ny. Gun loaded. Much danger."

She dropped the gun on the money in her lap, buried her face in her hands and began to sob. He hurried over and knelt before her, removed the gun and pushed it under the sofa.

"Tiff'ny," he murmured, sliding his hands up under her skirt and stroking her thighs.

She continued to cry. He kissed her knees and tried gently to pry them apart, but she wouldn't accommodate him. He climbed to the sofa and curled up with his head resting on the money in her lap. He felt her body shaking as she tried to bring her crying under control.

"All this money," she said, wiping her eyes and sniffling. "A loaded gun. You're a criminal, Bo, a criminal."

"Is not true," he soothed, reaching down and caressing a calf. "Bo not criminal. Tiff'ny must believe."

"You don't care about me," she sobbed. "You're only using me. I see that now."

Warm tears fell against his skin. He sat up and kissed the fingers hiding her face, kissed her hair, kissed her neck. Her squirming excited him and he began stroking her legs more urgently, but she kept them locked together. His head began throbbing. His temperature rose. He had to have her right now or he was going to explode.

He stood and tried to get her to her feet. Still weeping, she attempted to pull away, but, fully aroused now, he dragged her up from the sofa and wrenched her toward him. He lowered his shoulder, lifted her off the floor and stumbled with her through the bedroom door.

"Bo," she cried in alarm, "you'll hurt yourself."

He released her so that she fell backward onto the bed. Before she could roll away, he clambered on top of her, pinning her wrists and using his legs to force hers apart. He began licking and sucking her neck.

"No, baby," she moaned, heaving in an effort to free herself but succeeding only in inflaming him further.

Past caring, he pressed his hot cheek against her wet one and, rubbing his whole body against hers, blurted, "Bo love you forever."

She stopped struggling. A strange silence settled over them. He felt himself rising and falling with her breathing.

"What did you say?" she asked in a tremulous whisper.

"For truth," he told her, releasing her wrists. "Bo love you forever."

"You mean it?"

"Forever." He imagined biting down on the plastic capsule, releasing the sudden searing pain . . .

"Tell me again, baby," she said.

"Bo love Tiff'ny forever."

"And you're not a criminal?"

"Bo not criminal, loved one. Bo explain everything."

"But that's a real gun, baby."

He slid off and curled up next to her. "Real gun, yes. But not my gun. Tiff'ny. My swear."

"You never told me before," she said, touching him with her fingertips. "You know, what you said."

"Bo love you forever," he told her. It got easier each time. Forever would be two days, three days . . .

She took his hand and pressed it to her breast. "You still want me, baby? Now, I mean."

His lust, which had deserted him, returned at full throttle. He reached in and grasped at her panties with both hands. She raised her hips to make it easier for him. He burrowed down beneath her skirt and her raw hot smell enveloped him. He crawled hungrily toward it.

"I need to bathe first," she said, trying to push his head away.

When he wouldn't stop she kicked off her shoes and stroked his back with her feet while her trembling fingers struggled with the buttons of her blouse.

CHAPTER FORTY-FIVE

It was a little after seven when Fink got up to the suite. Marissa had guests: a thin black guy in his forties and an Asian girl, pretty, Laotian, Fink thought. Then again, maybe not: The nose was wrong.

"Mel," Marissa said, swirling over like Loretta Young, "say hello to Zack and Mee Yang. Zack, this is Mel, the detective I was telling you about."

The men shook hands. Fink had a funny itch; there was something familiar about the guy's face.

"Guess where Mee Yang is from?" Marissa asked playfully.

The girl seemed nervous. She had beautiful hair, nice hands, big eyes. Fink reconsidered.

"Cambodia," he said.

Marissa clapped delightedly. "See," she said to Zack, "what did I tell you? Come on, come on, sit down, everyone."

Fink wondered why there was so much tension in the room. He checked to make sure his gun wasn't showing.

The man eased himself down on the sofa next to the girl. Fink hadn't realized they were a couple.

"How long do you know Marissa?" Fink asked him.

Marissa answered: "We just met today. Zack and Mee Yang are staying here at the hotel. We have a mutual friend."

"Where are you coming from?" Fink asked the man.

"We were in Los Angeles, California, but only for one day."

"And before that?" Why did this guy look so familiar? Mug shot? Fax? What the hell was Marissa up to?

"Asia," the man answered.

"Big place," Fink remarked. "How long were you there?"

The man hesitated, then said, "Twenty-four years."

Fink glanced at Marissa. She nodded.

Jesus Christ, Fink thought, it's him.

When his head cleared, Fink discovered he was on his feet. He looked over to make sure the door was closed. His mind was whirring.

"Who else knows you're here?" he asked the man.

Marissa responded: "Just the *hombre* who sent them, me of course, and now you."

"We're sure of that?" Fink asked.

Zack nodded.

"And who's she?" Fink asked, indicating Mee Yang.

"Hey," Marissa said sharply.

"What?"

"Where are your manners?"

Fink walked over to the sofa and put out his hand. "Welcome home, Mr. Johnson."

"Thanks," Johnson said with a shy smile.

"Hi," Fink said to Mee Yang, extending a hand.

Johnson nudged her and she reached up and shook Fink's hand. "I have passport," she said. "Go head, Doc, show."

The passport looked genuine. Fink opened it. "Mee Yang Johnson," he read.

"My name," she said. "See picture?"

Fink looked, made a face. "You're much prettier than this," he said, hoping to make amends.

"Is true?" she asked, springing up and peering at the passport in Fink's hand.

Fink saw that Johnson was smiling. It was the same smile that made page one of the *Times* and the covers of *Time* and *Newsweek.* Jesus Christ, Fink thought, it really is him. No wonder Marissa was acting so frisky. But how the hell—?

"Zack has to be in Washington a few days from now," Marissa explained. "He's going to appear before the Grantham Committee."

"And I have to get him there?" Fink asked, catching one of many racing thoughts: security precautions, travel—there were a million things to consider. This was incredible.

"Why don't we talk about all that over dinner?" Marissa suggested, playing it to the hilt. "I thought a Cambodian restaurant, for Mee Yang."

"Sure," Fink said. With the four hundreds in his wallet he felt like Donald Trump. "Mr. Johnson—"

"Zack," Marissa said.

"Zack doesn't want anyone else to know he's here, is that right?"

"Everything's going a little fast for me," Johnson admitted.

"That's fine," Fink told him. "I understand. But if I'm going to be responsible for your security—"

"Do what you have to," Marissa told him.

He got Barton on the phone and asked him if he knew any good Cambodian restaurants.

"Come again," Barton responded.

"We're having dinner tonight at a Cambodian restaurant,"

Fink informed him. "Find a good one and get us a reservation for—" He looked to Marissa— "nine o'clock."

"I'm seeing Rhonda."

"Good. Bring her along. There'll be six of us. I'm paying. Make the reservation and call me here at Marissa's."

"Why six?"

"Friends of hers. You'll like them."

"Swell."

"Come on, Barton, get with the program."

"I hate it when you're in a good mood," Barton said.

Fink took Johnson aside. They talked. Johnson was as nervous and fragile as a bereaved child. He answered Fink's questions, explaining haltingly about his capture, the way he'd been moved from place to place, how he had finally been saved by Colonel Ransom, about marrying Mee Yang. As he spoke he became increasingly agitated. He confided that he didn't want to go to Washington and appear at any hearings. The prospect of reporters and cameras and microphones clearly frightened him. He insisted that he had nothing to say to those people. He was no hero. He had told that to the colonel maybe a million times. What had he done that was so special?

"You survived," Fink told him, taking his wrist.

"Maybe," Johnson mumbled, his eyes darting around the room.

"Now what can I do for you?" Fink asked, releasing him.

"Find my mother," Johnson said simply. "If you're as good a detective as the lady says, find my mother."

"I will," Fink told him, resisting the urge to touch him again, to comfort him, to take away his fear.

CHAPTER FORTY-SIX

Rhonda was wound tight. She'd planned an elaborate dinner at her place—wine, candles, the works—and then Don springs this on her at the last minute. She didn't mind having dinner with Fink, who was harmless, or even Marissa, who was rich and good-looking and, thankfully, past her prime, but now Rhonda was faced with this willowy young thing with a flat belly, no hips and drop-dead hair. To make matters worse, both women were draped in designer silk and Rhonda was wearing *pret-a-porter* cotton. Cambodian restaurant, Don said, so she'd dressed for Chinatown. Except this place was like fancy French. And this Zack: a hayseed, but look at him with this Mee Yang. How old could she be? Twenty? Twenty-one?

The evening was not going well for Barton either. He had begun fuming the second he saw Zack. He didn't like being an au pair black, didn't like it one damn bit: resented the hell out of it, as a matter of fact. He couldn't figure how these people got to be Marissa's friends. The guy was about her age, but he acted like a dweeb. His threads were good, but he wasn't comfortable in them, almost like they were someone else's. The girl was nervous, too nervous. Barton had never been out with an Asian. This one was pretty enough, but there was nothing there to grab on to. Her hair reminded him of an old 33 rpm record: shiny and black, with a zillion little grooves. It was her eyes, though. There was something wild in them, a little desperate, like a teenager collared for the first time.

The waiter poured champagne. Fink made a welcoming toast to the odd couple. Fink was full of himself, he loved rubbing Barton's nose in it. Something had to be done.

"You hear?" he asked Fink. "Looks like they picked up that MIA."

Marissa's head snapped around.

"They who?" Fink asked mildly.

"Chicago PD. Heard it on the way over. They caught a guy boosting a car, identified himself as Isaac P. Johnson."

"Believe nothing of what you hear," Marissa recited, "and half of what you see."

Barton didn't need *her* advice either. "Yeah?" he challenged. "Well, listen—"

"Son of Sam," Fink offered.

Everyone looked at him.

"I was at the seven three in Brooklyn when we had that Son of Sam thing—a serial killer—a little before your time, Barton. Once the media got revved up we were getting five maybe six calls a day, guys turning themselves in, hoping to get on TV. My guess, we're going to see a lot of Isaac P. Johnsons in the next few days."

"Chicago's about a thousand miles from here," Barton grumbled. "That's pretty fancy detective work."

"I'm a pretty fancy detective," Fink replied.

Marissa motioned over a small chubby Asian in a dark

suit and whispered something to him. The man became effusive, bowed to Mee Yang, mumbled some strange words, then insisted in English that she allow him to give her a tour of the kitchen. With Marissa's encouragement, Mee Yang went, but she pulled Zack along.

"What the hell is going on?" Barton demanded as soon as they were out of earshot.

Fink sipped his champagne, looking twinkly.

"This guy is from outer space," Barton said. "You expect us to believe these are friends of Marissa's."

"Why not?" Fink reached over and refilled Barton's glass.

"Look," he said to Fink, "if this is a security detail—"

"You're some detective," Fink teased.

Barton sat and seethed. What the hell was this all about? What could he be missing? Why was Fink grinning like that? Some detective, he said. A black dude in his forties going by the name of Zack with a Cambodian girl young enough to be— Zack?

As in I-Zack? No, no, no, it couldn't be. Could it? Where the hell would Fink . . . ?

When Zack and Mee Yang returned to the table Barton jumped up to hold Mee Yang's chair. As she was sitting he leaned forward and asked her last name.

"Johnson," she was pleased to inform him.

"I wasn't sure you were married," he explained, feeling muscles in his arms twitch as a commotion erupted nearby.

Plates crashed. Chairs fell. There were cries. Instinctively, Fink slid from his chair, drew his gun and moved to interpose his body between Johnson and the noise. The restaurant was too damn dark to see what the trouble was. People all over were standing.

"Help," someone cried.

Fink reached back to make sure Johnson was there. Nothing. He spun around. Johnson was gone. Barton was gone.

Fink held the gun flat against his thigh and began shouldering his way through the crowd.

The woman was about sixty and enormous. When Fink arrived, Barton had her from behind and was applying the Heimlich maneuver, each sharp grunting pull lifting her off the floor. It wasn't working. Her thrashing became frenzied. Fink scanned the area for Johnson, couldn't find him.

"Hold her tight," Johnson said, stepping up and grasping the woman's jaw with one hand and working his other hand far into her mouth. It looked grotesque—people in the crowd gasped—but a tense moment later he eased out something odd-shaped. The woman collapsed back against Barton. There was a collective sigh of relief, a smattering of applause. Fink discovered the gun in his hand, quickly holstered it and moved around trying to get the woman some breathing space.

With Johnson's help, Barton lowered the woman to the floor. She was wheezing. A man fell to his knees next to her and began frantically patting her hand, pausing to adjust the shoulder straps of her dress. The woman began to cough. Someone called for water. Fink's heart was pounding, but other than that, everything was okay.

A man tried to force his way past Fink into the little clearing.

Fink squared a hand on the man's chest. "Police," he said. "Stay back."

"Press," the man said. "I'm with the *Daily News*. I'd like to interview these people."

Fink kept the hand in place. "I can't let you do that," he said. "We've got a medical emergency here."

"C'mon, officer," the man cajoled, "this is a good human interest thing." He dropped his voice. "White woman, two black Samaritans. C'mon."

Fink stepped close and whispered: "One of those guys is on the job. Back off."

Two paramedics in whites arrived and took over. Johnson and Barton helped them get the woman onto the gurney. Fink eased over and told Barton there was a reporter nosing around. He told him to take Zack straight back to the hotel, no fuss, no muss: just go. Fink would bring the women back after dinner. Barton could order room service.

There was loud murmuring as people returned to their tables. Oriental music was playing, louder than before. Fink went back and reassured the women. Marissa seemed more nervous than the others. As they watched, the victim was wheeled out to general applause, like an injured athlete being carried off the field.

With her departure, the air in the restaurant settled back to normal. Following Fink's request to act natural, Marissa was sipping champagne and Rhonda was talking to Mee Yang.

"Sure," Mee Yang said, "Doc deliver plenty babies."

"Were you ever there?" Rhonda asked.

"Two time," Mee Yang said proudly, holding up fingers. "But only remember one."

Barton rolled the quarter back and forth across his knuckles, trying to decide whether to make the call. Johnson was asleep inside, all curled up like a ball, twitching and mumbling. The poor guy was fucked up in a major way. Barton was sure he'd be better off in an army hospital, where they had people trained to deal with his kind of problem. And telling Captain Reynolds would get Johnson into a hospital that much faster, would actually be better for the guy. That was one way to look at it.

He flipped the coin into the air and slapped it down on the back of his other hand. Heads or tails? He couldn't make up his mind.

He heard whimpering from the bedroom and went in. Johnson was clutching a pillow to his chest. He was trembling. Barton sat on the edge of the bed. Johnson's eyes were active behind closed lids. Barton's little sister Marlene used to have incidents like this: Night monsters, their mother called them. He reached out and tentatively touched Johnson's shoulder, then began rubbing his back the way he used to do Marlene's.

It worked. Johnson relaxed. He made soft smacking sounds with his lips, moved the pillow up to his head and snuggled against it. Barton stood, tiptoed back inside and sat staring at the phone. He felt for this guy, but if he didn't tell Reynolds, his career was Drano. Ten years in a toll booth, Reynolds had promised him. Or he could quit and go become a deputy in some one-horse town. Or go into private security work, taking Polaroids of middle-aged white guys getting it on with hookers, or videotaping their wives kicking the ceiling for delivery boys. Damn.

CHAPTER FORTY-SEVEN

"Let's agree on some ground rules," General Olden suggested, raising the window and shutting out his driver.

Shane Reilly put down her pad, crossed a leg and tried to ignore the thumping of her heart.

"Attribution," the general said. "How will I be identified in the piece?"

"How about name, rank, and serial number?" Shane joked, hoping to sound like someone for whom private nighttime briefings from air force generals were de rigueur.

Olden chuckled as he poured them each a soft drink. The limousine moved smoothly through the Virginia countryside. Shane used the time to review Mitchelson's instructions: agree to his conditions, never interrupt, never show surprise, never argue, never be confrontational, be grateful but don't kiss ass. It was a lot to remember.

He handed her the club soda. "How about calling *me* 'an informed Pentagon source'?"

"That's fine," she smiled, setting her glass into a plastic

caddy, opening her pad, making a note. She still couldn't believe she was actually doing this.

Olden began by reaffirming the military's commitment to resolving the fate of every Vietnam MIA. Next, he sought to put the issue in perspective by pointing out that there had been far more American MIAs following Korea and the Second World War, and that thousands of those had never been accounted for. War, he reminded her with a wry smile, was hell.

Which, he said, led him directly to the point of this briefing. He sighed. Passing along this information was his worst task in more than twenty years, when he'd been the incarnation of people's worst fears, appearing unannounced at their front door to tell them that a loved one had been captured. Or was missing in action. Or worse.

Shane fingered her pencil, chewed her lip. She knew what was coming: Johnson was dead. The story was over. Shit.

Olden turned and stared out into the darkness for a long moment. There was no way to sugarcoat this, he declared. It appeared that Corporal Isaac P. Johnson was a collaborator.

Shane felt chills. She wrote the word in block letters, put it in quotes, underlined it. "COLLABORATOR". Wow. This was great.

Olden explained that the evidence, though largely circumstantial, was overwhelming. He would detail it for her in a moment, but first he felt compelled to state, from a purely personal point of view, that continuing to treat Isaac Johnson as an American hero would be the grossest possible insult to the millions of brave—

His words poured out, propelled by a passionate intensity. Shane, writing furiously, was getting it all down. Her teeth moved to a fresh section of lip.

"Oh, hell," he said, abruptly regaining control of his emotions. He shook his head and pointed to her pad.

Shane reluctantly crumpled the page and stuffed it into an ashtray: "Never argue," Mitchelson had said.

Olden cleared his throat. "The Snosset report," he announced, drawing a manila folder from his briefcase.

He turned on her reading light and handed her a photocopied document stamped "SECRET." Shane read rapidly. The report closely paralleled what Snosset had told her over breakfast, but the appended "Psych-Eval" section was new to her. According to this analysis, Snosset's incident report "lacked candor." Follow-up interviews had established "to the satisfaction of the examiners" that he was "protecting" Corporal Johnson, though precisely what he was protecting him from remained "an enigma."

Shane recalled Snosset spilling his silverware and dribbling his juice.

"These next ones," Olden said, passing her a series of thin folders, "are reports of wartime prisoner interrogations."

There were nine of them, each stamped "TOP SECRET." She flipped through them, noting that all were dated between 1969 and 1973. In each report, more than half the text had been blacked out. Scattered among what little remained were statements referring to a rogue American medic whose description—though it varied from report to report—seemed consistent with Isaac P. Johnson.

When Shane put these aside Olden handed her another "TOP SECRET" document, this one an "ExecSum" of the debriefing of the five hundred ninety-one American POWs who were released by North Vietnam after the war. It consisted of more than a hundred pages, most of them completely blacked out.

"In the interests of time," Olden explained, "I took the liberty of marking the operative portions. There are sixteen separate instances where returning POWs report hearing about an American GI living with and providing medical treatment to the enemy."

Shane leafed through it, pausing to read a few of the short, yellow-highlighted passages, and noting that anything that might have helped identify individual POWs had been blacked out, making corroboration virtually impossible.

"One more document," Olden told her. "This one is a military attaché's report of a meeting between representatives of the American and Vietnamese governments. Most of it, I'm afraid, is censored, including the date, but you will find a highlighted reference to an American medic who joined the Cambodian forces in the late sixties. According to Vietnam, this American remained with the Cambodians—specifically, with a highly mobile cadre of Khmer Rouge—throughout the war and the years of terror that followed. The Cambodians referred to this American as '*l'ange noir*,' or 'the black angel.' You can draw your own conclusions."

Olden popped open another can of Pepsi. "Okay," he said, sounding relieved. "In case you're interested, we're driving southwest, through Virginia horse country. Ask me some questions."

She referred to her notes. "Why did the U.S. military wait until now to release this information?"

"That's an easy one. We remained silent to avoid causing pain to Corporal Johnson's family and to the men who served with him. Our reticence has been overcome by events."

"Which events?"

"The fingerprints, your stories, the media avalanche, the possibility that Corporal Johnson may be seeking to return to the United States to testify before a Senate subcommittee."

"There has been a great deal of speculation concerning the Pentagon's opposition to the Grantham Committee."

"The speculation is unwarranted. There is no opposition. We share their concern, we appreciate their interest, we are anxious to cooperate."

"And if Corporal Johnson does testify?"

"Same response."

"General, why is the Pentagon releasing this information through a single source?"

"To maximize accuracy and minimize sensationalism," he replied mechanically.

"You speak of minimizing sensationalism, General," Shane declared, hoping to prod him into something quotable, "but don't these reports reveal that Corporal Johnson is a traitor?"

Olden sat up, adjusted his jacket, forced a tilted smile. "No comment."

CHAPTER FORTY-EIGHT

After Barton left, Fink put in a call to John Crowley, a homicide detective with the Detroit PD. A few years back Fink had brought in a guy who was wanted for a double murder in Detroit. Crowley had flown to New York to pick him up. While the papers were being typed up, they'd had dinner and a few drinks and had kept in touch ever since. Crowley was now chief of detectives.

"Is this Axel Foley?" Fink asked when Crowley came on the line.

"Screw you, Fink. You better make this fast. I'm watching *Deep Space Nine.*"

"I'm trying to locate someone."

"This someone have a name?"

"Adelaide Johnson."

"You and everybody else," Crowley told him. "You mind telling me why you're looking for her?"

"Can't," Fink told him. "Sorry. That's why I'm calling you at home."

Crowley sighed. "Give me a number."

Fink hung up and started getting ready for bed. Marissa told him to hurry up. Ten minutes later the phone rang.

"Under torture, Mel, you never heard this from me."

"Scout's honor."

"The word I get is that you might want to check with Senator Grantham in our nation's capital."

"Live long and prosper," Fink told him.

Fink went inside, called the senator's office and left his name and number on the machine.

"What was that all about?" Marissa asked when he returned.

"I was just asking Mee Yang if she had a friend."

"She does," Marissa said. "Get into bed and I'll introduce you."

"This is Bob Cardanzer," an annoyingly chipper voice said at six-thirty the next morning. "Please identify yourself."

Fink did, then swung his legs out and sat at the edge of the bed. "I need to speak with Senator Grantham," he said.

"I'm the senator's chief of staff. How can we help you, Lieutenant?"

"This call is unofficial," Fink told him, trying to shake the sleep from his head.

"All right. What's your problem?"

"I'm looking for someone."

"Why call us?"

"Because I think you know where this someone is."

"And what makes you think that, Lieutenant?"

"A party in Detroit suggested it, Mr. . . ."

"Cardanzer. Call me Bob. I don't know what you're talking about, Lieutenant."

"Call me Mel. Let me put it this way, Bob: the person I represent is anxious to renew old family ties."

"Are you saying that the person you represent is a relative of this person you're looking for?"

"Immediate family, Bob. Couldn't be closer."

"Convince me."

"You already know name and rank," Fink said, reaching for his pad. "Here's his serial number."

He read it slowly. It was one of the few things about Johnson that hadn't been made public. It shouldn't take Cardanzer long to verify.

"So," Fink said, "if I came down to Washington, say, later this morning, Bob, would there be any reason for us to meet?"

"None that I can think of at the moment. But you better tell me how you will be getting here, Mel, just in case."

Fink woke Marcia at home and told her he would be taking a personal day. Yes, he'd keep his beeper on, but it only had a fifty-mile range. Never mind where he was going. If she couldn't get him she could always get Barton. He asked her how Vinny was doing.

"Okay this week," she replied, dropping her voice. "Going to his AA meetings, doing his NordicTrack. Keep your fingers crossed."

"I will," Fink promised.

"This MIA thing," Marcia said, "it's hitting him hard. He's been glued to the TV. It brings back a lot of memories, I guess. He's really rooting for this guy."

"Yeah," Fink said, "me too. Tell Vinnie hello."

Marissa burst from the bathroom looking radiant. She was planning to storm the Madison Avenue shops with Mee Yang. Could Fink believe that girl was a size three? Three! Marissa couldn't wait to get her into Miyake. When was he leaving for Washington? How was he getting there? What did he think of this hat?

He had never seen her this excited about shopping. Johnson's arrival had her really revved up. He reminded her that Zack was not to leave the hotel.

"You already said that, *caro*. How about these shoes? Too red?"

"Stunning. Remember, Barton is in charge of Zack's security. Don't get crazy on me, Marissa."

The phone rang. Fink picked it up.

It was Barton. "Turn on the TV," he said. "CNN."

"Why?"

"Just do it. I'm on my way over."

"Tell me," Fink demanded, searching for the remote.

"We got problems. They're saying Johnson was a collaborator."

Chapter Forty-Nine

A man too well-dressed to be a chauffeur was standing at the gate with a cardboard sign that read "FINK."

"Are you Mel?" the man asked when Fink stopped.

"Only if you're Bob. That fur collar is a nice touch."

Fink followed him down a corridor and through a nondescript door into a small empty lounge.

"Have you eaten?" Cardanzer asked, locking the door. "Please, help yourself. The orange stripe is decaf."

"Thanks."

"We can talk here," Cardanzer said. "I mean, it's safe. Oh, may I see some identification, please?"

Fink showed him. "Are those things supposed to be bagels?"

"Try a muffin. They're low-fat. How was your flight?"

Fink chose an easy chair and rested his coffee on a nearby ledge. Cardanzer stood fingering his expensive tie.

"I'm here to take her off your hands," Fink said.

"Would that it were that easy," Cardanzer sighed.

"It can be," Fink said. "She should be with her son. You know that."

"Last night we were protecting Mother Teresa and today we're harboring Ma Barker." Cardanzer tried to laugh. "Well, you're right, of course. She should be with her son. That was our intention all along. We simply wanted to shield her from the media. You understand."

"Of course."

"The senator made a humanitarian gesture, bringing her here to await her son's arrival. Frankly, I didn't see any downside. Goes to show you." He turned and stared through the curtained window at an empty runway. "I knew Snosset, by the way. I met with him only a few days before he died. He seemed all right. Normal. This whole thing," he said, shaking his head.

"I'll take her to her son," Fink said. "I'm a cop. No one will know anything. The senator will be off the hook. You too."

Cardanzer turned. "Here's the quid pro quo. Corporal Johnson has to be here in three days for the hearings. He's scheduled for Thursday at eleven. You get him here by ten. Do we have a deal?"

"Deal. It would be nice if he could see his mother sometime today."

"It would," Cardanzer agreed. "And you will take full responsibility?"

Fink gave him the smile he usually reserved for ball-busting clerks in the evidence room.

"We'll need to speak with him, say, tomorrow," Cardanzer said, pacing as he spoke. "Review his testimony. Make sure we're all in synch. I'll coordinate the time with you, then set up a conference call: the lead counsel, one or two others. But let's leave that until tomorrow. You and I can handle that. Let tonight be all theirs." He forced a smile.

"You have to be gentle with this guy," Fink said. "Tell your people. He's been through hell and he's very fragile."

"Of course."

"I think seeing his mother will help, but I'm worried about him. You might want to have a shrink on the conference call."

"Noted," Cardanzer said. "I'll see what can be done. But how is he physically? How does he look?"

"He looks okay," Fink said. "A little frayed around the edges. But overall he looks good."

"Excuse me for asking," Cardanzer said, perching on the edge of a chair, "but how did you find . . . ? I mean, why you?"

"Just lucky, I guess," Fink told him.

Cardanzer took a deep breath. "Tell me," he said, "please, if you can. Is it true?"

"Is what true?"

"What they're saying on the news this morning: that he was a collaborator."

"He told me the Cambodians mostly kept him in a bamboo cage. More than twenty years in a bamboo cage."

"But did he help them? That's what I'm asking. Did he provide aid and comfort? That's the real issue."

"Is it? Look, when they captured him he was setting a kid's leg: a kid around six. Was that kid the enemy?"

"I don't know," Cardanzer answered earnestly. "Was he?"

"Listen," Fink said, pushing to his feet, "this figures to be a pretty busy day for me. Where is the lady?"

"We'll have to go get her. It shouldn't take long."

"Okay. How often do these planes run?"

"You can't take her on a shuttle!"

"Why not?"

"Her photo has been everywhere. She would be recognized. Instantly. No, no, Lieutenant. Public transportation is out of the question, I'm afraid. You'll have to rent a car."

"Sorry," Fink told him. "New York is a five-hour drive, minimum. I can't spare the time. You want her driven, you drive her."

"Actually," Cardanzer said, considering, "I do know someone who can take her, someone she will be comfortable with." He was suddenly overflowing with nervous energy. "She'll have to pack and—We'll do it today, as soon as possible. You have to tell me exactly where to deliver her."

"Here's a phone number," Fink said. "Have the driver call me when he gets to Manhattan. I'll give him the address then."

"That seems a sensible precaution. Oh, let me prepare a short note for you to sign," Cardanzer said, hurrying to the desk. "It will simply state that—"

"Give it to the driver," Fink told him. "I'll sign it on delivery."

"This is a good thing we're doing," Cardanzer said, hurrying back and pumping Fink's hand. "Reuniting loved ones. I feel really good about this. The senator will too."

Fink chose an empty row near the tail and slid over into the window seat. The plane had a chilly mustiness about it. Fink was tired. He spread out and closed his eyes. There was a lot to think about.

"This seat taken?"

"No, go ahead," Fink muttered, righting himself by pushing on the flimsy armrests. He glanced around. There was no one else within three rows of them.

The man stowed his attaché case in the overhead compartment and settled into the adjacent seat. He was about Fink's age and height, with a dark blue suit, longish black hair and a short full beard. There was something about his eyes. Fink hoped to hell he wasn't gay.

"They're saying he was a collaborator," the man said, adjusting his seat back. "Did you hear that?"

"Yeah." Great: a talker.

"You know what surprised me, though?" the man said. "You interested in discussing this?"

"I haven't been following it," Fink said, hoping to turn him off.

"That's okay," the man said, reaching into Fink's seat and feeling around.

Fink squeezed himself against the bulkhead.

The man located the other end of his seat belt and sat back. "Who do you think is responsible?" he asked. "For this collaborator crap, I mean."

Fink looked at him. "What are you, a reporter?"

"No, a businessman, international variety. There go the engines. You'd better buckle up."

The plane disengaged from the umbilical. A stewardess came down the aisle checking seat backs and tray tables. By habit, Fink looked around for the nearest emergency exit.

"See, what I'm wondering," the man said, "is whether the Pentagon is acting alone or if the strings are being pulled from somewhere else? New York, maybe. What do you think?"

Fink didn't respond.

The man grinned. "Do I make you nervous?"

"Why did you sit here?" Fink asked him.

"I don't know," the man shrugged, scratching his beard, "maybe I'm fascinated by detectives who launder thousand dollar bills."

The plane swung onto the runway and stopped. The engines revved. The fuselage shook.

"Who the fuck are you?" Fink demanded.

"Ransom," the man said, offering his hand, "Everett G."

"The colonel?" Fink exclaimed, grasping his hand, relieved but incredulous.

The plane lurched forward, first lumbering, then barreling down the runway. Its nose came up and it lifted powerfully into the air. Fink saw buildings, water, heard the landing gear retract.

"How's Doc holding up?" Ransom asked.

"Not too well."

"He needs to see his mother. Did you have any luck with that?"

"Some."

"How soon before they're together?"

"If everything goes right, early tonight."

"In New York?"

Fink looked around. "Yeah."

"You've been great, Lieutenant. I mean that. Mee Yang, Zack—it was a lot to ask. How's Marissa, by the way?"

"That reminds me, how exactly do you know Marissa?"

The plane hit an air pocket. "I don't like planes," Ransom remarked. "You?"

"Parker Global," Fink said. "Is that how you know Marissa?"

Ransom peered up the aisle. "Christ, where's that cart? I could really use a drink. Yes. We occasionally work together."

"What kind of work?"

"Sales. I peddle Parker Global's products to people they can't."

"Such as."

"Anybody on the excluded list. You name it. PLO, IRA, PRC, Iran, Iraq." He smiled. "Just plain folks."

"How does Marissa fit in?"

"We're a team. I get an order and pass it along to her. She

has Parker Global invoice the merchandise to clients with whom understandings exist."

"Paraguay and Peru," Fink suggested.

"*Beaucoup* understanding there," Ransom allowed. "Man's done his homework."

"Then what?"

"End-user certificates, to cover everybody's ass. The *baksheesh* gets paid, and by the time the goods get delivered I've arranged to have them transshipped."

"Sounds simple enough. What went wrong?"

"You remember what happened with the USS *Iowa* a few years back?"

"Remind me."

"The *Iowa* was the last active World War Two destroyer. It was on maneuvers when the whole forward turret blew up, killed thirty or forty kids. You must remember it. The navy brass tried to blame the whole thing on a conveniently dead gay sailor with a nickel-dime life insurance policy."

"Oh, yeah," Fink recalled. "I saw it on TV. I couldn't believe they were still using those big canisters of dynamite to load the guns."

"That's it. Well, something like that happened to one of my regular customers: DRV, the Democratic Republic of Vietnam. That Subic Bay stuff was crap; that's why it was so cheap. I told them to spring for better quality, but communists are very cost-conscious; always a mistake."

"So?"

"So during a training exercise a few months ago some of the Subic shipment spontaneously combusts. Two dozen young heroes of the state become body parts, including a government honcho's eldest son." He shrugged. "Daddy got angry."

"But why didn't they come after you? You sold it to them."

"Communists are plodders. They've been working their way up the chain: Grelling, Trang. If I can't stop them, Marissa would be next on their list, then me. Rank has its privileges."

"About Marissa . . ."

"Oh, she knows, has known for some time. She's being very careful. I'm close to resolving the situation. Could happen today." He took a small round tin from his pocket. "French pastilles," he said. "You want one?"

"What flavor?"

"*Fraises de bois*. Strawberry, to you."

"Sure." Fink took one of the little hard candies and popped it into his mouth. He shouldn't like this guy, but he did.

A cart pulled up: a stewardess collecting fares. Ransom pushed Fink's arm away and paid for both of them in cash.

"My buddy here needs a receipt," Ransom told the stewardess. "I need a drink."

"The beverage service will be commencing shortly, sir."

Fink waited until she left. He was tempted to ask the colonel when Marissa learned she was a target, but he decided he didn't want to hear the answer. "Explain something to me," he said instead. "Why does Vietnam want to do business with an American company?"

"Half their weapons are American. We left them enough to equip three armies."

"How do they pay you, in rubles?"

Ransom laughed. "Lieutenant. Please. Do you know how much gold we left in the South Vietnamese treasury when we bailed out?"

"No."

"More than fifteen tons. Round numbers, that's about a billion dollars. Anytime—"

"Hey," Fink said, suddenly remembering, "you mind telling me why you had me followed?"

"I needed to know who Marissa was hanging out with. I had Zack to worry about."

"But you found out I was dirty."

"Hey," Ransom smiled, "nobody's perfect."

The plane shuddered violently. The seat belt sign came on. Ransom's eyes darted around the cabin.

"Turbulence," Fink said, holding on.

"Yeah?" Ransom challenged. "Listen."

He was right, there was something different about the sound. All the passengers were twisting around. Fink looked out the window. Nothing but white.

"We lost a fucking engine," Ransom said. "Who knew you were on this flight?"

"No one. Wait a minute! Grantham's office knew. You think—?"

The plane started listing. Fink was pressed against the bulkhead. Someone screamed. Fink's chest constricted.

The captain came on the loudspeaker. There was no cause for alarm. A warning light had come on and number two engine had shut itself down. All systems were operating normally, but regulations required that they return to Washington. He apologized for any inconvenience. An excellent view of the Capitol would be coming up for those on the left side of the aircraft.

"Okay," Ransom said, wiping his forehead with a handkerchief, "let's finish our talk. We may not get another chance."

Fink was feeling light-headed. "They'll transfer us to another plane," he said.

"Not me," Ransom told him with a nervous laugh. "You'll have to say hello to Zack and the girls for me. I hope to see them later."

"Later how?"

"You know," Ransom said, stretching, "I met Marissa in Florida once. She tried to sell me a condo. You're a lucky guy."

"Yeah."

"By the way, how many more of those thousands do you have?"

"None of your fucking business."

"That's the spirit. You go to New York. I'll see what can be done on this end."

"You know people in Washington?"

"Oh yeah," Ransom assured him. "You think the Pentagon doesn't know everything Parker Global is doing? Listen, you have questions, now is the time to ask them."

"Let's start with how you and Zack got hooked up."

"Fine. How much do you know about tigers?"

Fifteen minutes later the tires squealed and they were down. People up front began applauding.

"I have more questions," Fink said.

"They'll have to wait." Ransom made a move to get up and then dropped back down. "It's funny," he said, "but when Doc first said he wanted to go home I told him he couldn't, that he'd been gone too long, that nobody would want him back. You know what he said?"

"What?"

"He said his mother would want him." Ransom shrugged. "He was right. But so was I. You ever feel like an asshole, Lieutenant?"

"Some days more than others."

"You'd think I would have learned," Ransom said disgustedly. "Too damn long: I told him that. Hearings," he muttered. "Congressional goddamn hearings. I don't know what the hell got into me."

"I think he'll be okay at the hearings," Fink said. "Once he's seen his mother. He's a sweet guy."

But Ransom didn't seem to hear him. "This goddamn country," he said. "After the war ended, the guys who were prisoners with me, six of them, pilots, decent guys, they were all killed, every one of them. Hanged. Well, I got mad and I got even. I made my own goddamn rules and I never looked back. But Doc . . . Jesus. What can you do with a guy like that?" He shook his head. "Fucking Doc," he chuckled. "He doesn't know which way is up. But I should have known better, Lieutenant. I goddamn well should have known better than to get him into this."

"So what happens now?" Fink asked him.

Ransom unbuckled his belt and stood in the aisle. "I got him in, I'll get him out. Stay tuned," he said. "I've got a lot to do. I'll call you tonight. Be ready."

"Ready for what?"

"Sir," a stewardess called to Ransom, "you must remain seated until the aircraft comes to a complete stop."

"At the gate," he told her. "You're supposed to say 'comes to a complete stop at the gate.' " He reached up and opened the overhead compartment.

"Sir," she said firmly, "you can't do that."

He smiled. "You just watch me, sister."

CHAPTER FIFTY

Adelaide made another tour of the apartment, fluffing cushions, tucking corners, smoothing wrinkles, waiting for the knock that would take her out of here and send her on her way to her little Isaac, praise be Jesus.

Truth to tell, she was happy to be leaving this place. It wasn't fun here anymore. They wouldn't let her use the telephone and she'd had her fill of watching TV and eating sweets. She still talked with the Lord, of course, and she knew He listened, but it didn't seem the same without the church around her. She never thought she'd live to say it, but she even missed working. It was boring here. They kept sending over that same scaredy-cat young girl to keep her company, but they never took her out anymore. And then this morning the TV started in with all this foolishness about how her Isaac was helping enemy people over there all these years—collaborating, they called it—as if her boy wasn't as loyal an American as any of them, as if he hadn't volunteered to wear the uniform, as if her Isaac had done something wrong by being cooped up against his will halfway around the world all these years.

Mean-spirited, evil people, that's what these TV people were, scandalizing her boy as if he was some kind of she-didn't-know-what. Hadn't even let the boy talk yet—hadn't so much as laid eyes on him—and already they knew everything there was to know about him. Judging, judging, judging, as if the Lord hadn't been clear as glass about that.

She rechecked the closets, neatened up the hangers, squared the extra pillows up on the shelf. Where were those people? Come on bell, ring.

The trip had started well enough. The airplane ride from Detroit had been exciting and that nice young Jared boy reminded her a little of her Isaac, what with all his "Yes, ma'am's" and "No, ma'am's." And that late-night kerfuffle in the senator's office, all those people fussing over her like she was some kind of movie star, and then getting her set up all hush-hush in this fancy apartment in this high-toned project. She thought they were having her on, but come to find out this was it, the actual Watergate itself, where they had that robbery way back when that ended up with President Nixon resigning in that helicopter and going off to China and what-all. Still, even though this was such a famous place, she was more than ready to leave.

She looked down at her new Timex watch, the one that nice Mr. Cardanzer had given her. She pressed the little button and watched the dial light up like a Christmas tree, just like they showed on TV. She couldn't wait to see the look on Isaac's face when she showed him this.

Twenty-four years! Dear Lord, it didn't seem possible. It all still seemed like a dream. The phone call had come almost exactly when Ev said it would and just like that it was Isaac, talking as calm as you please. She couldn't recall much of what he said after his soft "Hello, Mama"—it was all like a blur in her mind—but she would have known his voice anywhere—anywhere—even after a million years. A mother knows, and that's the God's truth. Now all she wanted was to see her boy with her own two eyes and hold him and praise the Lord for his deliverance. She was ready to get on out of here. More than ready. The Lord knew she didn't mean to cast any spersions on anyone, but she had the feeling these people would be happy to see her going. There was such a thing as overstaying your welcome.

There was a knock at the door. She straightened her hat and hurried to open it.

"Why, it's you!"

"Yes, ma'am. Jared Hansen."

"Are you the one driving me?"

"Yes, ma'am. I hope that's all right."

"It surely is. Now where did I put my purse? Young man, there's someone I'd like for you to meet when we get to where we're going. Can you guess who it is?"

"Yes, ma'am, I believe I can. Is this all your luggage right here?"

"This big old thing, yes. I can carry it."

"No, ma'am, I won't hear of that. What you could do, ma'am, is to put down that veil, just until we get into the car."

Jared lugged the suitcase down the hall to the elevator. His nerves were all jangled. He hadn't been able to reach Zeiss even once since getting back from Detroit, and the voice that returned his calls was always gruff, impatient, unfriendly. But Jared had a feeling that Zeiss would be back today. He sure hoped so. He hadn't called yet because all he'd been told was that it would be a long trip and that he and the passenger would be traveling alone. He'd guessed it would be Mrs. Johnson again, but he hadn't been sure until she'd opened the door.

The car waiting out front was a new Hertz Thunderbird with bucket seats, dual air bags, a full tank and under two thousand miles. "Unobtrusive blue," Cardanzer described it before handing Jared an envelope with three hundred dollars in crisp tens and twenties, a roll of quarters and two telephone numbers, the first to call for instructions when he reached Manhattan, the second after he delivered his passenger.

Cardanzer was on the other side of the car saying a few final words to Mrs. Johnson. Now that Jared knew what was happening, he was anxious to get going. He adjusted his seat belt and decided that he would make an early pit stop to place a call to Zeiss. It was funny, but he missed the guy. He reminded himself to make a note of the T-bird's plate number before he made his call. A good agent always noted the license plate number. Zeiss would appreciate that.

CHAPTER FIFTY-ONE

Bo was surprised when the door was opened by a thin young Asian girl in a T-shirt and blue jeans. Yes, he replied as he rolled in the cart, he was indeed from Indochina. No, not from Vietnam, though many guessed that: Laos. Yes, he thought she might have been from Cambodia: a most beautiful country. No, no, he knew it only by reputation.

He set the cart near the window. She tagged along and introduced herself: Mee Yang and a surname that sounded like Ginseng. He told her he was Bo. She shook hands like a man. Yes, he agreed, it was nice to meet a neighbor so far from home. Her friendliness was disarming. For such a skinny girl, she was not unattractive.

He snapped the sides of the cart into place, smoothed the white cloth and began setting out the food. Her questions continued. A few months, he told her, and yourself? Only a few days, she declared: first in Hollywood, California, and now here in New York. She guessed Bo's age. He smiled and corrected her. Really? she exclaimed, he did not look it.

She had only twenty years. And how, she asked, had he come to America? When he hesitated she lowered her eyes. Ah, she understood. And apologized for asking. The fruit salad looked delicious. And everything else. He was doing a fine job. She was hungry. Her eyes were once again wide. She had married an American, she said, and had been told that she would now be an American too. Did Bo think that was really true? Ah, he had heard the same thing. She clapped her hands: Good, good.

Impulsively, he told her that he too was living with an American. A woman, he added quickly, making himself feel doubly foolish. Grinning, she asked if this American of his had yellow hair. She did? Ah! And blue eyes? Ah! What a lucky fellow, to have such a colorful woman! When he asked if her American was also blond, she covered her mouth and giggled. Well, Bo remarked, at least Mee Yang's husband was rich. No, no, she insisted, these rooms belonged to a woman who was a friend of a friend—a story much too complicated for a country girl like herself to understand. She and her husband had a room downstairs: "*très jolie*," but not nearly so grand as this. Her husband was a good man, she declared, but not rich. At least not yet. But who could foretell the future? She then startled Bo by opening her arms and launching herself backward at the sofa.

Look, she exclaimed, collapsing back against the cushions, here she was in New York! She popped up and twirled about. What energy! She planned to have a baby soon, she declared, right here in America. Did Bo know any good American names?

What was that? Yes, certainly Bo could open the wine now. Her friend was inside putting things on her face and would be out in a moment.

Twice now, Bo reflected, he had been in this suite without seeing the elusive Mrs. Grelling.

Excuse me? What had she said? No, he did not think she needed to put things on her face.

Did she care to examine the label? Which label? Oh, the wine. Ah, it was French. That was good. Perhaps, she said playfully, Bo should marry his yellow-haired American and then they could all be Americans together. That was the way it worked, or so she had been told—had he not heard the same thing? Ah! Good, good.

No, no, she could not sign the check—she knew nothing of such things—but if he wished she would take it inside to the woman.

Bo smiled as she bounded off like a forest deer. He would have talked with her more but there was little time before his appointment. When she came back with the signed check he wished her a hundred springtimes. She wished him many sons.

Chapter Fifty-Two

The intercom buzzed.

"Mr. Schaeffer to see you, General."

Robbins smiled and flicked off the TV. Olden and the others had carried out their assignments well. This phase of the operation was complete. An element of the public would continue to support Johnson, of course, regardless of—in some cases, because of—his collaboration, but the media had been turned against him. Things could proceed. This entire sordid business would soon be behind them. He only wished they had allowed him a larger role.

He opened a folder and reviewed his checklist. Danbury still had to be briefed, but other than that, everything was set. They were working with an ETA of eighteen-thirty: More than enough time. Robbins hoped the boy was a careful driver.

The general stood and smoothed his jacket. "Franklin," he said, turning to his bodyguard, "please wait outside."

The disappearance of Zeiss and his entire team had been

a setback, no question about it. The general had always known that Ransom was resourceful, but he was evidently a good deal tougher than anyone had realized. Robbins had no intention of underestimating him again. There were a hundred places, from Andorra to Zanzibar, where a man with money could disappear. Ransom could have gone to any of them, but the general's quickening pulse told him that Ransom was here in America. Nearby. Close, and getting closer.

Though the general had always relished a hunt, part of him regretted having to eliminate a man who had consistently done good work. Ransom's relationship in Cambodia with the Pol Pot regime had been exemplary, for instance, and more recently he had forged strong bonds in the Middle East with Hamas. But Ransom should have known that his connection with this medic presented an unacceptable risk; disclosure of Parker Global's extralegal activities was simply not a viable option: not for the company, and certainly not for the senior Pentagon staffers who routinely facilitated them. In a real sense, Ransom had sealed his own fate.

"Harold," the general said enthusiastically, coming out from behind his desk as Schaeffer entered, "I'm glad you dropped by. This is developing into a most eventful day."

"Tell me," the company president replied. "I could use some good news."

Robbins glanced over and made sure the door was closed. "As we speak, Harold," he confided, "Corporal Johnson's mother is en route to New York."

Schaeffer was flabbergasted. "Are you sure?"

The general smiled indulgently. "One of our people is driving her up from Washington. He called in soon after passing through the Baltimore tunnel, a little over two hours ago. Have a seat."

Schaeffer tugged at his shirt cuffs: a nervous habit. "That

means Johnson is here in New York," he said. "Do we know exactly where?"

"Not yet. But our man will be calling us as soon as he is told where to deliver his passenger."

"What if he doesn't call?"

"He will."

"But if something happens, and he doesn't . . ."

"I have been on the phone, Harold. Steps have been taken. There is an inexorable logic to this: The mother will lead us to Johnson, and Johnson will lead us to Ransom. All we have to do is wait."

"I just wish it was over," Schaeffer fretted, sitting down, pulling out his handkerchief and dabbing at his upper lip.

Parker Global's president had not been sleeping well. The prospect of Ransom's activities becoming public filled him with dread. Late at night, when the fear clawed at his insides, he imagined a nightmare future in which he was being carted off to jail while his wife was flying down to that hairy tennis pro in Puerto Vallarta.

At such moments, rather than contemplate the abyss, Schaeffer planned his defense. His best chance would be to plead ignorance, to have the lawyers present him as a harried executive betrayed by trusted subordinates, men like Frank Grelling and Herbert Trang, whose naked greed drove them to file false end-user certificates and sell weapons to America's enemies. Could anyone seriously believe, he imagined himself challenging the committee or the grand jury or the court, that Harold Schaeffer would have countenanced any of the sales this man Ransom claims to have brokered, sales to North Korea, Red China, Libya, Iran, Serbia . . . the list went on and on! With the wounded self-righteousness of Clarence Thomas, he would assure his inquisitors that he welcomed their scrutiny, he would inform them that thorough investigations were already under way, he would promise them that when the truth was uncovered he would let the chips fall where they may. The American people, he would declare, deserved no less.

Who knew? It might work. It had certainly worked in the past. It had saved dozens of defense executives whose firms had been caught red-handed: faking test results, padding cost overruns, hiding shoddy workmanship, billing the government for everything from vintage wines to abortions. This business with Ransom was the same thing, more or less. Deniability was the key. Schaeffer knew the drill: Accept full responsibility but steadfastly deny all knowledge. It worked for everyone. Well, almost everyone. And if it hadn't been for those idiotic White House tapes, it would have worked for Nixon too. It—

"Harold?"

"Oh, pardon me, General. Would you mind repeating that last part?"

Robbins was standing. "Mr. Danbury, our new security chief, has been waiting to see me."

"Of course. Danbury. Good man." He stood and tugged on his shirt cuffs. "So everything is set, then? You feel confident that this time . . . ? I mean, that your plan . . . ?"

"Harold," Robbins said, "I believe our interests are in good hands."

CHAPTER FIFTY-THREE

Antel Grantham paced the blue carpet, getting nowhere. The senior senator from Alaska had spent the day a virtual prisoner in his own office. Out beyond the closed door, his frazzled staff was doing its best to cope with the fallout from this morning's media bombshell. The phone lines were jammed. The fax machines had broken down. Reporters were swarming. In the midst of the storm Bobby Cardanzer had left for National Airport to see what could be done about Johnson's mother. Sadly, Bobby was right: Sheltering her had suddenly become an unacceptable political risk. Grantham had wanted to speak with her on the phone this morning, but Bobby had been adamant and, given the current climate, probably right. Grantham tried to imagine what the poor woman must be going through, but it defied his imagination. He walked past his message-strewn desk, noting the full bank of blinking lights on his telephone. The three calls he was waiting for would be coming in on his unlisted line. More than two dozen of his fellow senators had phoned today, including every member of his subcommittee. Grantham had not spoken to any of them. He wanted to wait until he had a handle on the story's genealogy and, more importantly, until he and Bobby had assessed its implications for the upcoming hearings. Grantham was still finding it difficult to accept that a single word—albeit one with five syllables—had reduced his months of careful planning to rubble.

He stopped and watched the silent, madly blinking lights. Where the hell was Bobby? Where the hell was that Reilly woman? Where the hell was Buzz? In a burst of frustration, he wrenched the receiver from its cradle and pressed a random flashing button.

"Good afternoon," he said.

"I want Grantham," a male voice demanded.

"You've got him. To whom am I speaking?"

"This is really Senator Grantham?"

"That's what they tell me. Now what can I do for you, Mr. . . . ?"

"Peabody. Randolph I. Peabody, calling from Fairbanks. It's about this Corporal Johnson business. Senator, my sister lost her youngest boy in that miserable war."

"I'm sorry to hear that, Mr. Peabody."

"This man was a collaborator, Senator. He aided and abetted."

Grantham calmly and patiently explained his position. The practice was good for him; he'd have to be doing it in front of TV cameras soon enough.

"I see what you're saying, Senator," the caller responded, "but you're fixing to make this guy a millionaire, that's what riles me. No matter how it turns out, this corporal is going to get his book deal and his miniseries. All my sister gets is to sit home at night and look at old pictures and cry."

"Mr. Peabody, I'm trying to do the best job I know how."

"Yes, sir. I just wish to hell this fellow wasn't a collaborator. I hope they shoot the son of a bitch. That's all I wanted to say."

That call proved to be the high-water mark. As the senator answered a dozen more, he felt the hatred bubbling up through the wires like some fiberoptic witch's brew. Several callers accused Grantham of being a communist. One shrill woman ordered him to "Love it or leave it!" An enraged man called him "a pinko, nigger-loving, Eskimo cocksucker."

Grantham put down the phone and made a note about beefing up security in the committee chamber. Bobby could see to that. Where the hell was Bobby, anyway?

The private line rang. He grabbed it.

"Shane Reilly, Senator, what can I do for you?"

"Tell me your source for today's story."

"You know I can't do that, Senator. But if you recall, sir, I offered you a chance to comment and you declined."

"True, but I also recall asking you to call General Olden over at the Pentagon to verify your facts."

"Yes, sir, and I did."

"What happened?"

"He said he was not at liberty to make a statement."

"You spoke with General Olden personally?"

"Yes, Senator."

"And explained that you were calling at my behest?"

"Yes, Senator, but in all fairness to the general, I don't know what he was doing when I called. They might have pulled him out of a meeting or—"

"Did he offer to get back to you?"

"No, he didn't." She changed voices. "Senator, now that you've had the day to reflect, would you care to make a statement concerning Corporal Johnson?"

"No, thank you, Ms. Reilly."

"Senator, several of your congressional colleagues are using the word 'treason' to describe—"

"Ms. Reilly, I really must go. I'm sure we'll be speaking again soon."

He hung up. The noise from the outer office came rushing back at him, reminding him of a long-forgotten line from Yeats. How did it go again? Something about "the ceremony of innocence . . ."

So Buzz had been muzzled by someone upstairs, some bastard who knew Buzz didn't believe that Johnson was a collaborator. Buzz Olden would have prevented this—

The private line rang. Grantham grabbed it, hoping for Bobby.

It was Olden, apologizing for not calling back sooner.

Grantham didn't mince words. "I've been bushwhacked, Buzz. What can you tell me about it?"

"At this point, not much. I've been checking—"

"Don't try to snow me, Buzz. We had a deal. Your people broke it. I want to know who's responsible."

"We're trying to find out, Antel. Believe me—"

"Damn it, Buzz, you can't massage me. This was orchestrated. By your people. Now what the hell is going on?"

"I swear, Antel—"

"What exactly did you say to her, Buzz?"

"Her who?"

"Reilly. That gal from the *Washington Post*."

There was a fraction of silence before Olden said, "I've never spoken with her."

"Never spoken with her? Are you sure?"

"Wait, let me double-check. Reilly, you said? What was that first name?"

"Shane." Grantham felt his anger hardening to stone.

"No, Antel. She's not even in my directory. Why?"

"No reason," he said mildly. "I thought you might have been one of the people she'd spoken with."

"Is she good-looking?" Olden joked.

"Tall and willowy. Right up your alley."

"I'll have to check her out. Listen, Antel, about this Johnson business: The people here are livid. We're tearing this place apart. Give me twenty-four hours. We'll know something by then. Heads will roll, I promise you."

"Fine. But you tell your people that all deals are off, and so are the gloves. As far as I'm concerned, nothing is off limits now, and no one. You make sure to tell them that: no one."

"I will," Olden promised.

Grantham carefully replaced the receiver. No fool like an old fool, he told himself. Where the hell was Bobby? If he was off with his damn mistress again . . . The new military, he thought ruefully, recalling Jack Kennedy's lament: "A general is a general is a general."

Yes, but what was this general up to? Twenty-four hours, Buzz had said. Something was going to happen in the next twenty-four hours. But what? Wildly disparate possibilities began jockeying for his attention. Where the hell was Bobby?

An aide poked her head in to alert him that the evening network news shows would be locking up soon. Peter Jennings and Dan Rather were both on hold. They had crews outside. If he—

"Get Bobby on the beeper," he told her. "Be sure to punch in my private line. Do it right now, please."

Why the hell hadn't he done that before? Getting old, that's why: Brain cells dying. Wonder why Brokaw hadn't called.

One idea elbowed its way to the front of Grantham's consciousness. He was shocked by its cynicism. They wouldn't dare! He went to his desk, sat down, pulled open a drawer and rummaged. He didn't want a damn Valium, didn't need a damn laxative and didn't deserve any Wild Turkey. He slammed the drawer shut. They damn well wouldn't dare, he told himself, glaring fiercely at his own thought.

But even if he was wrong, his hearings were finished. The question now was whether anything at all could be salvaged.

Twenty minutes later Bobby Cardanzer hurried in, shut the door, loosened his tie and dropped into a chair. "She's on her way," he said, expecting that would cheer the old man up.

It didn't. Grantham went to his desk and sat down. The slanting afternoon light made his skin look bad: saggy. Cardanzer made a mental note to add some curtains, soften the effect. Couldn't have the old man looking his age.

"That 'informed Pentagon source,'" Grantham said, tapping a pen against his blotter, "the one who leaked this morning's story?"

"Yes?"

"Buzz Olden."

Cardanzer was stunned. The old man wouldn't say it if he wasn't sure. Damn! Buzz Olden, the white knight. "Wait a minute, Antel. Didn't he know we had Johnson's mother?"

"Yes."

"Then we're damned lucky she's on her way to New York."

"I've been thinking about that, Bobby, and I don't like what I keep coming up with. Convince me I'm wrong."

"You look tired, Antel. When was the last time you had something to eat?"

"You want some think time, right? Okay, let's refuel. Order sandwiches and a pot of coffee. Tell me what happened with you. How did you arrange it? When does she get there?"

CHAPTER FIFTY-FOUR

Bo looked up and down the street. It was cold and gray. An old woman wearing a long mink coat and one clear plastic glove was standing in the gutter watching her poodle defecate. He dropped in the quarter and pressed the numbers. When someone picked up, Bo asked how things were in Khe Sanh, today's code city.

His controller came on the line. "We have located him," the man said.

"Where?"

"Fate has indeed smiled on us. He is staying at the hotel where you are employed."

"What does he call himself?"

"We do not know, but he is traveling with a young Cambodian woman who claims to be his wife. They should not be difficult to identify."

"A young Cambodian woman?"

"Did your injury affect your hearing?"

"Excuse me. Please continue."

"You will go to the locker after five this evening and remove a small zippered satchel, what the Americans call a gym bag. It will contain everything you require for your mission. You will leave the key and observe all the standard precautions. Any questions?"

"None. Continue."

"We have paid a great deal for this information. The mission must be completed tonight. You will decide where, when and how this is to be accomplished."

"And the Cambodian woman?"

"She is irrelevant. You are authorized to do whatever is necessary. The only requirement is that your actions must be conclusive."

"Understood."

"Absolutely conclusive. Anything short of that would be disastrous to our cause. Do you understand?"

"Yes."

"I am instructed to emphasize that it must be done tonight."

"Understood. What am I to do afterward?"

"Dispose of everything except the passport and the money. Get out of the city quickly and quietly. Consider yourself on paid leave. Do not attempt to contact us for at least six months."

"Where am I to go?"

"You are free to choose. Personally, I can recommend Disney World. The climate in Florida is agreeable. There are large numbers of foreigners and many diverting activities. California also has much to offer, as does Texas. All three have significant Asian populations and good food. Do not attempt to leave the country."

"Understood."

"We will be praying for your success tonight."

"Thank you."

"I wish you many sons."

"May you enjoy a hundred springtimes."

CHAPTER FIFTY-FIVE

Grantham ate only one quarter of the turkey club. They'd put bacon on it even though he'd asked them not to. He saw it as a sign of his waning influence.

"How well do we know this Hansen boy?" he asked Cardanzer.

"Not well. Junior committee staffer, the same one who picked her up in Detroit. We didn't want to use our own man, remember?"

"I'm not senile yet, Bobby. And I realize that if Buzz hadn't done it, someone else would have. The question I need answered is what the boys with the stars are up to."

"By planting this collaborator story?"

"Yep."

"Seems pretty straightforward: undermine Johnson's credibility before he testifies."

"Is that all of it, Bobby? Nothing else at work here?"

"Why else would—?" He stopped short.

"Go on," Grantham encouraged.

"You think they made all this noise to flush her out into the open."

"Keep going."

"They have people following her car to New York. They assume she will lead them to her son."

"Finish it."

"Technically, he's still on active duty. They will arrest him, put him in protective custody, hold him incommunicado. Bottom line, he doesn't testify at the hearings."

Grantham nodded. He and Bobby were on the same wavelength. Except Grantham's scenario went further; Bobby didn't know about Ransom.

"The only one who could override the generals would be the President," Cardanzer continued. "But this President won't go near anything to do with that war." He put up his hands with thumbs joined, framing a headline: " 'Draft Dodger Intervenes to Aid Collaborator.' Jesus, Antel, if he tried it, some nut like Dornan would introduce articles of impeachment. And he might have plenty of co-sponsors."

"The boys with the stars are pretty smart," Grantham conceded. "Can you see me sitting there with my gavel and my ice water, looking like a doddering old fool while witnesses read prepared statements? After all this buildup, Bobby, either we deliver a real live MIA or the networks will go right back to their soap operas. Game, set and match, Pentagon."

"I can try to stop her," Cardanzer suggested. "When Hansen calls, I can tell him—"

"This New York detective," Grantham said, thinking a few steps ahead, "I assume he's acting unofficially."

"Lieutenant Mel Fink. Homicide. I had him checked out. Maverick, but highly respected. A real pro. Vietnam vet, incidentally."

"Your assessment?"

"I like him."

"Can we trust him?"

"Yes."

"Good. Get him on the phone."

"He won't be there yet."

"Leave a message. I want to speak with him personally. My private line."

CHAPTER FIFTY-SIX

After Danbury left, General Robbins made a call and confirmed that the attaché case was ready. He was pleased with his deceptively simple plan. If discovered early, the case would cause anxious delay at what was certain to be a critical time. If discovered late, after their arrest, the case would provide the authorities with clear evidence of criminal intent. Either way, inserting Danbury was a wise precaution. Robbins was now effectively out of the loop. If things somehow went haywire and Schaeffer had to be sacrificed, the general would be available to step in and guide the company. For the good of the nation.

Robbins understood the Pentagon's concern about outside involvement at this stage. The Detroit operation had been an embarrassment and, in retrospect, an overreaction. Fortunately, no one serious had been hurt: one cargo plane, its two-man crew and a junior officer and his family were a small enough price to pay. And all the Pentagon had were unconfirmed suspicions. Every battle had casualties; Robbins understood that, even if today's armchair generals did not. Well, what could one expect from men who called that absurd mismatch in the Persian Gulf a "war." At least the Viet Cong had known how to fight.

The intercom buzzed.

"A Mrs. Vinh, General," his secretary said.

"Mrs. Vinh?"

"An appointment made by Mrs. Grelling, General. She said you had approved it."

"Oh, yes. Mrs. Vinh. Was that for today? I'd nearly forgotten. Please have Franklin show her in."

Robbins opened his center drawer, removed the red folder, checked his notes one last time and then fed them into the shredder. The mission clock was running.

The door opened. The general looked up, curious to see what Marissa was sending him.

She was wearing a blue suit, a white silk blouse and an abstract gold pin which suggested both a butterfly and the scientific symbol for infinity. Her hair was coiled tightly atop her head and held in place by what appeared to be a long ivory stickpin.

Robbins stood. "Mrs. Vinh," he said formally, inviting her to sit.

"General," she murmured, executing a slight bow before floating gracefully into the chair.

He came around the desk and took the facing easy chair. She lowered her eyes. Noting her superb hair, porcelain skin and delicate features, he imagined how exquisite she must have been as a child.

"How may I be of service?" he inquired, fingering an eagle cuff link.

"A friend," she began without looking up, her voice barely above a whisper, "gave me the number of Mrs. Grelling. I met with her and she suggested—" She brought a tiny fist to her mouth and coughed softly, glancing nervously at Franklin standing in the corner.

"One moment, please, Mrs. Vinh," the general said, nodding to the bodyguard.

Franklin would now deliver the silver tray with the decanter of plum wine, the two glasses, the thin vase with the single fresh bud rose. The general would pour. They would sip. Franklin would slip outside.

If the pattern held true, she would start by detailing her background, the hardships of life in her native land, the difficulties of arranging passage, the perils of the ocean voyage. The general would concentrate on remaining perfectly still. It was important to allow her to proceed at her own pace. Eventually she would mention her child.

A child? the general would say: an infant, surely. She would produce a photo. He would study it with polite disinterest. And how old is your daughter? he would ask. They would sip more wine.

She would broach the subject of documents. He would listen sympathetically, agreeing that government officials here could often be rigid and impersonal, that even for worthy applicants the procedures were distressingly lengthy and the outcome far from certain. He would concede that on those rare occasions when he had exerted his small influence the petitioners had met with success.

The general expected that the next step would prove difficult for one as shy as Mrs. Vinh. He would sit patiently, allowing her all the time she required. At least she had not come dressed as a child herself, the way some mothers did. He had once imagined having a card printed that read, "No Substitutions, Please."

To those women who broke down and cried or were otherwise unable to proceed, the general was unfailingly polite: offering tissues, promising to look into their situation, escorting them to the door. But he anticipated no such problem today. Mrs. Vinh struck him as a woman who knew what she was about; what she was here to do might be difficult for her, but she seemed prepared to carry it out with the appropriate dignity.

When he tuned back in to her, he was pleased to discover that she was already halfway across the Pacific. A few moments later, as her hands moved to her purse and extracted a small photograph, the general felt a deep tremble. As he reached for it he reminded himself to ask how recent it was, but when he looked down his mind went blank.

He stared, entranced. Time stood still. The clear eyes looking up at him radiated pure innocence. The mouth seemed about to speak to him. There was a mystical familiarity about the face, a hint of the eternal. Marissa had outdone herself this time.

"Of course," Mrs. Vinh murmured, "a photograph can be deceiving."

"Yes," the general agreed, unable to take his eyes from it. He could almost feel the supple young flesh. His very bones seemed to vibrate.

"I hesitate," Mrs. Vinh whispered, "to ask for any more of your valuable time, General."

Was it his imagination, or did that voice sound familiar: an echo almost? He had the sense of a pebble splashing in a deep well. Ripples. He couldn't pull his eyes from the photograph. His memory was running everything together: so many voices, so many faces, so many years.

". . . possible for you to conduct a private interview . . ." the woman was saying, her voice barely audible.

He held his breath.

". . . to determine if she is . . . worthy."

The general savored the moment, cradling the small black

and white photo in his palm like a tiny pet, looking down and watching the innocent eyes watching him watch them.

"Yes," he said, as much to the child in the photo as to the woman, "I believe that can be arranged."

When he looked up she had raised her glass of plum wine. She was smiling.

"I am so pleased, General," she said. "To your health."

"Thank you, Mrs. Vinh, and to yours."

The wine tasted especially sweet today.

"May you enjoy one hundred springtimes," she said, raising her glass again.

Her sudden effusiveness was charming. They drank.

"May she prove worthy," Mrs. Vinh said, and drained her glass.

He did the same. The sentiment and the wine left a delightful warmth in his stomach. He noticed he was still holding the photo.

"How long ago . . . ?" he asked, returning the picture.

She slipped it into her purse and took out a lace handkerchief. "Twenty-four years," she said.

"No, no." He smiled, assuming she was revealing her age. "I meant—"

"I have not cut my hair in twenty-four years, General. Here," and she reached up and grasped the ivory pin. "I will show you."

"That is not necessary," he replied warily, watching her hands.

As she slid out the long pin her hair sprang free, coil upon coil unwinding in sinuous bumps and tumbles. She reached up and pulled it over her shoulder, guiding it across her torso like a sash.

He slid his chair back beyond her reach. "I am afraid you misunderstood my question, Mrs. Vinh."

"I think not, General," she said, smiling sweetly and looking at him directly for the first time. "As I said, the photograph is twenty-four years old."

"But," he said irritably, and suddenly noticed that the woman was now wearing the same smile as the child in the photograph.

He felt a sharp constriction in his chest. He was about to speak when something clutched at his throat from inside, choking him. He opened his mouth wide, trying to breathe. He couldn't make it work.

"So soon, General?" she asked, calmly stroking her bandolier of hair. "Has it been sixty seconds already?"

She stood, put down the ivory pin and shook open the hankie. "Here, let me take that glass," she whispered, removing it from the tray. "I must now wipe it out carefully and pour in a bit more wine. Those were Mr. Ransom's instructions."

He groped blindly for her, missed.

"Are you in pain, General? How nice." She poured the wine and then tossed the glass to the carpet. "He is such a clever man, that Mr. Ransom. Please, a moment longer, General, while I finish arranging my hair. Oh, all right, go ahead and fall."

His face struck the carpet. Small, strange, gurgling noises came from his throat. He stopped moving.

She slid her hairpin back into place. "I will start to scream now, General," she said, poking him gently with her shoe. "I have no gag today. Perhaps this time someone will hear me."

CHAPTER FIFTY-SEVEN

"Look," Fink explained to the hotel's assistant manager. "I'm going to need some special services."

The young man smiled and gave his ballpoint a decidedly military click. "That is why I am here." His accent was early Schwarzenegger.

They were in a tiny, immaculate office adjoining the lobby. Fink was bristling with energy. He had just come in from the airport. Marissa and Johnson were safe upstairs. He had the outline of a plan.

"Not a problem," the hotelier declared when Fink finished. "I'll see to the additional suites, give instructions to the telephone operators, alert the garage, arrange for added security and contact the limousine service. Will there be anything else at this time?"

"What do I call you?"

"Gustav."

"Okay, Gustav, what we've got here is a fluid situation.

I'll need to be able to contact you. How late are you working?"

"Until eleven, but I will stay as long as required. This extension will reach me anywhere in the hotel. How will you be settling the bill?"

"Charge everything to Mrs. Grelling."

"Excellent."

"You know I'm a cop, right?"

"Yes, Lieutenant." He stood. "Shall we go and choose the new suites now?"

The assistant manager was built like an athlete. "You ever play ball as a kid, Gustav?"

"I grew up in Germany. We skied."

Fink gathered everyone into one of the new, unregistered suites. It was only four o'clock but the sky was already slate gray. Marissa had messages, Mee Yang had new clothes, Johnson looked shaky. Barton needed to speak with Fink alone: immediately.

"My mother," Johnson called before they could leave.

"It's all set," Fink told him. "She's on her way. Should be here in—" He glanced at his watch— "less than three hours."

Barton pulled him into the next room and shut the door. "He works here in the hotel."

"Who does?"

"Our perp: the Vietnamese kid."

"Jesus Christ! When did all this happen?"

"About half an hour ago, a tip from a restaurant owner hot for the reward money. Our boy goes by the name Bo Lee. He used to deliver Chinese for the tipster—an old man named Han—but left when he got a room service job here. You ready for the good news, Lieutenant?"

"Make my day."

"*Señor* Perp is scheduled for the graveyard shift tonight: eight P.M. to four A.M."

"How about a home address? A telephone?"

"He gave Han's restaurant on his application, but the old man claims he hasn't seen him in weeks."

"Great."

"It's funny," Barton said. "When Marcia gave me the message I wasn't going to return the call. But then I remembered Rotelli and I figured, you know, turn over every stone. Some coincidence he turns up here, huh?"

"Yeah," Fink said, distracted. Whatever the thought was, he lost it. "You say the kid's name is Lee? What else have we got?"

"The old man says small, wiry, black hair, twenties: really narrows it down. I thought about calling Reynolds for some—"

"Christ, no! That's all we need, that son of a bitch. What the hell is the matter with you? Reynolds would throw Zack in a holding pen and stand there posing for photographers."

"That's another thing," Barton said uncomfortably.

"What is?"

"I've been thinking, Lieutenant. I mean, what we're doing here, hiding him and all . . ."

"Yeah?" This was what Fink had been hoping for.

"Well, how long are we going to have to do this?"

"We?" Fink asked.

"Okay: me."

"What's the problem?"

"Well, what if it's true, that he was a collaborator, and he gets—? I don't know. Are we accessories? You see how I'm thinking."

"Oh yeah."

"Plus, here comes this lead on our primary and I can't follow it up because I'm stuck playing nursemaid."

"You want out of this, Barton?"

"I didn't say that. But I haven't got your years, Lieutenant. This blows up, the worst you get is a pension. But me—"

"Listen, Barton," Fink snarled, "I don't have time for your crybaby crap. Just do your goddamn job. When this is over I'll get you assigned to the canine unit, okay? Then you and your pooch can go around sniffing under little girls' skirts." He glared at him, then relaxed. "Now, you say our boy Lee is due in at eight?"

Barton was seething. "Right," he whispered. "Eight o'-clock."

Fink shooed him away. "Go downstairs. Canvass the staff. Play detective. I'll give you thirty minutes to get back here."

As Barton was stalking out, the phone rang. Marissa answered, waved him over, gave him the phone. It was Rhonda. She thought he and Fink would want to know: General Robbins was dead. Heart attack, right in his office, about an hour ago.

Chapter Fifty-Eight

Schaeffer tossed in the pills and washed them down with Perrier. He closed his eyes and imagined fluffy clouds, rolling fairways, palm trees swaying in a gentle breeze. He sensed the pills dissolving, rippling through his system, delivering an internal shiatsu massage. This was good. This was very good. In a few minutes he would go out and face the bright lights and read a prepared statement, a snippet of which might find its way onto the evening news as part of a total tribute of perhaps twenty seconds. Anything longer would tax the attention span of the average viewer. Americans today didn't want heroes, Schaeffer reflected, they wanted serial killers and beer commercials, axe murderers and collaborators. He opened his eyes and gazed out his window at the world of minnows below. That was why they were down there and Harold Schaeffer was up here.

He allowed himself one more deep breath. The pills were doing their job. The general was dead, but Harold Schaeffer would turn even that to his advantage. He picked up his phone and pressed Danbury's extension.

The acting security chief offered his condolences, then segued quickly: Would the general's death affect tonight's plans?

Schaeffer tried for the general's imperious tone: "Your instructions stand."

"I'd like to discuss that with you, Mr. Schaeffer."

"That will not be possible. Carry out your orders."

"Yes, sir."

"Is there anything else?"

"No, sir. I'm just waiting for that phone call."

Schaeffer hung up, his excitement bordering on giddiness. He had just green-lighted a mission designed by a military legend. Plus, when the mission succeeded, Harold Schaeffer figured to be the prime beneficiary. Best of all, whatever happened, Harold Schaeffer's deniability would be absolute. If necessary, he could take a polygraph: Did you formulate the plan? Did you choose the personnel? Did you know the particulars? No, No, No! This was perfect.

His secretary buzzed. They were ready with the statement. Did he wish to review it now? The media people were all waiting downstairs.

"All right," Schaeffer replied, trying out his bereaved sigh, and almost getting it. He told her to assure the media he would be joining them shortly. In the meantime, they should avail themselves of the open bar. She could send in the statement now. His second sigh was better, but it still lacked something. "Oh," he said, "I suppose that fellow with the makeup is out there. Might as well send him in too." He tried one more sigh: nailed it.

CHAPTER FIFTY-NINE

Fink went and rinsed his face. His skin felt like old shoe leather. When he came back out he saw Johnson standing in the corner with his back turned. Mee Yang was comforting him.

"Is he okay?" Fink asked her.

"Doc fine," she snapped, rubbing her husband's back. "Worry better by you."

Feisty little broad, Fink thought, remembering a tiny bright-eyed smuggler he'd met in Thailand . . . When was that? . . . almost thirty years ago. Christ, she was probably a grandmother by now. If she lived through the war . . .

"Messages," Marissa said, waving papers.

Fink bent and kissed her forehead. It was familiar, warm, reassuring. "Anything interesting?"

"Ransom phoned and talked to Zack. He said he would call you at six." She dropped her voice. "I think he wants to get them out of here tonight."

"What makes you think that?" Fink asked.

"I know how he operates, *caro*," Marissa replied. "Besides, he wants them all packed." She took Fink's tie between her fingers. "He told me I did good this time."

"With what?"

"With you, *viejo*." She gave his tie a little tug and released it. "Which reminds me, you're supposed to call a Bob Cardanzer in Washington. He left a number. Too bad about the general."

"You knew him, right?"

"Would you believe I talked with him on the phone yesterday? He sounded fine. *La vida*," she shrugged. "*Quién sabe*? You want me to dial that Washington number for you?"

"No, I'll do it inside. You stay and answer this one."

He took the message slip and started to walk off, then remembered Bo Lee. "Listen," he warned Marissa, "no room service. No one knows we're in here. Don't open the door for anyone but Barton. He should be back soon." He nodded toward Johnson. "And keep those two here. How sure are you about Ransom?"

Her eyes narrowed. "Sure how?"

"About his wanting to get them out of here."

"Ninety-nine percent."

"Okay. That means he probably figures to take Zack's mother along."

"I don't know," Marissa said.

"Don't listen to me, I'm just thinking out loud. Let me go see what this Cardanzer guy wants."

It took Fink a moment to locate the phone. Everything was coming at him too fast; it was like that day he'd been hit with five different homicides at once. There was only so much he could absorb. If Ransom was right, Bo Lee's presence on the staff here at Marissa's hotel was no coincidence. And maybe the general's death was no heart attack. Fink decided that he had better stay close to Marissa until this was over.

He sat on the edge of the bed, stretched his neck, listened to it creak. He felt rumpled from all the flying, and his sinuses were sore. The key question now was whether Barton would come through for him. Fink had gone out of his way to bruise Barton's ego, but would that be enough? He got an outside line and dialed the number.

CHAPTER SIXTY

Tiffany stroked Bo's silky hair as he poured out his incredible story. They were in bed, his cheek resting on her bare belly, his breath tickling her damp skin. She wanted him again, but right now talking this through was far more important. He was finally telling her the truth. Tiffany sensed that this conversation would settle their future; she would lose him forever or have him forever. She had no intention of losing him.

It turned out that Bo was a soldier in the Vietnamese army. He had been sent to America to assassinate crooked arms dealers whose defective merchandise had killed dozens of his countrymen. He had eliminated three people since arriving here. The first two had been evil men who sold munitions for profit, but the third had been an accident. Trapped in an office building, Bo had been forced to kill a security man, a former policeman. The money and the gun she had found in the hamper had come from that botched operation. There had been no thugs on a subway; the security man had struck him. He had lied to her about that, about his nationality, his name, his true purpose here—about so many things.

She was not upset that he had lied to her about those things—she had suspected as much—as long as he was not lying about the one thing that mattered most.

"Bo love Tiff'ny forever," he confirmed, kissing her belly and making her muscles quiver.

"Go on," she said. "With the story, I mean."

He had one more assignment, he told her, only one more. It had to be done tonight. After tonight he would have many months free. Months. Tiffany must quit her job and go away with him. He had much money: the ten thousand American dollars she had discovered, and five thousand more which had been left for him in a locker. Plus today was payday; there was a check waiting for him at the hotel. All she had to do was say yes. They could start with Disney World, and then travel to Texas, California, Las Vegas, the Mall of America—anywhere she wished! They could visit Hawaii. She could wear a grass skirt and learn the hula. He could dive for pearls and feed her oysters. Was this not wonderful? Were they not lucky? All she had to do was say yes.

"Tell me about this last assignment," she said.

He traced a lazy circle around her navel with his finger. "It is not important, loved one."

Her leg trembled. "They want you to kill someone."

"It is not important." He slid his hand up between her knees and began kneading the soft flesh of her inner thigh.

Her fingers brushed the wispy hairs at the base of his neck. "Tell me about the assignment," she said, trying to ignore his hand.

"No more talk," he said, working it higher.

"No more lies," she said, squirming away. "Promise me."

"Promise, loved one."

He moved around and brought his other hand into play. She felt herself floating backward toward ecstasy and struggled to delay it.

"We have to talk," she pleaded, licking her lips.

"After," he told her.

His hands were everywhere, moving over her like a tide.

"Now, baby," she moaned. "Please."

CHAPTER SIXTY-ONE

"I can't," Jared whined, cupping his hand around the mouthpiece of the pay phone. "I'm supposed to pull right into the hotel garage. Where's Zeiss? Listen, if I get caught—"

"You're coming up Park Avenue anyhow," Danbury told him. "Pull over at the northeast corner of Forty-eighth Street. There's a fire hydrant."

"Northeast? What the hell is northeast? No, look, I'm sorry. Really, I can't do this. I called Zeiss' beeper. I don't even know who you—"

"Calm down," Danbury said. "The whole thing will take five seconds. I've got the attaché case for him and an envelope for you."

"Envelope?"

"A small token of our appreciation. Now listen carefully, I'll walk you through it."

"Okay," Jared said, "give me a second here," patting himself for a pen and a scrap of paper. He found them, turned and waved at the double-parked car across the street. The interior was dark, but he thought he could see Mrs. Johnson returning his wave from the back seat. As long as they had an envelope for him he supposed he could stop for five seconds. But that was it: five seconds.

"Now," he said, scrunching up his shoulder and spreading paper against plastic, "tell me what—"

A gust of wind rustled the paper and peppered him with grit. He began to shiver. "This place scares the hell out of me," he admitted. "I'm from Illinois."

"I'm from Ohio," Danbury said. "Trust me, neighbor, this is going to be a piece of cake."

CHAPTER SIXTY-TWO

At ten to seven Bo turned the corner of Madison and Fiftieth and spotted two detectives in the front seat of an unmarked car. He was not particularly alarmed. This was a rich neighborhood. He had seen unmarked cars near the hotel before.

But five more strides brought him alongside a second unmarked car and five strides after that he saw a third. Three cars, six detectives, big trouble.

Bo maintained his casual pace, but his thoughts began to run. He had walked into a trap. Continuing at this rate would put him beneath the brightly lit hotel marquee in approximately one minute. More police would be stationed there. To keep going would be dangerous, but turning back and breaking the pattern of his motion might be worse. He glanced around but saw no doorway to duck into. He was the only pedestrian on the street, which suggested that several detectives were already following his movements.

"Make your choice," Tiffany had insisted tonight. "Life or death?"

"Life," Bo had declared, mounting her.

But afterward he had decided that he could have both, that Corporal Johnson's death would earn him a happy life with Tiffany.

Bo felt his lips tighten into a rueful smile. A happy life for a half-breed orphan? How could he have been such a fool? As he walked, slivers of cold sharp as broken dreams raked his face.

He jammed his hands into the pockets of his jeans. The only things in there were worthless American money and one wretched subway token. He had assured Tiffany he was going out only to collect his paycheck. She had believed him. The American police would not be so easily deceived.

The gun in Bo's waistband pressed against the small of his back, prompting an inventory; he had the Glock, plus his bracelet, plus his hands, his feet and his poor excuse for a brain. Not nearly enough.

Fifty meters short of the hotel Bo halted, leaned against a tree and pretended to examine the bottom of his sneaker. He sensed inquisitive police eyes appraising him from all directions. It seemed impossible that he could have been this stupid: Had he not told his controller there would be heavy security? In training, Bo's instructors had warned him that romantic entanglements would cloud his mind, that love could get him killed. He understood them now, but now was too late. Too late!

He closed his eyes and beseeched his maternal ancestors for one more miracle, vowing that if they granted him success tonight he would never ask them for anything again. The prayer lasted only a few seconds, but he sent it with all his strength.

He opened his eyes. The wind had stopped. It was quiet as a graveyard.

"Into the street," an internal voice whispered.

Eager to comply, Bo stepped quickly off the curb only to stop short. A vehicle was approaching. Its headlight beams were blurring its shape, but there was no mistaking the light on its roof. Police!

He retreated between parked cars. His ancestors had abandoned him, exactly as he deserved.

The police car was getting closer. It seemed to be slowing. Bo decided that when it stopped he would make a run for it, staying low and using the parked cars for cover. The tip of his tongue rubbed the hard capsule lodged inside his lip. When the time came to bite down on it he would close his eyes and picture Tiffany in a grass skirt, swaying for him.

As the car came alongside, Bo was splashed with yellow police light. His muscles tensed.

But, to his astonishment, the vehicle slid smoothly past, as apathetic as the huge old buffalo that used to haul water for his village. Bo's ancestors had not deserted him after all!

Tingling with relief, he inched forward and peered up the street. A man in a suit—another detective—emerged from the hotel garage, walked out into the street and stood there with his back turned, looking toward the far corner.

Could this have been what Bo's ancestors had wanted him to see? But why? What was—?

The hotel garage! Of course! They were showing him the hotel garage! With an elevator downstairs to carry him past the police-infested lobby and deliver him safely to any floor of the hotel. Yes!

Bo covered the remaining distance as inconspicuously as possible. The garage entrance was wide open. The big freight elevator was standing empty. The workers were gone. The detective in the street hunched his shoulders as Bo passed, but did not turn.

Bo entered the garage and quickened his pace. He knew the layout. The door at the back opened to a stairway which led to the parking area below. Once down there he would have to pass a small office to get to the hotel passenger elevator located against the far wall.

With a final glance toward the street, Bo grasped the chrome knob, eased the door open and slipped through to an enveloping darkness.

Corporal Johnson was as good as dead.

CHAPTER SIXTY-THREE

Fink stood in the street and watched his breath smoke into the chill night air. He'd given the driver good directions. Uptown traffic shouldn't be too bad at this hour. The blue Thunderbird with D.C. plates should have been here by now. Where the hell was it?

Everything had been all right until he'd spoken with Grantham. The senator had spooked him with that weird business about his son having been a lieutenant too. Forty-eight, Fink had told him, and Grantham had replied that his son would have been the same age. Then the old man had started rambling on about how the whole mad war had come down to this and how he was helpless to do anything but pass along a warning. The warning turned out to be a suspicion that Johnson's mother was being followed. There were people determined to keep her son from testifying, Grantham said, and there was no telling what they might do. But the people behind those people were federal, so there was no one Grantham could safely call on to intervene on Johnson's behalf. Fink was on his own. Grantham no longer wanted Johnson to testify, merely to survive. No matter what he'd done, Grantham said, he deserved that much.

Fink pushed up on his toes. A car stopped at the corner was signaling a turn. This had to be it. Fink reviewed his plan. When Ransom had called at six, they had worked out a timetable. Then, after Mrs. Johnson's driver had called from downtown, Fink had given Barton the specifics and had sent him downstairs to wait for Rhonda, providing him the opportunity to—

His plan stunk. It was too damned complicated, with too many variables. It was the best Fink had been able to come up with, but he knew in his gut it wasn't going to work. Poor Johnson. Rotelli had said it best: "Fuckin' world."

Thinking about Rotelli released a spurt of rage; Fink wished to hell he could stick around here tonight to take down that murdering Bo Lee bastard himself.

The light changed. Fink crossed his fingers, but it was only a cab, with nothing behind it. He checked his watch: five to seven. It was going to be tight. He had to have everyone out of the hotel by seven-fifteen; that was when O'Brien and the others would be arriving to take up positions for the Bo Lee collar.

He went back inside the garage and rubbed his hands together. Now where the hell were those two garage guys? Fink thought he had gauged Barton correctly, but maybe not. Who ever really knew anybody?

Unable to stand still, he braved the cold and went out to check the corner again. Nothing. There was a recklessness about what he was doing tonight that both excited and frightened him. It was the same dangerous impulse that had driven him since his childhood, from Vietnam to Atlantic City to . . .

. . . a trip to Coney Island, a long time ago. Fink remembered it all at once: racing his son along the boardwalk, the resilience of the wood, the mournful cries of the gulls, the wide deserted beach, the gray sea blending into gray sky, the salty wind in his eyes. It had been cold then too, but it had been a happy cold. Grantham's son would have been forty-eight. Fink's would have been twenty-one.

He raised his hand and inspected the finger where his wedding band used to be. There wasn't even the trace of a tan line. He thrust his hands into his pockets. He wanted to get back to Marissa. He wanted Isaac Johnson to have a life. He wanted to get this show on the road. Where was that goddamn car?

CHAPTER SIXTY-FOUR

Adelaide had never been to New York, and now that she was here she didn't care for it: all these buildings looking like they could fall over on you any second and not think twice about it. The air was cold, with a wet that made fuzzy little circles around everything, as if even the light was afraid to travel too far in this godforsaken place. She looked across the street and was glad to see Jared finally hanging up the phone.

"Only ten minutes more," he announced after hopping back in and locking the door.

Adelaide's belly went all funny, just like it had that first time she saw Isaac's daddy. She shook her head, amazed with herself; what a thing to be thinking about at a time like this. Forty-five years ago, that was. My oh my. Lord, she thought, You are some trickster.

The car was moving again. Adelaide fretted about whether Isaac would even recognize her with her hair gone all gray like it had. She had always imagined him as a little boy, but she now realized he wasn't a little boy, he was a full-grown man, forty-three years old. On the telephone, he had said he had a lady friend, a girl with a Chinese name Adelaide was sorry she hadn't written down and memorized. She'd tried to picture the girl but couldn't. A fellow Isaac's age should have a girl, she told herself, and not some gray-haired old lady fussing over him and getting in young folks' way. She surely didn't want to get between people, but after twenty-four years no decent woman would begrudge her a few minutes of the man's time. Not even a Chinese girl, whatever they might be like.

Stop and start. Stop and start. What kind of city was this where you couldn't go for ten seconds without hitting some bump or stopping at some red light? The people in charge ought to be ashamed. And now what was this? The boy was pulling over again. Were they here? Oh my. That hadn't been anybody's ten minutes. She wasn't ready. Where was her purse?

"This will only take a second, Mrs. Johnson," Jared said, putting down the front passenger window and filling the car with a mean cold.

She had a terrible fright when a big white man came running up out of nowhere and stuck his head through the open window. But it seemed like Jared had been expecting him. The man handed Jared an envelope and then laid a briefcase on the front seat, the kind that businessmen carried to hold important papers and such. Then the man backed out, patted the windowsill a few times and disappeared.

Strange doings, Adelaide thought as Jared raised up the window and the car started moving again.

Chapter Sixty-Five

Johnson pulled the mangled knot apart and crossed the room. Maybe if he tried tying it in the mirror.

Once again his reflection caught him unawares. It wasn't that he looked so bad, it was just that he didn't look like him. He wondered if Mama would even recognize him.

The bedroom door opened. He turned. Mee Yang raised her arms and did a pirouette. He watched her long hair fan out gracefully and then float back down, every strand magically finding its proper place.

"So," she asked, "what you think?"

"I love your hair," he murmured.

"Forget hair," she snapped, pouting. "Look at dress."

She turned again, slowly this time. The bright red fabric hugged her breasts and belly and cute little behind. The skirt was long, except for a wide slit on one side that ran all the way up to her thigh. Johnson thought his mother might faint.

"So?" she demanded.

He started to explain that his mother was kind of old-fashioned, but Mee Yang stormed out and slammed the door.

It wasn't only Mee Yang. Everyone was on edge tonight. It reminded Johnson of the mood in the village when Khmer Rouge patrols were rumored to be in the area.

He tried the knot again. The reversed image in the mirror was confusing, but he got the first two wraps just about perfect, then took a deep breath and attempted the big sideways loop. When that worked, he told himself he was halfway home.

The word stopped him. He stared at the mirror and silently mouthed it—Home, Home, Home, Home—until the eyes staring back at him fluttered and then went damp around the edges.

"Home," he whispered, and brought his face so close to the mirror that his features dissolved.

"Home," he said again and rested his forehead against the cool glass, closed his eyes and savored the word that had been his secret companion, his only comfort on terror-filled nights, the word that had seen him through sickness and storms and forced marches, the magic word that had the power to transport him out of himself and into a place where there was no pain and no time.

He attacked the tie with renewed energy. Maybe what these people on TV were saying about him was true; they all seemed so sure of themselves. He didn't care what they called him as long as it didn't upset Mama. He still couldn't believe he was finally going to see her. Tonight. Minutes from now.

Johnson stepped back to admire his handiwork. He had done it! A Windsor knot, Mama's favorite. Twenty-four years and he could still tie a Windsor knot.

There was a sharp knock on the door. Marissa poked in her head. Her earrings sparkled.

"Come on, *hombre*," she said. "We don't want to keep your mother waiting. It's cold in that garage."

CHAPTER SIXTY-SIX

It was so dark on the landing that Bo was invisible even to himself. The air was stale and smelled of sawdust and engine oil. Using the handrail, he descended the stairs on tiptoe, each tiny sound reverberating in the confined space.

When he reached the bottom he backed against the wall, pressed his palms together and sent a message skyward, first giving thanks for his safe passage here and then reminding his maternal ancestors that his target tonight was an American soldier, an invader of their sacred land, a despoiler of its virtuous women.

Bo pulled the door open a crack and heard muffled voices. At the edge of a clearing surrounded by parked cars a big black man was sharing a misshapen cigarette with a much smaller Latin. Both wore the brown and gold jackets of hotel garagemen. The Latin was not much larger than Bo.

An alarm bell sounded above Bo's head, giving him a start. The big black man grumbled, took one last drag on the cigarette and headed toward the stairwell.

Bo eased the door closed, stepped back, felt for his bracelet and carefully drew out the wire. Then, pressing himself against the wall, he raised his arms above his head and held his breath.

The door opened violently, striking the toe of Bo's sneaker and bouncing off. By the time he had a clear path the man was climbing the stairs and out of reach, leaving behind a foul odor of fried meat and hair oil.

The upstairs door squeaked and light spilled down the shaft. Bo watched the man lumber out. There were car noises. Others would be coming down here soon. Bo had to move quickly.

The Latin was seated behind a dilapidated metal desk studying a sex magazine when Bo slipped into the small office, eased the bills from his pocket and dropped them to the cement floor.

"Good evening," Bo said, smiling and displaying his hotel ID.

The man raised dull glazed eyes. "Yeah?" he challenged.

"You lose this money?" Bo asked him, pointing to the bills on the floor.

"Lemme see," the Latin said, coming around the desk.

Bo made room for him.

"Oh yeah, I musta dropped it," the man said, squeezing in front of Bo and bending for the cash. "Thanks."

"Welcome," Bo replied as he reached down, grasped the man's head and chin and wrenched them sharply in opposite directions. The neck snapped with a satisfying crunch.

Bo dragged the body behind the desk and stripped off the jacket. After retrieving the money, he left the office, skirted the clearing and, when he heard footsteps approaching from the back of the garage, ducked into the shadow of a parked car. Ten meters in front of him the freight elevator mechanism began clattering. A car was coming. He crouched down and eased the gun from his waistband.

CHAPTER SIXTY-SEVEN

"Two more blocks," Jared said, pointing to a street sign.

But the next thing Adelaide knew they were turning by a building with lights all over it like a movie house and a white man in a dark suit was waving the car off the street and into a narrow box-like thing. A metal curtain closed behind them. The lights went out. A mechanical noise started up, the whole contraption began shaking, and Adelaide realized it was a kind of freight elevator like they had in the buildings where she worked.

When it stopped they were in an underground garage. Up ahead, a good-looking black man in a suit was standing next to a pretty black girl. Adelaide didn't think that was her Isaac but she became frightened because she couldn't be sure.

The car jerked forward and stopped again. No, this wasn't Isaac, this was some West Indian boy. And the girl was surely not Chinese. Off to one side was a big limousine like Ev had that night by the church. Then before she knew it her door was open and she was being helped out. The same white man who had waved them into the elevator took hold of her arm and began hurrying her toward the limousine.

"Pop the trunk," he called out. "Let's get her luggage transferred. Barton," he barked, "help him out." He turned to her. "Hello, Mrs. Johnson," he said.

Adelaide couldn't even answer, the man was speeding her along so fast. Where was the fire? Couldn't he see she was no spring chicken? She looked back for Jared and saw him with her big suitcase in one hand and that little briefcase that came in through the window in the other.

"That's not mine," she called to him, but he didn't pay her any mind.

"Please, Mrs. Johnson," the man with her arm said, pulling at her.

He kept her moving forward, but she twisted around and saw Jared handing both things to the West Indian. She planted her feet and tried to pull her arm free. "Now listen here," she declared. "I preciate all this attention, but—"

"Mama?"

He was standing there big as life. Adelaide would have recognized him anywhere. Their eyes caught, her arms flew open and they both moved so fast she didn't know who got to who first.

Adelaide had never in her life held anything as tightly as she clung to her living breathing flesh-and-blood Isaac, her very own miracle of miracles. With her cheek pressed against his chest she listened to the beating of his blessed heart, remembering that first day she'd heard it through the doctor's stethoscope. This big strong man in her arms hadn't even been a real baby yet when that lickety-split rhythm in her belly had startled her to tears.

Suddenly afraid she would squeeze the life out of him, Adelaide ran her hands over his broad back and felt his bones. Alive! Her little Isaac was alive! Thank you, sweet Jesus!

She wanted to stand back and just look at him, but she couldn't make herself let go. She was so full of love and thanks that she thought she would explode into a million pieces and go flying off every which way.

A voice from above, so sweet it gave her shivers, whispered "Mama," and she gripped her boy even tighter.

The voice came again. "Mama," it said gently, "there's someone here I'd like for you to meet."

Fink caught himself staring and looked away, embarrassed. He had no time for that now.

"Back in the car," he ordered Jared, indicating the Thunderbird. "Rhonda, Barton," he called, "let's go."

"Go where?" Barton asked, angrily hefting the suitcase into the limousine's trunk.

"Thunderbird," Fink said. "Back seat. Come on!"

Barton caught up with Rhonda at the car. She was here at Fink's request: a precaution, he had said, so she wouldn't say anything to anyone.

"What the hell is going on?" Barton demanded.

"Change of plans," Fink told him. "Young Mr. Hansen here is driving you and Rhonda to the airport."

"Can't we all go together?" Rhonda asked.

"We're decoys," Barton muttered disgustedly, holding the door for her.

Barton saw the whole thing in one ugly splat: He'd been had. What he couldn't understand was how Fink had worked it out. Barton had called Captain Reynolds. Three unmarked cars were waiting outside to follow the Thunderbird. And to keep Fink from connecting it to him, Barton had arranged for the chase cars to hang back until they were far from the hotel. How the hell . . . ? Fink couldn't have had a phone tap; Barton had used a damn pay phone. Maybe—

Fink closed the driver's door.

"They said all I had to do was deliver her," Jared protested.

"You were misinformed," Fink told him.

"What do I have to do now?"

"Just keep the windows closed and drive." He turned to Barton. "Get him on the FDR north. Head for the Triboro and follow the signs to La Guardia. See how far you can get. Give the captain my regards."

"Look, Lieutenant," Barton said, "I want to—"

"I don't want to hear it," Fink told him. "Now get in the car. You told Reynolds La Guardia, right?"

"Right," Barton said glumly, sliding in next to Rhonda.

"Do this right," Fink said, "and I'll cover for you. Are we in synch on this now?"

"Sure," Barton grumbled.

"What's going on?" Rhonda asked.

"Nothing, Rhon. Everything is fine."

Fink slammed Barton's door, slapped the hood and pointed to the elevator. Jared drove in. Fink shut the gate and hit the red button, wondering why the Puerto Rican guy had to pick this time to go on a break.

Fink jogged back to the limousine. He had to rearrange the luggage to get the trunk closed. Mee Yang must have bought out the city.

He settled in behind the wheel and put on the black chauffeur's cap. It made him feel like a rookie going out on his first patrol. Marissa looked over at him, shook her head and laughed.

"Everybody ready?" he called over his shoulder.

"Shoe," Mee Yang replied.

"Zack?"

"Fine."

"Mrs. Johnson?"

"Praise Jesus," she sniffled. "Everything is fine and dandy."

Fink smiled and turned the ignition key.

"'Cept for that case," she added.

"Ma'am?" Fink asked, having trouble hearing over the engine.

"That boy gave me his case," Adelaide explained.

"What is she saying?" Marissa asked. "What case?"

Fink leaned his head back. "Ma'am?"

"You talking about your luggage, Mama?" Johnson asked.

"All I'm saying, baby," Adelaide told him, "is that they put that boy's briefcase in this car's trunk."

Fink reached down, released the latch and got out to check. He found a small attaché case wedged in a corner. When he pulled it out he was shocked by its weight.

"That's the one," Adelaide confirmed, and then explained about Jared stopping and opening the window and the man passing it through.

Fink held the case up to his ear and listened. Nothing. He didn't want to shake it.

"Give me a minute," he told everyone, and, carrying it carefully, hurried over to a house phone on the wall. The wall smelled of stale piss and old engine oil. He dialed the operator and got an outside line. He felt the seconds ticking away.

His next call was to the assistant manager. "Gustav," he said, "listen carefully. I'm leaving in the limousine now, for Kennedy Airport. There's a brown attaché case down here in the garage. I don't think it's anything to worry about, but I've called the bomb squad to come pick it up."

"Gott in himmel," Gustav gasped.

"It's probably nothing," Fink told him, "but I'd rather be safe than sorry. I'm leaving now, Gustav. In three minutes, you clear the garage. Okay?"

"Yes, of course. Of course. Should I evacuate also the hotel?"

"No, no, no. This thing is small. The worst it could do is take out a car or two. The bomb squad will get it out of here. Where am I going?"

"Kennedy Airport."

"*Danke.*"

Fink rang for the freight elevator and stood there waiting for the motor to start up. He checked his watch. Seven-twelve. He'd told Ransom eight. With luck, they could make Newark Airport in forty-five minutes. Then again, there was no guarantee that everyone outside had followed the Thunderbird. The attaché case suggested that Grantham's intuition had been right.

Fink banged the red button again and the elevator started to descend. He hurried back to the limousine and slid in. Marissa had shifted over to the middle of the seat. He glanced over at her and froze. There was an eerily familiar little Asian sitting next to her. Fink looked down. Marissa's arms were pinned to her sides by her seat belt. Bo Lee had a gun pressed against her ribs. He was looking at Fink and smiling.

Chapter Sixty-Eight

Jared stayed in the right-hand lane because New York drivers were nuts and because he liked watching the moonlight dancing across the water. He was doing about fifty. Sure, it was disappointing that he never got to shake Corporal Johnson's hand, but who had to know that? Jared could tell Zeiss anything he wanted. Besides, he'd opened the envelope at a red light and, holding it between his legs, had counted ten crisp hundreds. The sight had given him his second wind.

Suddenly the car directly behind them lit up and started to wail. Jared nearly jumped out of his skin. He wanted to pull over and let it pass, but he was already in the slow lane. The siren was piercing, the flashing lights like an insect swarm.

"What do I do?" he cried.

"Keep going," Barton told him.

He gripped the wheel hard. "Yes, sir."

The police car was tailgating him but Jared concentrated on maintaining his speed. The siren was maddening, the road was bumpy, and the flashing lights were making it hard to see. He swung the wheel and pulled into the center lane. The sound receded for a few seconds, but then the police car switched lanes too and the commotion seemed worse than before.

It was. Two more police cars had joined the chase, further back but weaving from lane to lane and gaining on them.

"Shouldn't I signal or pull over or something?" Jared pleaded. "Those guys sound angry."

"Keep going," Barton told him, leaning forward and grasping the back of Jared's seat.

Jared was totally frazzled. Between the sirens and the lights, it was like being in two discos at once.

"I think they're after us," he said. "I wasn't speeding, but—"

"Keep going," Barton said, making it an order.

"But—"

Police cars had roared into positions on either side. The car on the left was trying to nose ahead and cut the Thunderbird off, but at Barton's insistence Jared was staying right on the bumper of the car in front. He felt like he was in a movie chase scene, the kind that always ended in a fiery crash.

"Drive!" Barton yelled, and Jared was trying, but he knew if he kept this up he was going to die. In front of him stretched long red ribbons of taillights, but he saw fireballs, plumes of toxic smoke, twisted steel, mangled bodies. Jared began gasping for breath. His heart was beating so hard he thought it would burst. He didn't want to die.

His survival instinct took over and wrenched his foot from the gas pedal. The car in front pulled away and a police car darted into its place. Another one pulled up alongside and sealed them in.

"I'm sorry," he said to Barton. "I just . . ."

Barton patted his shoulder. "You did fine," he said evenly.

"Now keep your eyes on the road and listen to me. This is important. Keep both hands on the wheel where they can see them, even after you stop. Don't be surprised if they have their guns drawn. They don't know who we are. They'll chill out when they see my shield."

Jared's nerves were shot. He checked the dash. Their speed was down to twenty but his hands were shaking. He needed to pee. The police car in front started talking through a loudspeaker, instructing him to take the next exit. He raised a hand in acknowledgment, but Barton pushed it down.

"No sudden movements," Barton reminded him. "Both hands on the wheel. Put on your turn signal."

"Yes, sir."

"You're doing fine," Barton told him, glancing over to see how Rhonda was holding up.

She was huddled in the corner. Barton offered her his hand. The digital clock read seven forty-two. Fink would be in Brooklyn by now, cruising along the BQE in his fancy limousine, taking his sweet time getting out to Kennedy, probably getting off thinking about Barton taking all the heat.

Chapter Sixty-Nine

Fink steered the limousine down Seventh Avenue South through the West Village, past trendy restaurants and clots of tourists, past Sheridan Square's all-night newsstand, past the Gay Cruises billboard which this month featured two mustachioed men cavorting in a ship's swimming pool, past the Off-Broadway theater playing *Vampire Lesbians of Sodom*, past the ten-foot-high plastic margarita above the Tex-Mex joint whose entrance had the ass-end of an old Studebaker protruding from the wall, past the French bakeries and pasta joints, the Irish bars and Korean groceries, the falafel shops, health food stores, pizza parlors, souvlaki stands, kosher delis—past all of them to where—uh oh!—the three right lanes were backed up all the way to West Houston, a good six blocks from the tunnel entrance.

"Do not stop," Bo instructed.

"Okay," Fink replied, "but I'll have to reach under the seat."

"Go head," Bo told him, giving Marissa a quick jab with the gun.

Fink kept his eyes on the traffic. The little bastard was smart. If he'd shot Marissa and the rest of them in the hotel garage he would have had almost no chance of getting away. He had used the limousine to get himself safely out of the hotel, and he had agreed to let Fink drive to Newark because an airport would provide a good place to fire shots without attracting attention. The three passengers in back hadn't heard anything. The window separating them from the front seat was closed. If they even noticed Bo, they probably assumed he was a hotel worker sent along to help with the luggage.

Pulling over into the through lane on the left, Fink lowered his window, reached down under the seat and located the flasher, stuck it up on the roof and turned it on. Everything around them began to pulse red. When Fink came abreast of the front of the tunnel traffic he stopped and honked his way into the line. Up ahead, the uniformed cop in charge of feeding traffic into the tunnel saw the flasher and began waving Fink's lane through.

"I'm going to stop and do something here," Fink alerted Bo.

"Careful," Bo reminded him, keeping the gun against Marissa's side but draping the garageman's jacket over it.

Fink had been checking the mirrors regularly since they'd left the hotel and hadn't seen anything. Several cars had followed his flasher and forced their way into his lane behind him, but Fink didn't know whether they were merely aggressive drivers or something more sinister, and he was worried what Bo might do if he suspected their car was being followed.

Fink pulled up alongside the traffic cop, lowered his window and showed his gold shield.

"Listen," he said, waving the kid closer but speaking loud enough for Bo to hear, "starting with the car behind me, I want you to cut off this lane for the next fifteen minutes. I've got VIP cargo and I'm afraid of a tail."

"Okay, Lieutenant, no problem."

"Thanks."

Fink reached up, turned off the flasher and proceeded into the tunnel where he used the calm of the gently winding double white lines to take stock of their situation. It would take five minutes to get through the tunnel. Once they were in Jersey it was a straight fifteen-minute shot to Newark Airport, all on heavily traveled roads with no service or rest areas. Route 1-9 was the way to go; it would still be busy at this hour. The Turnpike would require two more stops: one to pick up a ticket, the other to pay the toll. Fink couldn't do anything while they were all in the car, so every stop was simply a chance for something to go wrong, to set Bo off and risk starting a bloodbath. For now, Fink counseled himself, the object of the exercise was to keep everything moving and to keep everyone calm.

He glanced at his watch. It was five to eight. Ransom should have the plane at the gate, all gassed up and ready to go. Once they reached the airport Fink would find a way to get this kid. He knew he would find a way. The arrogant little bastard hadn't even bothered to take Fink's gun.

Fink waited until he passed the next set of road signs, then glanced over and asked Marissa how she was doing. While she was answering he reached up, peeled the flasher from the roof, pulled it inside, bent forward and replaced it beneath his seat. Keeping his eyes on the road, he sighed as he straightened up, both to mask the sound of metal sliding against leather and to justify the slight hesitation required to position the gun between his legs before returning his hand to the wheel.

He and Marissa kept talking. Fink thought Bo would order them to shut up, but the kid just sat there staring at them with those cold flat eyes, looking as if a forked tongue was about to flick out from between his narrow lips.

Fink emerged from the tunnel and drove up beneath banks of synchronized traffic signals and past gas stations with garishly advertised prices. When the roadway split, he stayed to the left, following the signs to Route 1-9. So far, so good.

Up on the Pulaski Skyway the traffic thinned. They crossed a long looping bridge that afforded dramatic views back toward Manhattan. With its towers glowing in the clear night air, the city looked otherworldly, magnificent, serene. Fink recognized the Statue of Liberty by her torch, noting that from this side, her back was turned. He didn't take it personally.

"Muss never assume," Bo announced to no one in particular.

"What's that?" Fink asked him, noting the surprisingly nimble handling of the limousine.

"When I bring champagne to room," Bo explained, "I assume shoulder holster."

Fink felt a constriction in his chest.

"So now I surprise," Bo continued, extending his free hand, palm up, toward Fink. "You hold barrel, please," he said.

Fink reached down and passed the gun over as instructed. Bo checked the safety and slipped it into the pocket of the hotel jacket.

Nothing was ever easy, Fink reminded himself. If this guy wasn't a pro, Rotelli would still be alive. Fink consoled himself with the thought that Ransom would almost certainly be carrying.

An angled white arrow pointed toward Newark Airport.

Fink changed lanes and followed it, maintaining a steady fifty-five. The turn took them into a futuristic landscape of massive, brightly illuminated storage tanks. Single words painted in giant block letters on successive tanks delivered the message "OIL HEATS BEST." The spiraling metal stairways reminded Fink of the final scene in *White Heat* where a crazed James Cagney, trapped atop a tank just like these, fires his gun to start an all-consuming conflagration and cries out, "Hey, Ma, look at me! Top of the world!"

Someone in the back seat tapped the courtesy window. Fink looked across, received a nod, lowered it.

"Is that not Bo?" Mee Yang asked delightedly.

"Yes, miss," Bo replied pleasantly, his hard eyes never leaving Fink.

Fink, barely avoiding a swerve, forced his attention back to the road. The best explanation was that Bo had made another try for Marissa at the hotel and run into Mee Yang instead.

"Husband," Mee Yang was saying, "this is friend Bo from hotel."

"Pleasure," Johnson said.

Bo twisted around, reached over Marissa's shoulder and shook hands. Fink's skin began to crawl.

Johnson introduced his mother to Bo.

"Honorable mother," Bo said, bowing his head with what seemed to be genuine respect.

"Bo from Laos," Mee Yang announced. "Him have Merican girl with yellow hair and blue eyes."

"Mee Yang husband big hero," Bo declared. "I see picture all the time on TV."

"I'm not a hero," Johnson protested.

"Yes, you are," his mother insisted.

"I'm not, Mama," he said.

"Good son not argue with mother," Mee Yang admonished.

"Let's not fuss," Adelaide soothed.

"Hero," Mee Yang said petulantly.

"Tell us about your girlfriend," Johnson suggested to Bo.

"Sit back and enjoy ride," Bo said amiably, then looked over at Fink and murmured, "We close window now."

As Fink pressed the button he was struck by a revelation that set his insides churning. He suddenly knew as a fact certain that Bo was not here to kill Marissa, he was here to kill Isaac Johnson.

And in some way Fink did not understand, this struck him as even worse.

Chapter Seventy

"You're upset," Adelaide fretted. "If it's because of that hero business back there—"

"No, Mama," Johnson assured her, putting his arm around her shoulder and experiencing a feeling so elemental it distracted him momentarily from one even more basic: danger.

When the window had opened, danger had come streaming off this man Bo like electricity. Now, even with the window closed, Johnson sensed it sparking all about them. He glanced to the side and saw road signs, but they flew by too fast for him to read. It didn't matter. They were going to an airport to meet the colonel.

Johnson didn't want to frighten his mother, but he had to alert Mee Yang.

He released his mother and touched Mee Yang's arm. "This Bo," he whispered, "how do you know him?"

Chapter Seventy-One

"Buzz," Senator Grantham said cordially, taking the call at his desk, "thanks for getting back to me."

"Sorry for the delay," Olden replied. "I know it's eight o'-clock, but we've been working on terrorist simulations and I couldn't get away."

"Not a problem," Grantham assured him. "I've been keeping busy here in the office."

"How are things up on the Hill?" Olden asked him.

But the senator was too wound up for any more small talk. He thought he had a way out of this morass. "I'm prepared to offer a straight swap," he declared. "My hearings for your court martial. Does that sound interesting?"

"What do you have in mind, Antel?"

"All right. With regard to my subcommittee, I will agree to postpone all hearings, both public and closed-door."

"For how long?"

"Indefinitely."

"Define 'indefinitely.' "

"For as long as I am chairman. I can't commit beyond that."

"How will you explain it?"

"I've made a few notes: 'This subcommittee was established to help determine the fate of those Americans still unaccounted for in Southeast Asia. Public hearings at this time could impede the delicate negotiations now under way between representatives of our government and the government of Vietnam.' I'll flesh it out, of course, but that's the gist of it."

"I like it," Buzz said.

Grantham detected reservation. "But?"

"Nothing, really," Olden said, "though I suspect my people would prefer a more direct reference."

"Such as?"

"Your statement might refer to the continuing American efforts by representatives both military and diplomatic."

"Diplomatic and military," Grantham proposed, "and I'll make the efforts 'tireless.' "

"I think that will fly, Antel. I really do. Now what was our end?"

"Your people leave Corporal Johnson alone," Grantham declared. "No charges, no arrest, no protective custody, no debriefing, no court martial. You cut him a check for twenty-four years' back pay, issue him an honorable discharge and leave him the hell alone."

"And how do you suggest we justify that?" Olden asked.

"I don't know, Buzz. But I'm sure an 'informed Pentagon source' can come up with the right angle."

The silence crackled for a moment, until Olden spoke up: "By the way, Antel, did any of your committee people ever locate Corporal Johnson's mother?"

"Do we have a deal, General?"

"I'll have to make a few calls, of course. But, as we like

to say here at the Pentagon, Senator, the confidence level is high. Where can I reach you later tonight?"

"Home," Grantham told him, the word echoing inside him like footsteps in an empty room.

CHAPTER SEVENTY-TWO

They were in a dark, remote section of the airport. Fink slowed the big car and passed through the open gate of the chain link fence. Less than two hundred yards away, the jet's oval windows glowed like the bioluminescence of some weird deep-sea creature.

"Stop here," Bo said.

Fink hit the brake. "What's the problem?"

"No problem. Turn off engine. Turn off lights. Leave keys in car. We walk."

Fink reluctantly complied. This was bad. This was very bad. Up ahead, a long rectangle appeared in the jet's side. Fink looked away.

"Do not move," Bo said, opening his door.

The overhead light came on. Cold air rushed in. Fink saw that Bo was now holding a gun in each hand. He had more than enough bullets for the five of them.

"Open lady's seat belt," Bo instructed. "Slowly, please."

"Listen," Fink said, playing for time, "I want to—"

Bo jabbed her with the Glock. "Now, please."

Fink reached for the buckle. "I can give you money," he blurted, "a lot of money."

"How much money?"

Marissa's seat belt snapped apart.

"A hundred thousand U.S. dollars," Fink said. "All cash."

"Open your window, please," Bo told him.

Fink pressed the button, disgusted with himself. This guy wasn't a mercenary.

"Lady come with me, please," Bo said, backing out cautiously.

Bo walked her around to the driver's side. "How policeman have so much money?" he asked, standing clear of the door's arc.

"I stole it," Fink told him.

"Come out with hands on head," Bo said. "Where is this money? In bank?"

A jumbo jet passed low over them, whining in for a landing. Fink tensed but Bo's eyes never left him.

"The money is in my apartment," Fink said. "Back in New York."

Bo reached out and banged on one of the back doors. Someone inside opened it.

"Leave these people here," Fink suggested, "and I'll take you to the money right now."

"Maybe I do that," Bo told him. "All come out, please," he called into the back seat.

Fink thought he saw a shadow in the jet's doorway, but when he looked again it was gone. Behind him he heard people moving, snatches of conversation, sounds of surprise. He decided not to provoke Bo by turning around. The wind was making whistling noises, flapping his jacket and tie, rustling the tall grass nearby. Marissa was shivering. He glanced from side to side, trying to get a sense of the terrain.

It looked like they were standing at the dark edge of the world. If nothing else presented itself, Fink would have to yell for everyone to run and then go after Bo himself. He would take a bullet, but a few of the others might get away. He wondered if his daughter would get El Gordo's money. Even without it, his insurance would be enough to cover her grad school, with maybe a few bucks left over for a wedding.

He heard footsteps, took a chance and turned. Johnson was approaching, followed by Mee Yang in her new leather coat. Their hands were raised.

"Hurry," Bo told them, waving a gun, "we go to plane now."

"How about the luggage?" Marissa asked.

"Quiet," Bo snapped.

Johnson's mother emerged from the limousine. That was everyone. Fink knew he would have to make his move soon. He needed a diversion. Where were the feds? Where was Ransom? Where was goddamn Captain Reynolds? Fink knew that as soon as Bo got everyone together he would start shooting.

"We have a trunkful of luggage," Marissa said. "It would be easier—"

"Quiet! No more talk. Make one line," Bo ordered, directing Johnson with a gun.

"You stop that!" Adelaide cried in alarm.

"Mother be quiet," Bo told her.

"Don't you go pointing that thing at my boy," Adelaide warned, advancing angrily on Bo.

"Stop," he warned her, retreating a step and glancing at Fink over his shoulder.

"Mama," Johnson cried, starting toward her.

Bo raised a gun, freezing him.

"I told you to stop that," Adelaide said furiously, quickening her pace.

She was close. Bo aimed at her chest. His arm stiffened. Fink saw she wasn't going to stop.

"No, Mama!" Johnson shouted, rushing at her.

Fink hurled himself forward, hitting Bo obliquely but knocking him off his feet and hearing the welcome sound of metal skittering across pavement. He had tried to land on Bo but somehow missed. As Fink scrambled to his feet he was struck by a fierce barrage of blows to the body and face that took his legs out and sent the night spinning.

He heard isolated, distant sounds: cries, thumps, grunts. When feeling seeped back into his body something hard and sharp was digging at his side. He rolled off it and reached down. Above him two men were grappling in the darkness, their bodies a single, erratically jerking mass. The thing Fink grasped took on a familiar shape. It was Rotelli's Glock! Just then, Johnson went flying. Bo was about to go after him when he saw the gun in Fink's hand and stopped short.

Fink rolled to his belly and brought the gun up only to feel Bo's shadow pass over him and then see it sprinting for the safety of the darkness. Fink twisted, fired, heard the shot, a sharp cry, the thump of a fall.

Desperate to get to him before he escaped, Fink struggled to rise, fell over, tried again and then, with Marissa's help, made it to his feet.

Fink heard the sound of a punch, and then, "I've got him."

A moment later Ransom appeared at the fringe of the darkness dragging Bo by one leg. As they got closer Fink heard Ransom speaking Vietnamese. The little bastard wasn't dead. Good.

A quick look around satisfied Fink that everyone was accounted for and safe. His thoughts were still alternating with bursts of pain. Johnson was okay. Marissa was okay. It was cold.

Ransom wrenched Bo from the grass onto the blacktop and continued dragging him. In his other hand Ransom was holding the largest handgun Fink had ever seen.

"Did I really hit him?" Fink asked, limping over, wishing he had a set of cuffs.

"In the thigh," Ransom said, releasing the leg and stepping away. "He was lucky."

"I was lucky," Fink said, staring at Bo all crumpled up on the ground. "How bad is he?"

"Not bad enough," Ransom said. "He's still alive. Where's Doc?"

Johnson hurried over, rubbing an arm. Mee Yang was right behind him. Marissa was trying to help Adelaide into the back seat, but the old lady didn't want to go.

"Is that Ev?" she cried excitedly.

"Yes, ma'am," Ransom called, his eyes fixed on Bo.

"You get yourself over here this second," she demanded.

Marissa reached in and turned on the limousine's headlights. The beams trembled in the chill air.

"It's cold, ma'am," Ransom called without looking up. "You get in the car and I'll be right there. Lieutenant," he said to Fink, dropping his voice, "come watch this little prick."

Fink hurried over. Bo lay on his side with his knees drawn up and his hands clasped at his chin, almost as if he was praying. There was a long dark bloodstain on one leg. Fink knelt down, placed the gun barrel beneath Bo's ear and patted him down for weapons. He was clean.

"Hi, Colonel. Give me a little room," Johnson said, squatting down next to the body and leaning over to examine it.

Ransom backed up a few steps.

"Mama's waiting for you," Johnson reminded him.

"Okay," Ransom said. "Lieutenant, do you really need this guy alive?"

"Yes," Fink told him.

Ransom began walking off toward the car.

"Mel," Marissa said urgently, "I have to talk to you."

"Not now," Fink told her, stepping back to give Johnson some room, but keeping his eyes on Bo. The little bastard wasn't moving, but he had killed three people already.

"It's important, Mel," Marissa insisted, pulling at his arm.

"It can wait," Fink told her.

"It can't," she said, pulling harder.

"Look," Fink said, lowering the gun and turning to her, "you've got to—"

With a single catlike action, Bo sprang off the ground, swung himself onto Johnson's back and looped something around his neck. Johnson's hands rushed to his throat as his body arched backward and sideways with Bo clinging fiercely to him.

Fink pulled free of Marissa, raised the Glock and searched for a clear shot. Mee Yang flew past him screaming, blocking his view. Fink cursed and started forward but then heard a decisive thud as Ransom brought his gun down on Bo's skull, peeled him from Johnson's back, tossed him away and kicked him hard.

Johnson was okay. He was back in the limousine being tended to by the women. Bo lay on the ground where Ransom had flung him, his wrists and ankles now secured with heavy twine from the limousine's trunk. Fink was standing at a safe distance admiring the deadly bracelet when Bo came to.

Ransom offered to kill him.

"Come on, Colonel," Fink said, "I'll drive you to the plane."

"Corporal Johnson is dead?" Bo wheezed, struggling to sit up.

Ransom answered with a stream of mocking Vietnamese. Bo slumped back down.

"Let's go," Fink said. "This guy will stay put till I get back."

Bo made a harsh noise, either a cough or a laugh. Fink looked down at him. He decided to check his wrists one more time.

"Loved one," Bo murmured, and then did something with his mouth which made a sharp cracking sound. His body stiffened as if electrocuted, held that grotesque pose for a long second and then went limp. The wind carried a bitter smell.

Fink hung up the car phone and went to help with the luggage, wondering why the attaché case had contained nothing but cash, twenty thousand in small bills. And where were the feds Grantham had warned about?

He climbed the narrow metal stairs and ducked his head. Everyone was seated about the small lounge. He dropped into a swivel seat. Johnson's neck was raw, but other than that they all seemed fine. The door to the cockpit was closed. Fink counted eight seats aft of the lounge, four on either side. A wild idea flashed through his mind and kept on going.

Ransom pulled a curtain across the open doorway. Immediately the cabin began to warm. Fink told him about his call from Grantham earlier that evening.

"The senator said the military might do anything to keep from being embarrassed," Fink warned him. "You're not out of this yet."

"They won't do anything in Canadian airspace," Ransom assured him. "And we can be there in half an hour."

"Okay," Fink said, "but the senator said—"

"Drop it," Ransom told him.

"I'm just—"

"We're out of time," Ransom declared, raising his voice, "but from all of us I want to thank Lieutenant—"

"Listen," Fink said, "I'm just happy to have . . ." He lost the thought.

"You saved my life back there," Johnson said. "Mama's too."

Fink nodded. That's what he'd meant. He had to let these people get out of here.

"We have a small gift for you," Ransom announced.

"I can't."

"Yes you can," Ransom assured him, and handed him a package about the size of a shoe box, but heavier.

"Okay," Fink said, tucking it under his arm. "Thanks. I'd like to wish you all the best of luck. I hope . . . someday . . . maybe . . . Come on," he said to Marissa, ducking toward the door.

"You go ahead," she told him.

He turned and looked at her. Her fur coat was draped over the back of her seat.

"I'm going with them," she said simply.

The cabin got very quiet. Johnson was holding his mother's hand. Mee Yang was examining his neck. Ransom went forward toward the cockpit.

"All that luggage," Fink muttered, feeling very stupid.

"A woman needs things, *caro*," Marissa said.

"When did you decide?" he asked her, surprised that he wasn't more surprised.

She shook her head. "I'm sorry."

"Sure," he said, realizing that she had played it both ways; if something had gone wrong before they reached the plane she would have stayed with him.

The next thing he knew he had wished everyone luck and climbed down the little steps.

The cabin lights flickered and the engines began to whine. Fink stood by the limousine with his gift under his arm. The wind was ruffling his suit, mussing his hair, stinging his eyes. The sky was dark. The cold was going through him like a knife, but Fink was in no hurry to go back and collect Bo's body.

He stood there staring at the receding white dot in the sky until it became so small he was no longer sure it was even there.

EPILOGUE

CHAPTER SEVENTY-THREE

Marissa was in the galley trying to figure out how the microwave worked. People were getting hungry. The refueling stop in the Bahamas had gone smoothly; Ransom had taken some cash from a suitcase and gone out to greet the local officials. Twenty minutes later they were airborne again.

It was nice to see Johnson reunited with his mother. They were both shy, but she couldn't stop touching him—his hands, his face, his hair—as if she couldn't quite believe he was real. In a funny way, it reminded Marissa of that first night she and Frank spent together when she was seventeen. Seventeen. *Madre de Dios*.

Ransom couldn't seem to sit still. He kept going forward to confer with the crew, coming back to swivel distractedly in his seat, sip some champagne, stare off into space. Now he was making notes in that little pad he kept in his inside jacket pocket. He looked good, though: designer jeans, cowboy boots, black turtleneck, Armani jacket. His sideburns were going gray, which was new, and he was wearing his hair a little longer. She wouldn't have guessed it, but the beard worked. It brought out his eyes. Marissa had a feeling they would get along better this time. They were both a little older, trusted each other a little more. She liked the way he protected Johnson; it was a side of him she'd never seen. The idea of sending Zack to congressional hearings had been *loco*, of course, but Marissa thought she understood what Ransom had been after, though she could not have put it into words. Then again, maybe it was simply a macho thing. But now that Johnson was back with his mother, Ransom would return to his old self. The fire was still there, she was sure: for life, for action and, whether he realized it or not, for her. He was nervous now, but he'd be fine once they touched down in Asunción. Everyone would like the estate, she was sure of it. The staff had been there for weeks getting things ready. That was why she didn't want people eating too much now. She had called this afternoon and issued instructions. Cars would be waiting at the airport, and then the drive into the hills, and then a big dinner out by the pool: fresh langoustines, Argentine beef, paella, lots of local fruits and vegetables, plenty of wine, homemade desserts. A menu to make anyone happy. There was enough room in the main house for all of them. She would worry about the sleeping arrangements later.

Ransom was studying a chart. She went over and stood next to him. Their flight plan specified Newfoundland, but once out over the Atlantic they had turned south to Nassau. There would be a stiff fine from the FAA for the charter company, but Ransom would cover it. As far as the authorities knew from the manifest, there was only a single passenger on board, a Canadian named Andrews. Johnson's mother had no papers, but papers were no problem in Asunción.

Marissa put a hand on Ransom's shoulder and felt him

tremble. She wondered if it was her, and couldn't decide if that was good or bad. She gazed down at the top of his head. The swirl of his hair reminded her of one of those mad stars in a Van Gogh painting.

Absently, he reached up and patted her hand. Reassured, she returned to the galley, opened the freezer cabinet and checked the foil-covered entrees.

"Anyone for kosher?" she called.

CHAPTER SEVENTY-FOUR

Olden picked up the phone and identified himself.

"Yes, sir," the pilot replied, "the admiral said you might be calling."

"How's the weather out there, Major?" Olden asked.

"Excellent, sir."

"You enjoy carrier duty?"

"Yes, sir."

"The sea air is good for you, especially down there in the Caribbean. As long as you don't get seasick."

"I don't get seasick, sir."

"Good. You feel up to some flying tonight?"

"Yes, sir."

"Got yourself a good wing man?"

"First rate, sir."

"Your mission has the highest security classification, Major."

"Understood, sir."

"This is being logged as a standard night landing exercise, full weapons complement."

"Yes, sir."

"There is a small private aircraft headed your way, Major, a twin-engine Gulfstream. We have reason to believe it is carrying a cadre of international terrorists."

"Yes, sir."

"Get up there and find it for us, Major."

"Yes, sir."

CHAPTER SEVENTY-FIVE

"Where are we now?" Marissa asked, topping up Ransom's champagne.

She smelled nice. He checked his watch and did a rapid calculation.

"The Bermuda Triangle," he told her with a smile, taking her hand and rubbing it against his beard, thinking about tigers.

The bathroom door opened and Mee Yang came prancing out in another new outfit. She was wobbling on the high heels. Seeing her like this, it was hard to imagine her taking an Uzi and shooting a guy's face off. Women, he thought, glancing around the cabin. Marissa was having fun playing stewardess. Doc's mother was having a ball: couldn't stop grinning and wiping her eyes. Doc was like a happy puppy. Ransom was so pleased for all of them that it frightened him. He'd never been this happy for himself. It seemed dangerous.

Then again, he always felt vulnerable over the open

ocean, even on commercial flights. He felt safer over land, probably because of all his years living in the jungle: the canopy, the life, the sounds, the warmth. Up here it was empty and cold: exposed.

Okay, Ransom admitted to himself, the hearings had been a stupid idea. He'd had his head up his ass. Who knew what the hell he'd had in mind? But it had been Doc's idea to go back to the States in the first place. Well, they would all be happy in Paraguay. Marissa had been spending money like water. She must have fixed up a palace. He wouldn't be able to stay with them too long because he had that warhead deal pending in the Ukraine, and the Serbs always needed more stuff these days . . . Christ, he was tired. Probably shouldn't be drinking champagne: just put him to sleep. Speaking of money, he had to get back to Zurich pretty soon and talk to the gnomes. Maybe he would take Marissa along. He'd see how things went. It was time to start moving out of dollars in a major way. He didn't much like yen, but he had nothing against deutsche marks or Swiss francs or gold.

"Mr. Andrews," the intercom called.

Ransom pushed to his feet. "You need another Dr. Pepper, Mrs. Johnson?"

"You stop feeding me," she told him, slapping his arm playfully as he walked by.

"What's up?" he asked, poking his head into the cockpit.

"We've picked up two aircraft on radar," the pilot said. "You asked to be notified immediately."

"Show me," Ransom said, squeezing in, crouching down and pulling the door closed behind him. The cramped space smelled of aftershave.

"Here," the co-pilot said, pointing to a pair of green triangles on a small screen.

"You're sure that's two?" Ransom asked.

"Yes, sir."

"Military, then," Ransom said. "Flying in formation."

"Most likely Phantoms," the co-pilot agreed. "Night maneuvers off a carrier is my guess."

"How far away are they?" Ransom asked.

"Fifteen miles, on an intercept course, speed about six hundred knots."

"Let's get away from them," Ransom said. "Change our heading ninety degrees."

"If we've seen them," the pilot said, "they've certainly spotted us. We don't have the speed to outrun them."

"Turn the fucking plane," Ransom told him.

"As you wish, sir."

Ransom held on as they executed the turn, then watched as the tiny overlapping triangles changed direction as well. Each time the blip appeared it was marginally closer to the center of the screen.

"That device I gave you," Ransom said to the pilot, "turn it to standby."

"Yes, sir." He reached over and flicked a toggle switch. A yellow light came on, revealing Cyrillic lettering on a metal housing.

"Twelve miles and closing," the co-pilot reported.

"Any place nearby we can set down?" Ransom asked. "I mean, in a hurry?"

"No, sir. We're at least twenty minutes from—"

"Never mind."

"What shall I tell them?" the pilot asked, fiddling with his radio.

"Tell them you're carrying the president of Belize," Ransom said. "You're taking him home from a secret peace mission."

The pilot smiled. "What a lovely idea."

He broadcast the message on several channels, but received no reply. Ransom had him start reducing altitude.

"Nine miles and closing," the co-pilot reported.

"I'm going back to the cabin," Ransom told them. "Increase our angle of descent. Level off at five hundred feet. If they close to six miles before I'm back, turn off all the lights, engage the device and execute a series of random turns. Don't go back to our original heading until I say so. Understood?"

"Yes, sir."

"Good. Now repeat everything I just said."

CHAPTER SEVENTY-SIX

The radio squawked.

"Eight miles out," the major reported. "Shall I try contacting them, sir?"

"Negative," Olden replied.

"They can't reach us on this channel, sir," the major pointed out.

"Understood. Do you have target acquisition?"

"Affirmative. Target has commenced evasive maneuvers."

"Weapons systems hot?"

"Affirmative."

"Condition green. Repeat, condition green."

"Preparing to lock on target," the major reported. "Weapons armed and ready."

"Fire a Sidewinder when you have him in visual range," Olden ordered. "We need direct confirmation of the kill."

"Understood. Target in rapid descent," the pilot announced. "Now at fourteen thousand feet. We're following him down. Visual contact should be coming up."

CHAPTER SEVENTY-SEVEN

Mee Yang was modeling red silk pajamas with little embroidered pandas when the plane started to dive. She scrambled into a seat and clutched Johnson's hand. His mother, who already had his other hand, closed her eyes and began moving her lips in silent prayer.

Johnson pressed his feet against the floor, struggling to keep himself upright. Evasive action, the colonel had called it, though he said it might be useless against the type of missile he was expecting, something called a Sidewinder.

When the plane leveled off Ransom went back and pulled the life rafts from their storage compartments and dragged them to the emergency exit, assuring everyone it was simply a precaution. The rafts would inflate automatically upon hitting the water, he explained, and under that unlikely circumstance everyone could climb out on the wing and pile in. He told the women to take off their shoes. Before hurrying off to the cockpit Ransom got Johnson's attention and tapped his cowboy boot, reminding him of the papers he kept there.

Johnson felt himself sinking into a familiar shimmering emptiness. It began at his core and radiated outward through his skin. He squeezed Mee Yang's hand, trying to absorb her fear. She was frightened because she had never been where they were going, but to Johnson it was familiar territory. For Johnson, the best thing was that wherever they were going, they were all going together. He hoped the peace he felt was flowing into Mee Yang, and into Mama too. He didn't understand why these people were trying to kill them, but he had never understood such things. It was so interesting the way they could fold a raft up like that, to squeeze so much into so little. He closed his eyes and thought about how lucky he was.

CHAPTER SEVENTY-EIGHT

"Missile away?" Olden asked.
"Negative, sir."
"What's the problem?"
"There seems to be a malfunction in my targeting array. I'm switching to a backup system."
"Let your wing man take him," Olden ordered. "Do it now."
There was a short silence.
"He's experiencing the same problem, sir."
"What's your distance to the target?" Olden asked.
"Malfunction occurred at six miles, sir. I've got the backup system on-line, but . . . something's screwy, sir."
"Do you have visual?"
"Negative. Switching to— No, that's not working either."
"Do you think you're being jammed?" Olden asked.
"A jamming device, sir? On a Gulfstream?"
"What's your explanation, Major?"
"I think he crashed, sir. He was at five hundred feet when

I lost him. Maybe what our electronics is picking up is scattered debris."

"Scattered debris," Olden muttered, wishing he could believe it.

"Unless . . ." the pilot said.

"What?"

"I was switching radio channels and heard . . ."

"Heard what?" Olden demanded.

"Give me a moment, sir. Let me see if I can raise it again."

Olden waited anxiously for the pilot to come back on. He closed his eyes and sensed the twin Phantoms slicing through high icy darkness. He thought about his future. The long silence seemed ominous.

The sudden crackling startled him.

"Negative, sir," the pilot announced. "It must have been static."

"But you heard something," Olden insisted. "Before."

"Yes, sir, but—"

"What was it?" Olden demanded.

"Well, sir, I know this is going to sound crazy, but for a second back there I thought I heard someone laughing."